CORPS STONES

ALSO BY S.K. RANDOLPH

VARTERELS' UNIVERSE™

(as paperbacks)

Part I - UnFolding

1. DiMensioner's Revenge

5. ConDra's Fire

8. MasTer's Reach

10. Jaradee's Legacy

Agothany 1 (Companion Shorts 2, 3, 4, 6, 7, and 9)

Part II - CoaleScence

11. Incirrata Secret

13. Corps Stones

16. Mocendi's Gambit

19. Queen's Quest

Agothany 2 (Companion Shorts 12, 14, 15, 17, 18, and 20)

Part III - Quickening

(a work in process)

Told with words and art,

contained in novels and companion shorts,

available in print and eBooks.

CORPS STONES

ILLUSTRATED BY THE AUTHOR

VARTERELS' UNIVERSE
BOOK THIRTEEN

S.K. RANDOLPH

Cover and Illustrations by
S.K. RANDOLPH

Corps Stones: Illustrated by the Author (VarTerels' Universe Book 13)

ISBN
Paperback 978-1-962777-09-4
eBook 978-1-962777-36-0

Self Published by S.K. Randolph
CheeTrann Creations LLC
Suite 316-160
1410 Valley View Drive
Delta, CO 81416 USA

Web Site: www.skrandolph.com
Substack: skrandolph.substack.com
Facebook: http://facebook.com/S.K.Randolph11

Janet Gray 1951-2018

My good friend, my colleague, and my inspiration...

Janet and I worked together for over a quarter of a century. Her yearly trips to Interlochen Center for the Arts and St. Paul's School to work with my students were treasured by all who had the privilege of taking dance classes with her. She was unique in the way she approached her students, providing them with not only the gift of excellent jazz and tap technique but by also teaching them the skills necessary to pursue responsible and productive lives. Not a day goes by that I do not remember and cherish the friendship we shared and the joy we both found in teaching.

CORPS STONES

VarTerels' Universe ™
SCIENCE FANTASY

82nd Street
79th Street
77th Street
Riverside Dr
Old Mansion
West End Ave
Studio Apartment
Columbus Ave
Subway Hub
72nd Street
Apartment
Henry Hudson Parkway
Amsterdam Ave
Broadway
66th Street
West End Ave
65th Street
Lincoln Center
The Juilliard School
65th Street
62nd Street
Fordum University
60th Street
Lincoln Center Theater
Library
Philharmomic Hall
59th Street
Columbus Ave
Metropolitan Opera House
New York State Theater
62nd Street

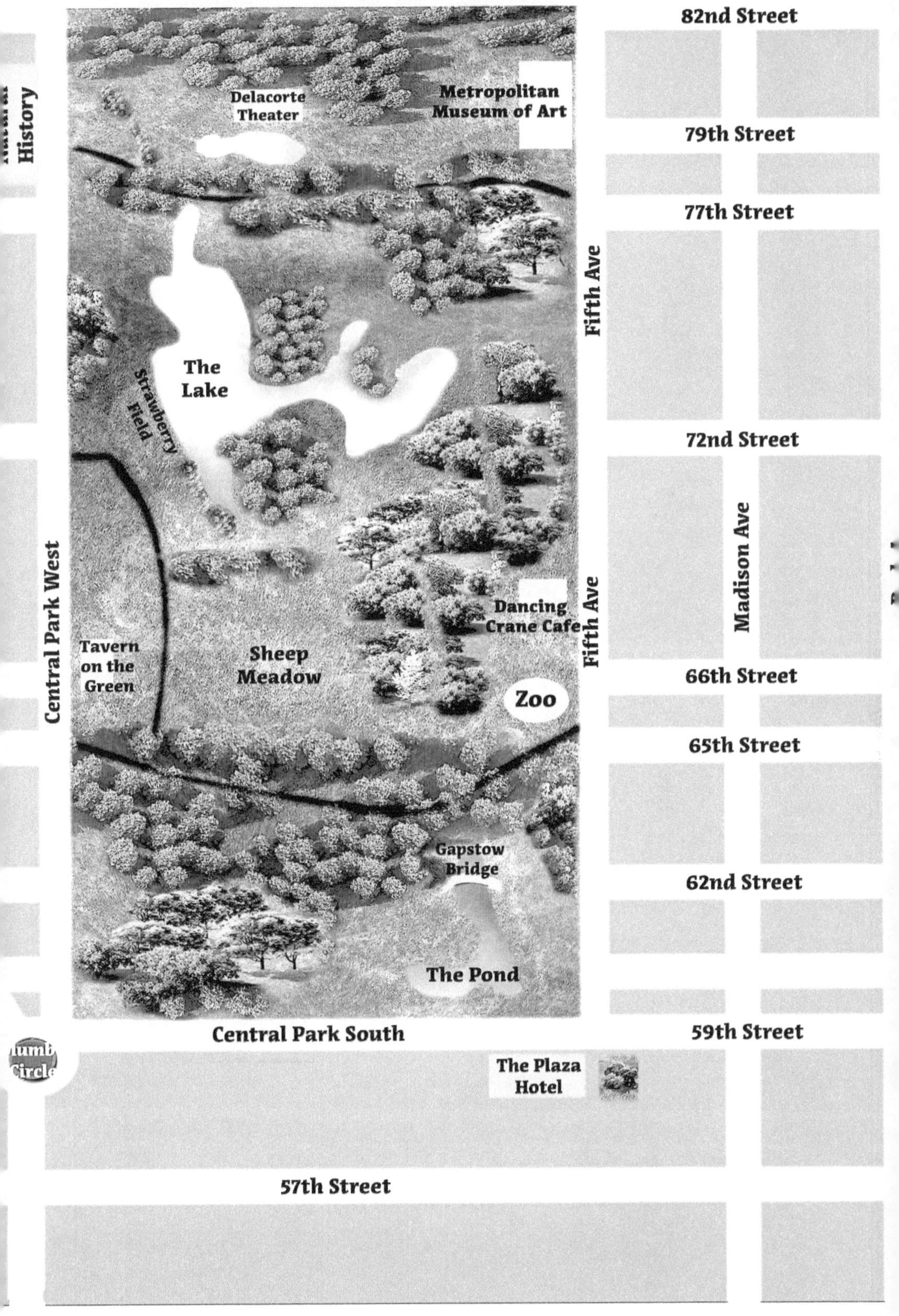

History
82nd Street
Metropolitan Museum of Art
Delacorte Theater
79th Street
77th Street
Fifth Ave
The Lake
Strawberry Field
72nd Street
Madison Ave
Central Park West
Dancing Crane Cafe
Fifth Ave
Tavern on the Green
Sheep Meadow
Zoo
66th Street
65th Street
Gapstow Bridge
62nd Street
The Pond
Central Park South
59th Street
The Plaza Hotel
Columbus Circle
57th Street

Prologue

Tao Spirian prophecies speak of a man
With two seeds of Carsilem, who must take a stand.
A journey through time with a young VarTerel
Will save his home planet and galaxy as well.

The single central eye in a *mammoth*, bear-like skull searched the dark mountain cavern. Straightening to his full height, Rikell, the RewFaaran Mindeco, snuffled the damp air. The scent of Human dropped him to a predatory crouch. A low-pitched growl rumbled deep in his throat.

From behind the large rock protecting the cavern entrance, a cloak-enshrouded figure stepped into the open, an envelope in its gloved hand. It stooped, then straightened, scanned the area, and retreated.

The Mindeco remained hidden and silent. He had no intention of falling into a trap. When the Human did not reappear, he stuck his nasal protuberance in the air, sniffed the ordinary odors of the RewFaaran cavern, and lowered his chin. Nothing shouted a warning.

Curiosity enhanced by the faint aroma of lilies propelled him to standing. His single oculus distinguished the pale gray envelope from the dark, slate-colored mud of the cavern floor. A loped stride brought him within reach.

He retrieved it and held it up in the light. The single word **RIKELL** written in block letters provided no hint to its scribe. Breaking the wax seal in two with his bear-like claw, he withdrew a single sheet of heavy, gray paper.

Sunrise over the Ocean of Mālie on the planet of Tao Spirian brought a lump to Esán Efre's throat. He gazed out over the harbor. *Capee Iwa*, his father Somay's sailboat, glided toward him through the sun-soaked water. Raising a hand to shield his eyes, he watched Somay drop the sail, shift the tiller, and let the boat's momentum bring her into the slip.

His father tossed him the bowline, then jumped onto the wooden finger with the stern line in his hand. Two quick half hitches secured it to a cleat.

"Hold her steady, Esán. I'll be with you in a minute."

Back in the cockpit, Somay secured the sail and boom, lashed the tiller amidship, and put the fenders over the side. Hopping back onto the finger, he took the bow line from Esán and tied it off at a forward cleat. After a quick visual check of the boat, he turned to his son, a father's smile beaming, and ran an eager eye over him.

Esán returned his appraisal with an appreciative grin. Their long, blond hair and stormy blue eyes marked them as father and son, a relationship he had never expected to have. His Aunt Merrilea had raised him in the Central Mountains on Thera. The fight to save Myrrh had introduced him to Somay.

"You look great, Esán. The last time I saw you..." His father tugged his wheat-colored braid. "...your hair had just started to grow back. Now, it's brushing your shoulders!" He became all business. "Are Torgin and Brie with you?"

"They're talking with the harbormaster. They wanted to give us some time."

Somay looked out to sea. "Your mother..." He cleared his throat. "She wished to meet your friends, especially Brie, but her role of birther had to take precedence." A smile etched the lines in his face deeper. "She hopes you will return home to Tao Spirian when it's the time to state your love and join with Brielle."

Esán gazed over the island-speckled ocean. "Tao Spirian's beauty pulses in my veins, Father. Someday, I *will* bring Brielle home, and we'll spend significant time here."

His father's expression softened, then grew somber. "Someday, but not today. Urgency snaps at our heels. Chealim has summoned me to a meeting while you collect your friends and bring them to our special place." He flashed from sight.

Esán hurried up the dock toward the harbormaster's hut.

❧ ❧

Rikell peered from the cave opening into the surrounding woods. Senses heightened, he made his way to the meeting place described in the letter. A dark-cloaked figure materialized near a rickety dock. Protective wards hummed around it.

The Mindeco strove to discern male or female, old or young. The cloak masked all but one gloved hand.

"You are here, Mindeco, so I assume you find my employer's proposal interesting?" The voice gave nothing away.

Rikell answered from the shadows. "How do I know I can trust you?"

The cloaked shoulder shrugged. "You can't. However, since you are unharmed, and I have come alone..." The words held a challenge. "Alone does not mean I am vulnerable, Mindeco. One false move and your turnings on this planet will end."

Rikell suppressed an overwhelming desire to merge with the figure's body and inched a step closer. "How will we travel?" He sidled into the open. "I am not small, nor am I likely to go unnoticed."

The figure raised the hand.

Blinding light flooded the clearing. Rikell stumbled. Dizziness spun the world. The ground flew up to meet him.

1

The Seeds of Carsilem stirred as Esán hurried to join Brielle AsTar and Torgin Whalend where they waited on the boardwalk outside the harbormaster's office. He hugged Brie and nodded at Torgin. "Chealim, Relevart, and my father are meeting us in one of my favorite places on the island."

He set a brisk pace along West Stafany Beach to a hut nestled in palm trees and kali rose bushes. Clasping Brie's hand, he nodded at Torgin. "Hold on." The walls of the hut blurred. A huge cavern took shape around them. On three sides, a seamless, clear wall provided a spectacular view of an undersea world brimming with fan coral, schools of tropical fish, and a diverse variety of aquatic life.

Brie gasped. "Oh, Esán, I see why you love it!"

Torgin walked ahead and whistled. "What a magnificent view!"

"Beautiful, isn't it?" Somay preceded Relevart and Chealim into the cavern and gestured to a cozy grouping of chairs. "Let's take a seat."

The Galactic Guardian Chealim his immenseness onto a couch. His sky-blue eyes narrowed, he looked from one expectant face to the next. "For everyone's safety, what I am about to share must remain among us and us alone. Do I have your solemn promise to hold this information in the strictest confidence?"

After each had made a vow of secrecy, he turned to the Universal VarTerel. "Please begin."

Relevart surveyed the group. "What do you know about the Crystal Laítise?"

Esán leaned forward. "Isn't it the means by which the planets communicate?"

Relevart nodded. "It's that and much more. The Laítise links the planets, solar systems, and galaxies and allows them to communicate over vast distances. Its most important function, however, is holding each celestial body or system to its place in the dark matter comprising the Universe. Were the Laítise to fail, planets would fly from orbit, solar systems would disintegrate, and galaxies would collide with one another. Chaos would ensue."

Torgin bristled with curiosity. "How is this Laítise constructed, Chealim?"

The Council's emissary pursed full lips. "The Fourth Galaxy is the largest in the Sirius Star System. The Laítise for this system comprises a network of quartz crystals in varying sizes. Corps Stones, the smallest crystals, are positioned at the core of each planet in the galaxy. They link to Demi Stones, larger crystals anchored on a central planet in each Solar System, which in turn connect to Prima Stones strategically placed in each galaxy. Evolsefil on Myrrh is the Fourth Galaxy's Prima. Of these three main stone types, only Corps Stones can change size to accommodate their environment."

Relevart withdrew a metal cylinder from an inside pocket in his loose-fitting jacket. He held it up. "A courier on horseback delivered this to me at my cottage on Persow, my home plate." He removed a note from the cylinder, unrolled it, and read:

"Galactic Council: Fourth Galaxy

"I have in my possession two Corps Stones, one from Tao Spirian and one from KcernFensia. By the time you receive this, I will have a third stone.

"If you wish to see them returned, you will fulfill the ransom request which will be forthcoming. To ensure your cooperation, press the blue star at the bottom of this note to see a memory image of the stones.

"I will be contacting you."

Relevart lowered the paper and pressed the star. Red and green swirls shimmered above it and coalesced into an emerald and a ruby, each enclosed within a clear quartz crystal orb. They hovered only long enough to register, then evaporated. He returned the note to the cylinder and passed it to Chealim.

"We are dealing with someone who either does not understand the ramifications of removing Corps Stones from their home planets, or who doesn't care if upheaval is created throughout the Inner Universe. Since I informed the Council, it has discovered several important things.

"As you know, RewFaar is the most technically advanced planet in the Clenaba Rolas System. One of its top research scientists went missing with no hint to her whereabouts. A moon cycle ago, your grandfather, Brielle, received a coded message from her, requesting a secret meeting. Lorsedi met with her, moved her to as safe place, and shared her information with the Council."

Chealim picked up the tale. "She had designed a time machine prototype. Her abductors, headed by a Pheet Adolan Klutarse named Upori Athai, forced her to build one for their use. We do not believe Upori is the thief; we believe someone associated with him is."

Brie tugged a red curl. "Do you think he sent the ransom note?"

"Our research scientist feels certain Upori Athai is not the man in charge." Chealim's elegant forehead furrowed. "What we know—Upori has taken the stones back through time to an ideal hiding place." A slight smile smoothed his brow. "He has a surprise in store. Lorsedi's research scientist programmed the time machine to stay in the past."

A thrill of excitement raced through Esán. "You want us to find the stones, right?"

"We thought you would guess the end point of this conversation." His father stifled a smile. "However, we have more to share before you get too excited."

Esán squeezed Brie's hand and controlled his enthusiasm.

Tapping a rhythmic cadence on his knee, Relevart gazed into the distance. The tapping ceased. His attention returned to the group. "Information we have gathered suggests that Upori has escaped to New York City on the American continent in the Old Earth year, 1969.," He paused to gaze at each member of the trio. "Since his passions comprise a love of the theater, music, dance, and dance history of that time, your youth plus your talents make you perfect for this mission."

Brie laughed softly. "That's why we've spent the past several turnings in the Galactic Library on Myrrh, studying New York in that time frame."

"That is exactly why." Chealim's twinkling eyes contrasted with his serious expression. "We want you to do a little time traveling."

Brie's emotions ran a relay race. Doubt, fear, excitement, and wonder passed the baton. She looked up to discover everyone's attention fastened on her.

Chealim's intimidating height towered over her. His stern gaze was unwavering. "You may not go to Earth as Brielle AsTar. Our enemies know what you look like and how to recognize your power and your energy's essence. Gaining control of you would be a triumph." He stepped away. "Share Rayna with us."

A shiver of expectancy raised the hair on her neck. She pushed back her chair and stood. With the help of the Star of Truth, she centered her scattered emotions. Esán's supportive presence buoyed her courage. She took a deep breath.

Rayna's appearance elicited a nod from the Galactic Guardian. Her confidence bolstered, Brie stared at Rayna's exotic reflection on the clear underground wall. Short, black hair with russet highlights framed amber eyes glinting in a porcelain-fair face. Rayna, tall and muscular, exuded physical power. Embracing what Rayna's persona offered, she turned.

Chealim nodded. She reversed the shift. The joy of returning to herself left her grinning.

Esán's embrace welcomed her back. Torgin's delighted laugh warmed her. She glanced at her reflected self, saw the expression on Chealim's face, and met his expectant gaze.

He returned to his seat, a smile twitching the corners of his mouth. "We have developed a plan we hope will give you each a cover story our enemies will not expect. Rayna Deejara will study ballet at the School of American Ballet. If you agree, Brielle, the Goddess Terpsichore will send someone to help you adjust your shifted form to accommodate your new role and to provide you with the skills you will require. Please take a moment to decide if being Rayna for an extended period is acceptable to you."

Brie folded her hands in her lap. Memory and desire made the decision for her. She met Chealim's inquiring gaze. "I've always wanted to dance." She tilted her head. "I like Rayna's surname."

The Fourth Galaxy's Guardian nodded his approval and turned his attention to Esán. "Nesá Zervos, you are the son of a Greek-American artist. You will study lighting design at the New York Studio and Forum under Joseph Shyro. Mr. Shyro is the head designer at New York City Ballet. It is our hope you will apprentice with him and thus gain access to the New York State Theater.

Torgin looked from one to the other. "This means we *are* going back in time!" Summer green eyes brimmed with anticipation. "I don't suppose I could study music at The Juilliard School?"

Chealim laughed, a sound reminiscent of distant bells tolling. "Yes, Torgin Whälen. Your story includes Finnish ancestry and studying music at Juilliard." He sobered. "You must not, however, forget your true reason for being in the New York City of 1969."

Brie observed her friend's excitement. The seriousness of the situation did not eclipse Torgin's delight.

Even, white teeth flashed against warm brown skin. "I promise, Chealim, to keep my duty to this time and place uppermost in my mind. May I ask a question?"

"You may."

Torgin straightened the papers stacked on a table next to his chair. "Why am I here? I understand Brie and Esán. They have talents that make them logical choices. But me?"

The Guardian's intense attention made him fidget. "You do not give yourself enough credit, Torgin. Think back to TreBlaya. Who trapped thirty Pheet Adole Mocendi in a prison created from a musical staff? How many times have you called into play your musical talent to save others? You are the descendent of a man named Kuparak. Did you know he could change shapes, teleport, use telepathy? We will explore these avenues before you depart. Your untapped talents may surprise you, but I doubt they will surprise anyone else."

The Guardian placed a ceramic whistle resembling a miniature flute on the table. "We also require a musician to help Brie and Esán create a time tunnel to carry you into the past."

Torgin picked up the whistle, which spanned his palm from finger tips to wrist. Its beautiful, fire-painted patterns glowed in the cool light. He looked at Chealim. "I presume someone will teach me how to use this?"

The Guardian's laugh tolled. "I believe playing it will come naturally. We will work with the three of you to create a tunnel to carry you back to 1969 and return you to this time when your mission is complete."

An elegant young woman walked into the cavern. She greeted Chealim with a bright smile and then addressed Brie. "I am called Étoile. If you will come with me, I will prepare you to join the dance world."

Apprehension-tinged excitement carried Brie to her feet. Étoile offered her hand. A blink later, Brie found herself in a room with ballet barres on one wall and floor to ceiling mirrors on the other.

*   *

Torgin looked up from examining the whistle and forced himself not to squirm under Relevart's serious scrutiny.

The VarTerel's solemn expression melted into a smile. "Go ahead. Play it."

Torgin placed his fingers, raised it to his lips, and blew a long high note. The atmosphere in the room grew taut. A lower note relaxed it. Playing the lowest note seemed to distance him from his companions. Again, a tone from the middle of the range returned things to normal.

Chealim nodded. "Good. Play a short tune. Nothing too fancy."

Torgin mentally composed a simple melody using the whistle's six holes. Clear, beautiful notes filled the space and faded. He gazed at the whistle in awe. "The sound is exquisite for such a small instrument."

Relevart reached for the whistle. "May I?"

"Of course." Torgin held it out.

The VarTerel blew a dissident note that left everyone covering their ears. He chuckled, then grew serious. "That, Torgin, depends on who's playing it. This whistle has been tuned to your energy signature. Only you can make the sound required to help Brie and Esán create the magnetic force needed for a time tunnel." He passed him the whistle. "Sparrow returned the Compass of Ostradio to you, correct?"

Torgin touched a leather pouch attached to his belt. "Yes."

"Good." Relevart looked at Esán. "The Seeds of Carsilem are the key to your part in this, Esán. We believe the whistle will set the seeds in motion. It will also vibrate Brielle's Star of Truth. Working together, these three things will establish the magnetic rotation required to carry you back in time. The compass will pinpoint your destination in New York. We will go into more detail when Brie returns."

The ground trembled. The ocean roiled against the clear wall. Fish darted in agitated patterns. Torgin grasped the whistle as Esán gripped the arms of his chair.

Chealim rose, his majestic height filling the space. "Relevart, Somay, and I have some things to attend to. I have arranged for you both to receive special training for the mission. Your tutors will arrive shortly. We will reconvene after evening meal.

The three men flashed from view, leaving Torgin gazing at the whistle and Esán staring at the tumultuous sea beyond the wall.

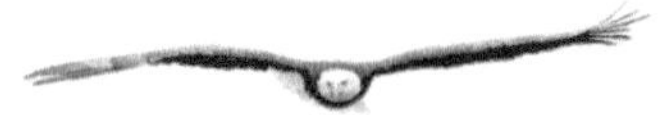

2

Brie walked around the ballet practice room, ran a finger along the rounded, wooden barre, and stopped in front of Étoile, who looked every inch the ballet dancer.

Her mentor's smile broadened. "You have questions, Brielle. Please ask."

Excited by the possibilities confronting her, she grinned. "I loved ballet when I took it as a child in Idronatti. Ari found it tedious, so we didn't continue. How can you help me prepare for dancing at a professional school?"

Étoile placed a wooden chair at the room's center. "Terpsichore chose me because I am the goddess who inspires and protects young dancers." Her dark gray eyes sparkled. "And ballet is my passion." She scrutinized Brie from head to toe. "The first thing we'll do is work with the Star of Truth to adjust Rayna's physical appearance and to provide the required muscle memory. Then I will place you in a trance and embed within your psyche the intellectual and emotional information you require to be a professional-level student. If you are ready, please take a seat. I understand you also have a renegade personality named Fisaco who has attached himself to The Master's gene. Make sure you tell me if he rears his head."

Brie sat on the straight-backed chair, her posture dancer perfect. Étoile's first step—altering Rayna's physique—took only a short time. Due to the goddess' quick reaction, Fisaco's tentative attempt to interfere ended with a speedy retreat. With a satisfied nod, she completed her work. The Star of Truth tingled. Brie stood, shifted to Rayna, and gazed in the mirror.

The changes were subtle but obvious. Rayna, her now long, dark hair in a bun, appeared more slender. Her calf and thigh muscles were well-defined and her feet beautifully arched. Amber eyes had darkened to brown with sparks of gold. Her peaches and cream complexion glowed.

Étoile stood back to observed the result. "I love your Eleo Predan coloring, Rayna. I kept it, but for the amber eyes. They would give you away to someone who knows Brielle's ancestry." Her easy smile grew serious. "Please have a seat again. It's time for a crash course in ballet technique."

Étoile allowed her to settle and relax, then placed her warm palms on either side of her head. The quiet in the studio intensified. Heat penetrated to her scalp and flowed throughout Rayna's body. Her mind flooded with information. Muscles twitched with a desire to move as Étoile's hands withdrew.

Rayna opened her eyes to find the goddess holding out a pair of pointe shoes. "Put these on. Let's see what you've learned."

The pink satin shoes fit like a glove. After tying the ribbons and tucking the ends neatly out of sight, Rayna faced the barre and rested her hands on the smooth, round wood. Placing her pointe-shoe-clad feet heel-to-heel in first position, she bent her knees in a *demi plié* and marveled at the ease with which she executed a *relevé* onto pointe. Over the course of the next hour, Étoile took her through a warmup at the barre and a series of combinations in front of the mirror.

At last, the goddess gave a congratulatory nod. "Nice work, Rayna. I believe you're up to the task. Please remember you must shape Brielle for a period every day. The spot where the Star of Truth is on Brie's neck will pinch when you need to shift. Is there anything else you wish to ask?"

"What happens if I have questions when I'm in New York City?"

Étoile smiled. "Simply take a moment, and the answer will surface. I have given you everything you need to know and more."

A final look in the mirror and Rayna shifted to Brie. "That was amazing!" She laughed. "Do you think I can dance in my own body?"

"You have the knowledge. Give it a try." Étoile gazed at her with interest.

Brie moved to the barre and performed the first several warmup exercises... *plié, tendu battement plié, tendu battement jeté.* She then walked to the center of the room, did a short jump combination, and turned to the goddess. "Not nearly as good as Rayna, but still... Thank you, Étoile. What now?"

"It's time for me to go and for you to rejoin your friends. Take care of yourself, Brielle AsTar. The mission you are about to embark on is as dangerous as it is important."

A flash of warm, pale peach light left the studio empty but for Brie and the echo of the goddess' warning.

His mind reeling with newly acquired knowledge, Esán returned to the undersea meeting chamber where Brie sat alone, her expression distant and thoughtful. He kissed her cheek and pulled his chair next to hers. "You look serious. How'd your session go?"

She held up a hand and studied it, curled the fingers, and lowered it. "The session went well. I think you will be surprised at how much information I assimilated in such a short time. What about you?"

Angling to see her better, he tucked his hair behind his ear. "As a student, I studied Earth's gods and goddesses but never thought of them as real until today. I met with a lighting specialist who works with Dionysus, the god of theater; you met with a goddess sent by Terpsichore; and Torgin is with Apollo's apprentice, who is helping him master the time whistle and preparing him for Juilliard. Are you as taken aback as I am?"

Brie focused on the vast sea world beyond the wall. Although her gaze returned to him, her distant look remained. "Training in DiMensionery has taught me that nothing is what it seems. Our lives are as fantastical as those we read about in books. Think about the vastness of this Universe. You and I are the tiniest specks of matter imaginable, and yet we are being prepared to save our galaxy and beyond. How much do we truly know about anything? Living gods and goddesses are no more strange than you possessing dual Seeds of Carsilem or my becoming the youngest VarTerel in the Inner Universe."

Running her hands through her hair, she interlocked her fingers on top of her head and raised a brow. "Which does not mean I'm not awed by everything we are experiencing." She let her red curls fall free to tumble around her face.

Torgin strode into the space, his excitement tangible. "Did I interrupt something? You look pretty serious."

Brie smiled at his obvious excitement. "Join us. We were discussing the magnitude of everything. How about you?"

"I just met the Greek demi-god named Allegro. He taught me how to play the time whistle, gave me enough musical training in an afternoon to fill years of my life, and helped me to recalibrate the Compass of Ostradio." He grinned. "The stars on the compass back are now those of Earth's sky in 1969.

Esán tilted his head. "Doesn't it bother you that you just worked with a deity from stories of old?"

His expression blanked. "I hadn't thought about it. I've been friends with you, Ari, and Brie for so long I guess I take the extraordinary for granted." He plopped down in a chair. "You have to admit you three are pretty amazing. Other kids in Idronatti certainly didn't teleport, use telepathy, or change shape." A deep inhale brought him upright. "Do you think I can do any of those things?"

Esán caught the glint of a reflection in the clear wall. "I believe we are about to find out."

T orgin met Relevart's knowing smile with a slight bow of his head. The Universal VarTerel took a seat. "Chealim and Somay will be joining us soon. While we wait, and since time is growing short, I suggest we see how much of Kuparak's gift you have inherited, Torgin. Please sit opposite me."

Forcing calm he did not feel, Torgin changed seats. "What do I need to do?"

"Relax, my boy. This will be a painless exercise, one which I believe may surprise you. Now, will Esán and Brie make you nervous?"

He shook his head. "To the contrary, sir. They will give me the confidence to try."

"Good boy. Calm your mind. Brie, on my signal, please place a thought in Torgin's mind. Let us know, Torgin, when you are aware of it."

Allowing Brie's calming presence to help him relax, Torgin waited for Relevart's signal. None came.

What if I can't—"

"Torgin, nod if you can hear me." Brie's quiet thought filled his mind.

He caught his breath and nodded.

"Good. The first concert we went to together in Idronatti...who was your favorite composer?"

The clarity of the question startled him. His eyes widened and sought Relevart's.

The VarTerel nodded. "You heard her question. Answer it in her mind."

Scrunching his forehead into furrows, Torgin concentrated on placing the answer. *"Wolfgang Amadeus Mozart."*

"You are so good, Torgin."

He gave a short laugh. "I had no idea. Why didn't I figure this out sooner?"

Relevart's serious expression suppressed Torgin's urge to jump for joy. "You assumed you didn't have the gifts your friends have. Your lack of belief in yourself kept you from trying. Let's see what you do with teleportation." He pointed to the ocean wall opposite the entrance. "Esán, please stand over there; Torgin, stand by the entrance."

Torgin, framed by the cavern's rough-edged entryway, barely held his jitters in check.

Esán's easy stance and serene smile helped. "Picture yourself beside me, Torg. Nod when you're ready."

Closing his eyes, Torgin imagined himself standing next to his friend. Breath held, he nodded.

"Will yourself here."

Esán's voice encouraged him to believe. He willed himself across the space, opened his eyes, and frowned. He hadn't moved, nor had anyone else. Relevart remained impassive. Brie merely watched. Doubt assailed him. Shoving it away, he pictured the spot next to Esán and willed himself there.

Silence told him he'd failed. Heaving a sigh, he peeked beneath his lids.

Esán grinned and slapped him on the back. "Race you to the entryway."

Torgin blinked. Laughter bubbled in his throat. Esán waved from the cavern entrance. Touching the clear wall's cool surface, Torgin pictured himself beside his friend. He arrived, gulped a surprised breath, and elbowed a grinning Esán in the ribs. "I did it! Wish Ari were here to see that I am not a Drotti!" He hugged Brie. His confident gaze fastened on Relevart. "You did say Kuparak could shape shift, right?"

Relevart's honey-gold eyes gleamed. "I did. It is the hardest of the three skills to master. If it doesn't work here, don't give up. Brie and Esán can work with you in New York City."

Brie interrupted. "You're sure we can use our gifts in another time and dimension?"

The VarTerel's white brow arced. "You can use your gifts; however, I caution you to be mindful of the situation. Don't call the enemy to your side."

Chealim marched into the space and scanned the group. His furrowed brow relayed his distress. Torgin shivered. He had never seen the Guardian rattled.

Towering over the group, Chealim frowned. "A third Corps Stone has been stolen. That means the ransom demand will be forthcoming. It also means the Solar System is at risk." Full lips pressed into a firm line. Shaking himself, he continued. "We had hoped to give you more time to assimilate all the information you've received, but we need you to locate the stones before the deadline."

He tilted his head, seemed to listen, and rubbed a hand on his pants. "I must go. Relevart will give you a quick course in how to create and use a time tunnel. I sent Somay on an errand. He wishes you well. Take care of yourselves." Inhaling a breath, he vanished.

Torgin clutched the time whistle hanging on the thong beneath his shirt. Insecurity nagged. *Sure wish I knew more about the science of time.*

3

Brie swallowed a knot in her throat and fixed her attention on the Universal Var Terel, who gave a key ring to Esán.

"These are the keys to your apartment in New York City. It's on the Upper West Side, a few blocks from Lincoln Center. Duplicate keys are in the desk drawer in the study. Family histories—which I suggest you commit to memory, maps, and subway schedules are on the dining table. Instructions regarding where to go to begin your New York City lives and a schedule for the first couple days in the city are there, too."

He handed Torgin a banking passbook. "Since you are the mathematical genius in this trio, you will be in charge of the finances. The council has deposited money for your use at a bank near Columbus Circle. All the information you require is in the passbook."

His somber gaze moved from eager face to eager face. "Do not let New York City's resemblance to Idronatti fool you. At this time in the city's history, crime ran rampant. Discrimination against race, religious preference, and gender, highlighted in riots throughout the city, put the population on edge. An unpopular war in Vietnam, a country on the other side of the planet, kept tempers flaring. You cannot let your guard down. Don't trust anyone except each other unless you are certain they mean you no harm."

Tapping his chin with an index finger, he again made eye contact with each of them. "I understand you have many questions. You're smart. You'll discover the answers. The primary goal of this mission is to locate and return the Corps Stones before the Clenaba Rolas System becomes unbalanced to the point of no return. Secondary is discovering who Upori's assistant is—who stole the stones for him." White brows bridged his nose. "We must know who Upori is working with. Every detail, no matter how seemingly insignificant, is important." He came to his feet. "Brie, you will need your VarTerel's staff. Torgin, please get out the time whistle and the compass. Let's get to work!"

Brie's staff flashed into being. Its tourmaline crown shot rays of rainbow light between the intricate weave of the rowan vines encasing it. Wonder washed over her. *I am a VarTerel.*

Relevart observed her with a slight smile. "Have you named the crystal?"

"I have christened it Musette, which means bright in Eleo Predan."

"Good. Have Musette take us into Mittkeer."

She gripped the staff. Torgin, Esán, and Relevart gathered around her. Stars and night sky embraced them. Quiet, as tangible as a spring breeze, held them silent.

Torgin, the first to recover his equilibrium, let out a breath. "I love Mittkeer. Now what?"

Relevart stepped apart from the group and withdrew a time whistle from his pocket. "Time as we perceive it is an illusion. Past, present, and future are all happening in this moment. Our goal, therefore, is to create a time tunnel which allows us to traverse the dimensional patterns of space-time. Mittkeer is the key to this. We must use two whistles to set up a coordinated harmonic. To travel forward, we will use high notes; to move backward, low notes. The rainbow tourmaline on Brie's staff will generate complimentary light waves, and the Seeds of Carsilem will provide the magnetic connection to hold everything in place. The compass will bring the destination point into focus."

Brie noted the gleam of appreciation in Torgin's eyes. She understood the concepts, but he realized how the principles worked together. Next to his love of music, mathematics and science fed his intellectual passion.

Esán pursed his lips in thought. "If we need two whistles to return to this dimensional time—"

A tremor rippled through the star-scape, cutting him short. Relevart's expression hardened. "We're working on it. You must go. Torgin, please play the low frequency scale Allegro taught you. The Compass of Ostradio will work on its own. Brie, shift to Rayna. Focus the light from Musette with this intent."

Rayna flashed into being. A picture filled her mind. Rainbow rays shot from the tourmaline crystal. Torgin played the scale. Relevart's whistle joined him an octave lower. Esán clasped the staff, his other hand on Torgin's arm. The stars shimmered brighter. The repeating scale vibrated through the night sky. Stars grew hazy and distant. Behind the trio, a tunnel spun into being, sucking them backward.

The last thing Rayna saw...Relevart growing smaller and smaller and smaller.

Esán, working with the energy emitted by the Seeds of Carsilem, created sustainable magnetic waves to keep the tunnel spinning in one direction at a consistent rotation. The rainbow rays from Brie's crystal did not waver. Low-pitched sound from the time whistle shaped the tunnel. Dimensions streaked by.

A distant blaze of pale magenta light sped toward them. Rayna moaned. Esán caught her as her knees buckled. Musette dimmed. The staff vanished. Torgin played a sustained note and gulped a breath. The light rushed closer. Another lower note held it steady. The tunnel's spin slowed. Darkness cloaked them. The tunnel dissolved, leaving them dappled in shadow beneath the wide, thick branches of a deciduous tree. Not far ahead, moonlight sparkled on the surface of a small lake. To one side, street lamps lined a gravel walkway.

Esán focused on Rayna.

She gripped his arm to help pull herself to standing. "Did you see that, Esán?"

"If you mean the racing blurs of light, yes." He saw only confusion on her face.

She peered between branches. "Weren't we supposed to end up in the apartment? Where are we, Torgin?"

"I'm not sure. Ostradio isn't responding." He scanned the sky. "The moon's in its final quarter, the right phase for our time frame."

A small dog's insistent yelping, pounding footsteps on the path, and a child's yell echoed through the night.

Esán pulled Rayna behind the tree. Torgin squatted behind a bush.

"Let me go." The youthful voice, more angry than afraid, mingled with a dog's threatening bark and a man's frustrated shout. A dark-skinned boy of ten or eleven sprinted across the grass on the far side of the path with a black and white rat terrier racing beside him.

A youngish, bearded man closed the gap between them, grabbed the child by the arm, and yanked him around to face him. His arm went back.

Esán stepped into the warm glow of a streetlamp. "I wouldn't if I were you."

The man gave a nasty laugh. "Who's gonna stop me? You?"

Torgin moved to his side. Rayna stood between them.

Esán ignored the question. "Let the boy go."

Jaw muscles beneath the ragged beard tensed. A shove sent the child sprawling on the ground. "Don't think I'll forget this, brat." Without a backward glance, the man sprinted up the path.

Esán hurried to the child's side. Ignoring his offered hand, the boy scrambled to standing and backed away. His dark-eyed gaze flitted from him to Rayna to Torgin.

Rayna smiled. "I promise we won't hurt you. My name's Rayna. These are my friends Esán and Torgin."

Suspicion quivered in his voice. "One minute ya weren't beneath that tree, the next ya were. I saw ya appear—outta nowhere. The guy caught me 'cause I was watchin' ya." An accusatory glare darted from Rayna to Torgin and stopped on Esán. Fear flashed. Curiosity eclipsed it. "Where'd ya come from?"

Esán kept his voice steady. "Please tell us where we are."

Uncertainty flickered across the boy's face. His gaze flitted along the path. He inched closer to the bushes.

"Please don't go." Rayna pleaded. "We're lost. We need your help."

Torgin withdrew a large, silver coin from his pocket. "This is yours if you'll explain where we are and what the date is."

The boy stared, his expression dumbfounded. A quick shake of his head left it blank. He licked his bottom lip. "It's Saturday, July 5, 1969." At a nod from Torgin, he took a halting step forward and snatched the fifty-cent piece. "You're on the west side of the park near 72nd Street and Central Park West." He stuffed the coin in his pocket, then shot them a penetrating stare. "Ya where ya expected to be?"

Rayna gripped Esán's forearm. "Close enough. What's your name?"

An internal struggle played out on his face. He swallowed. "Name's Gar. If ya tell me where ya need to go, I'll take ya."

Esán smiled. "Gar's a noble name."

White teeth flashed. Gar squinted up at them. "Ya ain't gonna tell me where you're from, are ya?"

Esán peered into the night. "Do you know the guy who was chasing you?"

Gar wrinkled his nose. "He's just some junky trying to make a score so's he can buy some dope."

Rayna scanned the trees. "Where's your family?"

The boyish face grew sullen. "Ain't got no folks. Just me and Spyglass." He gripped the dog's rope collar.

Footsteps crunching their direction on the gravel path brought a warning growl from the small dog.

Torgin pulled Rayna into the shadows. Gar's eyes narrowed. "Tell me where you need to go—"

With and urgent shake of his head, Esán beckoned him to follow. Gathered in a tight group behind a couple of trees, they watched a tall, muscular man in a uniform stroll closer, scan the area, and continue down the path.

His expression serious, Esán stooped to look Gar in the eye. "Can I trust you to keep a secret?"

The conspiratorial tone produced an enthusiastic nod.

"We're in New York City on a special mission. No one is to know where we are."

Gar swallowed. "I promise not to tell a soul."

Esán straightened and clasped Rayna's hand. "We're looking for the corner of 72nd Street and Broadway."

Gar jerked a thumb in her direction. "She your girl?"

He nodded solemnly. "She is. And don't you forget it."

A grin spread from ear to ear. "Never would. Let's go 'fore the patrol comes back." He trotted along a faint trail, Spyglass at his heels.

Rayna fell in step behind them. Torgin followed. Esán gave the area a final searching scan, obscured their energy signatures with a wave, and sprinted to catch up.

👁 👁

Muggy night air made Rayna's blouse stick to her neck as she and her friends trotted after Gar. Her attention flashed from one side of the path to the other. Her only experience with a city was Idronatti. It's pristine, peaceful, orderly streets were nothing like the one they were approaching. Suffocating smells and an abundance of unfamiliar noise overwhelmed her. She pulled Esán to a stop. Torgin and Gar glanced back as they reached the curb of the street bordering the west side of the park.

Rayna gulped a breath. "I'm sorry. I need a minute."

Esán squeezed her hand. "Take your time." He looked around. "It's a lot to assimilate."

Gar jogged up to her. "Ya okay?"

"I'll be fine." She forced herself to ignore her growing fear of being out of her element.

The light at the corner flashed from red to green. Gar grinned. "Good, 'cause green means go. We gotta cross the street 'fore it changes." He scurried back to Torgin. With Spyglass between them, they proceeded into the crosswalk. Esán's warm hand on her arm gave her the courage to follow.

At the next corner, the stoplight gleamed red. She met Torgin's inquiring gaze with a smile. "I'm fine, really." She peered down a deserted side street lined with tall, dirty buildings as far as she could see. Hazy, dim light made the blue-black asphalt glisten. Steam hovering over manhole covers reminded her of escaping ghosts. *What a peculiar place.*

A strange vehicle screeched to a halt at the crosswalk, music blaring from open windows. Deep bass vibrated through her. She shivered. Esán's arm around her waist steadied her.

Gar guided them to a busier intersection, where even the lateness of the hour didn't impact the non-stop flow of traffic.

Rayna read the street signs. "72nd Street and Amsterdam Avenue. I believe we're almost there."

The boy's smile took over his face. "Ya gettin' unlost?"

She couldn't help smiling back. "I think so. At least, I know this intersection isn't far from our building. Do you have the address?"

He beamed. "Torgin told me. It's this way." Gar led them through a small, triangular park near a bustling subway hub, then herded them across Broadway into a quieter neighborhood. After traversing another long block-and-a-half down 72nd Street, he came to a halt. "There it is." He pointed at a gray apartment building with a dark green awning between the sidewalk and the double glass doors.

Rayna smiled down at him. "Would you like to come in, Gar?"

A flicker of fright lit his features. "Nope. Me and Spyglass need to get goin'. Bein' inside makes us feel trapped. We'll meet ya in the mornin'."

Torgin held out a hand. "Thanks for everything."

Gar shook it, looked surprised, then he grinned and shoved his hand in his pocket. "See ya tomorrow." He trotted along the street, turned, waved, and merged with Spyglass into the night shadows.

Esán watched him go with a slight smile. "Did you give him a tip, Torg?"

"A small token of our gratitude. He deserved it." Torgin led them beneath the awning into the reception area.

After introducing themselves to the doorman, they took the elevator to their floor. The door thumping closed behind them made Torgin shake his head. "Elevators are nothing like the drop cars in Idronatti. I thought we'd never get here, and we're only on the fifth floor."

Esán led the way to apartment 5D, unlocked the three locks, and ushered Rayna inside. Torgin followed. The locks clunked into place. He lifted a chain and slid it along the metal track.

Embraced by the dim interior, Rayna shifted.

The boys vanished into the kitchen, giving Brie time to adjust. She wandered through a large arched entryway into the living room. *Whoever lives here must love ancient things.* The vacant eyes of the tribal masks covering a wall on either side of an oval mirror framed in seashells reminded her of classes in Old Earth anthropology. She ran a finger along the satiny wood of an intricately carved, waist-high cabinet and surveyed the rest of the room.

A comfortable, pillow-covered couch facing a coffee table and two overstuffed chairs formed a cozy sitting area. Beside a bookshelf filled with artifacts, a straight-back chair sported an intricate needlepoint seat cover.

She crossed to a window. The walk from Central Park had the earmarks of a dream. *Loud motor vehicles, foreign smells, and strange sounds...* A self-hug kept a shiver at bay. She studied the building across the way. *If the city streets didn't remind me so much of Idronatti, but dirtier, I might be tempted to wish myself back to my own space-time.*

Esán's arms encircled her. "What's going on in that head of yours?"

His warmth calmed her jitters. "I'm just trying to adjust to the strangeness."

He followed her gaze. "It reminds me of visiting Idronatti the first time, only it feels bigger and dirtier and it's much more noisy." His voice trailed off. "Don't worry, Brielle, we'll settle in."

She touched the long, slender leaf of a potted plant on the windowsill. "Where do you suppose Gar's sleeping tonight? I wish he had come up with us."

Esán kissed the top of her head. "I'm betting he's adopted us. Odds are he'll be waiting out front in the morning."

"I was so afraid when that man caught him." She looked up. "Thank you for helping him." Her brow wrinkled in thought. "There's something special about that boy."

Strong arms encircled her. Esán's eyes sparkled with mischief. "Rayna is sure beautiful. It's a good thing I prefer redheads."

His impish grin brought a gurgle of laughter. She pretended to pout, then gave him a playful punch in the arm. "Just remember the woman you love is always watching."

"Never forget, Brielle AsTar, how much I love you." He kissed her, then grinned. "Torgin's making a snack; then it's time to get some rest. I don't know about you, but the time tunnel experience took its toll on me." Questions wrinkled his brow. "What did you observe in the tunnel?"

She squinted. "I could have sworn I saw a woman's face. Are you sure you didn't notice anything?"

"Nothing, but I thought we were being watched in the Park."

"Hey, you two, foods up!" Torgin carried a loaded tray through the archway. "I say we eat at the coffee table." He set it down, sprawled in an overstuffed chair, and snagged a sandwich. "This is a pretty nice place. Can't wait to explore it." He took a healthy bite, chewed, and mumbled. "After we dine."

Esán picked up a thick ham and cheese sandwich. "If anyone asks, this is Rayna's aunt's apartment."

Brie sipped her lemonade. "Where is her aunt?"

"She's an archaeologist on a dig in Egypt. Her name is Maggie K. Dorain."

Torgin spoke through a mouthful. "That's why there's so much cool stuff everywhere. I love the masks."

Brie swallowed the last of her sandwich and wiped her hands on a napkin. "Speaking of Rayna's aunt, I'm ready to learn about our family histories."

Esán caught a dangling piece of lettuce between his teeth and chewed. "I'm betting the information we need is in the papers Relevart said would be on the dining room table." He nibbled a mustard-lathered crust. "We can look as soon as we finish eating." He wolfed another bite. "Great sandwich, Torg."

"Thanks. The kitchen is well stocked. Wonder who did it?" Torgin wiped his mouth and tossed the napkin on the tray. "Hey, did you see all those yellow cars with checkered stripes on the sides?"

Esán washed his last bite down with lemonade. "Those are cabs or taxis. You pay the driver to take you where you want to go. Sure were a lot of them."

Brie listened to the boys comparing notes on what they had learned in the library on Myrrh and what they had seen on their walk to the apartment. She stifled a yawn. *We are not in Myrrh anymore.*

Somewhat refreshed, Torgin carried the tray loaded with the dirty plates to the kitchen. Brie set about washing them. Esán dried them; Torgin put them away. When the last plate was in the cupboard, he grinned. "Time to explore."

The narrow entryway from the apartment door widened into a long hallway. Opposite the kitchen they discovered a small, elegant dining room. Two bedrooms on the left shared a bath. The large living room on the street side opened off the main hallway. Through a small archway next to the couch, they discovered a study with a desk and bookcases.

Torgin stopped by a closed door at the end of the hall. "What do you suppose is in here?"

Esán shrugged. "I suggest you peek inside."

Torgin turned the knob. "Oh my." His breath caught in his throat. "A Steinway!" Reverence filled the word. He stepped into the room. "In the Galactic Library, I found a book on how Steinway pianos are made. I read it from cover to cover." He ran his hand over the finish of the silky, dark wood. "The title of the book was *Piano: The Making of a Steinway Concert Grand* by James Barrow." He sighed and let his fascinated gaze absorb every detail of the beautiful instrument. Beneath the top board, it lingered on the gorgeous, deep red felt running crosswise to the strings. "I remember...."

Brie moved into his line of vision. "Are you alright, Torg?"

He smiled what he knew must be a dreamy smile. "I'm just captivated by the past. It never occurred to me, even when I read the book, I might see a Steinway baby grand in New York City, 1969."

She pulled out the padded bench. "Now, my dear friend, you get to play one. You can play it, right?"

"I believe so." He sat down and adjusted the seat. "I've only ever played an anopi, the keyboard the PPP allowed my parents to purchase for me." He touched the silky wood. "The designers fashioned the anopi after the piano—"

"What are you waiting for?" Brie's voice, tinged with expectation, almost unnerved him.

Esán, already seated in a wingback chair, came to the rescue. "Give him a minute, Brielle." He patted the chair next to his. "Sit."

Torgin lifted the fallboard and clasped his hands to his lap. "Did you know a grand piano has eighty-eight keys?" He pressed one at the low end of the keyboard. His hand flew to his heart. "Oh my. I never imagined how rich it would sound." He ran a finger over the white keys, then experimented with a

C major chord. Wide-eyed, he tried several more chords. The brightness of the sound left him laughing. Understanding and confidence increased. He played scales and then arpeggios, ascending and descending. He breathed a gratified sigh. When neither Brie nor Esán intruded into his artist's trance, he placed steady hands on the keys, and played in earnest.

Nothing in his experience as a musician had thrilled him like the magnificent sound of the Steinway. Each note produced a wave of pleasure. Mesmerized, he allowed the musical conversation and the artistry of the work to absorb him. Much too soon, he played the final note of the "Prelude in C Major" from Bach's *The Well-Tempered Clavier*, lifted his hands from the keys, and gazed at them as though they belonged to someone else.

Intoxicated by the breadth of the sound, he glanced up. Esán's delighted smile increased his joy. Brie, her tears overflowing, looked dazed.

Torgin ran a finger over the ivory keys. "My first piano teacher in Idronatti reported me to the PPP because I asked to learn classical music from Old Earth. The following week, a man I had heard of but never met, waited in the practice room. He began our lessons with Chopin's nocturnes." He lowered the fallboard. "I had no idea music would be so much richer played on an ancient instrument. Now that I think about it, I imagine I'll be playing a Steinway at the audition for Juilliard. Do you suppose Chealim arranged this?"

Esán stood. "You must ask him when we get back. You're pretty amazing, you know."

Their conversation released Brie from her stupor. "I knew you were good, but, Torgin, that was incredible. Who was the composer?"

"Johann Sebastian Bach." He gave them a short music history lesson. A yawn ended it. "I'm ready to get some sleep. This has been quite a turning."

"Don't forget a turning is a day in this time." Esán patted him on the back. "Bed sounds great. First, we have paperwork to go through." He led the way to the dining room and pulled out a chair. "Have a seat, maestro."

Torgin reached for a pile with his name on it. Fatigue fled as he read about The Juilliard School.

Her heart filled with music, her stomach full of good food, and her brain crammed with information, Brie peeked into her bedroom. A twin bed, nightstand, and matching dresser gave it a cozy feel. The contents of the closet and drawers delighted her. She had everything she needed for her stay in New York City. She held up a pair of bell-bottomed jeans with red poppies embroidered on the back pockets. Her smile of pleasure turned into a yawn. "If I weren't so tired, I'd try you on." More exhausted than she ever remembered being, she laid them over a chair in the corner, pulled off her clothes, and toppled into bed.

Before she knew it, sun warmed the one small window. Shifting to her alter ego, she pulled on the jeans with a red, tie-dyed T-shirt and slid her dancer's feet into red sandals. A glance in the full-length mirror caught her off guard. Glossy black hair to her waist, flashing brown eyes, and flawless skin made her smile. "Rayna, you are . . ."

A knuckle rapped the door. "Are you up?"

Rayna's deep voice replied. "Come in, Esán."

"Wow! You look great!"

She looked him up and down. He'd pulled his hair back in a queue at the nape of his neck. His dark blue T-shirt set off his eyes. Bell-bottomed jeans and a leather vest reminded her of the hippies she had read about in her research. "Not bad."

He grabbed her hand. "Come on. Torgin's ready to go. I wonder what he's come up with."

Torgin's low whistle told Rayna her attire was a hit. After smothering her with a hug, he stepped back and grinned. "What do you think?"

His short curls had lengthened into the full hair style that had grown popular in the mid-sixties. He wore a casual three-piece, dark green suit with a pale summer-green shirt. He looked at their astonished expressions. "What?"

"What did you do to your hair?" Esán demanded.

Torgin touched it. "I thought it longer."

Rayna couldn't hold back a laugh. "You *thought* it longer? Are you sure your name isn't Kuparak?"

Torgin laughed, walked around her, and grinned. "You look pretty *cool* yourself."

A soft knock on the door interrupted their banter. All three turned. Esán peered through the peep hole and began unlocking the locks.

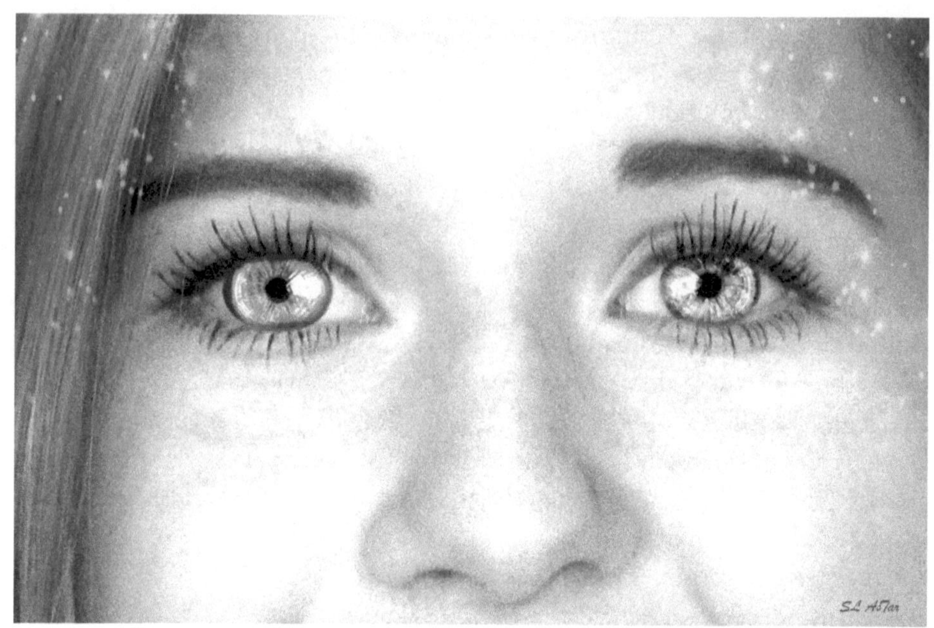

4

In the Research Library on Myrrh, Ari paced the aisle between book-filled shelves. An abrupt about-face brought her to the table where Elf poured over maps of New York City.

She peered over his shoulder. "Where *is* Relevart? Elae said he'd join us here." Impatience sent her in an agitated march around the table and back to Elf's side. She yanked the map from his line of vision. "How could he send Brie into the past without me?" A frustrated toss landed the map on the table. "She didn't even say goodbye." Ari halted her tirade to glare at Elf. "What are you looking at?"

"I'm watching you blow off steam. Tell me when you're ready to get busy." He folded his arms. "Chealim's source suggested Upori has hidden the Corps Stones somewhere in New York's dance community. New York City Ballet seems to be the most likely candidate." He raised a brow. "But we also need to research American Ballet Theater, The Joffrey, and several smaller companies. I have work to do." He picked up the map and resumed his examination.

She plopped down on a chair. "So, we do all the research. Then what? We're in this dimension. Brie, Esán, and Torgin are somewhere so far removed from today's Myrrh it makes my head spin."

A subtle atmospheric change brought Relevart into focus. "Perhaps I can help." He held out a ceramic whistle. "This is a time whistle. I'm here to teach you how to relay information to our New York team." He whispered the name of the crystal topping his staff, "Froetise, come forth."

A young man holding the VarTerel's staff in his hand materialized. A circlet of gold leaves nestled in his burnished curls. Dressed in a kilt-like skirt, hip-length cape, and sandals laced up to his knees, he resembled an actor on an old-fashioned movie set. He handed Relevart the staff, flashed Ari a gorgeous smile, and nodded to Elf. "I am Allegro. Apollo sent me."

Ari choked. "If you expect us to be—"

Relevart laid a hand on her shoulder. "It's true, Ari. Allegro is here to provide you with important information and to teach you how to play the time whistle. Please escort him to Veersuni. Return to the lab when you're finished. Elf and I have more research possibilities to explore."

She bit back a retort she knew she would regret and led the way from the Research level through the Reading Room to Veersuni. As the door closed, she rounded on the young man behind her. "Tell me the truth. Are you a god?"

"Just as you exist, Arienh, so do the gods. We live in a different realm, one you would call another dimension."

Ari eyed him up and down, shrugged, and gave him the benefit of the doubt.

The lesson with Allegro left Ari saturated with information. Somewhat contrite, she accompanied him to rejoin Relevart in the Research Lab. They found Elf buried in books and maps. The VarTerel had gone.

Allegro moved to the end of the table. "It has been a pleasure to meet you." His smile beamed. "Remember, Arienh, you are up to the task. Good luck."

Apollo's emissary vanished in a blaze of golden light.

Elf marked his place, closed his book, and fixed a penetrating gaze on Ari. "Something about you is different. What happened?"

She slid into a chair, her shoulders stooped. Restless fingers tugged a curl, then traced an infinity symbol on the tabletop. "I have just learned more from Allegro than I learned in the past several sun cycles. My sister and our friends are in horrible danger." She shivered. "I'm afraid for them and for us. Most of all, I'm terrified if I fail in my part, the Universe will come undone." She pressed her palms together. "What did Relevart share with you?"

Elf rubbed his temples. "He told me about Upori, why New York City, and why we must move so quickly. I wish we weren't at a crisis level."

"Wait... What about Upori? Why New York? Don't leave me in the dark."

Irritation made a fleeting appearance. A bland expression took its place. "Until a few Sun Cycles ago, Upori Athai was an unknown. Within the past moon cycle, his name has come up in connection with several recent robberies. Artifacts from museums and art galleries across the galaxy have gone missing. They identified Upori at the scene prior to the robberies on all but one occasion." He pursed his lips. "Why New York City?" His gaze fastened on the map. "Upori's an expert on ballet and theater on Earth. His favorite time period appears to be 1960-1980. A choreographer named George Balanchine, one of his idols, is connected with New York City Ballet." He tapped a stylus on the table. "Oh, one more thing. Balanchine created Upori's favorite ballet in late 1969-1970. Relevart was uncertain which one. I'm researching that now." Elf looked at her, his expression unfathomable. "What have you learned?"

She considered asking him why he seemed annoyed. Instead, she withdrew the time whistle Relevart had given her and played a low note. "When Allegro and I were working with this, I thought I saw Rayna, Torgin, and Esán. The image faded as fast as it materialized." She shook long, red curls back from her face. "Did Relevart tell you the third Corps Stone has gone missing?"

Elf's expression hardened. "He did. Our solar system is at risk. What do we do now?"

Ari slipped the whistle on its cord beneath her shirt. "We do the research. With the information Relevart shared and what we learn, we make an educated guess. Then I use the whistle to send a message telling Rayna, Esán, and Torgin where to concentrate their search."

Elf made no reply. With a shrug, he moved to a comp-screen.

From beneath her lashes, Ari watched him muttering to himself. *I wish you would tell me what's wrong.* Sighing, she began a search through her stack of books.

The almost silent flipping of pages filled the Lab.

T he urgent need to know what Brie and her friends were encountering in New York City, 1969 drove SparrowLyn up the stairs to her sanctuary. Chealim had paid her a dreamtime visit. He advised her to drink Elcaro's water from the fountain's alabaster ladle. Doing so, he had explained, would enhance her power. She crossed the room to the trunk, opened the lid, and lifted the ladle from its velvet cradle. "If I'm going to see into the past, I'll need all the help I can get."

A brown garnet cabochon the color of her eyes gleamed in the handle as she crossed to the fountain. Squaring her shoulders, she dipped the ladle in Elcaro's bowl. Cool water tingled down her throat. The ladle slipped from her trembling fingers. Its sharp clatter on the hardwood floor mingled with her startled hiss. Her racing heartbeat echoed in her ears. Heightened senses left her reeling. Instinct guiding her, she picked up the ladle, dipped it, and sipped. Her world stabilized. She returned the ladle to the trunk and ran a finger along its smooth, alabaster length. *How did I not know about your power sooner?*

The silence of water ceasing to fall from the statue's hands called Sparrow to Elcaro's side. A ray of sunlight shot through the window and dazzled rainbows from the fountain's pristine, white alabaster. At the bottom of the bowl, the point of Vesen, the crystal encased within the its pedestal, glowed radiant blue. Bubbles bobbed to the surface and burst, creating a vivid image.

A short, stocky man with a stubbly beard and bristling blondish hair searched the shore of a small lake. On hands and knees, he sniffed the ground beneath a deciduous tree. Bloodhound-like attention carried him on all fours to a bush across the path. Voices growing louder brought him to standing. An ugly scowl shaped the cruel mouth as he dodged behind a large tree.

Two girls strolled by. Their laughter mingled with lighthearted teasing made the man flinch. When they rounded the curve in the path, he walked back to the deciduous tree, dropped to all fours, and sniffed a patch of grass beneath it. He came to his feet, a malicious smile twisting his features. Calculation narrowed his gaze. A menacing laugh accompanied him along the path.

Sparrow gripped the fountain's rim. A terrifying realization sent goosebumps crawling over her skin. "I just saw Upori Athai at work." She eased her white-knuckled grip. "I am the Guardian of Myrrh." Gratitude replaced her terror. "I can warn my girls." Her stomach tightened. *"How do I get word to them?"*

The image of a young black boy with a small terrier at his side stepping from behind a bush provided the answer. Sparrow stared. "I've seen you before. Where?" She mulled it over, then smiled. "You were with Rayna, Torgin, and Esán when they arrived in New York. *You will be my messenger.*" She kissed her fingertip, touched the water's surface in Elcaro's Eye, and watched the ripples flow from the fountain over the lake in Central Park.

The child blinked. The terrier cocked its head.

She placed a message in the boy's mind. *"Look into the lake."*

His startled, dark-eyed gaze darted up and down the path.

"Please—look at the water!"

Curiosity dimmed the confusion on his face. He walked to the shoreline and knelt at the water's edge. Her image floated on the surface.

"Tell Rayna and her friends danger heads their way."

He gaped, rubbed his eyes, and croaked a strangled syllable. His hand hovered above the water. He lowered it to his side and nodded. Without looking back, he whistled for his dog and jogged down the path.

The image blurred. Glistening droplets spilled from the statue's palms. Sparrow exhaled. *I hope I can trust you.*

She retrieved the ladle from its resting place. "I know you are the reason I could send a message back through time." Holding it up to the light, she whispered, "I wish I knew your name."

The cabochon glowed deep chestnut brown. Alabaster shimmered in the sunlight. A single word floated through her mind. *VarLea.*

"Thank you, VarLea." She rested it on blue velvet and lowered the trunk's battered lid. "And thank you, Chealim."

Penee sat on a bench in the Plantitarium on the living ship El Aperdisa. Since Henrietta had brought her, Den, and Inōni, the K'iin Shaman's daughter, to TreBlaya, she had longed for time alone. Solitude amongst the flora of her home planet allowed her to digest the happenings of the past few moon cycles.

Two turnings earlier, genetic technicians created an embryo from her egg and Den's sperm. They implanted it in Inōni's uterus. Penee tilted her head. *It is odd to think our child will return to Neul Isle to take its place as a member of the K'iin.* A smile lit her eyes. *Inōni will birth a girl, one who will carry the Incirrata Secret into the future.*

Penee pressed her hands to her abdomen. *Will I ever have a child? If I do, who will father it?* Elf tiptoed into her thoughts. *We will always be close, Elf, but you love Arienh.* She sighed.

Den stepped through the hatchway. His charming smile flashed. "You look serious. Can I help?"

She moved to one side of the bench. "You can sit with me. Any news?"

He sat down, leaned his forearms on his knees, and interlaced his fingers. Another time his serious expression would have made her nervous. Today it made her curious. She waited.

His narrowed gaze wandered the bounty of foliage filling the Plantitarium, then came to rest on a glistening pool opposite their bench. "Brie and her friends are in New York City on the planet Earth in the Terran year 1969. Someone has stolen three Corps Stones. The Galactic Guardians are certain they're hidden in New York City in that time frame."

She studied his handsome profile. "I wonder what it's like going back in time?"

Seriousness cloaked him. "If they need help, we may find out."

The hair on Penee's neck prickled. She slipped her hand into his.

5

E sán ushered an agitated Gar into the living room. "Are you alright? You look like you've seen a ghost."

The boy pranced from foot to foot. "I just saw..." He bit his bottom lip and hiccuped a shaky breath.

Rayna offered her hand. "Let's sit, shall we? Torgin, please fetch Gar some water." She led the distressed boy to the couch. Esán locked the apartment door and joined them. Torgin returned, gave a tumbler of water to Gar, and sat opposite.

Hands trembling, Gar clutched the glass, his eyes as big as saucers. A shiver splashed water over the rim.

Rayna rescued the glass and set it on the table. "Where's Spyglass?"

"Hid him in the basement, b'cause his barkin' would give me away. I had to sneak in so's I wouldn't get caught." He tugged at his raggedy shirt and slouched deeper into the sofa cushions.

"Tell us what you saw, Gar." Rayna's soothing tone seemed to calm him. "Start from the beginning."

"This mornin' I went back to the park. Close to the place y'all appeared last night, I..." He licked his lips, then puffed out a breath. "Can't believe what I saw." Over bright eyes studied his palms. "A man was standin' on the path." Gar looked up. Worry creased his forehead. "Ya know how ya can tell somebody's trouble? This guy's trouble—shifty, reekin' of danger. So, I stayed hid. He searched every inch of the lake shore and the path. Even sniffed the ground like a hound dog. Under the tree—the one where ya appeared outta nowhere—he must've smelled somethin'. He stood up with the ugliest expression I ever saw on a face. Kinda know-it-all and full of meanness."

Esán leaned in. "Can you describe him?"

Gar rolled his eyes. "Course I can. He was short and kinda bulky. Lots of dirty, blond hair stickin' out all over his head; beady, mean eyes; a stubbly beard—" He shuddered. "Anyways, he took off."

Rayna kept her voice steady. "What else happened, Gar?"

Uncertainty made him shrink smaller. "I'm not crazy. So don't ya think I am, okay?"

"I promise we won't think you're crazy," Rayna coaxed. "Please tell us what happened."

Gar pressed clenched fists to his chest. "I heard a voice in here." He tapped his temple. "It told me ta look in the lake." He uncurled his fingers and rubbed his palms on his jeans. "When I didn't 'cause I *thought* I was hearin' stuff, the voice came again. I knelt by the water. A woman's face floated on the surface, like it was a lookin' glass. She told me ta find ya and warn ya you're in danger. I'm pretty sure the man was lookin' for ya." The frightened boy threw his hands in the air. "Then she up and disappeared."

Shaking fingers plucked at the hole in the knee of his jeans. "I promise I'm not crazy. That's what I saw."

Rayna gave him a quick hug. "We are so lucky you're our friend. Are you hungry?"

Gar gripped her knee. "Who was the lady in the water?"

Rayna caught Esán's eye.

His expression grew distant. "I believe you should tell him."

"She's my mother. Her name is Sparrow."

Eagerness glinted brighter. "She's not in New York City, right?"

Rayna took his hands in hers. "She's not in New York. Someday, I'll tell you where she is, but not today."

Small hands squeezed hers. "Like in the movies...ya wanna keep me safe, right?"

Torgin grinned. "We definitely want to keep you safe. Did the man see you?"

Lips pursed and relaxed. "Nah. I waited in the bushes ta make sure he was long gone." He shuddered. "Hope I never have ta meet him." He stared at Torgin. "Hey, what did you do ta your hair? Yesterday it was short. Ya ain't wearin' a wig, are ya?"

Torgin laughed. "You are one observant young man. I'm not wearing a wig. It *was* short yesterday."

Gar jumped up, his fists on his hips. "How d'ya get it long?"

Esán grinned. "Yeh, Torg, how did you get it long?"

Torgin put his finger to his lips and raised his brows. "Promise not to tell anyone ever, Gar?"

He gave an eager nod. "I promise."

"I imagined it long."

Gar pursed his lips and gave Torgin a hard stare. "Ahhh, ya pulling my leg?" He folded his arms across his chest. "We friends or not?"

Torgin smiled. "Wouldn't pull your leg. Give me your hands."

Gar hesitated. "You ain't gonna hurt me, are ya?"

"Never." Torgin clasped his hand. "Now, my man, imagine what you want your hair to look like."

Gar hesitated, then shut his eyes. Torgin's concentration created a soft glow around them. Esán caught Rayna's eye and grinned. Gar had an Afro to match Torgin's.

"You can open your eyes, Gar." Torgin's voice held a note of surprise. "Go take a look in the dining room mirror."

Gar scurried around the coffee table and into the next room. "Cool!" He came running back. "How did ya do that? You *really* aren't from the city." Worry consumed the small face. "We are pals, right?"

Esán drew him down on the couch. "We have no intention of hurting you or letting anyone else hurt you. Why don't we swear a pact? Will that help?"

The eagerness in Gar's face elicited a smile from Esán. "Everyone make a circle." He led the group to the center of the room. A small hand snuck into his, the other clasped Rayna's. Torgin stood opposite. Esán's serious gaze rested on the young boy. "Are you ready, Gar?"

A firm squeeze provided the answer.

Esán cleared his throat. "Repeat after me:

> *Four pals together, four pals for sure…*
> *We swear allegiance, heart-felt and pure.*
> *Protecting each other in our times of need,*
> *Protecting forever is our solemn creed.*

He remained silent for a long moment. Still holding hands, he knelt next to Gar. Brie and Torgin followed his example. "Arms up, one and all, and repeat together, Heart Promise."

Everyone's arms rose overhead. "Heart Promise" rang through the apartment.

Esán placed a hand on Gar's shoulder. "Better?"

Tears slipped down the boy's cheeks. "I never belonged before. I belong with ya, right?"

Rayna hugged him. "You belong with us."

Esán watched Gar's fear evaporate and wonder take its place.

❧ ❧

Rayna nibbled a late morning breakfast and listened to Esán and Torgin discussing the best way to use Gar's streetwise talents, where he should sleep, and how to keep him safe.

The boy cleared his throat. "Excuse me. I can take care of myself, ya know. Don't think anyone should see me with ya. I can watch ya from afar; get ya news when ya need it. We can have a signal, and I'll make contact."

Rayna handed him some grapes. "You sound twenty-five; you look about eight. How old *are* you?"

Gar squared his shoulders. "I'll be twelve years old in a couple months."

She smiled. "So, today you're eleven."

He shrugged and stuffed a grape in his mouth.

Following his example, she savored the crispy crunch and resulting juice. "Eleven going on twelve... Can you read?"

A scowl followed by a grimace made him appear younger. "I learnt enough to get by."

Torgin shoved a map across the table. "How about this?"

Gar shot him a disgusted look. "'Course I can read a map. I grew up with this street guy...an old man. He taught me so's I wouldn't get lost." Sadness soaked his expression.

Rayna saw him push it away with a shake of his head. "What else did your friend teach you?"

"He taught me all kinds of stuff." Gar squared his shoulders. "No one has ta take care of me." A glare darted around the table. "Why so many questions?"

Torgin cradled a cup of tea in his long-fingered hands. "We hope you and Spyglass might do a little spying for us, which means we need to know what skills you have."

The boyish face brightened. "Spyglass and me is good at stayin' hid. We can walk through a crowd unseen. People talk in front of us like we ain't there. We're good at gettin' lost in a hurry. And we can sniff out danger like one of them hound dogs." Satisfaction gave him a cocky smile.

Straight-faced, Torgin nodded. "Just the skills we require in our spy." He turned to Esán. "What's the plan for today?"

"Hold on." Esán grabbed a stack of paperwork from the desk, rifled through it, and held a piece of paper. "Our itinerary." He studied it. "Today we get acquainted with the city—where we need to be tomorrow—how to get back home. Mostly, we need to get used to being in New York so we don't act like we're from outer space."

Gar leaned forward. "But ya are from space, right, 'cause ya sure ain't from here." Stubbornness gleamed in the large dark eyes. He folded his arms.

Rayna smiled. "We are not from New York City." She let her expression grow serious. "I promise when it is safe to share more, we will. Until then, you'll have to trust us...like we trust you."

Gar squirmed, pressed his mouth tight, and thrust his chin out. His inner struggle became a shrug. "Guess I gotta trust ya. Only ever trusted Gin." He licked his lips. "I can show ya around. What else do ya need me to do?"

"Tomorrow, Rayna has her first ballet class at the School of American

Ballet; I have registration at The New York Studio; and Torgin has orientation at the new Juilliard facilities at Lincoln Center. As for you, Gar…" His brows formed a bridge over his nose. Silence built anticipation. His unwavering gaze fastened on the boy. "I have an important job for you, one no one else can do. Are you game?"

"What is it?" Eagerness erased any lingering distrust.

"Your job is to stick close to Rayna, see if anyone follows her, and make certain she arrives at SAB and home safely. Can you do that?"

"Sure can. What if someone is followin' her? What then?"

Rayna pressed a small quartz crystal in his hand. "You picture me, squeeze this, and think my name into my head."

He scrunched up his face. "Are you sure this'll work?"

"I'll go into the hall. Esán will tell you when to try it." She stopped just out of sight.

A tentative two words whispered through her thoughts. *"Rayna, trouble."* A questioning face peeked around the edge of the arched opening. "Did ya hear me?"

Rayna put a finger to her lips. *"I heard you, Gar."*

Blinking away his disbelief, he stared at the crystal. "Is it magic?"

She smiled. "Let's call it technology. I always name my crystals, so they know they belong to me. You should name yours."

He studied the gleaming stone a long moment. "I'll name it after Gin 'cause he's my guardian angel." A serious gaze met hers. "I promise to take good care of ya, Rayna."

She stifled the urge to ruffle his hair. "I feel safer already. Thank you, Gar."

When they completed the kitchen cleanup, Gar tugged at Esán's vest. "Can I go check on Spyglass? I bet he needs to go outside."

"Sure, but don't get caught. We need you."

Esán unlocked the door, watched until Gar dodged into the elevator, and slid the dead bolt back into place. He turned to Rayna. "You'd better shift while you can."

A soft inhale stimulated the change. Brie blinked in the dim hall. Torgin peered down at her. "What did you do to the crystal you gave Gar?"

Brie walked into the living room. "Nothing."

Esán joined them. "So, if you did nothing..."

She rubbed her palm with a thumb. "I had a hunch. Our little Gar is more than he seems."

Torgin paced to the window. "Do you suppose he's lying to us?"

"I think he believes he's exactly who he says he is." She cocked her head. Rayna materialized seconds before Gar's soft knock.

6

orgin followed a frantic Gar into the apartment. "Spyglass is missin'. I put him in the utility room by the laundry. Did they find him? What if they hurt him?"

"Calm down, Gar." Rayna put her hands on his shoulders. "I'm betting Spyglass is fine. Give me a minute." She released him.

He clutched her hand. "Please tell me he's okay. Please."

She crossed to the window and pointed at the street. "Look. Spyglass is on the sidewalk by the awning. While you calm down, Gar, Torgin will go down to get him. But first tell us more about *they*."

Gar fiddled with the tattered hem of his shirt. "Not sure why I said they. It just came out natural-like."

Rayna rested a hand on his shoulder. "Were you thinking of anyone just before you spoke?"

He brightened. "Yah. Inside my head, I saw the man from the park. Does that help? Can Torgin go, now?"

"It does help. Off you go, Torg." She clasped Gar's hand. "Let's find a treat for Spyglass."

Torgin unlocked the dead bolts. "Why do you suppose he imagined Upori, Esán?"

"I don't know." Esán frowned. "Watch your back. Sounds like our friend has a companion."

"Will do." To the sound of locks clicking into place behind him, Torgin walked to the elevator.

Glad to be alone, he leaned against the interior wall and allowed the elevator's slow descent to soothe his growing unease. On the ground floor, he nodded to the doorman and exited through the double glass doors.

A young man close to his age knelt on the sidewalk, scratching the terrier's ears. At the sight of Torgin, Spyglass, tail wagging madly, barked an excited welcome. The man stood up. "Hi. Is this your dog?"

Torgin smiled. "Nope. He belongs to a good friend. I was just coming to collect him."

A good-natured warmth infused the man's persona. He offered a hand. "Name's Cole."

"I'm Torgin. Nice to meet you."

"You new around here?"

"Just got into town." Torgin scooped up Spyglass. "Have you lived in this neighborhood long?"

Cole shook his head. "Arrived from Idaho yesterday." Excitement enhanced his good looks. "I'm attending Juilliard in the fall, so I came for the summer session to get my feet on the ground. What brought you to the city?"

Torgin hesitated a split second, sensed nothing alarming, and responded. "I'm also here to attend the summer session. I play the piano and the flute."

"I'm an actor. Juilliard just started a theater program. Can you tell I'm excited?" Cole laughed and hugged himself. "Registration is tomorrow morning, right? Want to walk downtown together?"

Torgin grinned as Spyglass licked his cheek. "Love to."

"Great. I'll see you here about 9:00." Cole gave him a clipped salute, grinned, and strode off down the street.

Torgin strolled under the awning.

The doorman held open the door. "Wondered whose dog that was."

Torgin scratched Spyglass's ears. "We're taking care of him today. He escaped from the apartment. Sure am glad he didn't wander far."

Nodding his agreement, the doorman returned to his desk.

On the way to the fifth floor, Torgin reviewed the conversation with Cole. Nothing made him suspicious. He frowned. *Would I know if something were amiss?* Instinct assured him he would. *I can't believe how much I've changed.*

The elevator jerked to a stop. Spyglass squirmed and jumped to the floor. Torgin pushed the outer door wide. The terrier gave a sharp yip and dashed into Gar's waiting arms. Torgin watched, his thoughts full of Buster and Shyllee. *Someday, I'm going to have a dog of my own.*

Esán and Rayna greeted them.

Gar snuggled Spyglass, his smile wide. "Look, guys, he's okay! Thanks, Torgin."

Spyglass wiggled free and padded down the hall. Gar dodged after him. "I gotta treat for ya, Spy."

Rayna watched him go with a satisfied smile, then turned. "Who was the guy, Torg?"

"Someone in town to attend the summer session at Juilliard. He's staying around here. We're meeting in the morning to go downtown. His name's Cole."

"Anything strange about him?" Esán walked with him to the dining room.

"Nope. Seemed ordinary to me. He's from Idaho. I sensed nothing amiss, but you can join us tomorrow and decide for yourself."

Esán rummaged in the sideboard drawer. "You'll be on your own, I'm afraid. I have to go to Greenwich Village, so I'll be taking the subway." He handed him a set of keys and gave another set to Rayna. "Don't want to forget these in case we get separated today."

Rayna examined hers. "Four keys...street door and three locks." She slipped the ring onto her thumb. "What's first today?"

Esán spread out a subway map on the table. "Let's take a subway to Greenwich Village and return via Lincoln Center. Gar, what route do you recommend?"

Gar joined them and pulled the map closer. He pointed. "We're here; ya want to go there. That means we travel downtown. Gin taught me to use the Empire State Building as my guide. He said if ya get lost, look for it. Figure out if you're up or down or east or west of it. That'll help ya know which direction to go."

Torgin grinned. "And which one is the Empire State Building?"

"Jeeze, Torgin." Gar shook his head. "It's the tallest building in the city. Can't miss it."

"Time to go." Esán folded the map. "How about you slip out first, Gar. We can join up at the subway station at Broadway and 72nd Street.

Rayna scratched Spyglass under the chin. "Can animals ride the subway?"

Gar put a finger on his lips. "Won't tell if you won't. This your first ride?"

"It is."

"Ya all got tokens?"

Torgin produced one from his pocket. "I do. I put it in the slot and go through the turnstile, right?"

"Yep. Rayna and Esán?"

"Got mine." Esán patted his pocket.

Rayna collected her shoulder bag from the living room. "Me, too." She tucked the keys inside. "Are we ready?"

Gar unlocked the door and whistled. Spyglass trotted to his side. "I'll lead ya to the right platform. We're gonna take a downtown express. Get off at Washington Square. Questions?"

Torgin held the door ajar. "I think we're fine. See you at the subway."

Gar, with Spyglass at his heels, slipped out. After giving them a few minutes to make it to the street, Torgin preceded his friends into the hall, buzzed for the elevator, and glanced back.

Esán kissed Rayna on the cheek. "Be careful out there."

She strode into the elevator. "You, too."

Torgin nudged his friend to follow her. "She'll be fine, Esán. After all, she is a VarTerel."

Near the stairs to the subway, Rayna merged into the crowd. Pushed, shoved, and jostled by the sheep-like herd, she found herself separated from her friends. Dodging from the masses to stand against the graffiti-covered wall, she searched for familiar faces. Her gaze brushed over an armed policeman, an old woman pushing a cart, and a teenage boy covered with tattoos. Insecurity rolled through her.

Gar stepped into view on the far side of the gate. Torgin and Esán stood close by, their expressions urging her onward. She swallowed her fear. The crowd surging toward the turnstiles carried her with it. A young man elbowed her ahead of him. She hesitated. He pressed closer. His warm breath tickling her neck spurred her into motion. She deposited her token and pushed her way to the other side.

Torgin caught her by the elbow. Together they followed Esán along the platform. Trying not to gawk at the chaos of people crowding into graffiti-decorated cars, she slipped a hand into Torgin's. Metal wheels clattering against metal tracks announced the approach of another train. A blast of air whipped her hair across her face. The train disappeared down the long, dirty tunnel.

New York subways are nothing like Idronatti's Ria Trains. A raggedy man shoved his way between her and Torgin. Separated from her friend's reassuring presence left her panting. She brushed hair off her face and hurried to catch up with Esán. His hand clutching arm gave her breathing space. She glanced back. Torgin made his way toward them. Down the platform, she caught sight of Gar leaning on a support column, watchful and alert.

She shuddered. Dirt, crowds, and noise, so different from the spotless, regulated stations in Idronatti, made her nervous. Another train racing by pressed her closer to Esán. The deafening clatter gradually faded. She sighed. *I miss the Ria Trains' soundless stopping on their cushions of air.*

Breaks squealing announced the Downtown Express. The double doors slid open. People poured onto the platform. Gar dodged into the end car. Spyglass, close behind him, hid under a seat. Torgin stepped aboard. Esán squeezed her arm tighter, moved into the crowd and into the car. A man shoved her backward onto the platform. The doors slide shut, cutting her off from her friends. The train shot forward.

Like a frantic child, Esán pressed his hands against the square window at the back of the train. A surge of panic roiled through her as he disappeared into the bowels of the city. Her heart raced. *I'm alone in the subways of New York.*

"Go to the apartment." Esán's faint telepathic message dispersed the fear.

"I will." She peered up and down the platform. "If I can figure out the way to the street."

A distinguished, older man in a well-tailored suit paused beside her. "You look lost. Perhaps I can help?"

Nothing about him alarmed her, so she drew in a breath. "I'm new to New York subways. Please tell me how to reach the street?"

He smiled. Laugh lines deepened. "I'll do better than that. I'll walk with you. What side of Broadway do you want?"

"The one closest to Amsterdam Avenue, please." She mustered a smile. "Thank you."

He walked ahead of her along the cement platform to the turnstiles and exit gates. "Go through the gate and take the stairs on the right. You'll exit on 72nd and Broadway on the side closest to Amsterdam." His pleasant expression became serious. "Take my advice: don't ride the subways alone at rush hour until you are better acquainted with them. A pretty girl like you could get in trouble if you got lost in the wrong place. Good day." He walked back to the platform.

Rayna hurried up the stairs into the mid-morning brightness. A young man leaning on a lamppost ran a lascivious gaze from her face to her feet with a brief pause on her chest. The temptation to leave him unconscious in the street dissolved as a ragged woman with a haggard expression shoved a flyer at her. A dirty-faced child darted from a recessed doorway, a grimy hand reaching for her bag. Rayna caught hold of the skinny arm, read the little girl's story in her body language, and pressed a coin into her hand. Surprise registered, then misted into fear. The child dashed from sight down the subway steps.

Pain from the Star of Truth stabbed, alerting her to the need to shift shape. Rayna hurried along 72nd, alert to everything surrounding her. *Please let me get to the apartment before...* She grimaced.

Midway to her building, she smiled at young children playing in water spraying from a fire hydrant. Their delighted giggles renewed her faith in humanity. A more insistent stab of pain urged her to lengthen her stride. A subtle mental scan of the street behind her assured her no one followed. She crossed West End Avenue at a trot. Halfway down the block, she keyed herself into her building. Disoriented, she ran a hand through her hair.

The doorman glanced up for his desk. "Good morning, miss."

"Good morning." She rubbed her neck, summoned a smile, and hurried to the elevator.

In the apartment, she locked the three locks and leaned, panting, against the door. The shift to Brielle left her gulping in air. When her breathing normalized, she walked to the living room window. Images of graffiti and filth, people fearful of being harmed, and armed policemen riding the subways made her shudder. *I've been to some strange places, but this is the strangest.*

E sán panicked. The words *'I will'* in his mind reduced it to manageable. Torgin's hand squeezing his shoulder steadied him further. A determined pivot brought them face to face. "I'm getting off at the next stop. I have to go back to make sure she's alright. I—"

Torgin folded his arms. "A time will come, Esán, for you to race to the rescue, but this isn't it. Rayna's a big girl. She'll get herself from the subway to the apartment. Besides, you sent her a message, right?"

Esán rubbed his hand on his thigh. "I did."

Torgin gripped the pole tighter as the train jerked. "If she needs us, she'll let us know. I suggest we continue our trek to Greenwich Village. We have things to accomplish today."

His friend's matter-of-fact attitude accompanied by their switch in roles made Esán smile. "You're right, Torg. It's just that..." He shrugged.

Torgin raised his brows. "It's just that you love her." His stared into the distance. "Maybe someday..." He sighed.

Gar slipped between them. "Next stop, ya wanna go back for Rayna, Esán?"

"Nope. She'll be fine. Besides, I can't wait to see the Forum."

Gar smiled. "Good choice. She's pretty independent, huh?"

"She is." Esán caught Torgin's eye. "*Very* independent. How many stops 'til we get off?"

"Three. Head left. The stairs'll take ya to the street. I'll be close." He seemed to melt into the dingy scribbles defacing the walls.

The afternoon in the Village proved to be full of interesting surprises. Tacos for lunch, a first time treat, inspired pleased grins from all. Gar gobbled his, sharing only a small bite with Spyglass. They found their way to the Forum, explored the neighborhood, and headed back to Washington Square. Esán liked the homier feel of this part of Manhattan and boarded the train, confident he could navigate there and back.

They arrived on the Upper West Side at sunset. Gar refused to join them for dinner, promised to be at the apartment early in the morning, and vanished into the dusk light dimming the New York street.

Silence met them at the apartment. Panic creeping closer, Esán strode into the hall. "Rayna?" The silence remained unbroken.

"Don't panic, Esán, I'm sure she's fine." Torgin's calm voice penetrated his frantic thoughts.

The front door locks clicked open. Rayna walked into the apartment with a large bag in her arms. "Hi! Look what I found."

"Rayna, you scared me." Esán crushed the bag between them. "Where have you been? We got home—you weren't here—"

"I'm fine." She ducked free of his embrace. "I wanted something fun for dinner. Come and help me, both of you."

Torgin grinned. "Good to see you." He took the bag and sniffed. "Smells great." With a mimicked bow, he followed her into the kitchen.

Esán collected his scattered wits, reestablished his usual calm, and ambled after them. Observing her from a place of love, not from the fear of losing her, he smiled. "You look happy, Rayna."

She put a container in the freezer. "I am." Dark brow bridged her nose. "When I saw you disappearing on the train, I almost panicked." The brows relaxed. She smiled. "I reminded myself I could find my way home."

Torgin stood behind her, grinning. He mouthed the word 'VarTerel' and gave a thumbs up.

Esán returned it.

Rayna removed the last container from the bag. "I suggest you stop talking behind my back, Torgin Whälen, and join us."

He winked at Esán, kissed Rayna's cheek, and looked at the banquet on the table. "Tell us about the feast."

She linked elbows with Esán. "We're about to try Italian food, so I hope you're hungry. I bought two main dishes, a salad, and fresh baked garlic bread.

The girl at the restaurant suggested tiramisu for dessert." She licked her lips. "It looks yummy. And gelato which I gather is similar to our iced cream. Is Gar with you?"

"Nope. He refused to come up. I'm not sure he trusts us yet."

Rayna stepped away from Esán. Brielle appeared. Red curls framing her smiling face glistened as she shook her head. "We materialized out of nowhere; we were lost and clueless about what year it was. He's lived a tough life. Trust takes time. He'll come around." She set plates on the counter. "Let's serve up, then you can tell me everything about your day."

Esán opened a container of noodles in a red sauce. "What's this? It smells divine."

Brie picked up a plate. "The red sauce is marinara; the creamy one is carbonara."

Torgin licked his fingers. His plate was full of salad, bread, and pasta in the creamy white sauce.

Brie filled her plate, shot a satisfied grin at both boys, and headed for the dining room.

Torgin grabbed another piece of garlic bread and trailed after her.

Esán marveled at the resilience of the woman he loved. A tremor of foreboding threatened to darken his mood. *This undertaking has only just begun.*

7

Torgin emptied his plate for the second time, pushed his chair back from the table, and beamed at Brie. "The spaghetti's great. I might have one more serving."

Brielle laughed. "If you eat much more pasta, you won't have room for dessert. The woman in the restaurant told me tiramisu is pretty decadent."

He gave his plate a rueful look. "Guess I can have leftovers later." He fiddled with his fork and observed his best friends.

Esán slid a hand across the table as he told Brie about their day. "We explored the West Village. It's homier than the Upper West Side." He blinked. "I wish we lived down there. But if the plan works the way the Guardians set it up, we'll all be working at Lincoln Center."

Brie's fingers touched his. "How did you like the Forum?"

"We didn't go in. I have a tour tomorrow, so I'll know more then." His fingers intertwined with hers. "We discovered several cafes, a bookstore, and a small park nearby. The subway ride isn't too bad on a Sunday. I imagine traveling during rush hour on a weekday is a different story."

Half-listening to the conversation, Torgin glanced at their linked fingers. *I wonder if I will ever fall in love?* He thought about being a younger teen. *I was so shy, I hid in my music. Ari and Brie were my only friends, and they were like sisters, always looking out for me.* He sighed.

Esán's voice interrupted his musing. "That was quite a sigh, Torg."

He shoved the memories into the background. "Just thinking about dessert." He raised a brow at Brielle. "Soon?"

She laughed. "You two clear the table. I'll get it ready."

Torgin carried dirty dishes into the kitchen. "Italian food is great, Brie. Thanks." He set them on the counter.

Esán trailed behind them. "I say let's clean up so we can relax after dessert."

The clatter of dishes mixed with easy banter ended with a clean kitchen. Soon the trio was sitting in the living room, ready to enjoy tiramisu and nocciola gelato. Soft music playing on the radio accompanied their first spoonful of lady fingers layered with whipped cream and custard.

Torgin swallowed. "Wow! Delicious!" He shoveled in another bite.

Esán grinned. "Ditto, Torgin. Thanks, Brielle. How did you come across this restaurant?"

She put her empty bowl on the coffee table. "I reached the apartment close to hysterics after you disappeared on the train. Eventually, logic reestablished itself. I decide to explore the neighborhood. The restaurant is on Broadway, not too far from the subway hub." She picked up her spoon. "I've concluded that New York City is a big, extraordinary place." A savored suck later, she returned the spoon to the bowl. "It's a lot dirtier than Idronatti but much more interesting. By the time we leave, I intend to have learned all I can about life in this city."

Torgin winked at Esán. "Told you she could take care of herself."

Exhausted from too many emotions and her panic earlier in the day, Brie excused herself. After a warm shower, she crawled into bed. Sleep eluded her. *You have to let go, Brielle. Think of something relaxing.* She imaged walking along the beach on the coast of Dast on Soputto. Memories of the ocean breeze caressing her skin, the smell of salty water, sand, and seaweed, and the sounds of the sea finally lulled her into a dreamless slumber.

Morning arrived with a stab of trepidation. *I have to take the subway.* She pushed her resistant body to sitting, yawned, and threw the covers aside. *Grow up, Brielle As Tar.*

A soft knock brought her to her feet. She pulled the door ajar. Esán kissed his finger then touched her lips. "Gar's here. Better shift before you come out."

A short time later, Rayna walked into the kitchen. Gar sat at the round table, nibbling jelly slathered toast. Torgin, wide awake and grinning, placed a plate in front of her and planted a kiss on her cheek. "Have a great turning...I mean day. Gotta go. See you at Lincoln Center." He hurried down the hall.

Gar munched his last corner of crust. "Is a day called a turning where you live?"

Rayna poured juice from a pitcher Torgin had left on the table. "Someday, we'll answer all your questions." She put her washed plate in the dish rack. "We need to go. I'll meet you at the stairs to the subway."

Wrinkles cluttered his forehead. An enormous sigh escorted him to the sink. Water sloshed over his dishes. He set them in the dish rack and dried his hands. "I'll be waitin' at Verdi Square, 'cross from the station." A soft clunk announced his departure.

Rayna brushed her teeth, put her hair up in a bun, and grabbed her dance bag.

Esán waited in the entryway. "I'll walk you to the subway."

The opportunity to be alone with him left Rayna smiling. She linked her arm through his. Together they strolled along the quiet street. Way too soon, they arrived at the subway head house at the junction of Broadway and 72nd Street. The sunshine reflecting off the building windows suggested a hot day in the making. Rayna shivered despite the rising temperature.

Esán nudged her ahead of him. Gar, who waited by the entryway, took the lead. She followed him to the downtown side of the tracks. On the platform, Esán kissed her cheek. "I'll see you tonight. Please take care of yourself today."

He hurried away, taking a piece of her heart with him.

Her nerves on edge, she watched Gar and Spyglass melt into the flood of bodies.

Wheels breaking shrieked an unnerving song. Doors slid open. People surging from the train mixed with those pushing their way into the cars. Rayna, jostled by the crowd, hugged her bag and allowed the flow of bodies to carry her on board. She gripped a sticky metal pole. Her gaze darted the length of the car. Gar stood halfway down the aisle, wedged between two teenage boys. The black and white terrier hid under a nearby seat.

The train screeched to a halt at the Lincoln Center Station. Rayna moved toward the exit, dodged an old woman flailing an umbrella, and pushed through the crowd to the steep cement stairs leading to the street. A labored hike carried her into a bright, sunny day smelling of car exhaust. She sniffed. *Better than the odor of trash and unwashed humans.*

Her peripheral vision picked up Gar and Spyglass waiting at the corner. He led her on a path that seemed somewhat familiar. Her first sighting of Lincoln Center Plaza left her shaking her head in wonder. *The Five Fathers' Performing Complex in the City of Idronatti on Thera is almost identical.* She smiled to herself. *It's a small Universe.*

The red light at the Broadway crosswalk gave her a few minutes to establish her bearings. Yellow blinked into green. She stepped from the curb.

"Rayna. Stop by Revson Fountain."

Gar's words in her head snapped her to attention. Tensed and ready for anything, she made her way to the fountain, walked its circumference, and paused.

"Man from the park by the crosswalk."

With the fountain's dancing water forming a curtain between her and Broadway, she scanned the street. A short, stocky man with bristling, dirty-blond hair climbed the steps and bustled toward the New York State Theater.

Rayna waited until he disappeared into the building, then made her way to the new state-of-the-art Juilliard Building and the School of American Ballet's new temporary home. A glance back gave her a glimpse of Gar slipping after Upori. *"Good, Gar. Go find out what you can discover."*

A group of girls, dance bags in tow, pushed by her. One stopped. "You look lost. Can I help?"

Rayna swallowed. "I'm from out of town. This is my second day in this city." She let her eyes widen. "It's all a bit overwhelming."

The girl smiled. "It's a big, busy place. You're a dancer, right? Whose class are you taking?"

Rayna read from her scribbled note. "My teacher at home wants me to study with Madame Dolavina and Miss Corsher."

A dark-haired girl studied her with an air of disdain. "Not just anyone can take a class with Madame Dolavina. You'd better try Corsher *if* you're even good enough for *her* class." She linked arms with the first girl and urged her toward the stairs. "Come on, Kelsia."

"You go on." Kelsia withdrew her arm. "*We'll* catch up." She motioned Rayna to join her. "Don't mind Lois. She acts stuck up, but once you get to know her, she's okay."

The next three hours flew by. Kelsia showed her the changing room and took her to the registrar's office. While they waited, she looked at her with a shy smile. "I'm taking Corsher's class. She doesn't scare me as much as Madame Dolavina. Besides, her class is the best one to take when you're new to SAB."

After Rayna signed up for Corsher's class, she followed Kelsia into the studio. Girls in black leotards and pink tights lined the barre. Several others stood talking in a corner. Rayna caught sight of herself in the floor to ceiling mirror. A wave of nervousness left her quaking. *What if I can't do this? What if I'm not good enough? What if...?*

Kelsia studied her. "You look terrified. Are you okay?"

"I'm a small-town girl." Rayna hung her towel over a metal brace. "This is a lot to take in."

A petite blonde woman entering the studio ended the conversation. She acknowledged the accompanist and faced the room full of expectant students. "Shall we begin?"

Miss Corsher set the warmup. Musician's fingers caressed the keyboard. Rayna smiled. *My first ballet class in New York City..* Exercise by exercise her confidence grew. *My body responds as though I trained my entire life for this moment.* The barre ended with *grande battement.* Sweat dripping down her face, she grabbed her towel and studied her fellow dancers in the mirror. *I fit right in. Étoile gave me everything I need.*

The ballet combinations in the center challenged her, along with everyone else. The *grand allegro* ending the class left Rayna feeling exhilarated. She performed *reverence* and clapped her appreciation with the rest of the students.

Miss Corsher thanked her accompanist and dismissed the dancers.

Rayna grinned at Kelsia. "That was wonderful. Thanks for recommending this class."

Kelsia, wreathed in smiles, gave her a quick hug. "You're amazing." She nodded toward piano. "I think Miss Corsher is trying to get your attention. I'll wait outside." She gathered up her dance bag and hurried from the studio.

Rayna stood motionless, unsure what to do.

Miss Corsher waved her over. "What is your name?"

"Rayna Deejara."

"Where did you train, Rayna?"

"I'm from the mid-west. I doubt you'd recognize my teacher's name."

Her pleasant smile broadened. "Try me."

"I studied with Marianna Alexandra."

A knowing nod accompanied an even broader smile. "No wonder you caught my eye. Come along, my dear, I have someone to introduce you to."

The walk into the hall brought Rayna face to face with a haughty Lois. "We've been waiting for..."

Miss Corsher glanced over her shoulder. "This way, Miss Deejara."

"Oh!" The girl's mouth clamped shut. The minute the teacher turned her back, Lois gave Rayna a nasty leer.

Ignoring her, Rayna followed Miss Corsher into another studio. At the grand piano in the corner, an older woman in a calf-length gray silk sheath and black character shoes clapped her hands, explained something Rayna could not hear, and clapped a new, more interesting rhythm.

A man with long, glossy black hair obscuring his face tapped the rhythm on his knee, then played it on the piano. A delighted laugh filled the studio. "That's it, Mr. Corvino! Thank you. I knew you would understand."

Miss Corsher paused. "Wait here, my dear. I need to speak with Madame Dolavina."

She crossed to the piano, acknowledged the accompanist, and spoke with the older woman. A graceful pivot turned Madame Dolavina to face Rayna. Her vibrant features, framed by permed blonde hair and highlighted by a matching pearl choker and earrings, hinted at the beauty of her youth.

Elegance accompanied her air of authority. Her attitude suggested an astute woman who missed little.

Miss Corsher waved Rayna forward. "Madame Dolavina, I'd like you to meet a new student at SAB. This is Rayna Deejara." Startling blue eyes scrutinized Rayna from head to foot. "Miss Corsher tells me you have received excellent training. Let's see what you can do. Mr. Corvino, please play an adagio for Miss Deejara." She indicated the center of the studio. "I will instruct you as he plays."

Butterflies slamming into each other in her stomach accompanied Rayna to her place. She stepped into *fifth position, croisé,* facing the front of the room. The accompanist shook his hair away from his face. Her butterflies settled. Corvus Karrew Castylim's confident smile deepened the dimple in his cheek. His unexpected presence gave her the courage to smile at the revered teacher.

Madame Dolavina nodded. Music accompanied her instructions. Rayna, immersed in the beautiful movements, experienced a love of dance that carried her through the long combination to its conclusion. Mesmerized, she held the final pose. As the music faded, she returned to fifth position, her attention on the two women.

"You may relax, my dear." Madame Dolavina ran manicured fingers over her pearls, spoke to Miss Corsher, and motioned Rayna to join them. "You have excellent training and a beautiful facility. You use both with an artistry I find lovely. I'd like you to be a part of SAB's Lecture Demonstration Program. Toward that end, you will attend my classes, one in the morning and one after lunch. Your rehearsals begin two days from today. Miss Corsher will provide you with a schedule. Do you have questions?"

Corvus nodded his approval. Rayna smiled a shy smile. "Thank you so much for this opportunity. If I do have questions, I'll ask Miss Corsher."

"Good. I'll see you in class at ten sharp. Don't be late. You may go."

Rayna walked into the hall, her thoughts in a whirl.

Kelsia caught hold of her arm. "You are so lucky!" She pulled her into the dressing room. "Do you know what just happened?"

"What?" Rayna sank onto a bench, tugged off her leotard and pulled on her tie-died shirt.

"Madame Dolavina invited you to take part in the Demo Program. That almost never happens." Kelsia pursed her lips. "I can't wait for Lois to find out."

On cue, Lois Jean strode into the room, disbelief written all over her face. "Who are you, anyway? Dolavina rarely bothers with new students. I can't believe she selected *you* for the Demo Program."

Rayna finished dressing, stuffed her dance attire in her bag, and flashed Lois a warm smile. "Let's start over." She offered her hand. "I'm Rayna Deejara. It's nice to meet you, Lois Jean. I look forward to getting to know you."

Lois stared at the hand, took it, and, looking puzzled, cleared her throat. "I...Ahh. Sorry, I didn't mean to be a bitch. It's nice to meet you." She picked up her dance bag. Head high, she left.

Kelsia seemed at a loss for words.

Rayna rubbed her neck and shouldered her bag. "I need to go. I have a lot to think about. Thanks for your help today, Kelsia. I'll see you tomorrow."

Her new friend sighed. "Since you're taking Madame's class, I won't see you. We could do lunch?" She looked hopeful.

Rayna gave her an enticing smile. "Why not take Madame's class with me?"

Kelsia paled. "I can't. She terrifies me. I'm not good enough."

Rayna gave her a quick hug. "I'll be there to protect you, Kelsia. Besides, I bet you are every bit as good in your own way as I am in mine." She moved to the door. "See you here at nine-thirty sharp."

Without waiting for a response, she hurried along the hall, down the stairs into the open air, and wandered toward the plaza. Pain shot down her neck. *I need to shift.* She looked at the crowd milling around the fountain. *Another pain made her flinch.* She made her way to a recessed area beneath an arch, her thoughts filled with Gar's image.

A sharp stinging sensation left her gasping. She dropped her dance bag, gripped her knees, and forced a calm she did not feel. *Can Fisaco take over if I don't change soon enough?*

A small shadow moving into the sunlight morphed into Gar. He dodged into the milling crowd and vanished amongst couples holding hands, children laughing in delight as the water leapt and fell, dancers, businessmen, tourists. Her frantic gaze froze on a man making a thorough search of the crowd. He tensed. His head jerked from side to side.

Rayna could not move. A small hand gripped her wrist, pulled her behind the building, and handed her the bag. Freed from her unexpected immobility, she jogged with him to the opposite side of Lincoln Center and ducked around a corner.

Pain shot down her neck. She gasped.

Gar tugged her arm. "Are ya okay? I heard ya call."

She fought to hold her fading awareness in check. "Tell me when we are alone. I need to change. I have..." She pressed her lips together and made herself concentrate. "Gar, I have to trust you with a secret. Torgin and Esán know, but no one else. It will put you in more danger. I'm sorry..."

Through clenched teeth, she repeated. "Tell me when we're alone."

He shot a worried glance behind them. "Too many people here. Can you make it across the street?"

She offered her hand. "With your help, I can. Hurry."

His smaller one clasping hers, he led the way through a labyrinth of buildings to the corner of 70th and West End Avenue. A red light held them captive. Gar pranced from foot to foot. Green flashed, sending him sprinting with her across the street. Halfway up the block, he darted into a narrow space between two buildings. "We're alone. Spyglass'll guard the way in."

Rayna inhaled. Brie exhaled into being. Gar's eyes bulged in shocked surprise. Fear carried him backward to the far side of the pass-through.

Brie sagged, felt a rough brick wall supporting her, forced herself to orient, to remember who she was.

Gar's gaze darted to the street and back. Trembling hands covered his mouth, trapping the astonishment Brie knew choked him. She wanted to reassure him. Words refused to form.

Clarity emerged one drop at a time. Blinking back tears of relief, she pushed away from the wall. Shaky hands smoothed red curls back from her face. A long, heart-felt exhale eased the tightness in her throat. She looked at Gar. "My name is Brielle. Rayna is my shifted form. She is my protection against a threat to my life and the lives of those I love and to the planets in my solar system and galaxy. I'm so sorry I frightened you, but I am so glad you are here with me. Thanks for keeping me safe." She opened her arms.

Gar took two hesitant steps, shook his head, and whistled. Spyglass trotted to his side. He dropped to his knees, wrapped his arms around the terrier, and sobbed. The hiccuped ebbing of his fright brought him to his feet. Spyglass licking her hand seemed to erase the last of his fear. He regarded her in silence, then cleared his throat. "I told Torgin and Esán ya were in trouble. They might meet us at the fountain." He gave her a crooked grin. "Can I get a hug now?"

She gathered his slender body in her arms. He rested his head on her chest. An urchin's grin lit his face. "You gotta a heart, just like me. I can hear it."

She released him. "See, we aren't so different."

His expression told her he didn't quite believe her. He scrubbed a hand over his hair. "Better go meet Esán and Torgin." A steady stare wavered. "Ya gotta change, right?"

"Right. No one must know Brielle is here. Are you ready?"

A timid nod.

Rayna looked down at him.

He gave a soft laugh and took her hand.

8

At the New York Studio and Forum of Stage Design, Esán received his registration packet and sat down in a quiet corner. Grateful for the chance to explore lighting design, something he had always found intriguing, he filled out the forms and returned them to the receptionist. "I understand there's a tour today."

The young man placed his packet on the top of a pile. "Schedule's on the bulletin board. The tour starts in about ten minutes."

A quick check sent Esán off at a trot. He arrived as a small group of students prepared to follow the tour guide, who welcomed them all with a harried smile. After a brief introduction, he escorted the group through classrooms, labs, a black box theater, a cafe, and a small library, answered a few questions, glanced at his watch, and excused himself.

Esán left his fellow students to get acquainted with one another. A stroll to the subway made him wish again he and his friends had an apartment in the West Village.

At Washington Square he paused, transfixed by a world so foreign he found it hard to absorb. A pair of musicians sat side by side, playing music on matching guitars. A small crowd responded with enthusiastic applause. Older men at cement tables played chess, a game he had read about in the Galactic Library on Myrrh. The playground rang with the joyful laughter of young children. Women pushed baby carriages along the sunny paths. After two earth years in seclusion on Myrrh, the life energy flooding the area overwhelmed him.

"Rayna trouble. Lincoln Center, Revson Fountain." The telepathic words in his mind wiped the bemused smile from his face. Hurrying across the square, he jogged down the stairs to the subway in time to catch a train to Columbus Circle. *Hurry. Hurry. Hurry.* The mantra played non-stop in his head as he watched stations flash by.

Torgin finished his day at Juilliard with a schedule in hand and a grin on his face. Passion for music and the excitement of being in New York City during a time when the arts flourished left him dizzy with delight. A solitary bench provided him a place to catch his breath. He reread his schedule, ticking off his classes on his fingers. *Composition, conducting, flute, piano, and music theory. What great luck!* Enthusiasm bubbled into a joyous laugh. Murmuring to himself, he tucked the schedule in his notebook. "Remember, Torgin Whälen, you are in New York City, 1969 to recover the Corps Stones and return them to their planets."

His thoughts wandered to his morning walk to Lincoln Center. Cole, who had proved to be a fun companion, painted vibrant verbal pictures of life growing up in a large family on an Idaho farm. Torgin shook his head. *What a different life from mine in Idronatti.*

He opened his notebook to review his notes. The day started with the music major's meeting, which had been interesting and informative. His music auditions had left him feeling exhilarated. *Sure am glad I familiarized myself with the Steinway at the apartment.* Overcome at the prospect of all he might learn, he walked through the school he had until now only read about in history books.

"Rayna. Trouble. Revson Fountain."

Gar's telepathic message tore him from all thoughts of his day. He arrived near the fountain, his heart racing. His searching gaze halted on a stocky man with bristly blond hair. A shiver careened up his spine. Upori Athai took a final drag on a cigarette, crushed it beneath his heel, and scrutinized the throng of people. His intense study of a woman near Torgin ended with a frustrated shrug. Upori crossed the plaza as Esán rounded the corner and stopped at the crosswalk.

Torgin held his breath. The light changed. The crowds surged forward and merged. Esán and Upori almost brushed shoulders. Upori continued across Columbus Avenue to Central Park West. Esán hurried up the steps toward the fountain.

Relieved, Torgin moved into a patch of sunlight and waited.

      👁 👁

sán barely noticed the late afternoon sun washing the plaza with warmth or the sparkling droplets sprinkling the fountain's surface. Rayna's absence nagged him to pick up his pace. Torgin's presence in front of the opera house drew him forward through the mix of students, dancers, and tourists enjoying the day.

A young man walked from Philharmonic Hall, waved at Torgin, and hurried to meet him.

Esán paused within hearing.

"Hi, Cole." Torgin's worried look brightened. "How was your afternoon?"

As fair as Torgin was dark and almost as tall, Cole grinned. He held up a stuffed legal sized folder. "About as packed as this. What a great orientation! How about you?"

Spyglass, tail wagging, trotted to Esán's side and licked his hand. Esán glanced over his shoulder. Rayna ambled in his direction. He caught Torgin's eye. *"Meet you at the apartment."*

"Right." Adjusting his leather satchel to a more comfortable position, Torgin smiled at his new friend. "Let's get a quick bite and compare notes." The two, deep in conversation, strolled toward Columbus Circle.

Noting the fatigue in Rayna's step, Esán considered meeting her halfway. A tiny shake of her head kept him stationary.

Without a sidelong glance, she strolled toward the intersection of Broadway and Columbus Ave. When she reached the steps, he wandered after her. Spyglass trotted at his heels.

Near the corner, the terrier darted into the late afternoon shadows cloaking Gar. Esán dipped his chin. Furtive as the fading light, dog and boy tailed Rayna up Broadway.

Esán fell in step behind them, his gaze never leaving Rayna's dancer-straight spine. Half-way to 72nd, she paused to look in a bookstore window. He dropped back to read the menu outside a Thai restaurant.

A man strolled by, almost passed her, then stopped. A hesitant smile transformed to delight. "You're Rayna. I saw you do Madame Dolavina's adagio. Wow, are you good!"

Rayna edged backward. "You are?"

"Name's Dwight Anders. I study at SAB. Heard you're joining the Demo Program. That's way cool. I'm a member." Ignoring her silence, he hurried on. "How about we grab some dinner? We can get to know each other. I'll tell you about the program."

With a tired smile, she hefted her dance bag to the other shoulder. "Perhaps another time. I've had a long day." She sighed. "Tomorrow might be even longer." She side-stepped to walk past him.

He grabbed her arm. "Come on. It won't take that long." His firm grip belied his coaxing expression.

Esán struggled with a desire to interfere.

Her gaze moved from Dwight's face to his hand. "Please let go of my arm."

He released her, seemed to inwardly shake himself, and frowned. "Sorry, Rayna. See you tomorrow."

She moved past him, walked to the corner, and waited for the light.

The young man stared after her until she rounded a building onto a side street at the end of the next block. A shrug turned him back toward Lincoln Center. Without a glance, he hurried past Esán.

Uncertain what to make of the strange encounter, Esán ducked into the restaurant, made his way to the counter, and placed a takeout order. *I have a feeling everyone will be hungry.*

Rayna detoured over to Columbus Avenue and walked uptown an extra block. A glance in a store window confirmed Dwight hadn't followed. Relief lightened her step. At her building, she rode the elevator to the fifth floor. Esán framed in the apartment entrance eliminated the last vestige of her concern. She flashed him a tired smile and slipped past him into the entryway.

He locked the door behind them, took her dance bag, and escorted her to her room. "Gar told me what happened. I'm glad he was with you." He put her bag on the bed. "Why don't you freshen up."

She started pulling pins from her bun. "How about dinner?"

"It's all taken care of. I brought home a surprise."

She sniffed the air. "That must be what I'm smelling. Torgin?"

"He'll be home soon. Get a move on. Gar's stomach is growling." He kissed her cheek. "So's mine." He cocked his head. "Was that yours I just heard?"

Brie materialized and tipped her face up for a proper kiss. She leaned against his muscular chest, grateful for his soothing warmth. He kissed her one more time, then left her to unwind.

Showered and refreshed, she pulled on a baggy shirt with a pair of sweatpants, slid her feet into plush, pink slippers, and padded down the hall.

A smiling Torgin greeted her. "Nice slippers, Brielle."

She flopped down on the couch and lifted a foot to eye-level. "Whoever picked them out did great." She smothered a yawn. "Where's Gar?"

"Helping Esán." Torgin poured her a glass of water. "I imagine you could use this. Sounds like you had quite a turning." He scrunched up his face. "I mean...day."

Esán's muffled voice drifted down the hall. "We'll be right in." Moments later, Gar arrived bearing a stack of plates, gave Brie a shy smile, and set them on the coffee table. Esán unloaded a tray laden with takeout boxes and joined her on the couch.

Brie inhaled. "What's that mouth-watering smell?"

Esán handed her a pair of wooden sticks, I'm introducing us to Thai cuisine. "These are chop sticks. The girl at the restaurant showed me how to use them." He positioned his in the crook between his thumb and index finger, dipped them into a box, pinched them together, and carried a small pink shrimp to his mouth. "Dig in!"

The delicious meal, consumed with lots of laughter and a large dose of teasing, helped diminish what remained of Brie's unease, but not her weariness. After cleanup, she trailed the boys into the living room. Snuggled up next to Esán on the sofa, she stifled a yawn. "We have loads to talk about." She beamed at Gar. "You were my hero today. Thank you."

He grinned from ear to ear and flopped down on the couch. "I learned stuff. Wanna hear?"

Torgin settled in an over-stuffed chair. "Sure do."

Gar tempered his excitement with a dose of Esán-like seriousness. "I followed the man into the theater. He met a guy on the stage. I followed 'em to a dark corner. They talked a bunch. Seems they're lookin' for a red-haired gal." He peaked under his lashes at Brie. "They're bettin' she'll show up soon." His direct, worried gaze examined her. "They're after ya, right? They want ya bad. Who are ya, really?"

She slid her palms over the soft fabric of her sweatpants. "Please don't worry. I have all of you to keep me safe. What else did you learn?"

"Only that someone or somethin's in place, whatever that means." He bit his lip. "Oh yah. They're worried about some dude, a pianist who showed up about a week ago."

Brie massaged her temples. "Corvus is here...in New York."

Esán angled his body toward her. "You know this because..."

"He was Madame Dolavina's accompanist today. I wonder if he's aware *they* know he's here?"

"Bet he is." Torgin stretched his long legs and crossed his ankles. "He doesn't miss much."

Gar raised a hand.

Esán nodded. "Go, young friend."

"Who's Corvus?"

"He's a good friend of ours."

"Not from here, right?" Dark features twisted into a frustrated grimace.

Esán regarded him with a half-smile. "When we can, Gar, we'll share who we are. Be patient. The important thing is to keep you safe."

"Hrrumph." The only answer he gave accompanied folded arms and a slight pout.

Esán looked at Torgin. "Did you discover anything interesting?"

"Only that a quartet is being formed as part of the Demo Program established by SAB. Auditions are tomorrow. How about you?"

"I'll be taking a class from Joseph Shyro, SAB's head lighting designer. Rumor has it he's looking for an apprentice who will work with him at the New York State Theater. If things work out, we'll all be near the target area.

"We need more information about Upori's connection to the dance world, in particular New York City Ballet." Torgin held up crossed fingers. "If we're lucky, that will help us discover who his boss is."

Brie yawned. "It's been a long couple of days. I need sleep." Another yawn overtook her. She rested her head on Esán's shoulder. "Anything else before we turn in?"

Torgin reached behind his chair and pulled out a large green bag. He held it up. "This is for you, Gar."

The boy took it in unsteady hands. "What is it?"

A twinkle glinted. Torgin grinned. "Open it and find out."

Gar peeked in the top. "Ohhhh." He pulled out a pair of new jeans and a T-shirt. "These are mine?"

"If they fit, they're yours. There's new underwear and socks in the bag. Try everything on in the bathroom. Come back and model them for us."

Gar scrambled off the sofa, stuffed the clothes in the bag, and scurried into the hall. The sound of the shower ended in a brief silence. A few minutes later, a new Gar sauntered into the room.

"Hope it's okay, I showered. I never had new clothes. Didn't wanna get 'em dirty." He stuffed his hands in his pockets and posed like a magazine model. "What do ya think?"

Esán winked. "You look like a new man!"

Torgin walked around him and copied his stance. "Lookin' good, my friend"

He crossed to Brie, his expression anxious. He bit his lip.

Brie grinned. "You look handsome, Gar. I'm so glad Torgin bought you new clothes."

Torgin sank into his chair. "You'll blend in better when you're guarding Rayna at Lincoln Center. Tomorrow, I'll take you to get new shoes. Now, where do you plan to sleep tonight?"

"I don't wanna get my clothes dirty." He walked to the window and back. "Can Spyglass and me stay with ya?"

A teary-eyed yawn prompted Brie to make sleep a priority. "That's a grand idea." She scrambled to her feet. "I'll let you boys figure it out. My day..." She smiled at Gar. "...our day starts early tomorrow."

Another yawn propelled her down the hall. After a trip to the bathroom, she wiggled into pale pink pajamas the same shade as her slippers. Her head touched the pillow. Sleep snatched her into dreaming.

Gar refused to sleep on the couch, so Torgin helped him create a bed beneath a front window. After folding his new clothes into a neat pile, he nestled into the blankets with Spyglass. A yawn morphed to a shy smile. "Thanks, Torgin. I never expected to have new stuff." He squirmed beneath the sheet and wrapped an arm around Spyglass. Sleep heavy eyelids drifted shut.

The quiet apartment seemed oppressive. Not ready to head to bed, Torgin wandered down the hall to the music room. The grand piano made his heart skip a beat. He traced the curve of the cabinet and touched an ivory key. *How lucky am I!* Humming to himself, he used the time alone to inspect the rest of the room.

Shelves were filled with more classical music scores than he had ever seen. An antique trunk beneath the window contained sheet music. On a stand in the corner, a guitar gleamed in the moonlight filtering though the sheer curtains. Fascinated, he picked it up, caressed the silky finish, smelled the faint odor of wood, and plucked a string. "I never expected to see a guitar, let alone hold one. Sure wish I knew how to play it."

"I can teach ya."

Torgin swung around. "Thought you were sleeping."

Gar, with a blanket draped over his shoulders, peered into the room, blinking sleep from his eyes. "Woke up worried about being trapped. Haven't slept inside a building for as long as I can remember."

"Better come in." Torgin placed a chair next to the piano. "Have a seat. I can't wait to hear how you learned to play a guitar."

Gar shuffled to the chair. Torgin straddled the piano bench.

"So tell me."

"My friend, Gin, loved music. He taught me to sight read. I play the guitar and the harmonica. We used to perform on street corners for donations." A tear slipped down his cheek.

"What happened to your friend, Gar?"

"Gin was an old guy...old enough to be my granddad. He found me hiding in a trash bin when I was three. He gived me my name. After that, I stayed with him. One morning about half a year ago, I woke up and found him dead." He wiped a tear away. "Old age ain't pretty. I watched Gin lose interest in livin'. Worst thing—he forgot how to play his guitar. Just forgot, like he never knowed how. If it didn't hurt so bad, I'd be glad he died." He wrapped the blanket tighter and slid off the chair. "Can I hold it?"

Torgin swallowed a lump in his throat. "Yes." Torgin stood beside him.

Gar's shoulder rose and fell. He reached out a tentative hand. "It's a Taylor, Torgin. Wow! Sure is lots nicer than Gin's and mine." He gave it a hungry look. "Ya sure it's okay if I hold it?"

"I'm sure Maggie won't mind." Torgin handed him the instrument.

Gar settled the strap over his shoulder. "Who's Maggie?"

"The woman who owns this apartment. Play something. Do you have a favorite artist?"

"I kinda like the Beatles, but Gin played classical music." Gar tipped his head and plucked each string. "Nice sound." Placing his fingers, he played a series of chords. An affirming nod later, music with a Spanish flavor floated through the room.

Torgin listened, transfixed. "That was fantastic, Gar. How long have you been playing?"

Skilled fingers strummed a set of chords. "Began playin' soon after Gin found me. You play the piano, right?"

"I do. Why?"

Gar bit his bottom lip. "Ya think we can play together sometime?"

"You bet we can." Torgin smiled. "Not tonight. We both need sleep. Let's plan to play tomorrow after dinner. What do you say?"

"I say *yes!*" A yawn caught him off guard. He squelched it with a grin and returned the guitar to its stand. "Can I sleep in here? Maybe with music all around I won't feel so queasy-like."

"I think that's a good plan."

Together they collected blankets and a pillow from the front room. Soon, Gar and Spyglass were sound asleep beside the Taylor Guitar.

Torgin marveled that this boy, who grew up on the streets of New York, could read music and play a guitar like a pro. Humming the tune Gar had played, he crawled into bed.

9

B rie woke to the morning's gentle light and a rat terrier licking her cheek. Gar nudged her door further ajar. "Esán said to tell ya breakfast's ready." He whistled. Spyglass delivered one last lick and scampered after his master.

A thrill of elation spiked with anticipation brought Brie to sitting. She threw back the covers. *I get to take Madame Dolavina's class. Am I ready?* As her feet touched the floor, she shifted to Rayna. *I am.* Humming a cheerful tune, she dressed in bell bottomed jeans and a yellow flowered T-shirt. A glimpse of her taller, dark-haired self prompted a grin. "I am definitely ready."

Merry giggles and the sharp snap of a flicked towel greeted her as she stepped into the hall. A panting Gar dashed from the kitchen. Torgin followed, a dish towel in hand. Twisting it for a stinging blow, he took aim. Gar dodged behind her.

Rayna threw up her hands. "This isn't my game, Torg." She stepped aside. Gar, clutching her waist, moved with her.

"Breakfast is ready." Esán called from the dining room. "Play or eat. Decide."

Torgin snapped the dish towel in the air. He grinned. "Another day, another try, right Gar? Let's eat."

An hour-and-a-half later, Rayna walked into the dressing room at SAB. Kelsia sat on a bench, hugging her towel with trembling hands. "Hi, Kelsia, I wasn't certain you'd be here."

"I decided I can take class from a woman I've worshipped all my dance life, especially since you'll be there." She glanced at the clock. "Better hustle."

Rayna changed into pink tights and a black leotard. After putting on her ballet slippers, she glanced in the mirror, adjust a bobby pin, and smiled. *I look like a dancer.* Nervous excitement conveyed her from the changing room into the hall. Dwight's presence brought her up short. His attention strayed in her direction.

He spoke to his companion and came to meet her. "I'd like to apologize. My behavior yesterday was out of line. I'm sorry. My excuse..." He shrugged. "...I wanted to meet you." He extended a hand. "Truce?"

Rayna, her smile guarded, shook it. "Truce. Thanks for the apology."

Curiosity flickered across the handsome face before he turned away.

Kelsia met her at the studio door, her gaze serious. "I hear he can be a real stinker. Better be careful." She bustled ahead.

Rayna, butterflies doing a jig in her belly, hesitated. The packed studio sent a wave of doubt rushing over her. *I can do this.* She squared her shoulders and marched to the place next to Kelsia at the barre. Her friend's jitters were palpable. Rayna kept hers in check.

Sudden silence erased the quiet chatter in the studio. Mr. Corvino held the door for Madame Dolavina, then followed her into the room. After a brief conversation in Russian, he settled at the piano. She perched on a tall stool at the front of the room, her astute gaze missing little. "Let us begin."

After a long, thorough warmup, Madame divided the dancers into groups of eight. She assigned Rayna and Kelsia to group one. A nervous Kelsia slipped into the second line. Rayna found herself in the front row. *Adagio, petite allegro, grand allegro*...the class flew by.

Rayna enjoyed every combination, absorbed every correction, and finished the class dripping wet. Pleased with herself, she grabbed her towel, wiped the sweat from her face, and walked into the hall. A bemused Kelsia hurried to meet her.

"Guess what! Madame invited us to attend the Company Trainee's *pas deux class* this afternoon."

Rayna draped her damp towel over her shoulder. "What about Madame Dolavina's second class?"

"She's the one who gave me the message. Aren't you excited? I am. I never expected to take *that* class." She wrinkled her brow. "Did you arrange this?"

Rayna laughed. "How would I do that? What time does it start?"

"Two o'clock. Wow. This is so cool." Kelsia grinned.

Rayna nudged her toward the dressing rooms. "We'd better grab lunch while we can."

They arrived back at SAB to find Lois waiting. "You're both taking *pas de deux* this afternoon, right?"

Kelsia tensed. Rayna smiled. "Madame asked us to attend. Are you in the class?"

"Dwight invited me. Mr. Tansley said he could pick his own partner." She pulled her point shoes from her bag. "Dwight's supposed to be the best partner ever. Guess I'm about to find out." Nose in the air, she strutted down the corridor.

Kelsia finished tying her pointe shoe ribbons. "Something weird's going on. Dwight's snubbed Lois since he arrived a few weeks ago." She stared after her friend. "I wouldn't trust him. Sure hope he doesn't hurt her."

Rayna rose onto pointe to test the comfort of her shoes. "Lois is a big girl. We'd better hurry."

Except for Lois and Dwight, a room full of unfamiliar faces met Rayna as she entered the studio. Several dancers smiled a welcome; others stared, their expressions cool and calculating. Fear of competition crackled like an electrical current through the studio. Lois shot her a haughty smile. Dwight ignored her.

Rayna joined Kelsia at the barre, performed several simple exercises to warm up her feet, and forced herself to breathe. *What am I doing in a pas de deux* class? *Will I know what to do?* She turned her focus inward. *Étoile said if I had questions to listen; the answer would come.*

Kelsia touched her hand. "Mr. Tansley is here."

Rayna reined in her stage fright and assessed the man standing just outside the door. He spoke to someone in shadow, pocketed his pipe, and walked into the studio. A female accompanist followed, slid onto the piano bench, and arranged her music. The dancers moved to the barre and grew quiet.

Mr. Tansley, an unassuming man of moderate height and build, surveyed the studio. His astute gaze brushed from Kelsia to Rayna. A brow raised and lowered. "Good afternoon. We have a lot to accomplish today." He turned to his accompanist. "Shall we begin?" The short, intricate barre prepared the dancers for the work to come. They finished a limbering stretch and turned their attention to their teacher. Mr. Tansley made a slow circuit of the room. With meticulous care, he paired men and women to partner together in the center. He gazed at Lois and Dwight, gave a clipped nod, and moved to Kelsia, whom he chose to work with a shy boy named Peter. Rayna stood alone at the barre, the only dancer without a partner.

Mr. Tansley regarded her with an intense stare. "Your name?"

"Rayna Deejara, sir."

"Ah. Madame Dolavina's new protégé. Let me see." He surveyed the couples standing ready to begin. "Peter, you will partner both Kelsia and Lois. Dwight, please work with Rayna." He walked to his place at the front of the class.

Lois flushed deep red. Dwight whispered something. Rayna focused on repositioning a hair pin in her bun. The slight sneer twisting Dwight's mouth as he turned his back on the angry girl transitioned to a wide smile. Three long, confident strides brought him to her side. Afire with conceit, he escorted her to the head of the class.

Mr. Tansley cast an appraising look around the studio. "We are seeking two couples to perform the new ballet, *Gems*, with the company. I will now teach a section of it which you will perform at the end of class. Consider it an audition. Please do your best not to massacre the choreography."

He set a long combination, answered a few questions, and let his gaze travel from couple to couple. "I'll give you a few minutes to get used to each other. When I return, we'll see what you have accomplished."

Dwight led Rayna to a corner. Much to her relief, she responded with ease to his excellent partnering skills. After working on the most difficult sections, they did a final run through. Dwight grinned down at her. "Nice work. We're the best in the room."

Rayna tried not to show her growing dislike. "You're an excellent partner."

A sudden hush made her turn as Madame Dolavina led two men to chairs positioned at the front of the room.

Rayna forced herself to remain calm.

Upori Athai sat between Madame Dolavina and the ballet master of the company.

⁂

"Esán Zervos."

Esán raised his hand. "Here."

The slender, dark-haired man at the front of the room added a check to his list, called three more names, and placed his clipboard on the desk. "I'm Joe Shyro." Piercing blue eyes scanned the room. "My job is to turn you into the best lighting designers you can be. Toward that end," he perched on the front edge of the desk, "we will start our relationship off with an exploratory assignment."

He glanced at the clock above the door. "You have what remains of the morning to create a synopsis of a lighting design for a theater production of your choice.

If you choose a play, I suggest you work on one act. If you choose a ballet, I recommend you disregard the older classics."

He retrieved his list. "By the time you return this afternoon, I will know your face, your name, and your lighting design history. We'll meet after lunch in the black box theater, where you will treat me to a demonstration of your genius." He surveyed the room. "Questions?"

The stunned silence brought a twinkle to his eye. "Good. I suggest you get to work. The actual design and lighting plot will be presented within two days' time. For those of you who wish to get a head start on your plot, the Drafting Lab will be open until 9:30 p.m. Class dismissed."

The minute the door clicked shut, the silence erupted into nervous chatter. Esán gathered his notebook and pencil, stuffed them in his book bag, and prepared to slip away. A hand on his shoulder kept him seated.

"Where do you think you're going?" A heavy-set boy glared down at him. "We stick together in this class."

Esán glanced at his classmates. No one else had moved. Fear scented the room. The energy flowing from the boy shouted 'bully'. Esán fastened the strap on his bag. He brushed the boy's hand from his shoulder, pushed his chair back, and rose. "I have work to do, don't you?"

Anger flushed the puffy face red. A flash of pain lit the boy's eyes. He rubbed his palms together. "What did you do to my hand?"

Esán shrugged. "Wouldn't try to bully anyone else if I were you. See you this afternoon." He walked into the hall.

A loud bellow exploded behind him. "What are you laughing at?" A chair crashed to the ground. A painful yelp ended in muffled muttering.

Students poured from the classroom. A short girl with tightly curled scarlet hair, big earrings, and crazy glasses caught up with Esán at the Drafting Lab.

"Hi." Magnified eyes blinked. "I'm Summer. What did you do in there? Dugun's been bullying everyone for the past three years." She trailed him to a table in the corner. "He steals our papers and takes our ideas. If anyone even thinks about telling the teacher, they take the chance of getting beat up." She stacked her books on the floor beside her chair, regarded him through her thick lenses, and smiled. "You don't have to tell me what you did." She sat down. "I'm just glad you did it." Without another word, she opened her notebook and went to work.

Esán reviewed what he had learned in his lessons with the demi-god of theater. Surprised at how much he knew, he focused on how to put the knowledge to use. *What ballet...*

An obscure choreographer from the early twentieth century rose from his mental files. Her piece, *The Gift of Balance*, had won several awards. The Library Archives on Myrrh had produced a V-chip of the work in rehearsal. He had found it intriguing and pertinent to the teachings of Trilemma. He smiled to himself. *It speaks to the importance of maintaining balance in the Universe.*

Listing the scenic elements he would use and the lighting changes he felt would augment the choreography, he got busy with creating the synopsis for the design. When he finished, he adjusted the ballet's time frame to accommodate 1969 and started his plot. A bell ringing startled him from his creative daze.

Summer caught his eye. "Lunch bell. You hungry?"

"Gosh. Time sure flew by." His stomach growled. "I am hungry."

"Care to get something to eat together?" Her tentative smile broadened as he smiled back.

"Sure would." He picked up his pencil. "Let me put a couple of finishing touches on my design, and I'll be ready."

"Great." She bent over her work.

A quarter of an hour later, Esán slipped his lighting plot and notebook into his book bag.

Summer's head rested on her arms. An occasional soft snore ruffled a stray curl. Not wanting to startle her, he sent a telepathic thought. *Wake up, Summer.*

She raised her head and yawned. "Oh. Sorry, I didn't mean to fall asleep." A searching hand sent her glasses skittering off the table.

Esán picked them up. "Here you go. I'm ready to leave when you are."

They were soon seated at a picnic table in a nearby park, enjoying pizza and a Coca-Cola. Summer concentrated on her food. Esán savored each bite of his first pizza ever and watched the world go by.

Summer finished eating and stuffed the trash in a bag. "I'm so nervous. I hate doing presentations in front of the class."

Esán tossed their rubbish in a garbage can. "Tell you what. I'm edgy, too. You present your project to me; I'll present mine to you. That way it won't be so nerve-wracking."

A shy smile welcomed his suggestion. "Sounds good. Better get going." She froze.

Esán followed her frightened gaze. Dugun walked their direction, an ugly look on his face. Placing his book bag on the table, Esán squeezed her hand. "Stay put. Watch our stuff."

Her freckled face paled. "Be careful."

"Don't worry about me, Summer." He walked to meet the angry boy, reminding himself not to do anything foolish.

10

Torgin studied the schedule board in the corridor at Juilliard. He found nothing detailing requirements for the quartet being formed to work with the Demo Program at SAB. *Guess I'll just stand in line and see what happens.*

Flute case in hand, he strolled down the wide corridor. He couldn't help but compare Idronatti's strict PPP control to the freedom of expression he witnessed all around him. *Sure am glad Idronatti's evolving.*

Torgin joined the line outside the audition studio and prepared to wait. A slender, dark-haired woman stepped into the hall.

"May I have your attention, please?" She scanned the length of the line. "You will be auditioning for a piano quartet. If piano, violin, cello, and viola are not your instruments, thank you. Enjoy some time to yourselves. For those remaining, the audition will begin shortly." She withdrew.

A murmured response—frustration and disappointment mixed with excitement and the prickly energy of nervousness—accompanied her departure. Torgin leaned against the wall, prepared to wait his turn.

The boy behind him tapped his shoulder. "No flutes. Didn't you hear?"

Torgin smiled. "I also play the piano." He noted the boy carried an instrument case. "I always wanted to play the violin. Somehow, life is always too busy. My name's Torgin." He offered a hand.

"Davy." He shook it and grinned. "Torgin! You're the guy Cole told me about. Didn't mean to sound pushy."

Torgin advanced with the line. "You didn't. How do you know Cole?"

"We grew up in the same town in Idaho."

A frowning student marched from the audition studio. Another young musician entered. One by one, students auditioned until Torgin arrived at the head of the line.

A disgruntled looking boy exited the studio and walked past him, muttering.

The woman appeared. "Next." She ducked back inside.

Davy frowned. "She didn't look happy." He smoothed his long hair. "Good luck."

"You, too." Torgin calmed his edginess, entered the room, and paused, awaiting instructions.

Three heads turned his direction; three pairs of eyes appraised him.

The woman picked up a pencil. "Please join us." She made several notes on her clipboard. "You realize we are not looking for flutists, so I presume you play the piano. Name?"

"Torgin Whälen."

Her unexpected smile surprised him. "Ah. Mr. Whälen. You auditioned with Mr. Larsen and Miss Tary yesterday, did you not?"

"Yes, Ma'am, I did."

She scribbled a note. "I am Mrs. Sydner. To my left... Professor of Music, Mr. Wallace...to my right... Professor of Music, Mr. Morsillo. Please leave your flute on the table. Take a seat at the piano."

Torgin left his flute case where she indicated, adjusted the piano stool to accommodate his long legs, and sat down.

Mr. Morsillo looked up from his note pad. "What are you playing today, Mr. Whälen?"

"I have selected the 'Prelude in C Major' from Bach's 'Well-Tempered Clavier', sir."

Mr. Wallace raised a brow. "Why Bach?"

Torgin smiled, "I love the intricacy of his work, sir. Someday, I hope to compose my own work. He is my inspiration."

Mrs. Sydner placed her pencil on her clipboard. "Please begin."

The cool ivory keys beneath Torgin's fingertips steadied his nerves. By the end of the first phrase, his performance jitters melted away. The music lifted him out of himself and carried him to the place where passion, bliss, and awe reside. He played the last note and lowered his hands to his lap.

Hushed stillness pulled him into the present moment. He looked up. A tear slipped down Mrs. Sydner's cheek. No one said a word. Confused, he rose to leave. Mr. Wallace cleared his throat. "Please play the flute. I understand you played one of your own compositions yesterday. We would love to hear it."

Torgin moved to the table. The case contained two instruments. He left the wooden flute Somay had carved nestled in the velvet lining and picked up the silver flute his father had obtained for his lessons in Idronatti.

Mr. Morsillo leaned forward. "Excuse me, Mr. Whälen, what is the other instrument."

Torgin ran a loving finger over the silky wood of the Tirips Tree. "My friend's father made it. I always keep it with me."

The professors conferred. Mrs. Sydner turned to Torgin. "Would you be willing to play the flute your friend made?"

"I would love to play it." Torgin put the silver flute in the case. He lifted Somay's gift and placed his fingers. "I call this piece *Memory.*"

Melodic pictures of woodlands, mountains, and grasslands, of the laughter of friends and the reuniting of loved ones filled the room. As the last note faded into the soft quiet, he lowered the instrument.

The panel of stern-faced professors had relaxed. Mrs. Sydner sighed. "Lovely, Mr. Whälen." She handed him a folded note. "Please be at this address tomorrow at eleven. Thank you for sharing your talent with us."

Torgin returned the flute to the case. "Thank you for allowing me to audition."

How he reached the hallway was a mystery.

Davy looked awe struck. "That was you on the flute, right?"

A voice from the room called, "Next."

Torgin whispered as Davy shuffled into the studio. "Good luck."

His flute case hugged to his chest, he slipped into an empty room and sat down in the back row. His performance high abated little by little. Reality focused. Torgin gazed at the small stage area several rows below him, placed his flute on the seat next to him, and stared at the note in his hand.

R ayna fixed her attention on Mr. Tansley, who clapped for quiet and turned to his three guests.

He bowed over Madame Dolavina's hand, kissed it, and straightened. "You all know our own esteemed teacher Madame Dolavina. She is joined by Cerril Thompson, the company ballet master, whom most of you have met. Unknown to you is Michael Mazer, British dance and theater critic and renowned dance historian. Mr. Mazer is here researching his new book about the history of New York City Ballet.

"Today our guests will be helping to choose two couples to work with the company on *Gems,* our newest ballet." He regarded the dancers with an expert eye. "We have nine couples. You will perform two couples at a time. Dwight, I know I asked you to work with Rayna, but I would appreciate it if you would partner Lois in the first set. Peter and Kelsia will join you."

The couples took their places. The room grew quiet. The accompanist began to play.

Rayna ducked behind a tall boy and pretended to retie her point shoe, while studying Michael Mazer.

Observing the dancers with a detached attitude, he seemed almost uninterested. Something about him bothered Rayna. She looked closer.

Mazer, a man in his early fifties, wore a tweed jacket and plain pants, a silk shirt and bow tie, and shoes spit polished to a glossy shine. A squarish face would have been nondescript but for the hardness of his eyes and the unflattering twist of his thin-lipped mouth.

Rayna placed her hands on the barre and did a series of *relevés* onto pointe. In the mirror, she continued her analysis. Something about him felt familiar and wrong. *Sure wish I could use DiMensionery.* The steel-hard gaze swept her direction. She executed a tendu series to work her feet. *I don't dare.*

The music stopped. Mr. Tansley gave corrections and selected the next two couples. They took their places; the music began.

Mazer's unpleasant gaze drifted her direction again. Rayna's instincts buzzed beware. Careful not to draw attention to herself, she marked the combination with the other couples.

Dwight showed up next to her. "You nervous?"

"Of course, aren't you?"

"Why should I be. We're a shoo-in."

His haughty attitude should not have surprised her, but it did.

In the park in the West Village, Esán walked to meet Dugun, who tromped along the sidewalk, stopped feet astride, and glared.

"What did you do to my hand, you s-o-b? Every time I try to use it, it hurts." He took a menacing step. His pudgy features twisted into an agonized grimace. "Tell me what you did."

"You're a bully, Dugun." Esán looked him square in the eye. "That tells me you're weak, and you're scared. Hurting others makes you feel better about yourself. I did nothing you hadn't already put into action. Think about it. When does the hand hurt?"

Dugun's mouth puckered. Narrowed, puffy eyes considered Esán. Thick fingers curled into a tight fist. Realization shifted his angry demeanor to puzzled. Esán waited. Dugun opened his fisted hand. "It only hurts when I want to hit someone." A flush crept up his thick neck. "Or if I'm about to steal someone else's ideas. What the heck?"

Esán spoke in a soft, non-threatening voice. "Somewhere along the line, you became convinced you aren't worth anything. Your need to prove you are the best turned you into a bully. I know you're smarter than you give yourself credit for and more talented than most of the kids in your classes. I can demonstrate it to you if you promise to quit the bullying. What do you say?"

Broad shoulders hunched. Dugun dropped his chin to his chest, chewed his bottom lip, and mumbled under his breath. He huffed. His chin jerked up. "What about today? I don't have a project. I was gonna make Summer give me hers."

"We have a little over an hour. Go back to the Forum. Work on your own synopsis. Don't even consider stealing someone else's idea. I'll tell Mr. Shyro, you'll be late and would like to go last."

"Ya right, he'll let me, his least favorite student, come in late and present." His flat tone spoke volumes.

"You promise to present your own ideas; I guarantee Mr. Shyro will let you go last."

Dugun ran his tongue over his teeth. His nostrils flared. "I promise. But if he won't allow me to show," he scowled, "I'll beat the crap outta ya." He winced and cradled his hand. "Guess we'd better get back. What about Summer?"

"I'll take care of Summer. Go. Get to work."

Hefting his overweight body in a half turn, Dugun scuttled down the street.

Esán accepted his book bag from his astonished new friend. "What did you do? I was sure he'd beat you up."

"We just talked." He shouldered his book bag. "Let's go. I have things to do before the showing."

Summer fell in step beside him. At the Forum, she halted in the reception area. "I have to fact check something in the library. See you in the theater."

Esán hastened to a study lab and dumped his bag on the table. *Dugun's more than a bully. The guy has a good brain.* He smiled to himself. *And a good heart. The trick is how to get Mr. Shyro to let him go last.* He sank into a chair, his fingers drumming the tabletop. *I need to plant the idea in his mind. A simple touch worked with Dugun. Mr. Shyro's different.* The drumming continued. *I can...* Drum, drum, drum— "Got it!"

A few minutes later, he walked into the black box theater with an envelope bearing Mr. Shyro's name and placed it on the instructor's table. Students gathered in small groups. The buzz of their chatter broadcasting their nervous excitement. Mr. Shyro strode into the theater, picked up the envelope, and withdrew a folded sheet of paper. A timid student approached the table. The envelope and paper disappeared into a notebook. Esán smiled. A subconscious thought was already at work.

11

Dwight led Rayna to the center of the performance space. They were the last couple to audition. The accompanist watched for a signal from Mr. Tansley. The trio at the front of the room prepared to watch.

Pain radiating from the Star of Truth left Rayna shaking. Dwight shot her an inquiring frown. She shook her head, gripped her knees, and fought to breathe.

Mr. Tansley's voice cut through her maze of frantic thoughts. "Are you alright, Miss Deejara?"

A hand pressed to her stomach, she suppressed a gasp of pain. "If you'll excuse me for a few minutes, I'll be fine."

A student entered the studio. "They require you down the hall, Mr. Tansley."

"I'll be right there." He walked over to the guest panel. "I suggest you take a short break."

The three murmured their approval and gathered their notes. Mr. Tansley turned to Rayna. "Are you certain you can perform?"

"Yes, sir. I just need a few minutes."

"Good. Be back here in fifteen." He hurried from the room.

Dwight grabbed her arm. "Don't mess this up, Rayna." Raging arrogance escorted him from the studio.

Mr. Corvino entered, spoke with the accompanist, and brushed past Rayna. *"Back exit."*

Relieved, she grabbed her dance bag, hurried through the exit into a secondary hallway, and ducked into the woman's restroom. In a locked stall, she shifted. The pain in her neck receded. The familiarity of Brie calmed her shattered nerves. Clarity returned. She glanced at the sprinkle of freckles on her hands.

Two chattering girls entered the restroom. Their bags plopped on the floor. "Did you see the expression on Lois' face earlier when Tansley told her she had to partner with Peter."

Another voice chimed in. "Lois is such a bitch. Too bad she got to dance with Dwight, after all."

"Can't wait to see Dwight with the new girl. Rumor has it she's pretty good."

The second girl chimed in. "I heard amazing. Better get back. We don't want to miss the show."

The door clicked shut. A smooth, painless shift left Rayna staring at pale hands. *No freckles.* She tidied her hair, hefted her bag, and slipped into the hall. At the main entrance to the studio, she reminded herself to breathe. Inside, she left her bag in the corner and joined a worried Kelsia at the barre.

"Are you alright?" Kelsia touched her arm. "You looked awful pale."

Rayna smiled. "I'm fine."

The panel filed to their seats at the front of the room. Michael Mazer's penetrating gaze examined her from head to toe. She feigned shyness right down to the soft pink flooding her cheeks. Madame Dolavina distracting him with a question gave her time to regroup as Mr. Tansley entered.

After a brief conversation with the panel, he crossed to her. "Are you able to perform, Miss Deejara?"

She nodded. "I'm ready anytime you are."

He returned her nod and strode to the front of the room.

Dwight grinned down at her. "Neat trick, Rayna. Now, everyone is hyped up to watch."

Before she could reply, Mr. Tansley moved to stand near the piano. "Please, Rayna and Dwight, we're ready to begin."

Silence settled over the studio; all attention focused their direction. Dwight led her forward. They stepped into the opening pose. The pianist held their gaze, lifted her hands, and placed them on the keys.

Immersed in the wonderful choreography, Rayna soon forgot who watched. She even forgot her dislike of the young man whose flawless partnering made her movements appear effortless. Although slender, Rayna was tall. Dwight handled her length without difficulty, lifted her like she weighed nothing, and showed her off to her best. Vaguely, she noted the oohs and ahhs of her fellow artists. A triple *pirouette* into an *arabesque promenade* ended in an overhead lift and a carry into the wings.

Dwight lowered her to the floor. "We did it." His excited whisper matched by the gleam in his eyes made her smile.

Applause exploded from the watching dancers. The panel clustered. Mr. Tansley joined them.

Kelsia caught her eye and grinned.

Michael Mazer checked his watch, broke from the conferencing group, and hurried from the studio. A final hasty glance over his shoulder raked over Rayna. Madame Dolavina and Cerril Thompson left shortly thereafter.

Mr. Tansley raised a hand. "May I have your attention, please?" He peered at his notes. "The panel continues its deliberations in my office. I will post the results in the morning. Thank you all for coming." He followed his accompanist from the room.

Several dancers complimented Rayna and Dwight; others shot them furtive glances and left talking in subdued voices.

Dwight gazed down at her. "I think we wowed them." His subtle change of position pressed Rayna's back to the barre. A hand rested against the mirror behind her. "Come on, Rayna, tell me I did great."

She forced a sweet smile. "You did great, Dwight." She attempted to move.

His other hand shot over her shoulder. Annoyed, she reviewed her options.

"Excuse me, Mr. Anders?"

Dwight scowled and glared at a boy's reflection in the mirror.

Rayna ducked under his arm, gathered her personal items, and walked from the room. She listened to Dwight taking his irritation out on the young pre-teen delivering him a message.

The boy dodged from the room and scurried to catch up with her. "Excuse me, Miss Deejara, I wanted to tell you I think you're beautiful."

She flashed him a dazzling smile. "Thanks! What's your name?"

"I'm Phillip." He turned shy. "Better go." He darted to the stairs, looked back, and waved.

"It appears you have an admirer." Michael Mazer stepped from Mr. Tansley's office.

Rayna's skin crawled. He pushed the door wider. "Mr. Tansley gave me permission to interview you. We can do it now, or I can take you to dinner."

Revulsion crawling up her throat, she moved to the dressing room door. "I am flattered, but I have plans tonight."

Mr. Tansley joined them. "I'm certain you can change your plans, Miss Deejara. It's not every day you earn the opportunity to interview with Michael Mazer."

Rayna fought the urge to walk away. "I'll need to call my friend."

"You can use the phone in my office." He smiled. "I'll leave you to make your plans."

Triumph gleamed in the journalist's eyes. Rayna met his gaze. "I need to change, Mr. Mazer. I'll meet you in Mr. Tansley's office." She edged by him into the dressing room.

Lois met her with an inquisitive half-smile. "An interview, huh? Lucky you."

Rayna sank onto the long bench between lockers. "I would be happy to let you go instead..."

Dark curls bounced around Lois' round, pixie face. "I'm sure Mr. Mazer wouldn't be too happy. What is it about you that has everyone in a twitter? I mean, you are a beautiful dancer, but..." She shrugged.

Rayna finished dressing and stuffed her damp leotard in her bag. "I'm just a new face, Lois. Like you, I've had good training. Who can say why me?" She looked at the disheartened girl. "Don't give up. You know how fickle people in the dance world are. See you tomorrow."

The short walk to Mr. Tansley's office gave Rayna no time to prepare. She knocked on the door.

"Come in."

A whiff of the familiar strangeness made her hesitate. Fumbling with the strap of her bag, she noted how out-of-place Michael Mazer looked behind Mr. Tansley's battered desk.

He pushed the phone toward her. "Please take a seat. Make your call, then we can decide the best place to conduct our interview."

She dropped her dance bag beside the chair and sat facing him. "Mr. Mazer, I am flattered that you chose me to interview. I checked my friend's schedule. He's in class. We had planned to meet for dinner. If you and I talk here, I can still meet him. Even if I'm a bit late, he'll understand once I tell him about you." She gave him her warmest smile.

He stroked the stubble on his chin. "I have a better idea. Why don't you introduce me to your friend?" His mouth twisted as he rounded the desk.

Alarm tightened her stomach.

Esán waited until the student talking to Mr. Shyro took a seat before crossing to the desk.

Mr. Shyro glanced up. "May I help you, Esán?"

"Yes, sir. Dugun asked me to tell you he'll be late. He would appreciate it if he could go last."

"Dugun?" Blue irises glinted. Mr. Shyro rested a hand on the notebook containing the envelope. "Ah, yes. I received a note that he will be late. Thank you."

Esán walked back to his seat and prepared to watch his fellow students present their work.

Mr. Shyro faced the class. He pointed at a boy in the back row. "John Petrose, you are number one. Everyone starting with John, please count off."

Voices chimed in: one, two, three... Esán, in his turn, called out nine. A breathless Summer slid into the chair next to him in time to call out ten. Eleven and twelve followed.

Mr. Shyro nodded. "Dugun will be number thirteen. I will hear everyone's presentation." He regarded each student. "Three of you will be selected to show your work tomorrow." He took a seat at the instructor's table, facing the black box theater. "Please, John, introduce your project."

John Petrose, a tall, lanky boy from Maryland, didn't try to hide his obvious frustration at having to go first. "I designed the lighting for the first act of *The Odd Couple* by Neil Simon." A lack of inventiveness laced his entire presentation. After a mumbled thanks to the class, he returned to the back row.

By the time Esán walked to the stage, half the students looked like a nap was next on their agenda. He cleared his throat. "Ballet, the classics in particular, have always fascinated me." He smiled. "My preference is to design a complete work, so I took Mr. Shyro's advice and set them aside. During my research, I came across an obscure choreographer from northern Michigan, whose ballets intrigued me. I will create a design for one of her works, a nine-minute piece entitled *The Gift of Balance*. As he described his lighting ideas, the drowsy atmosphere in the room changed to wakeful interest. Several students asked intriguing questions, which he answered. A promise to share the music at his showing completed his presentation.

Summer shared her design concepts for *Glass Menagerie*. A soft-spoken boy named Nick reached the conclusion to his presentation as Dugun slipped into the back row.

Mr. Tansley acknowledged Dugun with a clipped nod. "I am glad you could make it. Please share your design ideas with us."

Dugun's face, a picture of surprise mixed with nerves, turned redder. He walked to the stage area, caught Esán's eye, and stared down at his notes.

A quick glance at the class deepened the blush. "I have always loved musicals, so I designed a light plot for act one of *West Side Story*, highlighting the Dance in the Gym and the scene on the fire escape." His description grew more animated as his nervousness abated. He finished with everyone in the theater, including the instructor, showing interested surprise. Dugun returned to his seat, looking dazed.

Mr. Shyro shuffled through his notes, jotted a few more, and faced the students. Anticipation rippled through the black box theater. "The majority of you impressed me with your presentations. Those of you who fell short of expectation will hear from me." He allowed the tension to build. "Three of you have captured my imagination. Tomorrow, we will see work by Esán Zervos, Dugun Lawson, and Summer Miles, who will meet with me now. Everyone else is excused." Mr. Shyro rose. "I'll be back in a moment." With a nod, he walked into the wings.

The room emptied. Students darted curious glances at Dugun on the way out. One whispered, "I wonder whose ideas *he* stole."

A flushed Dugun joined Esán and Summer. He gave them a defiant look. "I did my own work."

Mr. Shyro, accompanied by an energetic younger man, walked across the stage area. "It's about time you figured out you have talent, Dugun. I hope you realize you need not steal anyone else's ideas. You have brilliant ones of your own." Not giving him a chance to respond. He introduced the man with him. "This is Richard Haze. He will help with the lights for your presentations tomorrow. I'm expecting great things from you." He completed the sentence with his attention on Dugun. "Don't let me or yourself down, young man."

The trio spent the next two hours with Richard, discussing their lights for their individual designs. When they finished, the lighting tech gave them each a scheduled time to hang and focus their lights and excused himself.

Dugun prepared to leave. Summer regarded him with interest. "I liked your presentation. Want to get a bite. I'd love to hear more about it, then we can work until the lab closes." She waved at Esán as they left.

He watched them go with a smile. *I knew you had talent, Dugun.* Quiet enveloped him. He surveyed the small theater. *This is magical.* He froze. *"Beware Michael Mazer."* Rayna's message triggered a wave of foreboding.

Hurrying from the Forum, he made his way to the subway.

Torgin dropped his flute case in the instrument room and strolled from the building as Rayna and Upori, under the guise of Michael Mazer, exited through the door marked SAB. The hair on his neck spiked. His skimming gaze picked out Gar and Spyglass ambling along 65th Street in his direction.

Without a word, they trailed the pair from Columbus Circle down Seventh Avenue. Torgin followed a short distance behind them. Midway along the block between 54th and 55th streets, Upori ushered Rayna ahead of him into the Carnegie Deli. Gar glanced backward.

Torgin took the lead, ducked into a dime store, and made his way to a rack of greeting cards. He beckoned Gar closer. "We're going into the deli. If they sit at a table, we will sit at one behind Mazer's back. I'll go first. You take care of Spyglass, then come find me."

They left with Torgin leading. The terrier darted between buildings. Torgin paused just inside the deli, assailed by the delectable smells of spicy meats, aged cheese, and sourdough bread baked on site. His stomach growling, he wandered through the narrow, dimly lit space to a table in a dark corner.

Gar slipped into a chair beside him. "Sure smells yummy in here. Don't suppose we can eat somethin'?"

Torgin smiled. "Not today. I promise we'll eat here another time, though."

From behind open menus, they watched Rayna and the 'columnist' prepare to order.

A server approached the table. "Mr. Mazer?"

Upori nodded. "I'm Michael Mazer."

"You have a call, sir. The person says it's important."

A scowling Upori followed him to a wall phone, turned his back to the room, and listened. Anger bristling, he slammed the receiver in the cradle, returned to Rayna, growled something, and marched from the restaurant.

Torgin caught Rayna's eye. *"Follow him?"*

She answered with a nod. *"Take Gar. See you at the apartment."*

Gar's eyes sparkled. "We tail him, right? I'll go first." He grinned. "Don't lose me, bro." Keeping to the shadows, he sauntered into the warm glow of the day's ending.

Torgin made his way between the packed tables. Outside, sunset silhouetted the city against a canvas of deep golden orange. Up the block, Upori attempted to hail a cab. When none stopped, he continued his angry march toward 59th Street. Torgin crossed at the corner and trailed half a block behind; Gar shadowed their quarry, midway in between.

Across from Central Park, Upori turned right onto Central Park South. Gar dodged a man in a fancy suit, then fell in step behind a young woman in expensive jeans. Torgin continued to hold back. At Fifth Avenue, Upori disappeared into a fancy-looking building.

Gar waited in the shadows for Torgin to come alongside. "That's The Plaza Hotel. Spyglass and me can't go in there, Torgin."

"Stay here. If I'm not back in fifteen minutes, go to the apartment. Tell Esán and Rayna where I am."

The boy gave him a sideways look, dug in his pocket, and held up his crystal. "I'll tell Rayna. Ya better go."

In the ritziest hotel lobby he'd ever seen, Torgin stepped behind a tall, potted palm and peered between the fronds. To one side, Upori, his back rigid and fists clenched, listened to an older man whose thin-lipped mouth pressed into an angry line left no doubt as to his mood.

Upori stiffened his spine, jerked his head up, and pivoted. His steely gaze swept the reception area and stopped to scrutinize the potted palm. The green fronds quivered.

Torgin sucked in a breath. *Who are you really, Upori Athai?* A casual rotation brought him around to face the florist's reflective window. His mind blank, he observed the taller man put a hand on the shorter man's shoulder. Upori shook it off. Without a backward glance, he marched from the lobby. The tall man strode after him.

Torgin peered at their retreating backs in the florist's window until they disappeared. A walk down the hotel's shop-lined hall brought him to the Fifth Avenue entrance. Glad to escape the confines of the building, he ignored his inclination to run and stepped into the twilight and bustling traffic. Concentrated effort forced his long legs into a slow walk to the corner and an aimless stroll down Central Park South. The need to put distance between himself and the enemy jabbed like an insistent elbow in the ribs. *Don't give yourself away, Torg.* His mental admonishment kept him from teleporting post haste to the apartment. Halfway down the block, he caught sight of Gar pressed into a darkened recess with Spyglass. They followed him at a discrete distance to the corner of the Avenue of the Americas.

Torgin crossed over to the park and strolled along a shadowy path. Gar, his dark features filled with questions, jogged to his side.

Amongst several trees at a bend in the winding path, Torgin stopped. A quick survey of the area assured him they were well hidden. He bent to look Gar in the eye. "I need you to hold on to me and to Spyglass. NO noise."

Gar started to speak. Torgin put a finger to his lips. "Now."

The boy gripped Spyglass' collar, clasped Torgin's hand, and squinted up at him.

Torgin visualized their destination. The next instant, they arrived in the living room at the apartment.

Eyes rounded in astonishment, Gar jerked his hand away. "You coulda told me what would happen. You coulda…" His voice shook.

Torgin knelt. "I didn't have time, Gar. Our enemies were too close. One of them sensed me. We had to put distance between them and us." He kept his voice light, his eyes unwavering. "I realize it's a lot to take in. I promise we'll tell you everything the minute it's safe."

Gar sputtered between quivering lips. "W-w-what's it c-c-called?" He swallowed. "What we just did?"

"Teleportation." Torgin rested a hand on the small shoulder. "You know nothing about it, right?"

White teeth gleamed. "Right."

Torgin put a finger to his lips. "We got company. Can you tell me who?"

12

Rayna's heavy mood lifted at the sight of Esán entering the deli.

He pulled out a chair, looped the strap of his book bag over the back, and sat down. "Did I see Torgin leaving?"

She shared a brief update of the day's events.

A glance toward the exit furrowed his brow. "I wonder where Upori's off to in such a hurry. Guess the boys will tell us later." He opened the menu and perused the multitude of choices. "I bet Torgin and Gar will be hungry when they get home. Why don't we surprise them with a deli dinner?"

"Great idea. Gar told me Reuben sandwiches are yummy." Rayna stared at the list of unusual entrées, side dishes, and desserts. "I hope they're being careful."

A short time later, she followed Esán from the deli. Brown bags full of succulent treats didn't keep her from fretting over Torgin and Gar. The walk uptown to Columbus Circle seemed to take forever. She picked up her pace. Esán linking his arm through hers held her in check.

They had almost reached the subway when Dwight stepped from a nearby store. Recognition lit the handsome face.

Rayna groaned.

Esán glanced at her. "We'll keep it short."

Dwight hurried to intercept them. "Rayna, you left so fast today."

Esán extended a hand. "Hi, you must be Dwight. Rayna told me what a brilliant partner you are."

"She did, huh? Well, she's pretty amazing herself." He shook the offered hand. "You her boyfriend?"

"Nope, just a good friend." He held up a brown bag. "We'd love to chat, but we have to deliver this uptown to a friend's birthday bash before either of us can go home. Nice meeting you."

Frustration muted Dwight's effusive smile. "Don't want to keep you. See you tomorrow, Rayna." He let them pass. "Hey," he called, "what's your name."

Esán whispered, "Turn and wave."

Gluing on a smile, she looked over her shoulder, waved, and matched her step to his. "He's following."

"Come on." Esán led the way down the stairs into the subway. Bypassing the turnstile, he guided her to the exit steps that would take them to the opposite side of Columbus Circle. When they reached the street, he hailed a cab.

Rayna climbed in. A backward glanced caught Dwight exiting the subway and searching the crowd. The taxi eased away from the curb into traffic.

They rode to their apartment building in silence. Esán paid the driver and escorted her into the elevator. Rayna frowned. "Dwight was following us."

Esán's expression confirmed her fear. "He was following you. Now he's curious about me."

The elevator jerked to a standstill. He motioned her into the corridor. "Torgin and Gar are home. Can't wait to hear what they learned.

Gar grinned at them from the apartment entryway. "I told Torgin it was you. Come on in." He locked the door behind them. "We learned important stuff." The grin turned to a grimace. "Least Torgin did. I had ta hide."

Torgin relieved Rayna of her bag of goodies. "I'll put these in the kitchen. You look beat. What I learned isn't going anywhere, so go freshen up."

"Thanks, Torg."

She trudged to her room, dumped her stuff on the bed, and kicked off her sandals. A blister on her little toe prompted a frustrated sigh. She shifted to Brielle. "Time to shower."

A quarter of an hour later, she walked into the living room to find the boys nibbling big, juicy pickles and sipping cold, bubbly soda called root beer. Plopping down on the couch, she folded her legs under her and accepted a frosty, brown bottle from Esán. A long, delicious drink made her grin. "This is yummy." She eyed thick sandwiches stacked on a plate, a carton of potato salad, and another of coleslaw. "We all have lots to share, but I'm starving."

Her statement was met with rowdy enthusiasm. They filled their plates to overflowing with the tantalizing treats. Brie bit into a thick sandwich called a Reuben. The mix of unique flavors inspired a murmur of delight. "I love the rye bread. Corned beef is better than I expected." She swallowed another bite. "This sandwich tastes unlike anything I've ever eaten at home."

Torgin licked his lips. "Nanny used to feed me Nouri Pouches all the time. We only ate actual food on special occasions."

Gar eyed Torgin with interest, belched, and grinned. "I only got to eat this kinda food if Gin and me made a few extra bucks performin'. Even when we did, we had ta be careful 'cause we never knew what the next day would bring." He sighed. "I sure miss Gin."

Brielle washed down a bite of potato salad with root beer. "It sounds like Gin was pretty good to you."

The dark head nodded. "He used to tell me he loved me like a grandkid."

Esán cleared his throat. "I think it's time to exchange information. Tell us where Upori went, and what you learned?"

Torgin lowered his sandwich. "Sure am glad you bought a variety of Reuben sandwiches." He pulled out a dangling piece of pastrami and popped it in his mouth. "We followed Upori to The Plaza Hotel, an upscale establishment on Fifth Avenue. He met a gentleman I think might be his boss." Another bite of sandwich preceded his detailed description of the older man.

Brielle's brows arched. "Sounds a lot like Skultar Rados." She shivered. "Wonder if they're related?"

Torgin shrugged. "Who is Upori Athai? He reminds me of someone—a dangerous someone—that's why I teleported us to the apartment."

Esán's brow shot up. "You what!"

Gar wiggled. "One minute we was in the park, the next in the livin' room. Shook me up plenty." He winked. "I don't know nothin' about teleportin'."

Torgin looked from Brielle, whose gaze remained fixed on Gar, to Esán. "There were too many unknowns. I can't explain it, but I'm certain danger stalked us. Safety became my priority."

Esán nodded. "Your instincts have gotten better and better, Torg. I trust you made the right choice."

Brie licked her fingers clean and pressed a napkin to her mouth. "I think it's time for dessert." She placed large slices of New York cheesecake in front of each of her friends. "I hear this is delicious." Lifting a large bite on her fork, she smiled. "A toast." Three full forks joined hers. "To good friends and incredible food."

Murmurs of appreciation followed a chorus of "hear, hears". Gar licked an escaping morsel from the corner of his mouth. "Torgin and me wanted to try the food at the deli. Thanks!"

Brie studied the boy's happy face. "Gar, what do you remember about your life before Gin found you?"

He pursed his lips. "Not much. Sometimes I feel like parts of my mind are empty. You'd think a guy could remember even one thing between bein' born and three." He shook his head. "Can't find anythin'."

Brie fingered the Remembering Stone in its velvet pouch. "Maybe someday we can help with that." She smiled at Torgin. "Tell us what else happened today."

His expression grew distant. "What else? Oh!" He held up the note given to him earlier in the day. "I auditioned for the string quartet that's being formed to work with the SAB Demo Program. Afterward, Mrs. Sydner gave me this and told me to report here tomorrow."

Esán leaned closer. "So where's 'here'?"

Torgin's face blanked. "Don't know. I couldn't get up the nerve to read the note." He unfolded it and gasped in surprise.

Gar squirmed in his chair. "Come on, Torgin. Tell us."

"At ten o'clock tomorrow morning, *I'm* supposed to report to the conductor of the ballet orchestra."

Esán grinned. "I guess we gotta wait to find out what's up. I have a hunch it's good though."

Torgin reread the note. "Sure hope so." He stuffed it in his pocket.

Brie washed down her last bite of cheesecake with root beer. "How about you, Esán?"

Esán shared details of his day. "I have to finish my plot tonight to present in class tomorrow. Cross your fingers. With luck, Mr. Shyro will select me to work with him at the theater at Lincoln Center. Brie?"

Brie shared her news. "It seems our next adventures will be revealed tomorrow."

Torgin paced the length of the hall and back to the music room. His nerves throbbing with anticipation would not let him relax. Music would calm him. He peeked into the music room. Gar and Spyglass lay snuggled together by the Taylor Guitar.

With a sigh, he eased it shut and shuffled toward the bedroom. A soft 'psst' halted him.

"You wanna play, right?" Gar's whisper brought him about-face.

"I do, but you need to sleep." He peered at the young boy. "Tomorrow might get crazy."

Gar pulled the door wider. "Can't make myself relax. Maybe music'll help."

Torgin eased onto the piano bench. "Why can't you sleep?"

The boy sat cross-legged on the floor. "Do ya ever feel like a storm's gonna break any minute, like you're waitin' for somethin' and ya aren't sure what?"

Torgin swiveled to face the keyboard. "It's been happening to me a lot lately." He played four notes. "How did you know I couldn't sleep?"

Large, dark eyes filled with earnestness gazed up at him. "I sense ya, kinda like you're part of me somehow." He shrugged. "I felt Gin that way. I sense Rayna, too." He pursed his lips. "Not Esán. Not sure why." Scrambling to his feet, he repeated Torgin's four notes an octave higher on the piano keyboard.

Torgin played them again. Gar echoed him. Torgin played a simple melody. Gar repeated it. They went back and forth several times. Gar hit a discordant note.

"Oops, got lost." He smothered a yawn.

Torgin reminded himself they both needed to rest. He looked at the sleepy child. "I didn't realize you played the piano."

A dark finger rested on a white key. "I don't. Least not 'til I watched ya." He smothered another yawn. "Think ya can sleep now?"

"I'm certain of it. Thanks, Gar. It helped to make music."

The boy grinned. "It was fun. See ya in the morning." He sank into his blankets, curled up around Spyglass, and slept.

Torgin stood in the relative quiet of the hallway. "The better I get to know you, Gar, the more curious I become." Another yawn produced tears. "Time to sleep."

In bed, he lay reviewing the day. Heavy lids drooped. The last thing he remembered was looking at Esán fast asleep across from him. *Why can't Gar sense you?*

*   *   *

Esán had worked late in the small office off the front room. He woke up early, padded down the hall to the living room, and crossed to the window. Dawn's light softened the edges of the buildings on the street. The misty blue sky suggested a clear day in the making. In the office, he reviewed his work of the previous night. A slight tingle in his mind made him pause. The words '*Esán, Gar*' tiptoeing through his brain set him in motion.

A soft knock on the music room door brought no reply. "Gar?" He pushed it ajar. The boy's soft snores welcomed him. The innocence of a child sleeping touched him in a way that surprised him.

Dark eyes flew open. An alarmed gaze darted to Esán. Gar scrabbled to sitting, his blanket clutched under his chin. "Had a dream. You were in it." Wrinkles clouded his brow. "Why did ya..." Bewilderment left him wide-eyed.

"You called me. I came to see what you needed."

The wrinkles dug deeper. "I called *you*? But I was sleepin'."

"You put a message in my head. *You* used telepathy."

Shaky fingers pulled his crystal from under his pillow. "Musta been this." Relief lathered his tone.

Esán held out a hand. "Come on. Let's make tea. Torgin and Brielle will be up soon."

.   .   .

Breakfast, a nervous though merry meal, finished with a lingering silence that ended in a flurry of activity. Rayna and Gar, with Spyglass at their heels, scurried to the elevator. Torgin changed his clothes three times, threw Esán a desperate look, and pulled on bell-bottomed slacks with a cotton sports shirt in a deep green. He reread the note, stuffed it in his pocket, and left to walk to Lincoln Center with Cole.

Esán checked to make certain his lighting plot was in his book bag. Halfway to the elevator, he did an about face, retraced his steps, and double-checked the three locks. The ride to the first floor gave him time to catch his breath. He shook his head. *What a crazy morning.* Exiting the building, he strode along 72nd Street to the subway.

In the Forum's black box theater, he found Summer and Dugun chatting with the ease of long-time friends. He waved and headed backstage in search of Richard Haze. The experienced stagehand listened to a description of two important changes to Esán's light plot, nodded his approval, and got to work. Esán thanked him and joined his friends as lighthearted chatter announced the arrival of their fellow students.

Mr. Shyro appeared from backstage. "Good morning, class. Although you will all present your projects by week's end, today's trio is under pressure to perform at peak. I have three important positions to fill: an apprentice to work with me at New York City Ballet, a teaching assistant, and a research assistant for a special project." A quick check of his notes left him nodding. He looked up with a smile. "Summer, at the risk of sounding cliché—ladies first."

Summer, her dangly earrings swaying in time to her walk, took her place at a mic set up on one side of the stage. Clearing her throat, she adjusted her large glasses and viewed her fellow students with a tentative smile. A synopsis of her project set the mood. She signaled Richard. The lights on stage dimmed. Action by action, she described what was taking place in the scene and called the lighting cues. After answering a barrage of questions, she sank into her seat with a relieved smile.

Throughout the presentation, Mr. Shyro jotted on a notepad. His only question had little to do with her light plot. "Why *Glass Menagerie?*"

Summer's expression grew serious. "My mother died two years ago, sir. It was her favorite play."

"Thank you, Summer. Dugun, please share a 'musical' moment with us."

Dugun shuffled to the front of the room, sweat beaded on his brow. The hand holding his notes trembled. He licked his lips, squared his shoulders, and made a tentative start. The nervous tremor in his voice lessened as he became engrossed in his subject. Enthusiasm soon took the place of fear. He finished to loud applause that brought a deep red hue to his face. He mumbled his thanks and sat down.

Mr. Shyro waved Esán forward. "Last, but not least." He grinned. "Another cliché but apropos."

Esán walked to the mic. "I have set the lighting for *The Gift of Balance* to the music. As it progresses, I will give a brief description of what is occurring. The ballet opens on a blank stage. The backdrop is lit to suggest a storm on the horizon." He waved a hand. Lights came up and Henryk Gorecki's beautiful music filled the theater.

"The piece begins with a single male dancer running with total abandon from the wings upstage right into wings upstage left. He exits as a female dancer, head thrown back and arms opening wide, runs across the center and into the stage right wings. Two dancers, one male and one female, enter from opposite corners, meet at center stage, and exit together. Six dancers enter and coalesce into three couples who perform a complex *pas de trois*, emphasizing the importance of balance for the dancers and for us as human beings. The last strains of music send the dancers into a floating lift sequence that carries them to the floor in an equilateral triangle, single point to the audience. They melt into their last pose, the music softens into silence, and the lights fade to black."

In the silence following the last note, a breathless quiet exploded into applause. Esán expressed his appreciation, answered several questions, and slid into his seat.

Mr. Shyro thanked the trio, requested that they stay, selected three students to show the following day, and dismissed the class. As the room emptied, he motioned them to join him at the table. "You all surprised me. Your work changed my perception of who should do what. Summer, you will apprentice with me at New York State Theater. Dugun, I would like you to be my teaching assistant. Please plan to meet with me tomorrow to learn your duties and to discuss expectations."

Dugun blanched. "But sir, I..." He clenched shaking hands in his lap.

Mr. Shyro nodded. "It will be a challenge to teach students you have bullied. I have faith in you." He smiled. "You and Summer may go."

With a curious look in Esán's direction, they gathered their belongings and disappeared into the hall.

Mr. Shyro shuffled through his notes, placed a slip of paper on top of the pile, and regarded Esán with an understanding smile. "I know you were hoping to be my apprentice, however, I have a client who needs a research assistant. Your sensitivity to light and sound makes you the perfect fit."

Esán swallowed his disappointment. "What type of research?"

"He's interested in how light, sound, and time work together. His name is Karl Sorda. He's an out-of-towner, a bit arrogant, but lots of money, or so he would have me believe. He will pay us well. You may use your research to add depth to your thesis project." He studied his folded hands and continued. "One more thing, Esán. Mr. Sorda wants his researcher to stay with him at The Plaza Hotel. You will continue your classes at the Forum..."

The Plaza, the words ringing in Esán's head, elicited a response from the Seeds of Carsilem. He grasped the strap on his book bag, felt the smooth strength of the brown leather, let it fall back into place, and gazed at Mr. Shyro. "I assume he will want to interview me."

An apologetic smile curved the corners of Mr. Shyro's mouth. "I had thought Summer would meet his needs the best, so I arrange a meeting with him at The Plaza at one o'clock this afternoon. A simple telephone call will alert him to the change."

Esán smoothed a stray tendril of hair back from his face. "This may sound odd, but I would appreciate it if you introduce me by my birth name: Nesá Zervos."

"I am happy to oblige. At the front desk, tell them your name and that Karl Sorda is expecting you. I'll be interested to hear your impression of him." Mr. Shyro pushed back his chair, collected his papers, and, with a brisk nod, departed.

Esán glanced at the clock on the wall. *Good. I have time to grab a quick snack.* He shouldered his book bag and strode from the theater. *I wonder if I'll discover the danger Torgin sensed at The Plaza?*

13

Rayna climbed the stairs to the SAB studios. Several dancers huddled by the Casting Board, giggling and talking in excited whispers.

Kelsia ran to meet her. "Guess who's performing with the company? You and Dwight and Lois and Peter. And guess what! They've invited me to join the Demo group. I am so thrilled!"

Rayna grinned. "I hear the happiness in your voice, but aren't you disappointed about the company?"

She shuddered. "Oh, no. Performing with NYCB dancers terrifies me. The SAB Demo Program is a perfect fit." She grabbed Rayna's hand. "Come look at the casting list. Of course, no one's surprised about you and Dwight." She continued to ramble until they reached the crowd gathering to check the bulletin board.

Dwight pushed his way to her side. "Congrats, Rayna! We made it. *I* knew we would." Arrogance cooled his good looks.

Rayna studied the posted list and schedule. "We have class this morning, we meet with Cerril Thompson before lunch, and we interview with Michael Mazer this afternoon. Rehearsals begin tomorrow." She shifted her bag. "I'll meet you at Mr. Thompson's office after class." Dodging his hand, she acknowledged those who congratulated her and slipped into the changing room.

Class with Madame Dolavina gave her the opportunity to lose herself in an art form that had become her passion. Jealous looks and whispered sneers did little to diminish Rayna's enjoyment. Sweaty and happy, she left the studio to prepare for her meeting with the Ballet Master. She arrived at his office as Lois rounded the corner ahead of Dwight and Peter.

"I am so excited. Aren't you, Rayna? I mean, we get to dance with the company. That is so cool!"

Rayna met her excitement with a smile.

A middle-aged woman stepped into the corridor. "Mr. Thompson is ready for you."

They filed into a small waiting area. The Ballet Master waved them into his business office. "Please take a seat." He indicated four chairs facing his desk. After speaking to the receptionist, he collected several items from a side table and returned to his comfortable-looking leather chair.

"First, congratulations. We are looking forward to working with you." He set a pile of papers in front of each of them. "Please look through the paperwork. On top are your apprentice contracts to perform with NYCB. You will receive a stipend. If we renew your contract or we select you to dance as a full-time company member, we will pay you a salary. Questions?"

Rayna noted her fellow apprentices were as tongue tied as she was.

Mr. Thompson continued. "Good. You are all over eighteen, so you can sign your contracts with or without parental approval. Your choice. Your packet contains schedules for apprentice classes: men's, women's, and pointe classes. It also includes your rehearsal schedule. You begin with us tomorrow morning at ten o'clock. This afternoon Michael Mazer will interview you one at a time. Please meet him in the office down the hallway. Don't be late. Check the schedule by his door." He rose. "Please return your contracts by the end of the day."

Peter and Lois hurried from the office to check the schedule. Dwight looked down at Rayna. A gleam crept into blue eyes which would have seemed cold, but for the warm, gray sunburst surrounding the pupils. "We are going to *wow* them." He paused. "Hey, who was the guy with you yesterday?"

She smiled. "A friend of a friend. He's studying lighting design at the Forum."

Dwight continued to regard her. "You disappeared."

"We ended up taking a cab to our friend's place."

Lois hurried toward them. "Peter is in with Mr. Mazer. I'm next in about fifteen minutes, then you, Rayna, and then Dwight. Aren't you excited? Michael Mazer... Coooool!" She tossed her head. Black curls bounced around her face. "My friends won't believe this." Turning on her heels, she reached the office as Peter came out, his face bright red.

She disappeared inside. He walked toward them.

Rayna sensed his distaste before he spoke. "Weird guy. Don't think he liked me much. Oh well. Hey, tell Lois I had to go. See you tomorrow." He dodged into the men's locker room.

Dwight raised a brow. "Peter's a pretty likable guy. This should be interesting. Weren't you supposed to interview with Mazer yesterday?"

"He received a phone call and had to leave before we got started." She leaned against the wall, her mind blank, her focus on the floor. Something about Dwight bothered her. From beneath her lashes, she caught him watching her with a strange, searching expression.

Lois exited the office, a smug smile on her face. "He said to send you both in. He's great. You're going to have fun."

Dwight grinned. "It's time to impress the master of dance history."

Rayna walked beside him, ignoring her misgivings about both men.

Torgin, flute case in hand, arrived at the ballet orchestra's rehearsal studio and knocked on the door marked *Conductor.*

"Come in."

He entered an office that seemed small for the imposing man behind the desk. "Good morning, sir. I'm Torgin Whälen."

Matt Harwood glanced up from an open file. A brow arched. "No one mentioned you're biracial."

Torgin remained silent.

Long fingers drummed the desktop. "Never mind. I've heard great things about you. Ah good, you brought your flute. Please sit. I'll explain our situation."

Torgin perched on the edge of a chair with the leather case resting on his knees. Mr. Harwood tapped the file. "This says you have been playing the flute since you were quite young. You're also a gifted pianist. Correct?"

Torgin gripped the case tighter. "I play both, sir."

Closing the file with a finality that made Torgin wonder if the meeting was over, the conductor folded his hands on top of it. "One of our flutists met with an accident and cannot play for some time. I need a replacement, someone who can start today. From your records, I gather you have played in an orchestra, correct?"

"Yes, sir, a small one in my hometown."

"You sight read?"

"Yes, sir."

"Good. There's sheet music on the stand over there. Please play for me."

Torgin removed the silver flute from the case. After arranging four pages of music for easy reading, he studied them, tried the fingering in a couple of difficult sections, and looked up. "I'm ready, sir."

Mr. Harwood nodded. "Please, begin."

The piece required nimble fingers and an expert's knowledge of the flute. Torgin immersed himself, allowing the music to inspire him. He played intricate passages with flawless precision. His musical sense brought a delighted glint to the conductor's eye. When he lowered his instrument, Mr. Harwood sat back and smiled, the first genuine smile Torgin had seen during the interview.

"I understand why Mrs. Snyder urged me to see you. How would you like to play with the ballet orchestra? Rehearsals are in the late afternoon; performances in the evenings with some matinees. If you're interested, I'll have my secretary draw up your contract."

His thoughts racing, Torgin returned to his seat. "It would be my honor to join the orchestra." He replaced the instrument in the flute case. "May I ask a question, sir?"

"You may."

"Did you write the composition I just played?"

Surprise flickered. "How did you guess?"

Torgin smiled. "I compose, too. Nothing as good as your piece, but I know the look when someone plays my work well."

"I'd enjoy seeing some of your work. Let's get you settled first, though. You should be able to maintain your schedule at Juilliard, except on matinee days. Stop by later to sign your contract. And lose the afro, Torgin. Let's not call attention to your youth and race. I have an orchestra member or two who are a bit immature."

Torgin left the office, his mind in a whirl. His mixed heritage had never been a problem in Idronatti. *What a strange time.* He shrugged, a grin spreading from ear to ear. *I'm playing in an orchestra in the year 1969. Cool!* He hustled to his first composition class.

R ayna and Dwight sat opposite Michael Mazer. His pudgy fingers fiddled with a pencil, picked up a piece of paper, and put it down. He scratched his unshaven chin and muttered under his breath.

Dwight's brows arched. "You okay, Mr. Mazer."

The man glanced up. His tongue flicked out. "Oh... Sorry. Got distracted." He flipped through the pages in his notebook. Pencil in hand, he raised bloodshot eyes. "Please describe how it feels to be selected as an apprentice with one of the best ballet companies in the world?"

Dwight jumped right in. "I felt certain we were a shoo-in. Rayna is a beautiful dancer. I'm a great... Are your sure you're alright?"

Michael Mazer bounced to his feet, sniffing the air like a bloodhound that's caught a tantalizing scent.

Rayna eased her chair back.

A soft growling sound brought her to her feet.

Dwight eased to standing. "Go, Rayna, I'll distract him. I've heard he has fits sometimes."

"You mean like epilepsy?"

He stepped around her. "Something like that. Go!"

She moved closer to the door. "I'll get help."

Dwight shook his head. "If I need assistance, I'll shout; otherwise, leave us alone."

A snarl whispered from Mazer's throat. Saliva dripped from his mouth.

He pressed his hands against the desk, hunched his shoulders, and sucked in air between bared teeth. A toss of his head ended in a full-bodied shudder. He dropped into his chair, motionless but for heavy breathing.

Rayna observed the behavior from a distance, a twinge of memory nagging. Intangible and fast fading, it left her searching for its trigger in the man behind the desk.

Eyelids fluttered. His dazed gaze wandered the room. An awkward swipe at his chin flicked the drool away. "Sorry you had to witness that." He stuffed his notes in a leather briefcase. "We need to postpone our interview." Heaving himself to his feet, he staggered from behind the desk. "I require a taxi."

Dwight caught his arm. "Go, Rayna. I'll help him hail a cab. See you tomorrow."

Rayna slipped from the office into the empty changing room. Grateful that classes were in session, she sank onto a bench to consider Mazer's behavior. *What is it about you that sparks memories?* She glanced at the clock. Gar and Spyglass waited for her by the fountain.

Shouldering her dance bag, she hurried down the hall to the stairs. As she stepped into the late afternoon brightness, Dwight assisted the ailing journalist into a cab and climbed in after him. *Are you two acquainted, or are you just being a good guy, Dwight Anders?*

14

Esán reached The Plaza Hotel ten minutes early. He found a quiet spot behind a potted palm, sank into a brocade armchair, and cleared his head of debris from the morning. Luxury surrounded him. Furnishings, plush carpets, and opulent decor were unlike anything he had experienced. People strolling by in expensive, stylish attire made him keenly aware of his bell-bottoms, leather vest, and t-shirt.

An angry voice cut through the foyer. "Let me go."

"Everything will be okay, Michael. We just need to get you upstairs.

The ensuing struggle drew everyone's attention to the Central Park South entrance of the hotel. Back rigid with strain, a young man attempted to assist an older gentleman, who yanked free, staggered, and collapsed. The concierge summoned two porters to help him into an elevator.

The hairs on the back of Esán's neck stood at attention. His gaze remained riveted on the retreating figures. *Dwight Anders, what are you doing at The Plaza Hotel with Michael Mazer?*

When the lobby had returned to normal, Esán approached the front desk, his mind working overtime. A man in a smart uniform cast a condescending look in his direction, finished sifting through a pile of envelopes, and cleared his throat. "May I help you?"

Esán smiled. "Mr. Karl Sorda is expecting me."

The man's superior sneer changed to a gracious smile. "You must be Mr. Zervos. One moment, please." He retreated to an inner office and re-emerged, a placating expression on his face. "Mr. Sorda is running late. He requests that you take a seat. He'll let me know when to send you up."

Speculation raced. *What if Dwight, Sorda, and Upori Athai are working together?* Esán returned to his brocade chair, cautioning himself not to get trapped in muddled 'what ifs'.

A porter peered down at him. "Mr. Sorda is ready. Take the elevator to the eighteenth floor and turn right. He is in The Penthouse Suite."

E sán exited the elevator and walked down the posh corridor to the elegant entrance of Karl Sorda's suite. A uniformed servant ushered him into a luxurious sitting room. Crimson curtains opened partway emphasized dust particles dancing like a sparkling *corps de ballet* in the bright rays shaped by the sunlight's attempts to enter.

A tall, angular gentleman walked through the glowing shafts, his saturnine features hidden or intensified by light and shadow. An effect, Esán noted, that would be dynamic in a theater setting. The imposing figure stopped with sunlight highlighting the elongated planes of his face. Strands of silver shimmered in his dark hair, mustache, and goatee.

A subtle signal bought a servant from the shadows. One window at a time, the crimson curtains swished open, flooding the room with brightness. The servant slipped away.

The man extended his hand. "Karl Sorda." His courteous smile combined with the warm light erased the harshness from his face. "I noticed you enjoyed my light show."

Esán clasped the hand. Power, strength, and something difficult to define pulsed through it. He summoned a smile. "I'm Nesá Zervos. I appreciated your dramatic lighting and your entrance."

The man gripped his hand a second longer, released it, and led the way to a sitting area. "Please, let us get acquainted." He waited for him to sit, then settled in a wingback chair opposite. "Mr. Shyro tells me you are a talented lighting designer with a unique understanding of how light enhances the subtleties of sound. Have you ever wondered how light and sound influence time?"

Esán thought back to Relevart's lessons. "I realize that light and sound travel through time at different rates." He focused on the man opposite. "The idea of researching how these three aspects impact one another is intriguing."

They continued their discussion, batting ideas back and forth and comparing thoughts until Mr. Sorda regarded him with a half-smile. "How would you feel about doing some research on the subject? I will specify certain things of particular significance to me. Mr. Shyro mentioned you are a senior. Anything you discover of interest may be used for your thesis. I'll pay you one thousand dollars up front. If you discover useful information, you will receive another twenty-five hundred when you complete the project." He pursed his lips. "There is one stipulation. You must stay at The Plaza Hotel."

Esán ordered his thoughts. "I am registered at the Forum. Can I continue to take classes there?"

"Mr. Shyro will meet with you here once a week. He will credit you for the courses you are registered in. I contributed to the science department at Fordham University. In exchange, they scheduled a lab for your use, along with access to their research library." He steepled his long fingers, pressed his thumbs to his chin, and waited.

"If I accept, will I have my own room?"

Mr. Sorda lowered his hands. "You will share a two-bedroom suite with my nephew, Dwight."

"Dwight Anders?" Premonition trembled through him.

Mr. Sorda squinted down his long nose. Suspicion bristled. "You know my nephew?"

"Only in passing, sir. He and a friend of a friend are partners at SAB."

Sorda's wary expression relaxed into a bemused smile. "Ah yes, Rayna. I have heard of nothing but Rayna since Dwight met her. So, Nesá, do we have a deal?"

"May I have tonight to think about it, sir? I'd be giving up a lot, but gaining a lot. I'd appreciate time to weigh my options so I can decide what is best for both of us."

A fleeting glimmer of frustration hardened the narrow features. A tolerant smile trumped it. Sorda glanced at his watch. "It is three o'clock. Leave me a message at the front desk by ten o'clock this evening. If you elect to join my team, I expect to see you, suitcase in hand, at nine o'clock tomorrow morning." He rose. "Jonas will show you out." He strode from the room.

Esán picked up his book bag. The young servant ushered him into the corridor and withdrew.

Instinct held Esán quiet. A search of his bag provided a reason for standing in the hall. He pitched his senses to pick up activity in The Penthouse Suite.

"You offered him too much, Karlsut." Anger soaked Dwight's accusation.

"I offered what it is worth to me."

"*She* won't like it. You are, after all, spending *her* money."

"Calm down, Dwight." Sorda's placating tone changed to a sneer. "He will never see the money."

R ayna merged into the crowd, her mind filled with plausible scenarios for Upori and Dwight as she searched for Gar. She almost smiled when he came bounding up to her.

"There's somethin' real strange about that Upori guy. Remember, I told ya he felt like trouble? He just walked by me." Gar wrinkled his nose. "He smells awful. Kinda rotten."

Rayna froze. Memories exploded: DerTah, Fera Finnero, the Tinga Forest in Trinuge. "We have to find Torgin. Fast! I know you sense his presence. You check the theater side of the plaza; I'll search the Juilliard side. If you locate him, tell him to meet us near the fountain."

Determination made him seem taller. He slipped a hand in his pocket, his attention focused on the theater.

Rayna's mental probe turned up nothing. Worry increased. She scanned the plaza. Gar had disappeared.

"Got him."

A sigh of relief dispersed her moment of disquiet. Gar and Torgin sauntered in her direction. Containing her desire to run to them, she waved.

When they reached her, she linked arms with Torgin and ambled after Gar to a quiet corner.

Torgin's impatience came to a head. He rounded on her. "You look ghost pale. Gar told me something he said scared you. Care to share?"

"We need to go to the apartment. I hope Esán's home. You're going to think I'm crazy."

"Take a breath, Rayna. Tell me what's upsetting you."

She shook her head. "Let's get the subway at 66th Street. As soon as we're safe, I promise I'll explain."

Esán slung the strap of his bag over his shoulder and walked toward the elevator. On the opposite side of the hall, a door opened. A wild-eyed Upori Athai darted forward. Strong fingers gripped Esán's upper arm and pulled him into the room. A well-aimed kick slammed the door shut. Upori leaned against it, panting. Distress, physical and mental, enshrouded him.

Esán, subtle shields surrounding him, maintained a safe distance.

The Pheet Adolan Klutarse shuddered. Beady eyes darted back and forth as he staggered toward the sitting area. "Please come away from the door. I won't harm you."

Esán let him pass, observed the tremors quaking through his body, and followed.

With a grimace of pain, the distraught man dropped onto a sofa. "I can help you locate the—" He groaned. Upori Athai blurred into an indistinct shape, one that vanished in the blink of an eye.

Memories swam into to focus. Realization dawned. *It can't be.* Esán scrutinized the trembling man. "Tell me what's hurting you?"

Another pain-filled spasm ended in a howl. Spittle drooled down Upori's chin. He growled through clenched teeth. "Hide. They're coming."

Esán, his book bag clutched to his chest, escaped into the bedroom as Karlsut Sorda and Dwight strode into the room. From behind the door, he peered at them through the narrow crack between the jamb and the frame.

Upori's befuddled gaze hurtled from Dwight, who placed cool palms on either side of his head, to the hypodermic in Sorda's hand. The shaking slowed. Confusion fled, leaving him expressionless.

Sorda approached. Upori whimpered. The medication administered with the precision of a professional produced immediate results. Full body tremors ceased. Upori's eyelids battled to stay open.

Dwight helped him to his feet. "I'll get him to bed, Uncle Karl. I know you have things to do."

"Don't take too long. We have plans to make." Sorda hurried from the suite.

Esán crept into the furthest corner of the bedroom closet and masked his presence by merging into the walls and clothing.

The sounds of stumbling, a moan, sheets rustling, and the sigh of the mattress implied Dwight had leveraged Upori onto the bed.

Esán held his breath.

The closet door jerked open. Dwight moved the clothes aside and scowled. Building tension held him quiet. The door closed. Silence settled over the suite.

The pad of heavy feet on carpet in the sitting area announced a visitor. "Excuse me, Mr. Anders, Mr. Sorda would like you to come *now*."

"Thank you, Jonas. Tell him I'll be right there."

Footsteps retreated.

Dwight peered into the closet, frowned, and moved to the center of the bedroom. "Whoever you are, you're good. I will find you, just not today."

Esán remained motionless until the Seeds signaled safety. He emerged to the sound of Upori's soft snores. Tiptoeing to the bed, he peered down at the slack features, glanced at the alarm clock next to the bed, and shouldered his book bag. *Five o'clock. I have to get to the apartment.* Soundless and alert, he moved to the exit. *I know this suite is being watched. A stroll to the elevator is a bad idea.* "Dwight or Sorda might feel me teleport, so the best thing I can do is *not leave a trail.*"

Protective wards scintillated into place. A subtle mental scan showed an empty elevator two floors down. The walls enclosed him. At the ninth floor, he exited the car into an empty hallway, took the stairs to the to the fourth floor, and teleported to the basement. *That should obscure my energy trail.*

In the alley, a large truck parked at the delivery ramp, with its loading doors agape, offered a means of escape. Unfamiliar voices approaching sent Esán scrabbling aboard. Ducking behind stacks of boxes, he squatted low. The loading doors slammed shut. The engine revved. Gears shifting rattled. Esán clung to a metal support as the truck pulled away from the ramp, rumbled from the underground garage, and turned onto the street.

One stop light... He held his breath. The truck eased to a stop. *Two stop lights...* Tension began to dissipate. *Three...* He pictured a dark, isolated corner in the subway hub at 72nd Street. A fake wall on the main floor provided the perfect cover. He materialized and merged into the crowd.

Midway to the apartment building, a raven swooped past him into a lightless pass-through between buildings. Esán dodged after it.

A hand gripped his shoulder. "Take us to the apartment." The soft whisper sent a chill up his neck.

15

Asurprised yelp rang through the apartment. Torgin hurried from the music room to find Gar staring from Esán to Corvus Castylim.

Brie hurried from her room. "Corvus?" She frowned. "Something's happened?"

"We need to talk. First, Torgin, please introduce your young friend."

"I can introduce myself." Dark brown eyes studied Corvus for a long, intense moment. "I'm Gar." He cocked his head. "Are ya messin' in my head?"

Corvus almost smiled. "I was. It's good to meet you, Gar."

"Hmmmm." He cocked his head. "You remind me of these guys."

Torgin squeezed his shoulder. "He's cool, Gar."

Brie slipped a hand into Esán's. "We can talk in the living room."

Corvus, seriousness cloaking him like a Mocendi's cape, waited for them to settle. His penetrating gaze fastened on Gar where he sat on the floor at Torgin's feet. "Since I know my friends trust you, I am going to share some things that are confidential. Anything we discuss stays in this room, understood?"

Gar pulled Spyglass closer. "Mum's the word. Promise."

Corvus dipped his chin. "You're a good lad." He returned his attention to the group. "Let me give you a synopsis of my time in New York City, 1969. Like you, the Galactic Guardians' governing body sent me to discover what I could about Upori Athai and the Corps Stones. Consider me the advance man. Almiralyn is working in the theater costume shop in the guise of Mira Weston. We're convinced the Stones are in the city. We feel certain they're in the vicinity of Lincoln Center. You have all positioned yourselves to help with the search." He grew more intense. "Karlsut Sorda has offered Esán a position which is important and more dangerous than we expected. Please, Brie and Esán, share what you discovered today."

Brie squeezed Esán's hand. "You go first. Your story is much more compelling."

Esán described his interview and the conversation he overheard from the hall. He glanced from Corvus to Gar.

Corvus fastened a steady gaze on the boy's face. Gar did not flinch, nor did he look away. "Good. Go ahead, Esán."

"You know what I'm about to tell you. Shall I continue?"

"Please. I am hoping you will confirm what I *think* we've discovered. Go on."

"I believe Upori Athai is possessed by a Mindeco. In fact, I am almost certain it's Rikell, the one who took over Desirol, the one Relevart sent back to the Trutore Mountains on RewFaar."

Brie interjected. "Dwight and I were with Upori when he experienced a convulsion. Dwight didn't seem surprised by it. He helped Upori get into a cab and left with him."

Gar wrinkled his nose. "They walked past me. The Upori guy stunk pretty bad."

Corvus studied him. "You have a good sense of smell?"

The boy grimaced. "Sometimes, too good."

Brie snuggled in the crook of Esán's arm. "I'm positive Dwight isn't Karlsut Sorda's nephew, so who is he?"

Corvus gripped his knees. "Mira and I believe he's the thief who stole the Stones. But we have no proof." He turned to Esán. "This is where you come in. We need you to accept the research position with Karlsut Sorda. However, Esán, it's your life that will be at risk—"

Torgin felt a surge of foreboding so strong it almost choked him. "Wait. They plan to kill him. How do we protect him?"

"He'll have a raven near at hand, the Seeds of Carsilem to warn him of danger, and the three of you close by." His inclusive gaze moved from Gar to Torgin to Brie and fastened on Esán. "Tell us your decision."

"I decided to take the position when I realized Upori, Sorda, and Dwight were a team."

Corvus leaned forward. "You understand that using your mystical talents could get you killed?"

"I realize that Dwight Anders is not what—who—he seems to be. His energy buzzes with a DiMensioner's potential. I promise to embrace my role as a scholar with every ounce of diligence I can muster." He picked at a lint puff on his pants and looked up.

All eyes were on him.

Corvus sat back. "You have another concern?"

"I do." Esán rolled the lint between his finger and thumb. "If I am a target, then Mr. Shyro is, too. How do we protect him?"

The dimple in Corvus' cheek deepened. "His wife just won a trip to Bermuda. They leave in two days. The head of the island's summer arts programs contacted Joe and asked him to design the lighting for the Shakespearean festival and the Civic Ballet performance during their stay. That should keep him occupied long enough for us to complete our business with Sorda and gang."

Gar squirmed. "What's Bermuda?"

Corvus smiled. "It's a beautiful island about seven hundred miles from New York." His dimple softened. "You have something to share, Gar?"

"I do, Mr. Corvus. When I was huntin' for Torgin earlier, two ladies in the costume shop were grumblin'. Seems the costume designer changed the design for the new ballet. One woman said somethin' about new glitz arriving soon. Not sure if it is important, but thought I should tell ya."

"Great work, Gar. Please call me Corvus, and like your friends, you don't know me, right?"

Gar's gaze darted to Torgin. "Torgin'll tell ya I'm good at secrets." He scrubbed fingers through his afro. "But I wish—"

Torgin shook his head. Gar pressed his lips into a petulant line and folded his arms across his chest.

Esán chuckled. "Kinda reminds me of a young Ari."

Gar glared. "Who's Ari?"

Brie laughed. "My twin sister. Wish she were here. Hey, Torgin, don't you have news to share?"

He grinned. "As do you, so please go first."

Brie sat up straighter. "The panel selected Dwight and me to dance in the new ballet being choreographed by the company's Artistic Director. We'll take apprentice classes and rehearse with NYCB."

Corvus dimpled. "Rayna is one beautiful dancer. I gather Dwight is an excellent partner. Sounds like you will be busy enough to distract him from watching Esán. Torgin, tell us your news."

Torgin described his audition and his subsequent invitation to perform with the ballet orchestra. He grinned. "I'm flattered, excited, and nervous."

"So, you will be at the theater. Excellent. Keep your ears open. Gossip can provide relevant information. Mira will be your contact there. Mr. Thompson invited me to play for company class. It's important that I'm not connected to any of you. Unless there's anything else, I believe we're done."

Gar scrambled onto his knees. "What about me, Corvus? Don't I get a job?"

"You have a very important job as Rayna's bodyguard. Keep her safe and don't attract Dwight's attention." He leaned down to look him straight in the eyes. "Do not second guess Dwight. He's a danger to all of us, but especially to you. Understood?"

Gar blinked. "Yes, sir. I promise to take care of Rayna and stay out of Dwight's way."

"Good." Corvus straightened. "I have to go. Get some sleep. I'll be in touch. If you need me, picture a raven. You, too, Gar." He flashed from sight.

Gar ran to the window. Torgin followed. A raven swooped from the roof of the building across the street, shot past their window, and soared upward. "Was that Corvus?"

Torgin squeezed the boy's shoulders. "You've learned a lot for one day. Remember, everything we shared tonight is between us."

Gar looked up at him, crossed his heart, and looked back at the street.

Torgin's throat constricted with worry. *Why are you a threat to Dwight?*

I n the aftermath of Corvus' visit, Esán slipped away to call The Plaza Hotel. He left a message for Karl Sorda, packed a suitcase, and returned to the living room. Brie stood alone by the window, listening to the soft melody floating from the music room.

She faced him, concern evident in her tentative expression. "What if Dwight realizes you're looking for the Corps Stones?"

He gazed down at the street. "He won't. You will be busy at the ballet. Besides, your crush on him will keep him focused your direction—"

"My *what*?" She glared up at him. "I don't have a crush on that arrogant—"

"Handsome, charming, talented man..." Esán grinned. "Kinda reminds you of me, right?"

She flounced away from the window, plopped down on the couch, and stuck out her bottom lip. A sheepish smile flashed. "That was a definite Ari moment." She sighed. "I miss her." She ran a hand over the nubby fabric. "If you promise I'll see you once a day, I can pretend Dwight is a... What's the word I'm after?"

"I think you want 'hunk'. That's me for sure."

Her brows raised.

He sobered. "I swear I'll be careful and contact you once a day." Pulling her to her feet, he kissed her. "I have to get some sleep; so do you. If I don't see you in the morning, enjoy your first day with the company."

He walked her down the hall. At her door, he cocked his head to listen. "No music. Guess our boys are in bed."

"Smart boys." She stood on tiptoe to kiss his cheek. "Sleep well."

The strong desire to hold her all night ushered him to the room he shared with Torgin. As silent as a mouse, he prepared for bed. Cool cotton sheets helped him release the day's tension, but not his yearning to be with Brie. He glanced at his roommate. *You'd better take good care of her.*

"I promise, Esán. Get some sleep."

Torgin's telepathic message made Esán smile. He checked the alarm, rolled onto his side, and let sleep cradle him.

. . .

ain's repetitive patter woke him just before the alarm buzzed. A quick shower later, he dressed, set his suitcase by the door, and went in search of breakfast.

In the kitchen Brie, Torgin, and Gar greeted him with smiles. Plates piled high with eggs, bacon, and toast made his stomach rumble.

He slid onto a chair. "Wow! Who cooked?"

Torgin grinned. "I did. Never expected to enjoy cooking, but I love it." He poured orange juice into tall glasses and took his seat. "Wish I could recall how Sibine gave thanks the time we stayed in her TreeOm."

Brie lifted her glass. "I remember. Let's have a toast."

Esán raised his glass. Torgin lifted his. Gar, his desire to question held in check, followed their example.

Brie took a silent breath and spoke in a soft voice:

"To the plants, to the Tree, to the Flowers and Vine,
For the food on our table, these presents divine,
We thank all who've given of body and soul
To keep our lives healthy, abundant, and whole."

After clinking glasses and enjoying a drink, Brie winked at Gar. "Sibine is a Wood Tiff, a guardian of forest trees. We'll tell you more about her someday." She set her glass down. "Eat up, one and all. We have a busy day ahead of us."

Esán sighed. *I wonder when I'll be with you again?*

16

Unwilling to battle the rain and the rush-hour subway ride, Esán, suitcase in hand, climbed into a Checkered Cab. A glance over his shoulder made his heart sing. Rayna blew him a kiss from the walkway of the apartment building.

He arrived at The Plaza as Dwight strode from the elevator. "Uncle Karl sent me to show you up. I understand we are to be roommates. Your name's Nésa, right?"

Esán smiled. "It is. I'm excited to work with your uncle."

They chatted on the way to the eighteenth floor. Dwight showed him their suite—a luxurious sitting room and two large bedrooms with private baths—handed him a key, and grabbed his dance gear. "Uncle Karl is waiting in The Penthouse. Just ring the bell. See you tonight."

Esán surveyed his room. He put his suitcase on the twin bed by the window, prepared himself for what was to come, and crossed the hall to The Penthouse.

Jonas escorted him to the sitting room. "Mr. Sorda will be with you shortly. Please have a seat."

Too nervous to sit, Esán peered out a window. The park's lush landscape, framed on all sides by tall buildings, reminded him of Idronatti's City Center People's Common, which he learned was a purposeful imitation of the Olmsted Brothers' design for New York's Central Park.

Footsteps softened by the plush carpet warned him he had company. He performed a casual about face. Karl Sorda stood to one side, observing him with a mix of interest and speculation.

"I chose this suite for its spectacular view." Karl Sorda didn't move. "Your application to The Forum, which Mr. Shyro shared, says you grew up on the West Coast. What brought you to New York?"

"My father was in the movie business. He wanted me to go to the University of California to study lighting. I did the research. The Forum has the best lighting design program in the country."

"Your father died?" Sorda studied him.

"He was a chain smoker." Esán let pain fill his expression.

Sorda moved to the sitting area. "Is the rest of your family out west?"

Esán waited for his host to sit before taking a seat. "My mother and younger sister have returned to Greece. I don't believe Mother was ever comfortable in the States. Dad was a second-generation Greek American, so this was his country. He met Mother in Greece during the war, married her, and brought her to California."

Sorda stretched his arm along the back of the sofa. "Any other family?"

"No, sir. I'm pretty much on my own."

Satisfaction settled over his host. "Not any longer." Sorda beamed a fatherly smile in his direction. "First, welcome to the team. You and Dwight have met. Michael Mazer, a British writer, whom I am sure Rayna has told you about, is a satellite member of our little enterprise. He's in New York to pursue his own goals, but has contributed a generous amount to our research fund. As I noted at our first meeting, a generous grant to Fordham University has secured us a lab and the privilege of using their science library resources." He placed a folder on the coffee table between them. "This contains your contacts and a list of topics to research."

Esán thumbed through the file. "May I ask a question, sir?"

Maintaining a patient, open expression, Sorda sat back. "Ask away."

"Well, sir, I want to plot my course of study in accordance with your needs. What are your goals?"

Shrewd eyes held his gaze. "Tell me how you met Rayna."

Esán didn't hesitate. "I met her through a good friend at San Francisco Ballet. Rayna was taking a summer workshop; I was working with Damian Clifford, a lighting designer freelancing with the company. Rayna's teacher in Kansas wanted her to study at SAB. Rayna wasn't sure. When she discovered I was coming to the city, I think it helped her decide. She's staying at her aunt's apartment. I'm rooming with a casual friend."

Sorda's narrow, hawkish face became more cunning. "You realize I have checked every detail of your application?"

"I wouldn't expect anything less, sir." He raised his brows. "Did I pass?"

Sorda laughed. "You have an appointment at Fordham this afternoon. I'd say that's a positive." He glanced at his watch. "I have things to do. Please settle into your room. You may take a cab to and from the University. Keep the receipts. I will reimburse you for all expenses." He rose and extended a hand. "Again, welcome. Jonas will show you out."

❦ ❦

Rayna shoved the last hair pin in her bun and walked down the hall to the apprentices' studio. The spacious room, lit by a bank of windows overlooking high-rise buildings and blue skies, felt welcoming. Female dancers sat in small groups, chatting and putting on pointe shoes. Others warmed up at the barre. Peter stood with a group of men gathered to one side.

Rayna steeled herself for the walk into the room. Glances, some curious, some hostile, flew in her direction. Ignoring them all, she made her way to the barre.

Next to her, a petite blonde smiled. "Hi. I'm Sherrie. Welcome to the apprentice class." She scanned the studio. "Don't let them bother you. Jealousy is just a show of insecurity. They'll get over it." She shrugged. "Or they won't."

Rayna draped her hand towel over the metal brace securing the barre to the wall. "I'm Rayna. Thanks. I needed the pep talk. You have a lovely accent."

Sherrie smiled. "I grew up in Paris. Yours is different, too."

Rayna returned the smile. "My mother's parents were missionaries in India. Mother was born there. How long have you been an apprentice?"

She performed a series of basic exercises. "Not long. Mr. Thompson is teaching today. Better warm up."

One exercise at a time, Rayna primed her body and mind for immersion into the art she loved. A commotion at the door interrupted her concentration. Lois marched into the studio with Dwight at her heels. She came to an abrupt halt. Dwight glared down at her. An argument ensued. Lois glanced her direction, stuck her nose in the air, and strutted across the studio. Much to Rayna's relief, she found a place at the barre several girls away.

Mr. Thompson's entrance ended the chatter. The pianist, a woman Rayna did not know, arranged her music and prepared to play for class.

The ballet master surveyed the room. "We have four new members joining us today. Please make Rayna, Lois, Dwight, and Peter welcome." He gestured to each of them. After a brief conversation with the accompanist, he set the first combination.

Class ended two hours later with *reverence*. Mr. Thompson escorted the pianist into the hall. As they exited, Dwight strode to her side. "How about lunch?"

Rayna pressed her towel against her throbbing neck. "I need to change. Where do you want to meet?"

"By the fountain?"

"Sounds good." She flipped the towel over her shoulder and left in search of a safe place to shift to her natural form.

The changing room, alive with women's chatter, drove her back into the hall. A door marked Costume Shop provided an escape route. She descended steep steps to a room filled with racks of costumes shimmering in the overhead lighting. Three long tables littered with scraps, glitter, scissors, and pins provided work areas. Sewing machines lined an adjacent wall. One seamstress sorted through a box containing various types of trim.

"Hello, Rayna." Mira spoke over her shoulder. "Your costume is hanging in the changing cubicle to your right."

Relief lightened Rayna's steps. Inside the cubicle, Brielle materialized. When the Star of Truth's tingling grew quiet, she shifted back to Rayna, slipped on a white tutu, and walked into the costume shop.

Mira's sapphire eyes telegraphed a brief warning. "Let's see what alterations I need to make." A tug, a fold, a pin here, one there left her nodding. She stepped backward to survey her work. "Have a look in the mirror."

Rayna regarded her reflection with a smile. "It's lovely."

Mira unhooked the bodice. "Please change."

In the cubicle, Rayna pulled on her leotard, draped her towel around her neck, and carried the tutu to Mira. "Do you need anything else?"

"Not today. Stop by tomorrow between class and rehearsal, and we'll do a final fitting. Nice to meet you, Rayna." She returned to sorting trim.

Dwight appeared at the top of the stairs. "Thought we were going to lunch."

"We are. I remembered I needed to see Miss Weston." The Star pinched. She rubbed her neck, moved past him toward the dressing room, and paused. "How did you know I was in the Costume Shop?"

"Lois told me."

Rayna covered her disbelief with a nod and hurried to change. *I will keep you focused on me, Dwight Anders. That's a promise.*

• •

Torgin's rehearsal with the orchestra left him grinning from ear to ear. Musicians who had looked at him with skepticism when he walked in showed definite signs of admiration at the end of the practice session. Mr. Harwood kept him afterwards to compliment him on both his playing and, in an off-handed way, his new hairstyle. He remembered to think it shorter before bed.

He glanced at his watch. "I've got time to find the costume shop before my conducting class." Lengthening his stride, he rounded the corner into the main hallway. Lois and Dwight huddled by a window overlooking Revson Fountain. Keeping his face averted, he ambled past, slipped into the studio across the hall. Concentration fixed on the pair opposite, he listened.

Dwight's irritated tone dripped with frustration. "I need you to be her friend, not her enemy, Lois. Find out her address and who she lives with, and I promise you a fantastic time."

"You're attracted to her." Jealousy drenched her low-pitched response.

"Why should I trust you'll keep your word?" She glared at him. "Why can't you get the information yourself? All you have to do is ask."

They moved down the hall, continuing to argue. Torgin heard Rayna's name mentioned several times.

Esán spread out the paperwork Sorda had given him on the dining table in his shared suite. Under the pretense of reading, he made a careful mental search, noted tiny video cams tucked in two places in the sitting room and another one in his bedroom. Satisfied he'd covered his bases, he prepared to depart for the University.

The rattle of someone trying to enter the suite brought him to his feet. He peered through the peephole, made sure his key was in his pocket, and opened the door. "May I help you?"

Upori Athai, dressed for his day as Michael Mazer, met his gaze with a tight smile. "May I come—

Esán pointed at Upori's door. When they were inside, he did a quick mental scan of the small suite.

Upori watched him with growing curiosity. "No recording devices. They put them in; I flush them down the toilet." He sat on one end of the couch. "They quit trying. You know who I am?"

Esán took a seat at the opposite end. "You are a Pheet Adolan Klutarse named Upori Athai in the guise of Michael Mazer." He analyzed the man's emotionless expression. "Rikell, the Mindeco, controls you."

Steely dark eyes blinked several times. The cruel mouth worked, baring his teeth. A shudder quaked through him. "What gave me away?"

Esán folded his arms. "You wished to share something?"

Upori clutched a throw pillow. "Yesterday, I could have taken you to the Corps Stones." An embittered scowl deepened the wrinkles in his square-jawed face. "This morning, they weren't in their hiding place."

"What do you want from me, Rikell?"

"Freedom. I wish to return to my own time and my home in the Trutore Mountains. You and your friends are the only ones who can help me." He put the pillow down. A shaking hand smoothed his shaggy hair.

Esán studied him. "Friends?"

A grimaced smile accompanied Upori's menacing change in posture. "You help me, or I'll tell Sorda everything, who you are, where you're from—" He groaned.

"Why threaten me?" Esán regarded him with interest. "You have access to a time machine. Steal it and go home."

The Mindeco's features made a fleeting appearance. Upori gripped his knees and panted. "You and I both know it doesn't work. Why else would Sorda have you researching time, sound, and light?"

Esán didn't answer. "Who's running this operation? Karl Sorda?"

Upori hugged himself and spoke through chattering teeth. "Don't know."

"When's your next shot?"

Rikell retreated. "Any time. Once they give it to me, I don't remember about the Mindeco until the medication wears off. You helping me or not?"

Esán walked to the door. "You help me find the stones; I'll help you get home. If they ask why I was with you—Michael Mazer was interviewing me." He slipped into his suite as Karlsut Sorda exited The Penthouse.

The silence of his bedroom soothed Esán's growing agitation. Calm breathing steadied him. He stuffed his paperwork for the University in his book bag, steeled his nerves, and stepped into the hall as Sorda exited Upori's suite, his expression less than happy.

"I understand you met Michael?"

"I did. He asked me some questions about dance lighting." He patted his bag. "I called Fordham. I'm meeting with the head of research in an hour. By the end of the day, I'll be set to begin our work."

"Excellent, Nésa. Check in with me when you come home. I'll be interested to hear how things went." He rubbed his chin. "I'd stay away from Michael. He's been having seizures. They can make him pretty mean. See you later."

Esán stepped into the elevator with a relieved sigh. At the main floor, he greeted the concierge and requested a cab. Settling into the well-worn seat, he reviewed his morning. *I wish we knew who's running the show, and why he's threatening the stability of an entire solar system?*

17

At the cottage on Myrrh, SparrowLyn glared at the cloudy surface of the fountain Elcaro's Eye. "I realize you can be stubborn, but why today? My daughter may be in trouble. I need to know how she's doing."

She scooped water into the alabaster dipper and held it up in the sunlight streaming through the window.

> *"Show me the past where my daughter resides*
> *Help me to know she is making good strides*
> *Provide a clear link for us to share news*
> *To help us know more of Upori's time ruse."*

A long drink later, she hung the dipper on the fountain's alabaster rim and looked up to find Ari standing in the doorway.

"May I come in, Mother?"

Sparrow shrugged. "You may, but I have little to share."

Ari kissed her cheek. "You look tired. How long have you been at loggerheads with Elcaro?"

Sparrow surrendered to her fatigue and sank into the one comfortable chair in the sanctuary. Cool palms pressed to her face revived her. "Too long, Ari. I'm about to give up." She lowered her hands. "Do you think Almiralyn ever had trouble getting the fountain to communicate?"

Amusement sparkled in Ari's chestnut-brown eyes. "Of course, she did, Mother. Elcaro's reputation for deciding the right time to share information and refusal to divulge it a moment sooner is well established." She held out a hand. "Let's try together."

Sparrow allowed her daughter to pull her to her feet. Side-by-side, they peered into the All Seeing Eye. Clouds obscuring the surface spiraled downward, leaving the water calm. Their mirrored reflections, captured in perfect detail, gleamed on the sunlit surface. Ari squeezed her mother's hand. A shimmering void erased their likenesses.

Three figures took shape in the fountain. Rayna Deejara and a tall young man performed an intricate *pas de deux* in a rehearsal studio. At the front of the room, a short, slender man gave instructions. A dark-haired pianist with a dimple in his right cheek accompanied the trio.

The successful execution of a difficult section of choreography produced a nod of satisfaction from the rehearsal director. Rayna and her partner listened to his corrections, then took the opening pose to prepare for a final run. A younger male dancer bustled into the studio, a folded note in his hand. The director took it with a nod of thanks.

The boy shot Rayna a shy smile. She winked. He blushed and darted out the door.

Ari smiled. "It appears Miss Rayna has a fan."

Sparrow put a finger to her lips. The rehearsal director passed the note to Dwight, who read it, tensed, and crumpled it into a ball. "I have to go. I apologize to both of you." He tossed the note in the wastepaper basket as he hastened from the room.

After a brief discussion regarding the following day's rehearsal, the director preceded the accompanist from the studio. Anxiety building, Rayna retrieved the note and smoothed the crinkled paper. The fountain zoomed in. The note read: 'Need immediate help. MM gone. KS'

Rayna hurried to the window.

The scene in Elcaro's Eye changed.

Dwight stood on the curb, his hand raised. A Checkered Cab exited the river of yellow vehicles to stop next to him. He climbed in. The taxi nosed its way into traffic.

The fountain rippled into a new image. Rayna retrieved her dance bag from the corner, dropped the crumpled note in the wastebasket, and left.

The image blurred. Another formed.

Esán sat at a well-used maple desk across from a distinguished, scholarly-looking gentleman. Animated faces and hands 'talking' along with their mouths illustrated their excitement. The phone rang. The man answered. A short conversation later, he cradled the receiver.

"My secretary tells me a young woman is waiting in the reception area. She has an important message for you. I suggest we meet at the lab on Monday morning." He stood up. "It's been a pleasure, Nésa. I look forward to beginning our work together."

"Monday?" Confusion left Esán flustered.

The man grinned. "Life gets away from us sometimes, doesn't it? Today's Friday. The weekend is upon us. Enjoy it." He offered a hand.

Esán shook it. "You, too. Thanks for your time."

Grabbing his bag, he hurried to meet Rayna in the outer room and escorted her from the office. At the end of the hall, Rayna urged him into an empty classroom, her body language telegraphing her unease.

"Dwight received a note from Sorda. It said MM's gone. Dwight excused himself in the middle of rehearsal. Please be careful when you go back to The Plaza."

Esán glanced at the closed door. "This may be a ploy to see if you contacted anyone. Are you certain he left the area?"

"He hailed a cab. I saw it leave. The driver could have driven him around the block, but..." She tipped her head. "I didn't make my way to Fordham until I reached the subway at Columbus Circle. If you hadn't been so close, I'd have alerted you via a telepathic message. Since you were, I sent Gar home and came in person."

Esán hugged her. "If Upori's disappeared, it's because the Mindeco got control."

Rayna's eyes narrowed. "Which means we have a big problem."

The image dissolved. The water stilled.

Ari glanced at her mother. "I'm thinking we need to let Relevart know what's up."

"He already knows. Look."

Relevart's countenance filled the fountain's bowl. "Arienh, meet me in the research library. Sparrow, I believe your art calls. See what you discover as you paint."

The image melted away. Elcaro's calm surface gleamed until the first drops of water falling from the statue's alabaster fingers sent ripples dancing in repeated, concentric circles.

A ri hugged her mother goodbye, pictured Veersuni in the Cave of Canedari in the Dojanack Caverns, and arrived in the blink of an eye. She gave a breathless laugh. "I can't believe I can do that." Giving herself time to stabilize, she reviewed what she had seen in Elcaro's Eye. A brisk walk across the Reading Room brought her to the staircase leading to the research area of Myrrh's Galactic Library.

At the bottom of the steps, she rounded the end of a glass case filled with artifacts. "What the heck?" She jammed on the brakes.

Penesert, tall and slender with fanny-length caramel-blonde hair and beautiful, mismatched eyes, met her surprised astonishment with a bright smile. "Hey, Ari, how do you like my *cool* new clothes?" She whirled to show off a long, full skirt, and a flowered shirt, smocked with lace trim.

"You look great! What are you doing in Myrrh? I thought you were on El Aperdisa." She sucked in a breath. "You're going to New York City, 1969!"

Penee pointed at a chair piled with clothing. "So are you."

Ari did a quick inventory. A shirt in her favorite red-orange lay atop bell bottoms with fringe on the hem of the pant legs. A pair of red sandals to complete the ensemble made her grin. She glanced around. "Are Relevart and Elf with you?"

The VarTerel materialized at the end of the table, staff in hand. "Relevart is."

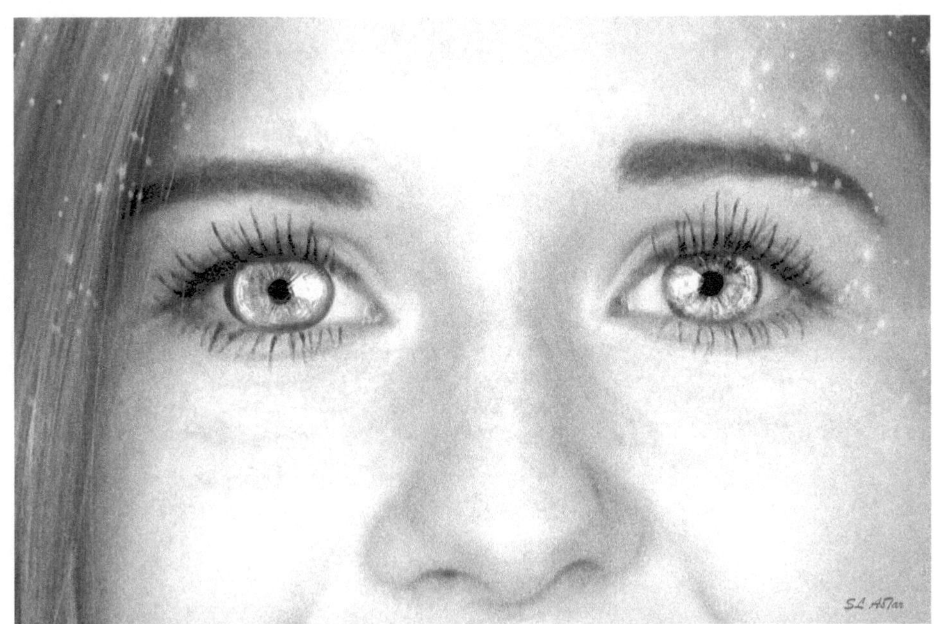

18

Esán escorted Rayna to her subway. Through the dirty window, she watched him exit the turnstile to take the stairs to the street. The clatter of her train echoed down the tunnel. At her stop, she allowed the crowd to carry her up the steep steps. Overwhelmed by the sheer number of bodies, she dodged from the stairwell onto the corner of Broadway, where an anxious Gar waited.

Spyglass trotted to her side. Gar examined her face. *"What's up?"*

She gave a minimized shake of the head.

He traipsed down 72nd to the apartment, dodged into the pass-through, and mouthed, "See you upstairs."

Rayna made a snap decision. A quick teleport left her standing in the center of her room. She dumped her gear on the bed and shifted to Brielle as the front door locks clicked, one after the other. Torgin had given Gar his own keys. The boy's happiness at being trusted brought her to tears. *What a gift you are, Gar.*

She entered the living room to find Torgin depositing his bag in a chair. Her young protector stood at the window, gazing down at the street.

Gar's chin shot up. He turned, his serious eyes fastened on hers. Small fists resting on his hips, he announced in a clear, steady voice, "I'm supposed to guard ya, Brie. Can't do my job when ya send me home without ya."

"You sent him home?" Torgin's brows bridged, framing a look teeming with questions.

Brie considered one then the other. "Let me explain." She told them about Dwight's note. "I had to warn Esán, Gar, and I didn't want to expose you to a possible tricky situation. I'm sorry I hurt your feelings."

"Ya didn't." He plopped down on the sofa. "Ya just got me all worried. If I don't know where ya are, it's as bad as not knowin' where Gin was. Don't do it again."

Torgin grinned. "You heard the man. Hey, is anyone hungry?"

"I'm starvin'." Gar looked anguished, then his face brightened. "Can I help ya cook?"

Getting to his feet, Torgin pulled Brie to hers, and marched into the kitchen. He had collected the makings for a shrimp salad when the locks on the apartment door clunked. A soft squeak ushered someone into the entryway.

Gar darted into the door. "Hey, Esán, I thought you was stayin' at The Plaza."

Esán flashed him a smile, dropped a kiss on Brie's cheek, and straddled a chair. "Dwight met me in the hotel lobby. Sorda sent him to ask if I'd mind staying at my own place for a couple of nights. I gather MM is creating havoc."

Happy to have all her friends close, Brie enjoyed their teasing chatter. Torgin put Gar to work washing vegetables. Wielding a knife like a trained sous chef, Esán cut them into chunks, while Torgin stuck a loaf of fresh French bread in the oven to reheat.

The normalcy of it all did not distract Brie from worrying about the Mindeco. *Has he left Upori's body?* The question sent a shiver to her toes and back.

Brie and Esán slipped from the kitchen to steal some time alone, leaving the cleanup to Torgin and Gar. The splash of dishwater juxtaposed the clatter of plates being stacked in the cupboard. Satisfied with their handy work, Torgin surveyed his domain. "I sure enjoy cooking."

Gar grinned. "Me, too." He whistled for his dog. "I gotta walk Spyglass. Don't share a bunch while I'm gone, okay?"

Torgin walked with him down the hall. "Mostly, we're guessing at stuff, so you won't miss much. Stay alert. Knock when you get back, and I'll let you in."

"I got my own keys, remember?"

With a grin, Torgin shooed him out the door.

Esán stuck his head into the hall. "Join us. We'll fill you in."

Torgin listened to an account of the day with a shudder of dread. "Any idea if the Mindeco still controls Upori?"

"You know what we know: MM is gone, which could mean a number of things. I'm supposed to check with the front desk tomorrow morning to find out if it's safe to return to The Plaza Monday after my day at Fordham. We'll find out more then."

The rest of the evening slid by. Brie and Esán headed for bed at an early hour. Torgin and Gar played quiet music until a full-bodied yawn sent the boy and his dog to snuggle up in their blankets in the corner by the guitar.

Torgin slipped into bed. Esán's soft breathing brought the brewing situation to the forefront of his thoughts. *Wish you didn't have to go back to The Plaza. Sure hope we find out what's up with the Mindeco before you do.* A yawn escorted him into dreaming.

He woke with a start, his heart racing and his hand gripping the time whistle. *How did I get the whistle?* He forced his mind to slow down. *What was I dreaming?*

Esán, propped up on an elbow, studied him. "You, too?"

Torgin stared at the miniature flute. "I think I dreamt something about the time whistle."

A soft knock interrupted. Brie stuck her head in the room. "Can I come in?"

Esán patted the mattress next to him. "You had a dream, right?"

"I woke up clutching my staff." She raised a brow at Torgin. "I didn't know you slept with the time whistle. How about you, Esán? Were the Seeds active?"

"Their vibrating woke me. Did either of you dream about Relevart?"

Torgin ran a finger over the whistle. "I didn't see him, but I heard his whistle. Did we travel through time?"

The door cracked open. "You didn't. We did." Ari nudged Penee ahead of her into the room.

"Arienh AsTar!" Brie threw her arms around her twin. "I've missed you both so much." She hugged Penee. "I'm so glad to see you." She looked from one to the other. "Why? How—"

A sharp bark cut her short. Spyglass darted into the room and sniffed each occupant in turn. Gar peeked around the door frame. His dumbfounded gaze jumped from one twin to the other. "There are two of ya." Scrutinizing them one at a time, he walked up to Ari, and held up his hand. "Hi, Ari, I'm Gar."

She touched her palm to his. "Good to meet you, Gar. How do you know who I am?"

He shrugged. "Just do." His gaze drifted to Penee. A hand flew to his mouth. "You're her—the girl with the Matriarch's Eyes." His brow crinkled. Confusion took him a step backward. He sidled closer to Torgin and slipped a trembling hand into his. Spyglass padded to his side.

Brie knelt. "It's alright, Gar. No one here will hurt you. Can you remember where you heard about the Matriarch's Eyes?"

The boy's mouth worked. He bit his lip and shook his head. "No." His fight for control telegraphed: don't touch me.

Brie held her desire to hug him in check. "Can you tell us why seeing Penee scared you?"

"Seein' her surprised me and sorta..." He bit his lip again. "It didn't scare me." With a quizzical tip to his head, he peeked over her shoulder at Penee. "It's more like she's a sign of change." He gave her a lame smile. "Good to meet ya, Penee."

She presented her palm. "I am honored to meet you, Gar."

He rubbed his hand on his pants, touched her palm, and placed his fist against his heart.

Torgin watched the exchange transpire with intense interest. The small hand holding his continued to tremble. *What does Penee's appearance mean to you, Gar? Something important, that's for sure.*

E sán yawned and looked at the clock. "It's six o'clock. I'm glad it's the weekend; we have a lot to accomplish. I don't suppose you two know your schedule?"

"It's on the dining room table. Why don't we let you get dressed? Gar can give us a tour."

With a sidelong glance at Penee, Gar dodged into the hall. She and the twins followed him.

Torgin threw back the covers. "You want to shower first?"

"Nope. Go ahead. I have some thinking to do. Besides, you have a crowd to cook for."

Torgin laughed. "One of these days, it'll be your turn in the kitchen. Today, I already have a plan simmering in my brain." He disappeared into the bathroom.

Esán put his arms behind his head. Picking a spot on the ceiling, he stared until the world blurred. *Where are you Upori Athai? Are you still using the persona of Michael Mazer, or are you fighting with the Mindeco? Your injections saved you. Without them...* Esán pressed his lips together. *If Rikell exits...* Memories of a body emptied of the Mindeco's presence decomposing on the ground in front of him left him shivering. He sat on the bed and pressed bare feet against the throw rug. *Ari and Penee... Relevart wouldn't have sent them unless we needed help. Is this about Rikell?*

Torgin walked into the room, scrubbing his short hair dry with a towel. "Sure am glad I don't have rehearsal until Monday afternoon. We can use the weekend to help Ari and Penee adjust."

Esán picked up his clothes and gave a soft laugh. "I lost track of Earth's week and got confused at Fordham. It reminded me to pay attention. Let's find out if the girls know why Relevart sent them to 1969. Then we'll plan our day. I'll shower and be right out."

"Sounds good." Torgin held up his towel. "Hang this up for me?"

Esán caught it at the peak of its arc and padded into the bathroom.

Wiping the steam from the mirror, he murmured to his reflection. "Hope we find the Mindeco before it does irreparable harm."

19

Ari carried a tray of delectable breakfast goodies into the dining room where Brie and Penee sat next to each other, talking a mile a minute. A twinge of jealousy tightened her jaw. She shook herself. *Grow up, Arienh AsTar. They spent intense time together on Soputto, dealing with the Incirrata's secret. Of course, they're close.* She gathered the reins of her self-control, let her resentment crumble to nothing, and placed the tray on the table.

"I bet you have a lot to catch up on. How's it going?"

Brie smiled. "We're almost up to date."

Penee came to her feet, unloaded the food, and smiled. "I'll see if Torgin needs anything. Better catch up while you have the chance." She slipped from the room.

Ari took her seat. "I missed you so much." She squeezed her twin's hand. "Do you sometimes wonder if we'll ever be in the same place for longer than a few turnings?"

Brie clasped her hand. "We seem to have different destinies, don't we? I suggest we make the best of the time we have. Tell me about you and Elf and Mother and Father."

Ari described their mother's frustration with Elcaro's Eye. "You'd think the fountain would be forthcoming. It is supposed to help, so—" Brie's serious expression stopped her. "What?"

"I believe it's all about timing. The fountain provides information at the right moment; otherwise, it remains quiet. Mom's lucky. Her paintings help her see what she needs to see. Aunt Mira didn't have that." She cocked her head. "Do you think Aunt Mira ever misses being Guardian of Myrrh?"

"I suppose we could ask her." Torgin entered with another tray. Penee, Gar, and Esán trailed him. He prepared to pile plates high with bacon, scrambled eggs spiced with fresh oregano and thyme, and crispy home fries.

Ari inhaled. "That smells divine." She pilfered a slice of bacon. "What do you mean we can ask her?" The taste filling her mouth demanded focused attention.

Chairs scraped. The boys and Penee sat down. Torgin handed her a full plate. "Mira works at the theater as a costumer."

"Corvus works at the theater, too. He's an accompanist with the company." Brie set her plate on her mat and picked up a fork.

Conversation continued between bites of Torgin's excellent cooking. When she had wiped her plate clean, Ari leaned back to study her best friend. "I did not know you could cook. What a great welcome to New York City."

Torgin began clearing the table. "I didn't know I could either. I love it." He picked up a laden tray. "Wait for me. I want to hear about your research and why Relevart sent you to join us."

Brie pushed back from the table. "We'll all help in the kitchen, so we can get to business faster."

Many hands made quick work of the cleanup. Soon, everyone sat at the table, ready to share updates.

Ari glanced at Gar and gave Esán an inquiring look.

He responded with a smile. "Gar is a full partner in this venture. You can trust him, Ari."

She smiled. "Great. Penesert, please fill us in on El Aperdisa."

Penee nodded. "Your grandmaman, Mairin, has finished physio-thérapie and is walking with only a small limp. She and Lanli are helping with the preparations for El Aperdisa's departure to El Stroma."

A soft gasp pulled her attention in Gar's direction. Dilated pupils turned his brown eyes black. His mouth worked around a garble of silent words. Trembling fingers gripping the table kept him from tumbling to the floor.

Torgin hurried to his side, scooped him up, and carried him to the sofa. A hand on his forehead produced a worried frown. "He's cold as ice."

"I'll get a blanket." Brie hastened from the room.

Esán sat down at Gar's feet, his hands resting on the boy's ankles. Penee and Ari moved to one side to give them space. Spyglass whined and licked Gar's cheek.

Brie returned to cover him with a soft, blue blanket. "Torgin, put Spyglass beside him to help warm him." She knelt. "Gar, can you hear me?"

Spyglass settled at his master's side. The boy's hand twitched. Black pupils constricted to normal size. The agitated rise and fall of the small chest slowed.

Torgin moved to kneel next to Brie. "Gar, we're all here. You're safe."

His eyelids fluttered. Glassy, brown eyes blinked. He licked his dry lips. "Torgin?"

The breathy word, though barely discernible, made Torgin lean over him. "I'm right here."

"Thirsty."

Penee scurried from the room and returned with a glass of water. She waited for Torgin to slip an arm beneath the boy's shoulder. When he had finished helping him to sip the cool fluid, she retrieved the glass.

Torgin lowered Gar to the sofa. "Take a minute to rest. We'll be close."

He motioned his friends to join him by the window. His concern-filled gaze rested on Brie. "We can't help him if we don't know who he is."

Brie's hand caressed the blue pouch hanging on its matching ribbon. Ari moved closer. "You have the Stone of Remembering, and I have Efillaeh."

The Stone of Remembering hummed beneath Brie's hand; the Star of Truth thrummed at the back of her neck. She walked to the sofa to observe the dozing boy. His eyelids fluttered open. "I need to know who—" Pain twisted his youthful features. His hand clutched at his chest. He groaned.

"What just happened, Gar?"

"Don't know."

"What triggers your pain?"

His brow crinkled. "If I think 'bout who I—" He gasped.

She put a finger to her lips. "Hug Spyglass. Concentrate on all the fun you've had together."

Hurrying back to the anxious group by the window, she pulled the blue pouch from beneath her shirt. "Whoever hid his identity set up an ambush to keep him from digging too deep. It will take all our talents to discover who he is. Penee, join Esán to create protective wards. Ari use the sacred knife to heal any damage and to help me find what triggers the trap. When it's safe to do so, the Remembering Stone will return his memories, leaving him unscathed."

Torgin cleared his throat. "What about me? How can I support the process?"

Brie clasped his hand. "Of all of us, Gar trusts you the most. You will be his personal guardian. I will channel his memories into your mind. Your job is to filter out anything that can harm him. I'll help. Between us, we'll figure out his true identity and why someone went to the trouble of hiding it."

Gar moaned. Spyglass wiggled closer, whined, and licked his cheek.

The group wasted no more time. Torgin took his place at Gar's side. Ari sat at his feet with Brie at his head. Penee stood at one end of the sofa; Esán stood at the other.

Torgin placed gentle hands on the whimpering boy's shoulder. "Gar, I'm here. Look at me."

Stark terror flashed across the boy's sweat-covered face. Moaning, he reached for Torgin.

Torgin sandwiched one small black hand between his brown ones. "Keep looking at me, no matter what happens. I promise not to let you go. Blink if you understand."

Gar blinked. His free hand gripped Torgin's wrist.

Brie caught Esán's eye. "Shields, now."

He held Penee's gaze. Together, they created a shimmering, circular shield surrounding the group.

Ari placed the sacred blade, Efillaeh, on Gar's chest.

"Efillaeh, the healing knife
Protect Gar from pain and strife
Keep his life tied to his soul
Keep him strong, keep him whole."

Amethyst radiance misting from the knife's handle spread out to surround the boy's body. Emerald etchings on the silver blade glowed. Tendrils of green light, like slender roots, encircled his chest. Ari glanced up at her twin.

Brie held up the smooth, blue Remembering Stone.

"Stone of recalling, Gar's memories revive.
Bring them from hiding, whole and alive.
Share them with gentle concern for this boy;
Keep him unharmed should the trigger deploy."

She placed the stone on Gar's forehead. He hiccuped a shaky breath as the stone's blue light saturated his mind and flowed through his heart into Torgin's.

Torgin shook from head to foot. An exhaled breath left him wrapped in stillness. A voice, not his own, filled the room.

"I am Marama, the keeper of the memories and history of Garon, son of Ralara Aureka and Tane Anaru. Garon is my sister's son. We are of the Giroblania from El Quil'Tran on the planet of El Stroma."

Astonishment registered on every face. Torgin gulped a breath. The voice continued.

"I speak through the great-grandson of my grandson, Kuparak Whalend. Torgin Wilith Whalend now carries our history to share with those who gather to protect Garon Aureka Anaru and the Girl with the Matriarch's Eyes."

The voice stilled. Gar whispered, "Aunt Marama."

Torgin released Gar's hand and sat back on his heels. Once again, Marama spoke through him. "My time ends, Garon. You are with those who can help you achieve your destiny." The voice quivered.

Ari returned the sacred knife to its scabbard, her attention fixed on Torgin's face.

Brie removed the stone from Gar's forehead. "You have completed your job, Marama. It is time to pass into the ever-life. We promise to take care of Garon." She looked at Penee. Together they chanted:

> *"Peace to the ancestors of the deceased.*
> *Now, in this moment, let her be released.*
> *We welcome your presence, the peace that you bring;*
> *We lift up our voices, your praises to sing.*
>
> *Be with us here in this circled-farewell;*
> *Escort Marama to the land where you dwell.*
> *We celebrate All and the lives you have lived;*
> *We honor your passing and all that you give.*
>
> *Ancestors, we honor your stories, your grace;*
> *Your feet that have walked in this glorious place;*
> *Your hands that have worked on the land and the seas;*
> *Your breath that has moved through the winds and the trees."*

At the end of the chorus, Gar exhaled a long, quiet breath. Tears streamed down his cheeks. "She's gone. Will I ever know my story?" He sniffed.

Ari smiled. "I believe, young Garon, our dear friend Torgin will share your story with all of us."

Gar pushed to sitting and touched Torgin's face. "We are kin?"

Torgin hugged him, then looked him in the eyes. "I have always known we share a connection, my dear cousin. Now we can celebrate it."

Gar's hand snuck into his. Shyness cloaked him as he gazed up at Penee. "We share a destiny?"

She took Ari's place on the sofa. "We do." She raised her beautiful eyes, one warm green, the other cool blue, to connect with each person in the room. "We all share a destiny."

Esán moved to Brie's side. Ari joined them.

Penee smiled. "I would like to hear your story, Garon. What do you say, Torgin?"

"I need to be alone." He released Gar's hand and came to his feet. "I'll be back in a few minutes." He walked from the room.

Realization washed over Ari. *You are no longer the frightened boy we first met in Idronatti, Torgin Whalend.*

Torgin crossed the music room and sank onto the piano bench. For a time, Garon's story over-saturated his mind. His fingers caressing the cool ivory keys helped to calm his turbulent thoughts. To the strains of Ravel's *Bolero,* his memories shuffled and resorted. Gar's story found its proper place. The repetitive nature of the beautiful piece helped him regain his equilibrium. As the last note faded, he walked down the hall.

He found his friends conversing in soft voices. Gar looked up, his expression showing his mixed emotions. Torgin angled a chair to face him. "Are you ready to hear your story, Garon?"

Doubt, fear, expectation spilled from every pore in his young body. "I'm scared, Torgin." He produced a tiny smile. "But I'm not alone anymore." Newfound confidence made its presence known in his straight spine and steady smile. "I'm ready."

Torgin, his attention never wavering, let Marama's memories speak through him as though she were telling her story.

"Garon was born on El Stroma as the RomPeer's plan to obliterate the Eleo Predan people came to a head.

"The ancient texts of our people, the tribe Giroblania, prophesied that the son of Charnlandian leaders would rise to walk at the side of the Girl with the Matriarch's Eyes. The RomPeer ordered soldiers to kill all Eleo Predan male infants and young boys. As his troops marched closer to Gar's village, his mother secreted him with me in the Gruseeno Mountains in Charnlandia on the continent of El QuilTran.

"In our culture, the elders selected girls in childhood to train as Time Singers, women who could travel through time. I was a chosen one. I promised my younger sister, Ralara, I would take her son away if something happened to her.

"Gar, an infant of six moon cycles, thrived in the mountains. When he was midway through his first sun cycle, an elderly peasant hiked to the retreat with news of the RomPeer's War. The enemy had killed Gar's parents. They beheaded his father, the headman of the village and executed his mother, a revered shameena, as she tried to help the village women escape from the prison wagon carrying them to slave camps.

"I knew leaving El Stroma with Gar via normal means was not possible. Time Travel seemed our best option. Concerned traveling might harm the child, we stayed in the village until word came that the soldiers approached the mountain pass leading to our valley retreat.

"In the cavern where the Time Singers worked their magic, I set my sights on the planet Earth, cradled my nephew in my arms, and chanted the song to create a time tunnel. We arrived in Central Park in New York City, 1959 in the last month of summer, beneath a full moon.

"Garon weathered the journey. I did not. My knees buckled. I fell to the ground with Garon hugged to my chest, my life force ebbing. A man knelt beside us and removed Garon from my shaking embrace. A shaft of light shooting between roiling clouds illuminated the wrinkled, brown face of an old man. His full, white beard and mustache stressed the gentleness in his smile. He spoke to me in an unknown language. Fear clutched at my heart. Would he kill us?

"The storm broke. Rain fell in torrents. He told me his name was Gin and half supported, half carried me to a small tent pitched beneath a stone bridge. After helping me to lie down on a tattered mat, he offered me scraps from a tin bowl. When I refused to eat, he fed Garon and placed him next to me. Gin picked up a string instrument of a type I had never seen. The gentle strumming relaxed us. Gradually, the rain ceased to fall, and the clouds parted. Moonlight soaked us with its cool beauty, bringing with it the knowledge of my imminent death. The man's wise, gentle expression told me he understood. I whispered a song to hide Garon's memories and to create a place for my spirit to reside until he was old enough to carry the burdens of his heritage. With the final chorus, knowledge of the man's language flooded my mind. I told him Gar's name, trusted him with a bit of our tale, and asked him to take care of the boy. Gin promised to raise him as his own. My breath caught in my throat; my spirit slipped from my body into Garon's."

<Story Break>

Torgin gazed at Gar. "Gin didn't find you in a trash can, abandoned and unloved. Your aunt made certain you were safe before she died. Look around you, Gar. We are your family."

The boy's wide-eyed gaze traveled the group. Tears streamed down his cheeks. He slid from the sofa. "I need time to be... I need..." He lifted his shoulders in a confused shrug.

Torgin moved aside. "The music room is a great place to think."

Gar whistled. He left the room with Spyglass trotting at his heels. The soft strains of the guitar whispered down the hall.

Torgin smiled. *We do share a connection, Garon Anaru.*

20

The aching beauty of Gar's music brought Esán's emotions tumbling to the surface. Empathy coursed through him. The memory of discovering Somay was his father warmed him. *Stories of my childhood and my home planet gave me roots for the first time.* A swell of happiness made him smile. *Gar's roots are sprouting.* He looked up to find his friends watching him.

Brie clasped his hand. "Memories are something, aren't they?"

"They are." He beamed, then grew serious. "We have a weekend to find the Mindeco and convince him to share what he knows about the Corps Stones. Relevart sent you, Ari and Penee, for several reasons, one being to help Gar learn who he is. Any idea what else prompted the decision?"

Penee tugged at her dangling earring. "I think the Clenaba Rolas System is about to destabilize. To save it, we must return the stones to their home planets."

Esán drew in a harried breath. "That's what I was afraid of. We need to define our goals and divide up the tasks between us."

Silence from the music room presaged Gar's arrival in the arched entryway. He rested his head against the frame, his expression distant. Spyglass waited by his side, puppy eyes fixed on his master. Gar shook himself, scratched the dog's ears, and crossed to the sofa. "Thanks for helpin' me. I'm so full of feelin's I think I might burst." He bit his lip. "Can't seem ta pin 'em down."

"Give yourself time, Gar." Esán drew him onto the sofa next to him. "I learned who I am and met my father the first time a couple of years ago. Just let it seep in. We're all here to support you."

Brie leaned forward. "All of us have a hidden history—things that slip from memory. Every person you see on the street can tell tales of their pain, their sorrow, their amazement, their joy. Honor your stories, Gar. They are like ligament to bone. They mold you into a cohesive whole. Before you know it, the things you learned today will seem as natural as breathing."

Torgin pulled up a straight-back chair. "If you feel okay, Gar, we need to decide the best way to find the Mindeco."

Gar slipped a hand into his. "Mindeco?"

"Mindeco?" Penee echoed him. "What is that, exactly?"

Brie cringed. "It's a creature found only in the Trutore Mountains on the planet of RewFaar. It snatches human bodies, and, keeping the mind and memories intact, it inhabits the physical body. The owner's essence is destroyed in the process. When the Mindeco no longer requires the use of the borrowed form, it sheds it like an old coat." She hugged herself. "The moment the creature steps free, the carcass decomposes."

The whites of Gar's eyes grew larger. "What's it look like?"

Torgin's brows met above his nose. "A Mindeco is over seven Earth feet tall. It has long, lean limbs with bulging joints and rarely walks upright. Instead, it leans forward, its clawed fingers brushing the ground. Its bear-like skull has a single eye known as an oculus in the center of the forehead." He wrinkled his nose. "Worst of all, it stinks of decay...like a rotting corpse."

Penee paled. "Are you telling me this is the creature we are looking for? How can we trust it not to claim one of us?"

Esán's somber expression did not waver. "We can't." A flashed image of the Mindeco's single eye fixed on his face caught him off guard. Crossing to the window, he stared at the street. "*His* name is Rikell." He turned, more serious than ever. "He's closer than we think. I'm not sure if he has abandoned Upori's body or not."

Ari shrunk smaller in her over-stuffed chair. "Penee and I aren't ready to venture out on our own, especially with Rikell on the loose."

Penee pressed her palms together. "I've never spent time in anyplace bigger than a village. Manhattan's endless dirty, building-lined streets terrifies me. I can't see the sky or feel the warmth of the sun. How will I ever navigate this enormous city?" She shivered.

"One thing at a time." Esán returned to his seat beside Brie. "Ari, tell us what you and Elf learned in your research."

She gripped the chair arms to pull herself upright. "We confirmed that New York City, 1969, is the correct time frame. As far as we can tell, New York City Ballet or an affiliated organization is where the thieves hid the Corps Stones."

Penee cleared her throat. "I also did some work in El Aperdisa's research lab. Karl Sorda is the bastard son of my cousin Skultar's father. Skultar and Karlsut are half-brothers and hate each other. I didn't find out much about Dwight, did you, Ari?"

"Nope. He's a mystery. It's almost as though he appeared out of nowhere."

Gar raised a hand. "What are Corps Stones? That's why ya came to the city, right?"

The phone in the study chimed. Conversation ceased. Esán hurried to the desk. Heavy breathing hissing as he pressed the receiver to his ear. A pause and then a smothered cough followed. "Who?"

"Nésa Zervos."

"Alone."

"No." Esán straightened the blotter.

"Friend or enemy?"

Esán faced his friends. After mouthing the word 'Upori', he mimed that Brie should listen on the phone in the kitchen. She hurried from the room. He timed his response to cover the click of her pick up. "Depends. Who are you?"

"Upori. Sorda and Dwight are closing in. If they catch me, you'll never know about the stones."

"What do you need from me?"

"Tell me where you are?" The man's voice grew eager.

Esán inhaled. "I'll come to you."

"I know your friends, the ones who stripped the Mindeco from Desirol, are with you. You saved him. You can save me to carry on the Michael Mazer charade. Release me from—" The line went dead.

Esán stared at the receiver, then replaced it in the cradle. Thoughts in a muddle, he gazed unseeing at his hand resting on its glossy black surface.

Brielle hurried in from the kitchen, led him to the couch, and sat down with Gar between them. She provided the group with a quick summary of the conversation.

Ari ran a freckled hand through her coppery curls. "Why do you suppose Rikell wants Upori alive?"

Esán's puzzlement cleared. "I can think of two reasons." He ticked them off on his fingers. "One, Upori knows more about the time machine than anyone. If he's living and thinking, Rikell doesn't need us to take him into the future. Two, he wants the Corps Stones for himself."

Torgin shook his head. "Wait. Why does a Mindeco need Corps Stones?"

The phone's persistent ring clipped the conversation short.

Esán hurried to answer it.

"May I please speak to Nesá?" Karlsut's curt question crackled with frustration.

"This is Nesá. Is that you, Mr. Sorda?"

"Please call me Karl. I'm calling to let you know you can return to The Plaza. We have work to do."

Esán flashed his friends a warning look and gripped the phone tighter. "You didn't require my presence, so my friend and I made plans to leave town for the weekend."

At the other end of the line, silence lengthened into a tense pause. "One moment." An apparent hand over the mouthpiece obscured whispering voices. A crackle accompanied Sorda's return. "Nesá, I didn't want to tell you this over the phone." He cleared his throat. "You are in danger. Michael Mazer is a sick man. For some unknown reason, he is focused on finding you. I'd feel better if you were where I can protect you." He paused.

The whispering voice hissed.

Sorda continued. "It might be wise to bring your roommate along."

Esán fingered the cord. "My friend knows nothing about Michael Mazer or my work with you. What do you suggest I tell him?"

More whispering at Sorda's end gave Esán time to collect his thoughts. "Nesá?"

"Yes, sir."

"Tell him I have invited you both to spend the weekend. It's ten o'clock. I'll order lunch to be served in The Penthouse at noon. See you then." A sharp click ended the call.

Esán placed the receiver in the cradle. "Looks like two of us will be spending the weekend at The Plaza Hotel." He sat next to Brie, his gaze fixed on Ari. "How do you feel about coming with me as Ira Raast?"

"Why me?" Ari's brow creased. "I don't have the gifts you require to protect you."

He smiled. "Don't doubt your abilities, Ari. I need someone who appears non-threatening to come with me."

Ari opened her mouth.

His stopped her with a tight smile. "And someone who is observant and smart enough not to draw attention. You qualify. So, what do you say?"

Ari muttered something under her breath and gripped her knees. "I'll do it. You understand he will check my family history. How do we get one for me?"

Brie smiled at her twin. "Étoile told me to concentrate on what I needed. You worked with Allegro, right?"

"I did. He said the same thing." She closed her eyes, pressed her palms together, and concentrated. A tiny smile tugged at the corners of her mouth. She blinked. "Gar, would you mind fetching the papers from the dining room?"

"You bet." He jumped to his feet. Within moments, he returned, clutching a pile of papers in each hand. He gave one to Ari, the other to Penee, and sank down next to Torgin. "So tell us."

Ari studied her paperwork. Her deep laugh filled the room. "I should have known. Allegro told me I had a surprise waiting for me when I got here." She looked somewhat smug.

Brie nudged her. "Don't keep us all in suspense."

Ari, uncomfortable shifting in a roomful of people, excused herself and hurried to the bathroom. Gazing in the mirror, she pondered her situation. Her head tilted; her lips pursed. *Who are you in 1969, Ira Raast?*

A slow nod of the head accompanied the beginning of her transformation. Red curls turned to shoulder-length brown, wavy hair. Her feminine body melded into a muscular male with broad shoulders and narrow hips. She examined Ira's reflection. "What's missing?" Calloused fingers rubbed his smooth chin. "Ahha." A mustache and trimmed beard materialized. She squinted. "You need a tattoo, my boy." The etched image of an eagle in flight appeared on his upper arm. A smile bared straight white teeth. "Not bad."

Unlike Rayna, who had total recall of Brie, Ira dismissed Ari from memory. *Better stay in control, Arienh, if you want to see their reaction.* Focused on her awareness of self, Ari pulled on bell bottoms with a tie-dyed shirt Esán had provided and hurried down the hall.

A gasp of surprise met her appearance in the doorway. The tickle of Ira's mustache framing a wide grin released her fully to her shifted persona.

Ira stepped into the room and performed a sweeping bow. "I'm Ira Raast, folk singer and guitarist." He sauntered over to Penee. "You are my younger sister, Wendi. Our parents, both teachers, raised us in Carson City, Nevada, near Lake Tahoe." His gaze swept to Esán. "I met you, Nesá, in San Francisco. We hit it off. When I discovered you were moving to New York, it provided me with an excuse to move here, too."

His twinkling eyes refocused on Penee. "Mother wouldn't allow you to come with me, Wendi, until we had a place to live in a safe neighborhood." A possessive hand squeezed her shoulder. "You're arriving soon, though." He strolled to the window, let the pause build interest, and turned.

His hands positioned as though holding a guitar, he strummed while he walked to Penee's side. "Our agent got us a gig! We're opening for some top performers at a folk music festival in Central Park in a couple of weeks." He surveyed his audience, gave another sweeping bow, and plopped down on the couch next to Brie.

Applause exploded. He laughed. "Thanks, one and all."

Esán shot him a knowing expression. "That settles it. You're coming with me to the party at The Plaza." He stood up. "You'd better collect your things so we can go."

"Wait." Torgin perched on the edge of his chair. "What do we do while you're partying?"

Esán raised a brow. "You find the Mindeco before he releases Upori's body, convince him to tell you what he knows about the Corps Stones, and try to keep him under control. We'll learn what we can from Karlsut and Dwight. If we discover anything important, we'll get a message to you."

Brie frowned. "How do you propose to do that? You know they'll watch your every move."

Ira patted her shoulder. "Everything's cool. We can take care of ourselves. You have your own worries to focus on."

Brie folded her arms. "If we need to get a message to you?"

Ira grinned at Esán. "You're the boss."

Esán crossed to the window and froze. In slow motion he stepped to the side, turned, and mouthed one word. "Upori."

Ira peered over his shoulder. On the sidewalk opposite, a short, stocky man surveyed the street. Beady eyes traveled from building to building, pausing, then moving on. "Is that our Mindeco?"

Esán nodded.

"How did he find us?"

"Good question."

Ira shuddered. "Now what?"

21

The tingle of the Mindeco's proximity triggered a piercing pain from the Star of Truth. Brie smothered a gasp and rubbed the small, star-shaped birthmark. "He knows we're close. I feel him searching."

Penee moved to Esán's vacated spot. "Can he find us? Can he use a mental probe?"

The image of the Mindeco flashing in her mind made Brie shiver. "He senses things in his vicinity, mostly with his acute sense of smell." She thought back to her encounters with the creature. "I think he's telepathic, but in a different way than we are. He can't talk to us, but..." She shrugged and closed her eyes.

Penee waited in silence until she opened them. "Is he still outside?"

"He is." She walked over to Esán. "How did he find this street?"

"Rikell got a good whiff of my scent during my visits to The Plaza. I bet he followed it here. He also knows our energy signatures."

Brie glanced at Gar. "He doesn't know Gar's or Penee's. They could help us figure out where he is."

Penee blanched.

Gar joined them. "I can go out through the basement. Spyglass'll sniff 'im out."

"This isn't a game, Gar." Brie rested her hand on his shoulder. "Rikell isn't like anything you've ever encountered. He's dangerous, he's mean—"

The phone rang. Esán answered it. "This is Nesá. Yes, sir. Something came up. It kept us longer than expected. Yes, sir. We're leaving now." He hung up. "Karlsut is a bit unhappy with his new research assistant. Lunch is waiting." His brows shot up. "Where's Gar?"

Brie moved toward the hall. "I bet he's gone to find Rikell." The apartment door standing ajar confirmed her fear. Hurrying into the hallway, she arrived at the elevator as it reached the basement. *"Gar, you'd better be careful."* She strode into the apartment, threw the locks and chain, and hurried to the living room. "Gar just took the elevator to the basement. What do we do?"

Esán slipped an arm around her waist. "We give him some time. He's smart and street savvy." He kissed her cheek and released her. "Ira, we need to go. I don't want to leave this building by normal means. Rikell will pick up our scent before we walk two feet. I know a secluded corner in the 72nd Street station. We'll teleport there, then take a cab to the hotel. Grab your stuff." He caught Torgin's eye.

"Don't worry, Esán. We can take care of ourselves. Watch your back. Karlsut is after something."

Brie touched his arm. "Dwight's a wildcard. Don't underestimate him."

Ira, backpack slung over his shoulder, entered the room.

Esán urged Brie closer to the window. "Look."

A raven perched on the roof across the way.

"Gar isn't alone." He kissed her cheek. "I'll call when I can. Ready, Ira?"

"Ready."

They flashed from view, leaving Brie with her attention riveted on the street.

Gar and Spyglass slipped from the basement to dodge behind the neighboring building. Chaotic, fearful thoughts galloped around his brain. The aroma of decaying flesh permeating the air magnified them. His nose wrinkled in disgust. A soft slap on his thigh called Spyglass to heel.

The Mindeco's odor filled the pass-through. Upori Athai rounded the corner. Frustration tainted with fear bristled around him. He glared over his shoulder. His nostrils flared. A snuffling sound hissed in chorus with the deep rumbling of a predatory growl. He pivoted, his attention fastening on Gar.

Spyglass's repeated bark rang out. Gar gripped his collar and edged backward. The man's enraged gaze drilled into him. The stench of decay washing over him left Gar gagging on the bile rising in his throat.

A hand closed on his shoulder. Darkness and the soft breathing of another Human surrounded him. Motionless and without thought, Gar waited.

In the apartment, Torgin paced. He sensed the Mindeco, felt Gar's fear, then the boy's essence vanished. Anxiety propelled him to the window. "Where are you, Garon?" He swung around to face Brie. "One second he was in the pass-through, the next—gone." He strode toward the hall. "I have to find him."

Brie caught his arm. "We can't go out there. The Mindeco will smell us the minute we step into the open. Gar's smart and capable, and the Star of Truth is quiet. Right now, we need Rikell distracted to give Esán and Ira time to reach The Plaza."

Torgin yanked his arm away. "He's a kid, Brie. What if Rikell takes him over? What if..." He gulped in a cleansing breath. *Remember, Torgin Whalend, Corvus is near.* Its slow release eased his agitation. A mental probe of the area showed him Rikell remained close; the boy and his dog were gone. *At least I know the Mindeco doesn't have him.*

He shook himself like Spyglass after a bath. "If I can't help, I'd better cook." He marched into the kitchen, pulled open the refrigerator door, and glanced back at Penee and Brie observing him from the hall. "Breakfast or lunch?"

"Something that will hold us for a while." Brie grabbed silverware, set the table, and slid onto a chair.

Penee added plates and glasses. "I'll love anything you prepare, Torgin." She sat down, plucked a napkin from the holder at the table's center, and began folding it.

Torgin peered over her shoulder. "Whatcha doing?"

She held up a paper bird. "I learned to make things from scraps when Skultar imprisoned me on TaSneach. It helps me to think." A distant memory clouded her expression. "I wonder..." The expression evaporated.

"You wonder?" Brie examined the bird Penee had set on the table beside a mug.

"I'll bet my cousin, Skultar, knows about the Corps Stones. He tracks everything Karlsut does." She pursed her lips, then held up crossed fingers. "Of course, he might still be wandering around the ocean on Soputto."

Torgin set down a large plate of sandwiches. "Bacon, egg, tomato, and cheese on sourdough bread. Ought to keep us going. I'll get juice."

They ate in silence. Torgin made himself bite, chew, and swallow. *"Where are you, Gar? If you don't get back soon, I promise to come looking."*

Ira waited while Esán paid the cab driver and pocketed the receipt. Transfixed by The Plaza Hotel's opulent entryway, the rushing traffic, and the obvious wealth of the hotel patrons, he wished, not for the first time, that he were back on Myrrh.

Esán brushing past him made him jump. Nervousness surged. His frantic gaze darted up and down Fifth Avenue. He gulped a breath and hurried into the hotel after Esán. The luxurious foyer left him gawking. Snapping his gaping mouth closed, he suppressed the desire to stare.

A lithe young man crossed the reception area. Steel-blue eyes met his.

Ira held himself steady, allowing unsophisticated thoughts to skitter through his mind.

Esán stepped into the breach. "Dwight, it's good to see you. This is my roommate, Ira Raast. Sorry we're later than expected."

Dwight gave him a quick nod and returned his attention to Ira. "My uncle is upstairs." He raised a brow at Esán. "He doesn't appreciate being kept waiting."

Esán's gracious smile juxtaposed the edge in Dwight's voice. "I will explain the situation to Karl. Shall we go?"

Dwight's full lips wrestled between a scowl and a smile. "Yes, of course." He led the way to the elevator, ushered them in ahead of him, and pressed the button.

Tension as thick as a winter blanket cloaked them. The conflict developing between his companions set Ira's nerves on edge. From under lowered lids, he studied one then the other. *I might have found humor in the situation another time. Today, too much is at risk.*

The door opened; the tension eased. Relieved, he followed his companions into The Penthouse Suite, where a uniformed man ushered them to a sitting room decorated in scarlet. In the cab, Esán had described his initial meeting with Karlsut Sorda. Ira's quick mind formed a vivid picture of that first encounter.

Prompted by Esán's example, he stood when their host entered.

Sorda extended a manicured hand. "I'm Karlsut Sorda. Welcome to The Plaza Hotel."

"Ira Raast. It's a pleasure to meet you, sir." Sorda's firm grip triggered a shiver Ira controlled by sheer will-power. Fighting the impulse to wipe his hand on the seat of his pants, he lowered it to his side. Sorda's intense gaze lingering on his face made him suppress the desire to squirm. His host's attention refocusing on Esán left him weak-kneed.

Sorda studied his research assistant. "I'm glad you could finally get away." The underlying question in the statement suggested an explanation was in order.

Esán ignored it. "We're sorry to be late. It was not our intention."

Sorda smiled away the growing awkwardness. "I suggest we adjourn to the dining room. We'll serve ourselves from the buffet, then get to know one another."

In the formal dining room, a woman in a starched burgundy uniform removed the covers from ornate silver serving dishes and stepped to one side.

"Dwight, why don't you start. Our guests can follow." He nodded to the server. "You may go. If we need anything, I'll ring."

She bobbed a small curtsy and left.

Ira realized, as he took his seat next to Karl and across from Dwight, that he was about to become the center of attention. *Don't volunteer any information. The less said, the better.*

Sorda took the lead. "We don't stand on formality, so please, Ira, call me Karl. I understand you are from Carson City, Nevada. Do you have family there?"

"I have one sister, Wendi, who is preparing to join me in a couple of days, and, of course, my parents."

Conversation remained easy and non-threatening. Mindful of an undercurrent of strain, Ira answered a stream of questions with an air of innocent openness.

Dwight took over the interrogation. "I understand you know Rayna Deejara."

"I do. We met through my sister in San Francisco. Rayna tells me you're a wonderful partner."

Preening like a peacock, Dwight brushed his longish bangs from his forehead. "I am. Of course, it helps if the girl's good too." He puffed out his chest. "Rayna and I make an excellent duo." He straightened his napkin. "You wouldn't know if she has a boyfriend, would you?"

Ira smiled. "She told me she's too busy for boys, but..." He let his smile widen. "She really likes you."

Sorda pushed back his chair. "Enough gossip. Esán and I have work to do. Dwight, why don't you show Ira to your suite. You can watch a movie or something. We'll be a couple of hours."

The beginnings of a stubborn glower tugged at Dwight's mouth. A stern, no nonsense look from his uncle sent it into retreat.

"Ah, sure. Come on, Ira."

When they reached the suite, Ira surveyed the room. "It sounds like you have things to do, Dwight. I had a pretty rough day yesterday, so a nap sounds mighty good." He rubbed his throbbing thumb and hid a grimace with a full-bodied yawn.

Dwight's eyes glinted. "I'll be back in an hour."

"Sounds good." Ira trailed him to the door.

He reined in the impulse to search for hidden recording devices and headed to the bathroom, locking the door behind him.

The change from Ira left Ari doubled over. Her rapid breathing gradually slowed to normal. She stared at a feminine hand gripping her knee and sighed. *I thought I had longer—* Footsteps in the suite jolted her upright.

The shift back to Ira sent a hissed breath between barred teeth. A shudder ran through his body. *Steady, Ira Raast. You've got a role to play.* With one more calming inhale, he flushed the toilet, washed his hands, and moseyed into the sitting area.

Dwight's head jerked up. His guilty gaze darted from the backpack in his hand to Ira's face. "I thought..." He dropped it on the settee.

Ira folded his arms. "If you wanted to search my pack, all you had to do was ask. I'm curious. What did you expect to find besides underwear and socks?"

Dwight blinked. "I found it on the floor." He shrugged. "Just picked it up."

Ira didn't move. "I see. Thanks. Thought you had work to do."

"I changed my mind. Wanna watch a movie?"

Clenching his teeth to squelch a response he knew he would regret, Ira gathered up his belongings. "I think I'll take that nap. See ya later." He escaped to the relative safety of the bedroom.

Conscious of the fact Dwight watched via a mini cam, he dumped the contents of the pack on the uncluttered twin bed. Making a show of refolding underwear and a clean shirt, he repacked and set the backpack on a chair. A sizable yawn directed his attention to the bed. His thoughts masked with fatigue, he lay down. An occasional snore floated through the room. In a distant corner of his mind, he wondered if he would get any sleep during his stay at The Plaza.

22

The hand released Gar's shoulder; his rescuer's soft breathing ceased. Gar knelt beside Spyglass, his hand still gripping his collar. Alert yet unafraid, he assessed his surroundings. *We're alone, Spy. But where?* He squinted. *Not in the pass-through.* His nose wrinkled at the aromas of sweaty bodies, a musty smell he did not recognize, and the subtle scent of a flowery perfume.

He whispered. "No noise, Spy. Stay."

The small dog dropped to his haunches.

Something prickly brushed Gar's bare arm. A thrill of fear shot him to his feet. His hand touched silky fabric. Tiptoeing forward in the pitch black, he tripped. Small, black wheels rolled over smooth linoleum. The soft swish of silk against silk whispered. He froze, alert and rigid with anticipation.

Quiet footsteps passed his hiding place. A single light came on. Metal scrapped the floor. Gar peered around the end of a rack of frilly dresses. A work lamp glimmered beside a mirror. On a chair in front of it sat the most beautiful woman he had ever seen. Her gleaming sapphire blue eyes observed his every move. Silver-blonde hair pinned up in a low bun highlighted the peaches and cream of her fair skin. Her dazzling smile, when she caught his eye, left him breathless.

From behind the rack of dresses, he calmed his racing thoughts.

"You can come out, Gar. I am a friend of Corvus. My name is Mira."

The melody inherent in the words tantalized his musician's heart. Still, he hesitated. A laugh trilled a soft song. He peeked around the end of the rack. Spyglass gazed up at the woman, tongue hanging out and tail wagging.

She caressed his small chin. "Hello, sweet pup."

Gar took a shy step into the open. She angled a chair away from the mirror and patted the seat. "Come sit down. I promise not to hurt you. Perhaps it will help if you realize I am related to Brie and Ari, like you are to Torgin."

He moved closer. "Ya know Esán and..." He waited.

She smiled. "I have known Esán since he was a boy, but have not met Penee."

He perched on the chair, ready to run. "Corvus brought me here, right?"

"He did."

Gar noted the row of mirrors and racks filled with costumes. "Are we in the theater?"

"We are. I work as a costume mistress. But you mustn't—"

"Tell anyone I met ya." He gripped the sides of the metal chair and squirmed backward. "Wish someone would tell me stuff."

"What would help you the most, Garon?"

"Ya know about me?"

She smiled. "I know lots of things."

After digesting her response, he counted off on his fingers. "I wanna understand where you're all from, what Corps Stones are, why Upori wants them, and why Dwight is a threat ta me. I need ta understand more about who I am." He curled his fingers into fists. "I'm only eleven going on twelve, but I'm part of this." The defiance in his voice made him glance at her from under his lashes.

She offered her hand. "If you will trust me to take us to a safe place, I'll answer all your questions."

He glanced around. "Where's Corvus?"

"He's taking care of Esán and Ira."

A narrow-eyed examination of the beautiful face, a nudge from his instincts, and Spyglass jumping onto Mira's lap cemented his decision. He took her hand. The theater dressing room disappeared.

E sán sat at a paper-littered table in Karl Sorda's study, his finger marking a passage in a book on Einstein's Theory of Relativity. Though important to the scientific community in 1969, it had, in the future, evolved beyond recognition. He found it fascinating to compare where it began to how it developed over the centuria.

Karl worked at his desk, his attention focused on a set of blueprints. He glanced up. "How did you get to New York City 1969, Nesá?"

"I beg your pardon, sir." Esán swiveled to observe the man over his shoulder.

"How did you come to be here and now?" The man's face showed no expression.

"I was born in 1950, thus my arrival in 1969." He smiled at his own humor. "I flew to New York on a plane. Why?"

"Dwight tells me you are not what you seem."

Esán shrugged. "I just met Dwight. I'm surprised I interest him at all."

Karl folded the blueprints and slipped them with a notebook into a large manila envelope. "Why do you think I want you to research space-time?"

"You have been unclear about your goals, sir, so I'm not sure. The theory of relativity fascinates me. I'm also intrigued by the impact of sound and light on time, and vice versa. That's why I accepted your offer. If you've changed your mind—"

"I haven't changed my mind, Nesá." Karl sighed. "Michael Mazer's behavior has made me suspicious of everyone. Although he came to us highly recommended, he's become a liability." Sorda smoothed his mustache. Piercing eyes fastened on Esán. "He's interested in you. Why?"

Esán frowned. "I have no idea, sir. We only met the other day when he interviewed me in his suite."

Staring into the distance, Sorda frowned. Restless fingers drummed the edge of the desk. He rose, picked up the envelope, and handed it to Esán. "See what you make of these."

Esán cleared a place and withdrew the blueprints. He set the envelope aside. The crinkling sound of the plans unfolding brought an eager expression to his face. He laid them on the desktop and stood to get a better look. Eagerness deteriorated to confusion. "What is it, sir? I've never seen anything quite like it." He lowered onto his seat and glanced at his boss, who regarded him with the intensity of a hawk analyzing prey.

Karl Sorda folded his arms. "Michael is the only one who can interpret these plans. Lately, something has distracted him from the work I hired him to do. We need to find him." He refolded the plans and stuffed them in the envelope. "The next time he calls, I plan to tell him you're here."

Esán tapped a pencil against the tabletop. "Are you using me as bait?"

"Mazer's help is vital to our work. Once he is back under my care, you may return to the research lab at Fordham." He placed the envelope in the desk drawer. "Until then, please work with the resources provided for you here."

"Am I to assume I'm in protective custody? What about Ira? Can he go back to the apartment?"

Sorda's sardonic smile said more than his words. "We wouldn't want to put Ira in danger, would we? I've ordered dinner from a restaurant recommended by the hotel manager. They should deliver it soon. Please bring your friend and Dwight and join me." He strode from the study.

With his thoughts scrambling, Esán rolled the pencil between his fingers and thumb, held it up, and placed it in the book to mark his place. Allowing only thoughts of collecting Ira to traipse through his mind, he ambled across the hall to the suite he shared with Dwight.

Torgin sat at the piano, playing the song he and Gar had composed. After the umpteenth repetition, he performed a series of arpeggios. Frustration made his fingers uncooperative. With a loud sigh, he lowered the fallboard.

The need to find Gar boiled over. Straddling the bench, he clenched and unclenched his fists. *If he weren't alright, I'd know. If—*

A faint oval the height of a man intensified beside the Taylor guitar. Torgin jumped to his feet, his eyes fixed on the portal's steady whirl. The center grew filmy. A sharp bark penetrated into the room. Spyglass leapt free. Gar darted after him and threw his arms around Torgin.

"Are you alright, Gar? Where have you been?"

"He's been with me, Torgin."

His chin jerked up. The warmth of Almiralyn's smile washed over him. Behind her, the portal vanished.

Brie pushed the door ajar. "Aunt Mira!" She embraced her aunt. "How did you get here? Teleport?"

Mira grew serious. "We didn't teleport. Dwight is far too sensitive to signature currents. Please remember that. I created a temporary portal to obscure our presence."

Penee arrived in the doorway. "Gar! We've been so worried."

Gar hugged her. "Almiralyn brought me home. Mira, this is Penee." He grinned. "We share a destiny."

Mira's smile lit up the room. "I am so glad to meet you at last, Penesert."

Penee looked bemused but happy. "I'm glad to meet you, too."

Torgin squeezed Gar's hand. "I suggest we move to the front room where we can get comfortable. I imagine we have lots to share."

Torgin listened to Gar's story. He shuddered at the idea of the Mindeco so close to him. *Thank goodness for Corvus.*

When Gar finished, Almiralyn regarded each member of the group in turn. "I can't stay long. Please listen. Esán and Ira are being held at The Plaza. Dwight senses Esán is more than he seems. Ira will be the next to come to his notice. We need to help extricate them *without* destroying their cover. Any suggestions?"

Brie rubbed her chin. "We could leave a message at the front desk."

Torgin shook his head. "He has established the fact that he's alone except for Ira. Who would call?"

Penee tugged at her hair. "Wendi might call. Perhaps she's getting to NY a day earlier than expected; perhaps she expects them to meet her at the airport."

"That sounds good." Torgin puckered his lips in thought. "How did she discover Ira is at The Plaza?"

"He called to tell her where to contact him." Penee grinned. "They are pretty close, after all."

Almiralyn raised delicate brows. "Why would Wendi be arriving early?"

Torgin jumped in. "I know! They've called a special rehearsal for the Central Park gig."

Brie shook her head. "Dwight can check that out."

Almiralyn moved to the window. "Corvus has made a contact in a recording studio near 57th Street and Broadway. What if Wendi is arriving early to meet with a company rep about a potential recording contract?"

Corvus walked into the room. "What if Rayna calls and asks Ira to call her? I believe it is important to keep Dwight away from Penee."

Mira tipped her head to gaze up at him. "And you've been eavesdropping how long?"

He chuckled and hugged her. "I've been close. When you mentioned a recording, I decided it was time to add my, uh, 'two cents worth,' as they say in 1969 New York." He passed a business card to Brie. "Give this number to Ira. Dwight is sure to be listening. Arthur, my contact, will confirm the company's existence as well as Ira and Wendi's appointment."

Brie placed the card on the desk by the phone. "How do we get Karlsut to cut Esán loose?"

Corvus put an arm around Almiralyn's waist. "That will depend on Michael Mazer's next move." His eyes narrowed. "Please open the portal, Mira, we need to go."

A faint oval took shape. Almiralyn handed Brie an envelope. "The address and keys to Ira and Esán's new 'digs'. Tell them this apartment is off limits."

Corvus nudged her ahead of him and followed her into the whirling light. The faint words "we'll be in touch" melted along with the gateway.

Gar shook his head. "She promised me answers." He peeked up at Torgin. "You gonna fill me in, or do I have ta keep feelin' lost?"

Torgin glanced from Brie to Penee. "What do you think, ladies?"

Brie leaned back in her chair and put her feet up on a footstool. "I believe it's time. What do you think, Pen?"

"Is the Mindeco still close?"

"Nope." Brie crossed her ankles. "He disappeared right after Gar vanished."

Penee curled her legs under her. "Then now is the perfect time."

Gar flashed a wide grin.

Torgin pulled him down on the couch. "Okay, what do you want to know?"

Gar took a deep breath. "Everything."

Torgin laughed. "Everything is a lot." His eyes twinkling, he tapped his chin. "Let me see... Where to begin?"

Esán entered the shared suite to find Dwight stretched out on the sofa, watching a television movie and the phone ringing.

Dwight swung his feet to the floor and strode across the room. "Hello? One moment." He held out the receiver. "Nice timing. It's for you."

Esán listened. "Yes, this is Nesá Zervos." He paused, picked up a pencil, and scribbled on the notepad provided by The Plaza. "I'll see that he gets the message. Thank you." He hung up and folded the note in half.

"Who was that?" Dwight's tone sounded more like a command than a question.

Esán fought the desire to make a terse, none-of-your-business reply. Ira, walking from the bedroom smothering a yawn, saved him.

"Did I hear a phone ring, or was I dreaming?"

Esán handed him the note. "It was the front desk. Rayna left a message. Wendi called. She's arriving late tomorrow night." He grinned. "Your sister, with the help of your agent, arranged an audition with a recording company Monday afternoon."

Ira looked stunned. "Wow! She's been busy." His shoulders sagged. "Will it be safe to leave the hotel?" He paced the room and plopped down on the sofa. "What's her flight schedule? I need to meet her at the airport."

Dwight's look of disbelief morphed into a pleasant smile. "When you said you were a folk singer, I didn't realize you were that good. We can talk to Uncle Karl. Bet he'll help you figure things out."

Esán watched Dwight observing Ira. Suspicion lurked at the back of his eyes, but he held himself in check. *What are you waiting for, Dwight Anders?*

As though he felt Esán's suspicious observation, Dwight switched his attention. "Why didn't Rayna call the room?"

Esán shrugged. "She probably doesn't know the number."

"I would have thought you'd give it to her." Dwight looked ready to pounce.

"Why? We hardly know each other. *You* could give it to her. I gather she's developing kind of a crush—"

A soft knock propelled Dwight across the room. "Where are we? Grand Central Station?" He pulled the door open.

Jonas made no move to enter. "Mr. Sorda asks that you join him."

Dwight opened the door wider. "Let's go, roomies. Dinner is waiting, and so is the solution to your predicament."

By the time Esán and Ira followed him into the corridor, Jonas waited to escort them into The Penthouse.

Karl greeted their arrival with a pleasant smile. "Dwight, I need to confer with you in the study. Esán and Ira, please make yourself comfortable in the sitting room. We will join you shortly."

Esán crossed to the windows and peered out over Central Park. "Come look at the view, Ira."

The assumption they were being spied on kept them from doing more than oohing and ahing over the park's beauty.

Ira pointed. "Ever since I arrived in New York, I've wanted to ride in a horse-drawn carriage. I might take Wendi in one as her welcome to the city."

The distant ring of a phone made them exchange glances. A short time later, Sorda preceded his nephew from the office. "Dwight's been telling me about Wendi's arrival and your interview. Let's talk over dinner. I'm betting we can find a creative way to distract Michael so you can attend the meeting. Of course, your sister should come to The Plaza for her own safety." He sat down and spread his pristine linen napkin across his lap.

Dinner proved to be an interesting meal. Great food from a fancy French restaurant presented with an elegant flair by a French waiter provided the backdrop for a game of dodge the question. The game played with fierce finesse by all involved ended in a draw.

Sorda and Dwight withdrew to the study for a brandy. Esán and Ira retired to their suite, where Esán stood guard while Ira slipped into the bathroom and shifted to Ari. When he returned to the bedroom, Ira announced, "I'm going for a walk. Tell Karl I'll be back in a half hour."

Esán stood up. "I'll go with you."

As they exited the room, Dwight stormed from The Penthouse. "Sometimes my uncle infuriates me. Where do you think you're going?"

"For a walk. Wanna come?" Esán held his breath.

"Great idea. Maybe I'll be able to walk off some of my anger." He strode to the elevator and pushed the button.

Ira paused. "You two go. I changed my mind."

Dwight smiled. "You'd think you didn't like me." He blocked the door from closing.

Esán linked his arm through Ira's. "Fresh air will do you good. We won't be gone long."

The strained ride to the first floor took an eternity. In the foyer, a doorman met them. "Mr. Anders?"

Dwight's scowl tainted his reply. "Yes."

The man handed him a note and departed.

He read it and stuffed it in his pocket. "I wouldn't leave the building if I were you." He hurried to the elevator.

23

To the faint strains of a piano/guitar duet, Brie paced from the window to the sofa and back. "The weekend is slipping away." A frown tugged. "We haven't even begun our search for Upori." She stared at 72nd Street. "I wonder how much longer the Mindeco will stay in his body. If he leaves it, will he take another one or hide or... Stop it!" She exclaimed through tightened jaws.

"Stop what?" Penee stood in the archway. "Are you okay?"

Brie flopped on the couch. "I'm worried. Esán and Ira are in more danger than we know. They're at The Plaza; we're here." With a frustrated groan, she folded her arms.

Penee lowered into an overstuffed chair. Hugging a throw pillow, she gave her a sympathetic smile. "You're in turmoil. How can I help?"

"Find Rikell. He's the key to everything."

Penee drummed her fingers on her knee. "We don't even know where to begin our search."

Brie smoothed her long, red hair into a ponytail, looped it through an elastic band, and gripped her knees. "We know he's hanging out near The Plaza. I'm not sure why, but he's fixated on Esán. Not only that, I bet the Corps Stones are close to the hotel. If we could lure Rikell into the open, we might convince him to help us."

Torgin watched from the entryway with Gar peering around him. Spyglass poked his head between them. "Did I hear the name Rikell?"

"You did." Brie patted the sofa.

The frisky terrier jumped up. Gar plopped down beside him.

Torgin sprawled in the chair next to Penee. "Let's have it, Brielle. What's the latest."

"If we're going to help Esán and Ira *and* recover the Corps Stones, we need to find the Mindeco. Penee and I think he is most likely hiding near The Plaza." She scratched Spyglass under his chin. "How do we lure him into the open? If we do, will he work with us?"

"Or if he's unwilling to play our game..." Torgin stretched out his long legs. "How do we neutralize him?"

Gar scooched to the edge of the sofa. "I have an idea. I told ya how Gin and I used ta perform on street corners, right? Torgin and me can dress raggedy and play in the park near the hotel. You girls can disguise yourselves as audience members. Ya told me Rikell could smell ya. If he's close, he might come out of hidin'."

Torgin nodded and flashed a knowing smile. "The Mindeco prefers not to have an audience for its antics. Gar and I will definitely draw a crowd, so we'll be a bit safer. Right, Gar?"

"Right. We can't use the Taylor guitar though 'cause it's way too nice, so we'll have ta collect Gin's. Ya could play the silver flute, your wooden one, or I gotta harmonica. I hid some of Gin's old clothes with the guitar. Ya can dress up so ya'll look like a street guy. What do ya think?"

Brie reviewed the details of the plan. "You two portray street people and play music in the park closest to The Plaza. Penee and I disguise ourselves as audience in the hopes my scent will coax Rikell/Upori to show himself."

She leaned back, her eyes closed. Wispy memories focused: sitting on the Throne of Netydis, images of Central Park, a musician playing a guitar— The vision ended, obscured by thick fog. She sat upright.

"It's a good idea." Brow wrinkled in concentration, she stared at the far wall. "But it doesn't feel quite right. I saw this event on Netydis. Just now, fog obscured something important." Uncertainty nudged. "I'm unable to sense the outcome. Do you think we should consider something else?"

Torgin shifted in his chair. "Gar has an excellent idea. Let's tentatively plan on executing it tomorrow. If we wake up feeling it's still a decent plan, we go. If we are uncertain, we don't. What do you think, Penee?"

She ran her hands along the smooth arms of her chair. "I agree with you, it's a good idea. Terrific work, Garon. If we decide to move forward with it, Brie, will you go as Rayna or Brielle?"

"Brielle, but somewhat disguised. We don't want to alert Dwight and Karl to Brie's presence in New York by accident." She regarded Penee with an inquisitive smile. "What about you? It's not safe to walk down the streets looking like Penesert. Skultar and Karlsut may dislike each other, but I bet they've discussed you."

Torgin turned to Penee. "Has Karlsut ever seen you?"

"I don't remember him." She frowned. "I would have had to be pretty young if he visited. I know he didn't come to my proxy parents' manor or to the prison on TaSneach."

Brie leaned forward. "Do you recall where you were before your cousin found you and placed you with Barlet and Coranna?"

Penee's nostrils flared. She flinched as though struck. "I only remember dark, filth, rough hands, and a voice filled with anger." She shook herself. "I doubt Karlsut was anywhere near. He grew up on Roahymn with a wealthy family."

Gar moved to her side, his gaze filled with such knowing Penee pulled him closer and rested her cheek on his head. "Thank you, Garon, for understanding."

A wave of empathy washed over Brie. "I didn't mean to bring up painful memories, Pen."

A tremulous smile surfaced, bringing a touch of color back to her friend's paled cheeks. "We all have things we'd prefer not to remember. Even unscrupulous people like Skultar and Karlsut have dealt with sorrow and loss." She hugged herself. "Let's change the subject. I'd rather concentrate on tomorrow's masquerade. I can't imagine my hair into another style like the boys, but I can make myself seem older."

The conversation grew animated. Details emerged. A plan evolved. Gar and Torgin left to retrieve Gin's belongings. Like a couple of giggling schoolgirls, Brie and Penee prepared to make a trip to a thrift store. In the building lobby, Brie handed Penee her dark glasses and ushered her through the lobby door into a waiting cab. Nose pressed to the window, Penee murmured soft sounds of surprise.

The West Side Thrift Store was huge. Brie took a deep breath and opened the door. Penee froze. Swallowing her own nervousness, Brie linked an elbow through her friend's. Soon, they rummaged through racks and shelves like they had done it all their lives. Brie grinned as they held up a variety of clothing for each other's approval and changed their minds a dozen times.

Penee caught her eye. "Are you having as much fun as I am?"

Brie laughed. "It almost feels like a holiday." She held gold loops up to her ears. "How about these?"

"Pretty cool." Penee set a wide-brimmed hat on her head. Red and white flowers decorated the rim. "This reminds me of your Aunt Henrietta." She grinned. "I'll get it."

They completed their rummaging by purchasing two shopping bags full. A short, giddy cab ride later, they entered their building to find the elevator waiting.

Penee leaned against the metal wall. "My initiation into the big city..." She hugged her bag to her chest. "It was much easier than I expected. I'm worried about tomorrow. Will it be overwhelming?"

The elevator came to a halt. Brie escorted her into the corridor. "You'll do great."

A grinning Gar pulled open the apartment door. The aroma of dinner drifted into the hallway. Soon, they all sat around at the kitchen table, eating Torgin's excellent cooking.

Brie chewed a bite of chicken and licked her lips. "This is amazing. What is it and how do you know what to cook?"

Penee chimed in. "You just get better and better, Torgin. What's your secret?"

"I explored Maggie's cookbooks and found this." He reached behind him.

Brie read the title. "*The Graham Kerr Cookbook by The Galloping Gourmet.*" She surveyed her plate. "So, what are we eating."

Eyes twinkling, Torgin flipped through the pages. "We are feasting on Chicken Whakatane and Otaki Potatoes. Pretty good, huh! I had no idea how much fun it is to cook. It's so..." He pursed his lips, then nodded. "It's creative, kinda like writing a music composition but using different skills and different materials."

Gar munched a potato. "This is yummy, Torgin! Will ya teach me how ta cook?"

Torgin stroked his chin. "I could certainly use a sous chef."

"What's that?" Gar stuffed another potato in his mouth.

"It's the assistant to the head chef. What do you think?"

The boy swallowed and grinned from ear to ear. "I think it sounds cool." Held out his plate. "More, please."

The companions, their expressions amused, returned their attention to their meal.

Brie finished the last bite on her plate and sighed. "What a long, full day. I gleaned more information about this culture at the thrift store than from all the books in the Galactic Library. I've never seen so much stuff in one place in my life." She laughed.

Torgin cleared her plate. "What made the biggest impression?"

"The variety of selections... In Idronatti, the PPP provided us with things specific to our level in the status quo: uniforms, furniture in the same colors, specifically designed toys, the food we ate. We never got to choose anything ourselves. At the thrift store, I realized how lucky people are to make their own choices. They get to wear what they enjoy in whatever color suits their mood, eat from mismatched dishes if they want, select their own furnishings, even paint their own walls. Do you know how many books on different topics we discovered? Oh, and musical instruments and figurines and lamps and jewelry and scarves and..." She threw her hands in the air. "Wow."

Penee, her demeanor thoughtful, rubbed a pale hand through her hair. "It never occurred to me that my erratic life provided opportunities to be myself. My proxy parents may have disliked my choices sometimes, but they let me make them." She sighed. "Skultar was a different story all together."

Brie drew in a breath. "Ari and I were lucky. Our mother encouraged us to be individuals."

Torgin placed dishes of chocolate ice cream on the table. "I lived under the close scrutiny of the PPP, but then I met Ari and Brie and gained two friends who became like sisters." He kissed Brie's cheek. "What a fortuitous break that was!"

Gar had listened with a rapt expression. "We've all had hard times, huh? I thought 'cause ya all can do neat stuff like teleport, your lives must be easier than mine. They haven't been though, have they?"

Torgin held up a spoonful of ice cream. "A toast to lessons learned and the wonderful friends who helped us out."

Brie raised her spoon, saw the love in Torgin's eyes, Penee's happiness, and Gar's delight to be part of a family who cared. "Here, Here."

After they washed their new clothes in the basement laundromat and folded them for the next day's masquerade, the girls crawled into bed and set alarms for early Sunday morning.

Penee murmured a sleepy goodnight.

Brie lay in bed, reviewing the happenings of the day. She marveled at how making plans to find the Mindeco, a trip to the thrift store, and talking over dinner had strengthened the bonds of friendship among four such different people. Penee's reticence to become a part of anything had melted. Gar's fear of abandonment disappeared. Torgin's blossoming leadership skills helped to bind the group together. *What of me... How have I changed?* She rolled onto her side. *I guess time will tell.* She drifted toward sleep. *Time, so intangible yet real, is how it all began.*

Esán stared after Dwight's disappearing figure, answers falling into place like tumblers in a lock.

Beside him, Ira's gaze flicked from Dwight to him. "What's going on?"

Esán nudged him into motion. Ambling through the foyer, he stopped to peer in a florist shop window. "I believe Upori has made a move. Let's go inside."

Ira walked to a display of spring flowers. "Do you think he's close?"

Esán stiffened. "More than close." He tugged Ira with him behind a carousel of floral bouquets. "See the man with the bristly hair and stubble?"

Between roses and lilies, they watched Upori's eyes darting from side to side.

Ira groaned. "He's got our scent, hasn't he?"

"He does." Esán kept his tone even.

"Can't we teleport?"

"I wish we could." Esán spoke in an undertone. "Remember, no teleporting. Not only will Upori feel it, so will Dwight."

A dark-haired man moved from behind the counter. A dimple in his right cheek deepened. "This way, please."

Esán nudged Ira ahead of him. They stopped in front of a row of refrigerator units.

The man's dimple smoothed. He nodded toward an exit door. His forbidding expression blocked any discourse. "If you'll excuse me, I am about to have a customer."

Esán opened the door wide enough to side-step into the hall beyond.

Ira slipped through after him and pulled it shut. He looked back. "How'd Corvus know?"

Esán shook his head. "Come on."

With the stealth of a soldier on patrol, he led Ira to a service entrance marked D&J Fine Jewelry. Easing the door open, he discovered a narrow, dim room lined with shelves stacked high with merchandise. Nothing triggered his internal alarm, so he tiptoed to the curtain covering the entryway to the main shop.

Ira peered over his shoulder.

Except for a young woman arranging jewelry in a case, the store appeared to be empty. A shout in the foyer drew her attention to the lobby windows.

Esán hustled to a display case near the door.

Outside, Dwight towered over Upori. Sorda, a hypodermic in hand, made several futile attempts to get closer. Two doormen hurried toward them. Upori's angry shout stopped them in their tracks. He threw his full body weight into Dwight. Athletic quickness came to the younger man's rescue as he caught himself mid-way to the floor. Without breaking stride, Upori ran for the main entrance, knocked a surprised doorman to his knees, and dashed into the busy evening gloom.

Sorda and Dwight, cornered by the hotel manager, followed him through the dispersing crowd to his office.

The clerk turned. Surprise flashed into doubt. "You weren't in here before the—"

"That was crazy." Esán gave her a wide-eyed stare. "We barely made it into the shop in time."

Ira flashed her a startled smile. "Wow! Weird!" He strode toward the exit. "Better hustle. Don't want Mom to worry."

Esán nodded to the astonished salesclerk and hurried after him.

Near the elevators, Ira regarded him with a slight frown. "Now what? Do we go or stay or—" His agitation made his voice hoarse.

"We don't want to blow our cover." Esán shrugged. "If we don't stay, we'll never know what Upori threatened them with or where the Corps Stones are or who their boss is."

Ira nudged him. "They're coming. I'll follow your lead."

Esán hurried toward them. "Dwight, are you okay? We saw Michael Mazer almost run you over."

Dwight scowled. "I'm fine. That idiot—"

Sorda cleared his throat. "We can talk upstairs." He pushed the button to summon the elevator. His anger built as he watched the numbers indicating that the car halted at every floor. Finally, it arrived in the lobby. An elderly couple toddled out. Sorda marched in. Dwight nudged Ira ahead of him and followed Esán. Tension built as the car trundled upward, stopping for passengers along the way.

At The Penthouse level, Sorda held himself in check until the doors closed. Eyes narrowed, he glared from one boy to the other. "Nesá and Ira, get some sleep. We'll talk in the morning. Nephew, come with me." The door to The Penthouse Suite slammed behind them.

Ira stared at it with disgust. "What's next?"

Esán yawned. "I suggest we follow Sorda's suggestion. Tomorrow is going to be interesting."

A sharp pain in his thumb woke Ira from a deep sleep. He considered shifting shape in bed, but thought better of it. His bare feet, soundless on the thick carpet, he stumbled to the bathroom. One small nightlight cast a yellow pool on the marble countertop. He gripped the rounded edge and smothered a groan. The temptation to shift without hiding sent gooseflesh flying over his skin. *Better safe than sorry, Ira Raast.* Unsteady legs carried him to the shower.

The darkness magnified the strangeness of the shift to Ari. She leaned against the cool tile, trying to remember why she was there. A line of light appearing at the bottom of the bathroom door triggered a panicked shift that sent a confused Ira darting from the shower to the counter.

The door handle turned. Dwight's silhouette filled the doorway. He flipped on the light switch. "What are you doing?"

Ira blinked in the sudden brightness and held up a toothbrush. "What does it look like I'm doing?" He took a gulp of water, swished, and spit. "Did you even consider knocking?"

Dwight shot him a dirty look. Facing Esán, who sat on the side of the bed, looking half asleep, he announced, "Breakfast at nine o'clock. See you both then." He marched from their room, slamming the door with a loud bang.

Ira shot Esán a wide-eyed stare. "What was that all about?"

Esán spoke through a yawn that disguised a wink. "Guess he thought he'd lost you."

Ira flipped off the bathroom light. "When can we go back to our place?" He plopped down on the bed.

The dull thud of fists plumping a pillow into a new configuration camouflaged the single whispered word, 'soon'. Esán squirmed onto his side. "Karl will let us know when it's safe. Get some sleep."

The soft sound of the air conditioner mingled with Esán's intermittent snores. Ira stared at nothing in particular, rehashing the events of the day. Something kept nagging at him. *Upori could have gotten to us in the floral shop. Was it Corvus' presence that stopped him? Or did he lure Karl and Dwight downstairs?* He rolled over.

Was the earlier phone call from Upori? Ira forced himself to lie motionless while his mind jumped from one thought to the next. *I bet they had an appointment to meet. Did Sorda's arrival with a hypodermic ready to use alert him to trouble?* He bit his lower lip. *No. I'm sure he knew Sorda would try to trick him.*

Ira replayed Upori's escape: the impact of his middle-aged, out of shape body against Dwight's younger, dancer's physique; Dwight's missed attempt to grab him; Upori's escape into the night. *Was it a setup?* He recalled the surprised anger on Dwight's face and Sorda's obvious frustration.

Rolling onto his side, he stifled a yawn. *"Upori wasn't after us. Ten to one Sorda will tell us a different story in the morning."*

24

The next morning, after a tasty breakfast, Brie retired to choose her attire for the day. Frowning at the pile of discards on the bed, she donned her fourth outfit and faced the mirror. "Not bad. Better hide that red hair, though." Deft fingers wrapped a minty green silk scarf around her head and the low bun by her left ear. She fastened on a gold and malachite choker. The large gold loops she purchased at the thrift store glinted in the room's artificial light.

She rotated, checking every detail. A jumpsuit in green, a shade darker than her scarf, accented the curves of her slender body. The cap-sleeved, scoop-necked top buttoned up the front. The shorts, known as hot pants, were much skimpier than she would normally wear. She raised a brow at her reflection. "Today isn't normal, is it?"

With a slight smile, she regarded her knee-high, black leather boots. The two-inch stacked heals made her appear taller and her legs longer. The smile became a grin. "This is sure better than wearing the same blue uniform day after day."

Her critical eye examined her shapely legs. "They're too pale for hot pants." She pictured her skin a nice golden tan and felt a wave of satisfaction as it changed.

Twisting to see herself from all sides, she smiled at her reflection. "Sure wish Esán could see me today."

She picked up her hat, woven yellow-gold straw with a wide green band, and grabbed her shoulder bag as the bathroom door opened and Penee strutted into the room.

"I love your outfit, Brielle." She spun around. "Will I do?"

Penee wore her long hair loose. Her white and red flowered blouse cinched in at the waist with a long red scarf matched her ankle-length skirt. Low-heeled red sandals minimized her height. On her wrist, several bangles shimmered. She sported three rings on each hand. Her dragonfly earrings complimented the dragonfly tattooed on her bare shoulder.

Brie clapped her hands in delight. "All I can say is wow!"

"How old do I look?"

"Early thirties, maybe." Brie cocked her head. "Your eyes match."

"Learned to put in a contact lens." She settled her hat at an angle on her shiny, long hair. "Let's show the boys, shall we?" She opened the door to the strains of flute and guitar floating down the hallway.

Like models on a catwalk, they paraded into the living room.

"Wow!" Gar gaped. "You're two super cool-lookin' chicks!"

Torgin played a long trill. "I'll say!" Arms wide, he pivoted to show off his costume. "Will I pass for a street musician?"

Brie circled the boys. Both had longer hair. Torgin, who appeared to be in his mid-thirties, sported the beginnings of a mustache and a couple days' growth of stubble on his chin. A younger looking Gar cast her a shy, vulnerable smile.

She grinned. "You look great. What do you think, Pen?"

"I want to hear 'em play." She sat on the arm of the sofa.

Gar strummed Gin's battered guitar. Torgin played the wooden flute made by Esán's father.

Brie blinked away tears of surprised delight. "I'm certain you'll draw a crowd. When do we leave?"

Gar put the guitar in a beat-up case and flipped the latches. "No one can see us together." He glanced up at his fellow musician. "Right, Torgin?"

"It's your plan, Garon. You call it."

Torgin's show of confidence produced a wide grin. "Okay. Torg and I go first. We'll take the subway. Since it's Penee's first time in the city proper, you two take a cab to the corner of Central Park South and Fifth Avenue. There's a path that'll lead ya to The Pond." He handed her a hand-drawn map and pointed. "I chose this open space so Upori can hide in the trees and 'cause there's room for a crowd ta gather." He glanced at the clock. "It's nine. We need ta be playin' by elevenish ta draw the lunch crowd."

Torgin pulled the One Man's sheepskin sheath from the custom flute case his father had given him and slid the wooden flute inside. "Excellent work, Gar. If Upori shows, we'll all follow our instincts. Nobody meets with him alone. Questions?"

Brie felt a wave of nostalgia. "You've sure changed, Torgin Whalend."

He grinned. "For the better, I hope."

She hugged him. "Definitely for the better. And you, Gar, are quite the strategist." She paused. "No questions come to mind, Torg. Penee, do you have any?"

"Is it possible to ride the subway part way? Then, if there's an emergency, I'll know what to expect."

"You two figure it out." Torgin looped the sheath's leather strap over his shoulder and picked up the guitar. We need to leave. Ready, Gar?"

"Sure am." He shrugged on a backpack and grinned. "See you at The Pond, ladies." Hurrying down the hall, he threw the three dead bolts. "We'll go out through the basement, Torgin. Wouldn't wanna worry the doorman, right?"

Torgin gave a soft snort. "Right, Gar. Lead the way." He kissed Brie on the cheek and hugged Penee. "Take care of each other. Spyglass, come."

Before either girl could respond, he was half-way to the elevator with Gar's terrier at his heels. Brie called after them. "You be careful." She slid the chain into place and followed Penee to the living room. "Since we're riding the subway part way, we'd better go."

Penee nodded. "What's your plan?"

"We'll ride the train to Lincoln Center. From there, we can catch a cab. It's Sunday, so it won't be too bad. Prepare yourself for lots of people and stay close to me." She handed her friend several subway tokens and some cash. "Put these in your purse. You did great yesterday with the money at the thrift store. We already talked about using tokens. Just do what I do. If we get separated, stay put. I'll find you. Got it?"

"Got it." Penee settled her sunglasses on her nose. "I'm nervous."

Brie grabbed her shoulder bag. "Better than being too cocky. Off to Lincoln Center we go."

Esán woke to the grating buzz of his alarm. Mumbled expletives accompanied him to the bathroom. He glared at his reflection. "Maybe, I'll feel ready to deal with Sorda after a long, hot shower. He stepped into the steamy cubicle and savored the hot water's cleansing effects. Dried, with the towel wrapping his waist, he wielded the hair dryer like a magic wand. Mesmerized by his long hair, he lowered the dryer to the counter. *I recall being bald because of the illness that almost ended my life.* He stared in the mirror. *I am so lucky to be symptom free.*

His serious face gazed back at him. He cleared his throat. "*Someday, I'll help children the way others helped me. That's a promise.*"

When he finished dressing, he took a final look in the mirror. *Bell bottoms, tie-dyed shirt, leather vest, ponytail...* He grinned. *I definitely look the part of a young artist in 1969.*

When he walked into the bedroom, Ira greeted him with the grumpy scowl of a petulant child.

"Good morning to you, Ira Raast. How d'you sleep?"

"Off and on. Done in the bathroom?"

"Yep. All yours. Take your time."

Ira slipped his feet into the slippers provided by The Plaza. Muttering about growing boys needing more sleep than he'd gotten, he shuffled into the bathroom. Moments later, he pulled open the door.

"Ya left some stuff behind. Better get it while you can."

Esán walked into the bathroom. Ira left the door partway open, then guided him to the far end of the counter.

"Gotta message: *The park. Near you. Today. Lunchtime.*" He handed him a couple of small bottles.

Esán nodded. "Thanks." He left, closing the door behind him.

With the sounds of the shower in the background, he considered the message. He knew about the twins' ability to share dreams. Fingers crossed that Dwight suspected nothing, he put on his shoes and prepared to meet with Sorda at breakfast.

Ira exited the bathroom, refreshed and happy. "Any idea what Karl plans to share this morning?"

Esán smiled at his friend's sudden mood change. "I guess we'll find out soon enough."

"Hey, I could help with the research you guys are doing. I'm pretty good at looking stuff up."

With his back to the recording device, Esán made a face. "Talk to Karl. He might take you up on it. Come on. Let's see if Dwight's ready to go."

Dwight had already left, so they crossed the hall and rang the bell.

Jonas answered. "Mr. Sorda and Mr. Anders are in the dining room." He shot them a warning glance and hurried away.

A silence, stretched thin by strain, met them when they entered the room. Karlsut Sorda greeted them with a tight smile. Dwight stood facing the window, his back tense and hands fisted.

Esán nudged Ira ahead of him. By the time they had filled their plates, Dwight had gone.

Sorda waited for them to sit down. "We ate earlier. Enjoy your breakfast. Then please join me in the study to discuss yesterday evening."

Silence, but for the intermittent click of sterling silver against fine china, reigned. Between bites, Ira shot fleeting looks at the door. Esán concentrated on eating. His thoughts alternated between what his boss might share and random thoughts about the food, Ira's loud chewing, and his desire to leave The Plaza behind. Sorda's strained relationship with his nephew did not bode well for anyone.

Across from him, Ira used toast to wipe up the remains of his eggs. He sat back, tossed his soiled napkin on the table, and heaved a satisfied sigh. "Tasty breakfast..."

Esán folded his napkin. "Shall we go see what Karl has to say?"

A soft knock on the study door brought an invitation to enter. Inside, they settled in chairs at Sorda's desk. Esán noted Dwight's continued absence and his uncle's strained demeanor.

The ticking of a grandfather clock seemed to magnify the uneasiness. Still, Sorda did not speak. Ira squirmed, rubbed his palms on his pants, and folded his arms across his chest. Esán cleared his throat. "Karl, why don't we come back later."

A piercing gaze moved from a pile of papers to examine his guests. Sorda sighed. "Dwight and I, as I am sure you can tell, have differing opinions on several things. Although I am his uncle, not his father, I helped to raise him. He's like a son to me. I'm finding that young men have minds of their own." He heaved another sigh. "Time will take care of it. Let's discuss Michael Mazer."

A brief pause lengthened into a tension-filled lapse in conversation. Sorda picked up a letter opener resembling an antique dagger, studied the intricate handle, touched the pointed tip, and laid it with careful precision on the desk. "Michael has expressed the desire to meet with you, Esán. You already know, he is having mental issues. When he called yesterday afternoon, he demanded I allow you to meet him alone. I, for obvious reasons, felt reluctant to do so.

"Dwight and I decided, rather than expose you to Mazer's unpredictability, it would be best to give him his injection. We planned to return him to his suite, where we could get him professional attention." He turned the letter opener over several times. "You saw the result of our attempt to help him. The hotel manager, though pleasant, has warned us Michael is no longer welcome at The Plaza, which leaves me with a dilemma. Michael is exceptional at what I hired him to do. He is, in fact, the best. I hate to lose his input on my project." He shook his head. "Hopefully, this helps you to understand why I want you under my care."

Esán heard truth and falsehood in Sorda's words. What he knew for certain—he and Ira were expendable. They needed to get out from under his thumb.

He raised innocent eyes to the man's face. "Thank you, sir, for sharing this with us. I imagine it's hard to know what to do next. I'm grateful for your willingness to protect me. However, my presence is taking its toll on your relationship with Dwight. Have you considered allowing me to work on this at Fordham and return to my apartment? We can schedule meetings bi-weekly or—"

"No." He came to his feet, the dagger-shape letter opener in his hand. "I want you here. That was our deal."

His eyes on the shaking point of the dagger, Esán rose. Ira, gasping in surprise, followed his example.

In the calmest voice he could muster, Esán said, "Mr. Sorda, I believe we should give you time to think about what is best for you. We'll be back in a while."

The opener clunked on the desk. Sorda's arms dropped to his side. Beady eyes narrowed. "Are you quitting, Nesá?"

"Well, sir, that depends on you. If you'll excuse us, we'll check back with you in an hour."

Inscrutability cloaked the man across from them. "How do I know I can trust you?" He hefted the dagger.

"Because, sir, we could have returned to our apartment on several occasions but honored your wish." Without waiting for Sorda's reply, he ushered Ira from the room.

25

Penee fought her escalating fear. The trip to the thrift store had proved manageable. An underground ride in an enormous city she didn't know inspired abject terror.

By the time they reached 72nd and Broadway, she stifled a panic attack in the making. Forcing herself to breathe, she gripped Brie's arm and glued on a smile. Together, they walked into the subway station.

"So many people." She almost choked on the whispered words.

Brie squeezed the hand on her arm. "Pretty overwhelming, huh? I grew up in a city, Pen, and New York still scares the heck out of me. Can you handle this, or should we return to the apartment?"

Penee swallowed her rising panic. "We can't turn back. I will do this." She sucked a long breath. "Give me a moment." Her gaze roamed the hustling throng. *They're just people. No one is after me.* A semblance of calm seeped over her. "I'm ready, Brielle. Lead the way."

Brie released her hand. "We're going downstairs and through the turnstiles onto the platform." Her brown eyes twinkled. "Don't forget to breathe. A little oxygen always helps."

Edging into the stream of humanity, they descended a steep cement stairway. People staring straight ahead hurried by, some hiking up the stairs; some scurrying down. At the bottom, lines formed at a row of turnstiles.

A boy dodging between Penee and her lifeline left her in panic mode. She peered through the crowd, caught sight of Brie's green scarf-covered head, and edged forward. A heavy-set woman cut in front of her, blocking Brie from view. Hysteria clawed.

Brie stepped into sight, her steady gaze demanding Penee's attention. She held up her token, then deposited it in the slot.

With a gulped breath, Penee followed her example, pushed through the turnstile, and stumbled to a stop.

"You gonna stand there all day, lady?"

The gravelly voice behind her jarred Penee into motion. She shot him an apologetic smile, fastened her attention on her companion, and moved to the side.

Brie clasped her arm. "We're going to walk down the platform. Stay close." With the ease of someone used to navigating crowded subways, she led the way through milling bodies, large and small.

The stench of human filth and urine wrinkled Penee's nose. Near her, an older man coughed open-mouthed, spewing spittle in the air. Brie edged her around a pile of dog feces to a spot at the edge of the platform. A young boy peeled paper from a sandwich, crumpled it, and tossed it on the ground. Penee hugged her bag close. *I need a shower.*

Strange, cartoon-like scribbles covering the stone walls added to the chaotic foreign atmosphere. She could almost see invisible protective barriers gleaming around the people scattered along the platform, their eyes staring straight ahead.

A loud clatter and a sustained whistle announced the approach of the train. Under cover of screeching breaks, Brie pulled her behind a metal scaffolding. "We're being followed."

Penee refrained from scanning the area. "Upori?"

"Not unless the Mindeco has taken another body. This is a younger, hippie-looking guy. I'll tell you if he gets on the train."

Brie's grip on her arm tightened. The metal doors slid apart. People poured onto the platform. Brie marched her into the car and nudged her onto a seat facing the front. Doors sliding shut, accompanied by a whooshing sound, preceded a jerk into motion that pressed Brie against her.

"Our pursuer is behind us: tall, patched bells, white blousy shirt, a leather vest with long fringe, and a matching leather headband. He's wearing sunglasses. Don't glance back until we stand to get off."

The train shot ahead, slowed, sped up, and eased into the next station. Penee studied the scribbled paintings. *Graffiti... I read about it.* She leaned closer to Brie. "How soon is our stop?"

"This is a local, so we're next. Hold on to me. We need to lose our escort."

Sooner than Penee expected, the breaks screeched, bringing the car to a jerky halt. The doors gaped wide. She clutched her bag and dodged onto the platform. Brie clasped her hand, pulled her around a corner, and up a flight of stairs. At the top, they ducked into a small cafe. Their pursuer jogged past, his head jerking one direction then the other.

Brie smiled at the man behind the counter. "Is there another way out?"

His eyes narrowed. "You in trouble?"

She shook her head. "We're dodging a guy who won't take no for an answer."

He looked them over. "I gotcha. Go out through the kitchen." He jerked his chin toward double doors. "Don't get underfoot."

Brie didn't hesitate. Penee, anxiety squeezing her throat, followed her through the swinging doors into a room bustling with activity and bursting with a variety of aromas. They skirted the high-traffic areas and dodged out the exit into a trash-strewn alley.

Penee looked around. "Where are we?"

"We're close to Lincoln Center. I planned to catch a cab there, but I think we're better off flagging one on Amsterdam Ave. We'll cut through the Juilliard School. If it's clear, we'll head west. Ready?"

"I'm right behind you." Penee sniffed her hand and grimaced. *I feel like I just walked through a garbage dump. Sure wish I could shower or, better yet, soak in a bath.* She picked up her pace and caught up with Brie at the end of the alley.

Brie sensed their tail getting closer. *Who are you?* She skirted a waist-high fence, led the way between buildings to 66th Street, and jaywalked to the Juilliard side of the street. A peek through the glass doors gave her the all-clear. She ducked inside.

Penee's soft breathing held a slight quiver. Brie gave her a quick hug. "We're fine; you're doing great. Let's catch a cab on 65th Street. Keep your eyes peeled. If you see our guy, grab my arm."

They walked down a narrow hallway to a wider corridor. After establishing her bearings, Brie strode toward the main entrance.

Penee squeezed her arm. "At the far end of the hall."

She guided Penee from the building as a yellow cab turned the corner. Stepping from the curb, she hailed it. Almost before it stopped, she had the door open. Penee climbed in.

Brie joined her. She leaned forward to give the driver instructions. "The northeast corner of Central Park South and Fifth Avenue, please." The cab eased into traffic. A backward glance provided her with the view of their hippie tail sprinting from the building to a standstill, his expression less than happy. Her alarm seeped away.

Beside her, Penee gazed out the window with the eager curiosity of a child. "You realize, Pen, being in a big city is good for you."

"Really?" Penee slid her sunglasses to the tip of her nose and peered over them. "Why?"

"The more you learn about what life offers, the stronger leader you will be. Have you thought about what you and Garon have ahead of you?"

"Not a day goes by that I don't wonder. Sometimes it scares me. More often, I feel anticipation at the possibilities."

The taxicab stopped at a red light. The driver looked in the rear-view mirror. "I can turn into the park at the Grand Army Plaza and drop you by the subway station?"

Brie's mind flashed to a mental map of Central Park. "That would be perfect."

Green flashed. The cab turned onto Fifth Avenue, made a quick left, and pulled into a parking spot. Penee climbed out.

Brie checked the meter and handed the driver a ten-dollar bill. "Keep the change. Thank you."

She stood with her friend, watching the cab pull away.

Penee regarded her through sunglass-dark lenses. "The fare wasn't that much, right?"

"I didn't want to wait for change; besides, he needs the money. The cab's clock said it's almost eleven." She tapped a spot on Gar's map. "We're here."

Penee peered over her shoulder, then pointed. "The path is over there."

Brie smiled as her friend took the lead. *The shock of the big city is wearing off.*

E sán led Ira past their suite to the waiting elevator. When they reached the reception area, he ambled down the hall to the main entrance, descended the steps to the sidewalk, and wandered toward the corner of Central Park South.

Ira sauntered beside him, his silence filled with questions. An occasional sideways glance told Esán his friend reined in the impulse to bombard him until they were a safe distance from The Plaza.

A yellow cab braked to a sudden stop at the crosswalk. Dwight hopped out. He shot a furtive glance at the hotel and hurried to block their way. "We need to talk."

His demeanor made Esán examine him with careful attention. Arrogance, a hallmark of Dwight's temperament, was absent. His usual condescending confidence morphed to uncertainty as Esán watched.

Ira scowled. "What if we don't want to talk to you, Dwight Anders?"

Esán laid a calming hand on Ira's arm and in a non-committal tone addressed their roommate. "Perhaps you can convince us what you have to say is important. Let's find a quiet place to talk."

Astonishment clamped Ira's mouth shut, though his expression telegraphed his desire to rebel.

A wordless Dwight nodded.

They crossed the street to the Fifth Avenue subway station and turned onto a shaded path heading toward The Pond. Esán pulled Ira down on a shaded bench, poised to listen. Dwight hesitated. He stood, clasping and unclasping trembling hands. His evasive gaze scrambled over the terrain. Jaw clenched, he sat down, rested his forearms on his knees, and stared at the ground.

"Karlsut Sorda is not my uncle. He's my foster mother's partner. Michael Mazer helped us to steal something important from another time and dimension. We transported it to New York City, 1969." He studied them with pleading eyes. "Please don't think I'm crazy. I am confiding in you because I'm positive you're not from 1969 either."

Confusion overwhelmed him. His attention riveted to the path, he murmured under his breath. "How do I know this?" He squinted into the distance. "I can sense others in the city, as well."

Conviction crept word-by-word into his voice. "Today, I went to the building where I'm pretty sure you live, hoping to discover something. Two women came out the front entrance. I recognized their energy like I recognize yours, Nesá." Hands shaking, he covered his face and moaned.

Esán kept his tone gentle. "Dwight, why are you telling us?"

He lowered his hands. "I overheard a conversation between Sorda and Mazer. They were negotiating a deal. They plan to sell what we stole and divide the spoils between them. Their goal is then to gain control of several powerful people. Mazer told Karl he's certain their targets are in New York City. The plan is for Mazer to capture them." A visible shudder quaked through him. Pallor robbed his face of color.

His frantic gaze jumped from Ira to Esán. "Do you know what a Mindeco is?" He rushed on. "I see by the expression on your faces you do. Sorda has promised a Mindeco named Rikell I will be his next victim if he delivers Brielle and Ari AsTar and Penesert El Stroma to him. They are also seeking Troms el Shiv and a boy named Rethson, although I doubt they are in this time."

His lips twitched into a sneering smile. "Sorda doesn't realize your power, Nesá, or the power of the young boy who hangs around with Rayna. There's another guy, too, who carries the taint of an Eleo Predan. His power is unusual and potent." He turned his head to peer down the path. "His power is—"

The strains of guitar and flute drifting their way propelled Dwight to standing. Realization fueled his long stride as he hustled toward the music.

Esán pulled Ira to his feet. "I'm certain that's Torgin and Gar playing, which means the girls are near. Find them; warn them. I'll stick with our roomie. Keep your eyes peeled for Upori." He jogged to Dwight's side and matched his stride.

A short distance along the path, onlookers gathered. Dwight and Esán stopped at the back of the crowd. A tall man with gray- streaked hair played a handmade flute. A young boy, with a small dog at his feet, strummed the guitar.

Dwight whispered, "There's the guy. His power is music."

The musicians performed three pieces that produced enthusiastic applause from their audience. Smiling, the older man lowered his wooden instrument. "Thank you for stopping to listen. We'll take a brief pause, then play some more. Have a wonderful Sunday."

The youngster leaned his guitar against a folding stool and sipped water from a battered thermos.

Ira ambled from the dispersing crowd to drop some change in the open case on the ground by the stool. Others followed his lead. Some hung around for the next set.

Dwight's nostrils flared. His keen-eyed gaze searched the woods. "The Mindeco is closer than we think."

Gar's dark-eyed gaze darted over the clearing, his nose wrinkling in disgust. He said something to Torgin, ordered Spyglass to stay, and reclaimed the guitar.

Torgin drank from the thermos, set it by the case, and raised his flute.

Music filled the air. People gathered in groups, swaying with the strummed rhythms of the guitar. Brie and Penee strolled into the clearing and merged into the small crowd. A stocky man hidden within the trees watched them with greedy, glinting eyes.

Dwight tensed. "Those are the women from your building, Nesá. We can't allow Mazer to kidnap them. I'll distract him. You tell them they're in danger."

Esán spoke under his breath. "Steady, boy. He won't try anything in this crowd. I don't think he's seen you, so stay out of his line of sight."

Slipping into the stand of trees, Esán circled behind Mazer and stopped beside him. "Mister Mazer, I gather you're a music lover."

The man turned his head, raised bushy brows, and glared. "I'm surprised Sorda let you escape from The Plaza, Nesá. Don't you have work to do?"

"Mr. Sorda needed a break, so I took a walk."

Beady eyes narrowed. "You had no idea there would be a music concert near The Pond, right?"

Esán smiled. "How would I know that, Mr. Mazer?"

"Ah. I don't suppose you recognize the woman in the green hot pants either?"

"No, sir, but I wouldn't mind meeting her. Why?"

His gaze roamed the crowd. "No reason. Thought she looked familiar, that's all." Mazer shook his head and edged away. "I have things to do."

Esán moved with him. "I saw what happened at The Plaza last evening. I gather you won't be staying there any longer. Have you found a new place?"

Mazer's expression froze; anger distorted it. With an obvious effort, he controlled himself. "Don't tell Karl Sorda we talked." He stalked off through the stand of trees, an occasional tremor shaking his body.

Torgin played a final note on the flute, Gar strummed a final cord on the guitar, and applause broke out.

The temptation to follow Mazer tugged. Esán ignored it. *Dwight's a wild card. I best not leave him on his own until we get him under control. The Mindeco will keep Upori nearby.*

26

Esán turned to find Dwight hurrying toward him, his expression a mix of confusion and anger. "Why did you let Mazer go, Nesá? His freedom gives him an opportunity to hunt down the girls. He knows what street they live on. He'll go there. No matter how long it takes, he'll keep looking until he finds them."

"Calm down, Dwight." Esán met the barrage with a slight smile as Ira join them. "You'll take the girls back to our apartment, won't you, Ira?"

"You bet."

Dwight frowned. "What about meeting your sister's plane?"

Ira opened his mouth, snapped it shut, and shot Esán a quizzical look.

Dwight's gaze flicked from one to the other. "Oh. You don't have a sister named Wendi, right? That's just part of the whole charade. It appears Karl, Mazer, and me aren't the only one's playing games."

Ira studied him. "I'm betting you and Nesá can find some common ground." He handed Esán an envelope. "The contents are self-explanatory."

He glanced across the clearing. "The girls are on the move. If I'm to escort them home, I'd better go. Call when you can, Nesá."

Ira intersected with his charges and hustled them along the path toward the subway station. Torgin and Gar had played a final set, packed their gear, and walked the opposite way with the black and white terrier trotting ahead of them.

Esán shoved the envelope in his pocket. "I suggest a stroll through the park while we finish our conversation, Dwight."

"Sounds good. I'm thirsty. The zoo has a great café. Why don't we walk that direction?"

As they ambled along in silence, Esán provided Dwight with space to sort through his feelings.

Dwight eyeballed him several times. He came to a halt with bridged brows and a face alight with questions. "What is the power I feel in you? It differs from Ira's or Rayna's."

Esán moved off the path to a large rock overlooking The Pond. "Let's talk." He scrambled to the top to sit cross-legged facing the water.

Dwight climbed after him. "I don't see why you should trust me, but I promise not to share anything we talk about with Karl. You aren't from this time and dimension. Neither am I. Clenaba Rolas is my home solar system. I'm presuming it's yours, too."

Esán kept his gaze on a pair of loons fishing near the center of the pond. "What else are you guessing?"

"I think I've figured out what brought you to New York City, 1969."

"I'm pretty sure you have. Look, we can get nowhere by dodging around stuff, or we can trust each other and figure how we're going to save our solar system. You tell me your true story; I'll tell you mine."

Dwight's expression turned distant and wistful. He plucked a long piece of grass from between two rocks and studied it through half-closed eyes. "If I'm truthful, I have no idea who I am, or where I'm from. When I was young, my foster mother told me that my birth parents abandoned me. Was she telling me the truth? I don't know." The grass fell from trembling fingers. "She raised me on..." He blew out a breath. "By sharing this with you, Esán, I'm putting us both in grave danger. If my uncle—Karl—ever finds out I've told you anything about him or me or Upori Athai, he will kill me. I mean it."

"You mean like he plans to kill me once he's done with me?"

Shame-laced surprise registered. "How did you know?" He shook his head. "I'm so sorry."

"I expect you aren't at fault, Dwight. It seems we're in the same boat. How about a little tit for tat to release the pressure? The planet of Tao Spirian is my home. You?"

"I grew up on RewFaar. Do you carry a Seed of Carsilem?"

Esán nodded. "I do. Is your foster mother... Was she a peasant or a LaChette?"

Dwight sighed. "A LaChette. If she discovers I told you, she will have me killed." Vertical creases formed between his brows. "Wait. You said something about saving our solar system. I don't understand. What's jeopardizing the Clenaba Rolas System, and how can we help?"

Esán's thoughts quaked, collapsed in on themselves, and reformed. "Tell me what Karl Sorda and Upori Athai brought with them from the past."

The creases deepened. "They had me steal three valuable gemstones worth a ton of money. Their plan is to sell them in this time and dimension. Wait. What's that got to do with our solar system being in danger?"

Speculation churned. Esán scrutinized the young man next to him. *Are you telling the truth? Can I trust you? Dare I share how important the stones are?* Inhaling a deep breath, he called on the Seeds of Carsilem to provide insight. A close look at Dwight's aura, his body language, and the confusion making the air surrounding him hum helped Esán to relax. He waited for his companion to break the silence.

Dwight looked away. He resumed eye contact with determination replacing his confusion. "I understand if you don't trust me, Nesá, but I haven't been dishonest since we began sharing. You have my word." He groaned. "My word is worth nothing, right?"

Truth and despair rang as loud and clear as bells in a cathedral. Esán heard it. "Your word, Dwight, spoken from a place of truth, is golden." He slid to the ground and offered his hand. "My true name is Esán."

Dwight shook the hand. "Thank you, Esán, for your belief in me."

Esán smiled. "Thanks for trusting me. Let's head to the cafe. We can talk more on the way."

Brie hadn't allowed herself even a small peek at Esán and Dwight when they walked past. Penee had hidden behind dark glasses and her wide-brimmed hat. Although Ira had alluded to a mysterious circumstance regarding Dwight's relationship with his uncle, she planned to keep him at a distance, especially in her present form.

They reached the Fifth Avenue station in record time. Brie handed Penee a subway map. "Find the route. Take us home."

Penee removed her glasses. "Are you kidding? I can't take us home."

Ira laughed. "Sure ya can. I'll help. Between us, we might even get us there."

They pored over the map. Ira grinned and pointed. "How 'bout this, Miss Brielle?"

"Looks good." Brie returned the folded map to her bag. "You lead the way."

A small dog's bark stopped them mid-stride. Spyglass ran from the trees straight to Brie, his frantic barking a message of distress.

The sound of racing feet pounded closer. Torgin burst into the square, guitar case in hand, and agitation exploding from every cell.

"Upori's got Gar." He gulped. "He threatened to hurt him if we don't do what he says." Fighting for breath, he handed the case to Ira, and gripped his knees. "I'm so sorry. I didn't see the man 'til it was too late."

Brie touched his shoulder. "Take us back to the bridge."

He inhaled. "They aren't there. He grabbed Gar. Told me to go home and wait for a call. Somehow, they teleported. Mindeco can't teleport." He straightened and squeezed the bridge of his nose. "We need to go home."

Brie picked up Spyglass. "No. We need to do the unexpected. Let's return to the path-side bench. You can tell us what happened."

Without waiting, she hurried the short distance. "Sit down, Torgin." She set the guitar case at his feet, placed Spyglass on his knees, and sat facing him.

Penee perched on the edge, her hand on his shoulder.

Ira winced and stared at his thumb. "I require some privacy."

Brie nodded. "Go. Then find the guys. I'd use telepathy, but I'm not sure what's going on."

"Got it. I'll send you a message when I catch up with them." He loped away down the path and disappeared into the trees.

Torgin rested his cheek on Spyglass' head. "Sorry, boy."

Brie pushed a flicker of sympathy aside. "No time for regrets, Torg. Tell us what happened."

Torgin picked at the fringe on his leather vest. "We were on the approach to Gapstow Bridge, figuring we'd circle the pond and make our way to Columbus Circle to catch the subway. Spyglass was sniffing up ahead. On the far side of the bridge, he growled, dashed into some trees, and started barking his head off. Gar ran after him. The barking stopped." Torgin raised despair-filled eyes to her face. "I expected them to reappear. They didn't. My instincts shouted danger, so I hid the guitar and crept through the trees."

I found Upori Athai and Gar facing each other like combatants in an arena. A red-faced Upori gripped Spyglass by the neck. Gar's expression, one of fear mixed with pleading, made me angrier than I can ever remember.

"Upori gave me a nasty look. "You come any closer—I kill the dog." He squeezed Spyglass' throat so hard the terrier went limp. Upori scowled at Gar. "Remember your promise, kid." Gar shot me a terrified look and nodded. Upori dropped the dog to grab Gar's arm. A menacing scowl twisted his features. "Go home and wait for my call."

"They disappeared. I don't understand how. Mindeco can't teleport, so..." He shook himself and scratched the terrier's black ears. Spyglass whimpered, rolled onto his belly, and jumped to his feet the minute they vanished. He brought me to you. End of story. I think we should go wait for that call."

Brie stood up, walked across the path, ordered her tumultuous thoughts, and strode back. "You and Penee take Spyglass to the apartment. I'll find Ira. If he hasn't found Esán, we'll find him together. He needs to know what's happened. If I discover we can trust Dwight, I'll contact you via telepathy. If not..." She shook her head.

Spyglass jumped to the ground. Torgin stood, arms folded. "I'm not leaving. Bet Spyglass wants to stay, too."

Brie copied his stance. "Don't turn stubborn on me, Torg. You're our connection to Upori. Go home. Wait for the call."

Penee pulled off her sunglasses and shoved them in her bag. "I agree with Brie, Torgin. The sooner we get back, the better. Can we take Spyglass on the subway?"

Torgin's intractable stance eased. He muttered under his breath. "Chill, Whalend." He whistled for Spyglass and picked up the guitar case. "We can. Let's go before we end up in the dinner rush. Didn't mean to be a pain, Brielle. Be careful. Please, stay in touch."

Ragged street performer, elegant young woman, and small dog walked away side by side.

Brie hurried down the path, her senses tuned to Ira's frequency range.

I ra waded into the midst of a group of older oak trees, sat down between surface roots, and shifted.

A ri materialized, stroked the roughness of bark, and smelled the dark, rich earth. She leaned her head against the tree trunk to gaze at the leaves overhead. She imaged the canopy in the Terces Wood on Myrrh, the Wood Tiffs in their TreeOms, the Nyti fluttering from branch to branch. The sound of voices on the path brought her back to New York City, 1969. *This feels like a dream.* She sighed. *Maybe life is just a dream. Maybe I'm somewhere else dreaming all this.*

A robin landed on a branch above her head, trilling a cheerful song. She heaved another sigh, made certain no one could see her, and shifted.

I ra stretched and climbed to standing. "Someday I'll remember why I don't remember." He gave himself a minute to get his bearings. "Find Esán and Dwight. Which way...? Right or left? I think they went to the zoo. I believe it's this way." He hustled along the path.

People meandered by. Dogs strained against their leashes. Children ran ahead and back at the whim of their parents. An old woman pushing her arthritic husband in a wheelchair got stuck in a rut. People wandered past without even looking their direction.

Ira walked over. "May I help?"

Her timid nod gave him permission. He maneuvered the chair away from the rut. "Can I help with anything else?"

The old man put a hand to his chest and mouthed the words, "Fine. Thank you."

Ira smiled at them. "Have a pleasant afternoon, madam, sir."

"Thank you, young man." The woman's relieved smile made him feel like a hero.

He ambled on, whistling until he reached the zoo. His stomach growling reminded him he'd missed lunch. The idea of Gar with Upori reminded him he had urgent business with his friends. *Hope Dwight and Esán found somewhere to talk over a meal. I'm starving.* He walked across an open space to peer in the window of the Dancing Crane Cafe.

At a table in the corner, he spotted Dwight's dancer-straight back. Esán waved him inside.

Ira slid into the seat beside him. He fixed a serious gaze on Dwight. "This is important. Are you friend or foe?"

Dwight met his gaze without flinching. "I am not your enemy; I never have been. What I realize now, after learning more about the stones, is that I've been a pawn in someone else's game. I just didn't realize it."

Ira faced Esán. "You told him we knew about the Corps Stones?"

His friend nodded. "I told him what the stones he stole for Karl and Upori actually are. We can trust him, Ira."

Ira held Esán's gaze a moment longer, before settling in his seat. "Upori has Gar. He says he'll hurt him if we don't cooperate. Torgin's taking the girls back to the apartment to wait for his call."

Esán shoved his half-eaten lunch toward Ira. "Eat while you can." He wiped his hands on a paper napkin and tossed it on the table. "I was just telling Dwight how we know about Upori and the time machine." He returned his attention to the boy across from him. "Is there anything else you'd like to share?"

Dwight placed his fork on his plate. "I will tell you everything, but Upori is unwell. We need to find Gar before it's too late."

Ira crunched a bite of bacon. "What about Karl? He has the stones. We don't want him to take off with them."

Esán rested his forearms on the table. "Dwight, you and Karl argued. Does he know you heard his conversation with Upori?"

"We fought because he's spending our money frivolously. He told me to mind my own business." His teeth clinched. "It is my business. My mother is financing this." He came to his feet. "We need to rescue the boy."

"Your foster mother is Karl's boss?" Ira caught the warning in Esán's eyes too late. Silence draped the companions. Cursing himself for his stupidity, Ira waited to see who would make the next move. He didn't have long to wait.

Dwight turned on his heels. "We're done."

👁 👁

Brie arrived outside the Dancing Crane to find Dwight storming from the cafe, his focus glued to the ground, his stride an angry march. Tensed to jump aside, she stepped into his line of flight. "Hello!"

His head flew up. His eyes widened with recognition. He braked to a full stop a foot away from her. Sarcasm, uncertainty, and anger melded together in his body language and his facial expression. "Who are you really?"

Her demeanor relaxed but cautious, she studied him. "I'm disinclined to trust you since it appears you are leaving the restaurant without Esán and Ira."

Esán strode up to them, Ira at his side. "If you will pledge to be one of us, Dwight, to help us rescue Gar and to find and return the Corps Stones, she will tell you what you wish to know."

He clenched his fists. "Promise to leave my mother out of this."

Esán's steady gaze did not waver. "Your mother isn't involved in this."

"Okay. I'm in. I vow to do my best to be a team player." He looked at Brie. "Please tell me who you really are?"

She pulled off the green scarf. Her long, red hair cascaded down her back. "I am Brielle AsTar. I presume you've heard of me."

"You're the youngest VarTerel in the Universe, right?"

"That answer will have to wait." Torgin sprinted from the trees, looking somewhat bemused. He caught Brie's eye and grinned. "Can't believe I can teleport." Seriousness flowed over him as he regarded the group. "Gar is in real danger. We need to go somewhere safe and private. I have an idea about how to rescue him."

Ira spoke up. "What about the apartment? It's private."

Torgin shook his head. "Upori already called to tell us he's watching it. If we teleport from there, he'll know. I pulled a Gar and left from the basement."

Brie turned to Dwight. "You've been in New York longer than we have. Any thoughts on a safe place nearby?"

"I know a place, but it will entail traveling the way Torgin traveled to reach Dancing Crane. Let's walk deeper into the park. We need to find a more secluded spot."

Esán smiled. "What are you waiting for? Lead on!"

Brie marveled at his ability to help people both see and accept truth. She walked at his side as the group traipsed after Dwight. Reminding herself this was business, not pleasure, she refrained from slipping her hand into his.

27

orgin's impatience roiled into a demand for action. Gar needed help, not sometime today or tomorrow. He needed it straightaway. *My plan's unconventional, so the others might think it's crazy.* Torgin bit back the desire to scream 'hurry' at the top of his lungs. *The plan will work. I'm sure of it.*

He walked with Ira, engaging in an internal monologue, urging their leader to get a move on. When Dwight dodged down the banks of a small stream to a spot well-hidden from passersby, Torgin almost shouted his relief.

Dwight scanned the area, then offered his hand. "Circle up, everyone. Hold on."

The sound of scurrying ended with Ira and Brie on either side of Torgin. He looked across the circle at Dwight and Esán. Power sparked, flowing from person to person. The park vanished. A dark, damp chamber wavered into focus.

Cold, oppressive stillness held everyone quiet. Torgin broke the circle to survey their surroundings. "Where are we?"

Dwight reached overhead. Light from a naked bulb glowed. "We're in a hidden room beneath the Natural History Museum. No one will bother us."

Esán walked over to a large, donut-shaped structure in one corner. "Is that what I think it is?"

Dwight moved closer. His expression inscrutable, he nodded.

"Someone care to share?" Ira peered from one to the other, his curiosity evident in his rapid-fire question.

Esán studied the structure from several angles. "This is the time machine Lorsedi's researcher built, the one Karl is hoping my work might help to fix." He turned to the group. "We have more important things to do. Torgin, explain your plan?"

"This may sound crazy. I realize changing anything in this time frame might create problems, however, since none of us are from 1969, nor are Upori and Gar, I suggest we go back to the past to rescue him."

Surprise, interest, and doubt flashed across the faces of his companions. He hurried on. "I've done the math. I've checked and double checked. We have two time whistles, Esán's Seeds of Carsilem, Brie's staff, and, we have Dwight's power to add to the mix. What do you think? Oh, the Compass of Ostradio is tuned to New York City, 1969."

Dwight looked dumbfounded. "Wait. What power? I mean, I can teleport. A friend of my mother's taught me. I can even sense telepathy, although I don't use it well. So, what power are you talking about?"

Torgin groaned. "First things first, Dwight. We'll explain when Gar is safe. Right now, the Mindeco has a pretty short fuse. We don't have time to waste."

Brie walked over to Dwight. "Come with me, Dwight Anders. I'll introduce you to your talents. You need to understand them to help rescue Gar." She glanced at Torgin. "Give us a minute. You, Esán, and Ira discuss the best way to do what you're suggesting."

The validity of her request didn't help Torgin feel less impatient, but it helped him do as she asked. He urged his friends to a corner opposite the time machine. "Will my idea work?"

Esán regarded him with an amused smile, then turned to Ira. "Torgin's plan will work, but..." He tapped Ira's temple.

"Ouch." Ira rubbed his thumb.

Ignoring Ira, Torgin reviewed his calculations.

"Hello, Torg."

A deep voice he recognized brought him about face. He blinked and chuckled.

Ari's crooked grin spoke volumes. "Esán says the plan to rescue Gar is yours. What happened to that scaredy-cat Drotti I used to know?"

Torgin grinned. "He grew up."

B rie recognized Dwight's restrained reaction for the fear it was. "Tell me why you're afraid? I won't do anything to hurt you."

He shook his head. "I'm not sure. My mother was always particular about who came near me and rarely left me alone with visitors. She warned me never to allow anybody to read my mind. Am I betraying her?"

Brie offered her hands. "You aren't betraying anyone. Unless, of course, you refuse to learn more about who you are; then you're cheating yourself. I am a VarTerel, Dwight. You have that potential. I can sense it pulsing in your blood. Shall we explore and discover who is deceiving whom?"

He rubbed his palms on his jeans. Decision came quicker than Brie expected. He clasped her hands. "I'm read—"

Power ripped through him. Brie saw it, experienced the full strength of it, and gasped. Recognition of the person whose hands she held ignited a flood of tears.

Eyes widening, he shuddered from head to foot. Pulling his hands away, he gulped a long cleansing breath. "Why didn't she tell me? Why didn't she want me to find out?" Confusion and dismay choked him.

"Dwight, look at me. I might know a bit of your story, but we have to rescue Gar. When he's safe, I'll share everything."

He touched the tears slipping down her cheek. "You're crying. Why?"

The Star would not let her fib. "I recognize your energy, Dwight. You are amazing. I can't wait to share what I've discovered. Let's rescue Gar, so we can talk."

His internal struggle showed on his face. Although she understood his indecision, she ignored it and walked over to their companions.

Esán read the amazement in her tear-damp eyes and put an arm around her. "More powerful than you realized?"

"Gar first, then I'll share what I learned."

Torgin considered the man across the room. "Is he in or out?"

Dwight joined them. "I'm in. Tell me what I—" Startled eyes gazed from Brie to Ari. "Who are you?" He searched the room. "Where's Ira?"

Brie smiled. "This is my sister, Ari."

"Oh. I get it. Ira and Ari are the same person." He stepped into the circle the companions had formed. "I gather I have a lot to learn." He raised a brow at Torgin. "Better find Gar before my curiosity gets the better of me."

T orgin's gaze encompassed the circle. He withdrew his time whistle on its long lanyard. From the leather pouch at his waist, he removed the compass and handed it to Dwight. "This is Ostradio. Your knowledge of Upori will help it pinpoint his location. We need your staff, Brie."

It flashed into her hand. "You got it."

"Ari, you have the bass whistle, correct?"

Withdrawing it from beneath her shirt, she held it up. "I do."

"Good. We will match pitch and tone to hold us to place and time. Esán will control how far into the past we go. When he gives the signal, Dwight, tell Ostradio to take us to Upori. Everyone clear?"

Dwight grimaced. "Humor me, please. I'm new to all of this. A brief explanation of the compass will help."

Torgin grinned. "Sorry, Dwight. Ostradio absorbs the geography of the place where it is located. We ask it a question; it provides an answer. When I give you the sign, you direct the compass to show us Upori's hiding place. Because it knows the city's geography, you know Upori, and I know Gar, it will locate them for us. Does that help?"

"Yes. Thank you. I'm ready whenever you are."

"Good. Brielle, take us into Mittkeer."

Brie raised the staff. The chamber morphed into the starry night sky.

Dwight, eyes rounded, scanned the vastness, and gasped in surprise.

Torgin shot him a questioning look. "Are you okay?"

"I'm fine. Just astonished."

Torgin raised the time whistle. "Ready, set, go, Arienh." He blew a long, high note that cut through the night quiet.

Ari lifted her whistle, repeating the note at its lowest octave. All Time and No Time swirled in response. Eternal darkness cycloned into a tunnel, surrounding them in a blur of stars.

Esán used the power of the Seeds to hold it steady. Brie's crystal, Musette, sent rays of light in a multitude of colors to encapsulate them within the mini tunnel.

Torgin fixed his attention on Ari. Together, they inhaled and worked their way to a note midway between the highest and lowest octaves. With each change in pitch, the spin slowed until, as they played the same note an octave apart, the tunnel settled in the present, its rotation slow and steady.

Torgin and Ari repeated the note at short intervals, keeping it long and sustained.

Esán focused on the Seeds to control the spin. "Go, Dwight."

Dwight held up the compass, his gaze fixed on the face. "Upori Athai and Gar."

The compass needle spun into stillness. A map formed and zoomed in. A hologram of a decrepit residence on Riverside Drive rose and steadied.

Torgin and Ari played their whistles an octave lower.

With purposeful intent, Dwight directed the compass to the next destination point. "Gapstow Bridge."

The golden needle spun. The multiple colors shooting from Brie's staff's crystal crown narrowed to a single ray.

Esán and the Seeds equalized the time tunnel's rotation. Light flashed, leaving them in a huddle at the center of the bridge.

Torgin sprinted into the trees, his heart racing. *Where are you, Gar?*

Spyglass' bark ripped through the air. Torgin pivoted toward the sound. Upori stepped from behind a bush, his attention riveted on the young boy, kneeling beside his dog. Darting forward, Torgin grabbed Gar by the arm, whistled for Spyglass, and sprinted back to the bridge. Brie, her staff raised, hugged Gar to her. Mittkeer formed, its star-spangled glory embracing them. Ari blew a note in the higher octave. Torgin matched her.

"Museum of Natural History." Dwight commanded as though he'd controlled the compass his whole life.

The light spectrum from the crystal Musette broadened. Esán and the

Seeds of Carsilem reversed the tunnel's spin. Mittkeer melted away. Darkness enshrouded them.

No one spoke.

With a shiver, Torgin tucked the whistle beneath his shirt.

The small terrier whimpered.

A soft click, as loud as a tip of a whip snapping, sounded. Light from a single bare bulb chased the darkness to the corners of the chamber beneath the Museum of Natural History.

Gar flew from Brie to Torgin. "I knew you'd come for me!"

Spyglass barked his joyous agreement.

Ari slapped Torgin on the back. "You did great, Torg!"

Esán embraced Brie. "Outstanding work, VarTerel."

To one side Dwight, his horrified gaze riveted to something beyond them, looked shell-shocked.

As one, the group turned. Torgin gripped Gar's hand.

Karlsut Sorda, his rapacious features triumphant, observed them from across the chamber. Esán, his mind blanked, awaited his adversaries first move.

Sorda glared past him. "You are a wimp, Dwight Anders. Right from the start, I knew you would turn tail at the first opportunity. I gave you numerous chances to prove me wrong. Unfortunately for you, you did not." His gaze swept the entire group. "However, dear boy, your parting gift is magnificent." He beamed as he turned to the twins. "Brielle and Arienh AsTar, I knew you would show up. I just wasn't sure when."

Esán stepped forward. "What is it you require, Karl?"

Piercing dark eyes narrowed. "Before you consider doing anything stupid, Nesá, allow me to tell you about my bargaining chip, one I believe you will not wish me to harm. Penesert El Stroma is my... let us say... my guest." His chilling gaze skimmed the group. "You should never have allowed her to stay at the apartment on her own."

"How did you find us?" Esán kept his tone neutral.

Sorda smirked. "Think, Nesá, how *did* I find you?"

"If I knew, I would not be asking."

Karl shot him a cocky smile. "My loving nephew led me right to you. I keep track of him at all times." His expression hardened. "Enough chatter. This is what I expect of you if Penesert is to remain alive and unharmed. Upori Athai has, once again, absconded with the Corps Stone. I want them found. And I want his helper, the Mindeco, destroyed.

"From this day forward, you will report *only* to me. Forget whoever sent you to this time and place. Play your individual roles to perfection. If you are unwise enough to veer from your expected course, punishment will be immediate."

He sauntered over to the twins. "Which of you is Arienh?" When neither acknowledged his question, he grabbed one by the chin. Unflinching, she stared straight at his face. He smirked and moved to the second twin, gripped her chin, and squeezed.

"Get your hands off me." She jerked her head away.

He grabbed her arm and pulled her away from the group. "I've heard about your temper, Miss AsTar. You will be accompanying me back to The Plaza. Please remain calm, or I'll make certain you do."

Esán interrupted before Ari could respond. "Will Dwight and I return to the hotel with you and Ari?"

Sorda's disparaging gaze switched from Ari to Esán to Dwight. "I would prefer to dispense with your presence altogether, Dwight Anders. However, you still have some value to me. Your charade will continue along with everyone else's." He regarded the silent companions. "Tomorrow, you will all play your individual roles, *and* you will continue the search for the stones. When they are in my possession, I will share the next phase of the plan."

He glimpsed Gar kneeling in the shadows beside Spyglass. "Tell me how you freed the boy and where Upori is hiding."

Torgin stepped in front of Gar. "We traced his energy signature and teleported him to us. Your presence has kept us from discerning where the Mindeco hid him."

Sorda's expression telegraphed disbelief. "You are…"

"I'm Torgin Whälen."

"Ah yes, the musician and mathematician. The time will come when you will help Nesá reprogram that machine; until then, play your part in our little drama." His large nostrils flared and narrowed. "Nesá, get over here. Dwight will teleport us to The Plaza."

Sorda's hand gripped Esán's upper arm. "Brie, I suggest you teleport your companions home. If you don't arrive in a prompt fashion, one of your friends will pay the price. Get a good night's sleep. You'll need it. By week's end, I want the stones in my hands." He shot Dwight a scathing look. "Get over here."

Esán's warning glance darted from Dwight, whose desire to rebel flashed like a beacon, to Brie. She nudged Dwight's tall, resistant body into motion. Sorda yanked him closer. "*Now*, nephew."

The trio vanished.

28

Her back to the entryway, Brie beckoned Gar to her side. "Hold on to Spyglass." Her gaze darted from Torgin's face to the chain on the bulb.

He reached overhead. Darkness enclosed them. Rowan wood warmed her hand. Power rippling through her, she called forth Mittkeer's star-sprinkled night.

In the stillness embracing them, Gar, wonder shining in his eyes, surveyed the endless star-scape. "Where d'ya bring us?"

"This is Mittkeer, the land where Time is Everything and Nothing." Brie pulled him closer. "Listen. We'll do what Sorda expects and teleport to the apartment. I've done an advance scan. Whoever kidnapped Penee left Sorda's calling card in the form of small recording devices hidden throughout the apartment. Once we get home, keep conversation minimal but natural. Torgin will prepare us a bedtime snack. Pretend you're super tired. Once we're all tucked in, I'll create a holographic scene of us sleeping. They didn't bug the bathroom, so we'll meet there. I'll take us to a place where we can figure out our plan of action."

She focused her attention on, The Penthouse Suite. "Sorda's getting impatient. Hold on."

They arrived in a storage room in the basement of their building and stepped into the hall. Spyglass sprinted to a closet door at the far end and sniffed the faint line of light glowing along the bottom edge. The fur on the back of his neck rose like a porcupine's quills. A growl rumbled. Paws scratched the door, then the cement floor at its bottom edge. Repeated frenetic barking echoed through the basement.

"Gar, call Spyglass to heel." Brie edged toward the closet.

He whistled. The terrier snarled, his paws scratching harder. Gar grabbed his rope collar. Spyglass broke away, barked louder, and ran back to the door.

Quick as lightning, Torgin snatched up the terrier and carried him back to the storage room entrance. Gar trotted after him, scolding his errant terrier.

Brie eased the battered door open a crack. Her lungs rebelled; her stomach churned. Heart pounding so hard she couldn't breathe, she closed the door. Leaning against it, she rested her head on an arm and forced her breathing to come in slow, even gulps. After regaining a measure of control, she crept back to Spyglass and the boys.

"Upori is in that closet. He's in trouble. Torgin, take Gar. Teleport to the apartment. Remember, to behave naturally. Oh, for Sorda's benefit, discuss my decision to pick up a surprise dinner for us."

Torgin stopped her. "What if Rikell is ready to switch bodies? I won't leave you to face him alone."

"You have to. I promise he won't hurt me. He wants Gar. Get him upstairs, Torg. I'll be there as fast as I can."

The desire to argue evident in every move he made, he took the boy's hand. "Hold on to Spyglass, Gar."

She gave them time to reach the apartment and herself time to calm her racing heartbeat, then flipped on the light and opened the closet door.

A sheet-pale Upori, reeking of decay, stumbled down the hall. "Take me to your place."

Finger to her lips, Brie beckoned him into the large storage room. "I can't take you to the apartment. Sorda bugged it. We can talk in here."

He growled. "You took the boy. He's my ace in the hole. I want him—" A convulsion quaked through his body, leaving him trembling. He groaned, hugged himself, and shot her a pleading look. "Mindeco's too strong. Can't fight him. Can't hold him off." He stumbled, knocked over a stack of empty boxes, and slumped against the wall. "Help me. I can't—"

The aroma of death and decay engulfed him. Terror shook his stocky body. Gurgled sounds boiling up his throat turned to spasmodic gasps that ended in sudden, complete silence as he crumpled to the ground.

Rikell, the Trutoran Mindeco stepped free of Upori's decomposing remains. The iris of the single, central oculus blazed fiery red around the large black pupil. Yellowing teeth gnashed. Razor sharp canines flashed. The immense creature shot to his full height; flexed his long, lean limbs; and swung his huge, skeletal head in her direction.

"You are unafraid, Brielle AsTar. Why?"

"Because, Rikell, if you take over my body, you cannot make use of my DiMensioner's power." She watched him digest her words. "I am not your intended victim."

A bluish tongue dripped slobber over his bony chin. He licked his teeth. "The Corps Stones have disappeared from their hiding place. Find them. If I do not have them by the week's end, I will select a human body a day to house my presence. When I release it, I will leave it mangled, bloody, and unrecognizable." His hideous laugh filled the space. "Panic will reign in the city, panic certain to be the worst in recorded history." One long stride carried him to the door. "Find the Stones, Brielle AsTar." With a quick look both ways, he loped down the hall.

The outside door banged shut. Horrified realization shuddered through her. *Rikell will do exactly as he described.*

• • •

Ari almost regretted her temper-ignited response to Sorda—almost. *At least Brie's free to determine what she needs to do.* A peek at the muscular, unkept man holding her arm in a vice-like grip made her cringe: *I think you're what's called a thug.* He hustled her ahead of him into a dingy apartment smelling of cigarette smoke; marched her straight to a second door; fumbled to unlock it; and, with a rough-handed shove, sent her stumbling into a small, dim room reeking of stale air and unpleasant odors. The key turning in the lock sounded so final it left her gritting her teeth.

A brief glance at her new surroundings left her grimacing. "Guess this is home."

A soft groan, the only response, drew her to a darkened corner. Penee lay curled in a tight ball on one side of a dirty mattress. Mismatched eyes opened a slit. "So cold." She squeezed them shut, shivering.

Unable to find a blanket, Ari laid down, matched the curve of Penee's back, and snuggled close.

An icy hand squeezed hers. "Th-thank y-you." The words whispered through chattering teeth, made Ari desperate to help her friend.

They lay in the silence, listening to the door-filtered sounds of TV and occasional male laughter. Ari squeezed her eyes shut, trying to pick up tidbits of conversation. The bits she could hear provided nothing of value.

Penee's hand squeezing hers brought her back from the edge of sleep. Ari strained to hear her whisper. "Let me turn over."

She stretched her legs and moved to the side.

Penee flinched as she straightened her limbs. "Thank you. I couldn't neutralize the drugs they gave me and maintain my body temperature. When they come in to give us the next dose, I'll distract them. You spit yours out." She stifled a yawn. "Do you know where we are?"

"Some seedy apartment complex. That's all I know. What's keeping us here? Except those jerks in the other room?"

"Karl made it clear if we try anything, he'll make us sorry we did." She bit her lip. "I'm pretty certain everyone can take care of themselves, but I hate to put them at risk."

Ari rolled onto her back. "Wish there was something we could do besides lie here."

The key clicked in the lock. A mean-looking man filled the opened doorway, surveyed the room, and entered. With a threatening glare, he placed a large, brown paper bag on an upturned box. "Dinner." The gruff single word pronounced without a glance their way preceded the door shutting and the key clicking in the lock.

Ari retrieved the sack and withdrew a burger wrapped in paper. "Smells good."

Penee pushed to sitting. "Whew. Dizzy. I'm not sure if they drug the food. This is the first time they've provided a meal."

Ari eyed the burger with doubt. "Maybe I should eat first. If it makes me sleepy, you can pretend you're drugged; if not, you can eat."

Penee smiled. "I have a better plan. Give it to me."

Ari handed it over. Penee held it between her hands and shut her eyes. When she opened them, she gave it back. "I detect nothing harmful. Hand me another one, and I'll check it too. Food would make me feel a lot better."

After checking everything in the bag, she found nothing of concern. Ari took a bite, chewed and grinned. "Not bad."

Esán glanced at the clock, apprehension clawing like a dog after a bone. Karl had taken Dwight to The Penthouse. *What's taking them so long?* He frowned. *I hope you keep your hatred in check, Dwight Anders.*

Half an hour later, the key turned in the lock. Dwight, a caricature of frustration, marched into the room, accompanied by a surly man Esán had never met. "This is Ricco. He'll be our constant companion from here on out. Don't know how he'll watch both of us tomorrow, but that's his problem." He shrugged and flopped onto the couch. "Have a seat, watchdog."

Undercurrents of anger negated the man's feigned disinterest.

Dwight flicked a glance over his shoulder, shot Esán a sideways look, and stared up at the recording device. "Since I'm in charge of the finances and the bank will *only* deal with me, Karl has agreed to let me live a while longer. Good thing my mother doesn't trust him." He jumped up. "Come on, Esán. I don't know about you, but I'd enjoy a slice of yummy pizza. Bet Ricco knows the best place to go, right Ricco?"

Their watchdog didn't move. "Mr. Sorda said to stay put."

"Ah, come on, Ricco. Aren't you hungry? If we eat, you eat. I'm *buying*." Dwight emphasized the word buying.

Ricco fumbled with a piece of chain looping his belt.

Dwight addressed the recording device. "We're going out for pizza, *Uncle* Karl. If you want to come, meet us in the hall. If not, it's okay. We'll see you in a couple of hours." He grinned at Ricco. "Satisfied?"

The man lumbered to his feet. "Guess so. A few blocks from the hotel there's a great Italian restaurant." He licked his lips. "They make the best calzones in the city." A glare wiped every hint of pleasure from his face. "You try anything dumb, I guarantee you'll be sorry."

"We promise not to get you into trouble with *your* boss." Dwight draped an arm over Esán's shoulder. "Right, pal?"

Dwight's wheedling innocence teased a slight smile from Esán. He turned away from the recording device. "All I want is food and sleep. Lead on, Ricco."

As expected, Sorda did not meet them in the hall. Esán's outlook brightened at the prospect of being beyond his influence, even for a time. A silent elevator ride ending in a stroll through the foyer into the muggy night intensified his sense of freedom. The lightness in Dwight's step suggested he experienced a similar feeling.

At the corner of 58th Street and Central Park South, Dwight pulled out a fifty-dollar bill and waved it at Ricco. "This is yours if you keep your distance in the restaurant."

The man looked doubtful. "The boss said you can do weird stuff and to watch ya close."

Dwight held it out to him. "I promise no tricks. Sorda will never know, and you'll be fifty dollars richer. What do you say, Ricco?"

The watchdog stared at his feet.

Dwight folded the bill. "Your choice. Okay, Nesá, send him into oblivion." He stepped back.

Esán shot him a quizzical look. *Stay or walk away.* His sense of humor tickled. *Play along.* "Really, Dwight? You realize I might not have the power to bring him back." He ran an appraising gaze over his quarry.

Eyes as big as fifty-cent pieces, Ricco held his ground.

Esán drew a symbol in the air. "But if you insist—"

Ricco paled. "Hold it. I'll take the money, but no tricks." He snatched the bill from Dwight's outstretched hand, turned on his heels as the green light flashed, and strode across the street.

Dwight winked at Esán. "Well, done. We need to talk fast. Karl has promised to let me live until he can convince the bank to change our accounts to his name."

"Can he do that?"

"Nope. Mother made it impossible. If something happens to me, the bank will freeze our assets until she gives the word." He laughed. "Which means never. I guess I should be grateful. What's the name of that board game with money and places to buy?"

"You mean Monopoly?"

"Yah. She gave me a 'get out of jail free' card like in Monopoly."

Down the block, Ricco stopped to study a menu in a glass case. At their approach, he waved them inside.

Dwight pulled open the door. The rich aroma of Italian cooking wafted onto the street. "Smells wonderful. We're about to have dinner. I'm starved."

Ricco tailed them into the restaurant and selected a spot near the door. Dwight zigzagged between tables to a booth in a dim corner. He slid in far enough to be out of Ricco's sight.

Esán sat opposite. "You were pretty good out there."

Dwight nodded. "So were you. I say we order and make plans."

The server arrived with a notebook in hand, scribbled their order, and hurried away. He returned with their sodas and left. Dwight picked up a straw, dipped it in his cola, and sipped. "Tell me about the Seeds of Carsilem."

Esán enjoyed the biting flavor of his ginger ale. "On my world, one Seed is rare; more than that has only occurred once in recorded history. You and I have similar gifts, although mine are..." He swallowed a mouthful of the effervescent bubbles. "It's difficult to explain."

Dwight's expression intensified. "Tell me who I am. I mean, who I really am not just Roween Rattori's—" He clamped his mouth shut. His fists clench. "You can't tell anyone, Nesá. If she ever finds out, I let it slip—"

Aware of his obvious dread, Esán remained silent.

Dwight leaned closer. "Please promise you won't tell a soul."

Esán held his gaze and his voice steady. Sympathy flooded his features. "I can't promise not to share important information with the people who are working to save our solar system. What I can guarantee is that they and my friends and me will protect you."

He sat back and waited as the server placed their pizza at the table's center. "Thank you."

The man smiled. "Enjoy your meal." He hurried back toward the kitchen, wiping his hands on his white apron.

Dwight made no move to eat, his attention fixed on white-knuckled hands gripping the table.

Esán bit into a thin crust, coated with tomatoes, basil, and creamy mozzarella drizzled with olive oil. "Wow. This is great. Eat up, Dwight. We have lots to accomplish in the next few days." He picked up another piece. "Please don't worry. Roween isn't here and neither are those I would share your secret with."

"Will you tell Brie and Torgin and the others?"

"Only if they need to know. I'd rather you tell them in your own way, in your own time."

Dwight lifted a piece of pizza, inhaled, and bit off a chunk. His brows shot upward. Several bites later, he licked his fingers. "I never came across pizza in our time, did you?"

Esán savored another bite. "Nope. Let's enjoy it." The sounds of chew, swallow, and slurp through a straw lasted several minutes. Esán took a final drink of his soda and sat back. "Tomorrow, you and Rayna will find a place to talk in private. She will tell you what she learned earlier."

Dwight finished the last of his pizza in silence. When the server brought their dessert, a delicious scoop of gelato, Dwight requested he include Ricco's meal in the bill.

"Thanks for the splendid meal, Dwight." Esán laid his soiled napkin next to his plate. "Any more questions?"

"Nope. If you're done, we'd better get back." He left a generous tip and paid the bill at the cash register.

Ricco joined them on the sidewalk. "How'd ya like the food?"

Dwight smiled. "Best pizza I've ever had."

The man's body language threatened. "You tell your uncle I let you sit alone, and I'll make certain you pay a bigger price than fifty bucks."

Dwight faced him square on, arms at his side, demeanor non-threatening. "I suggest a truce. We share a secret. Esán and I trust you not to tell. The only reason we would inform my uncle is if your behavior forced us to do so. What do you say?"

Sorda's watchdog walked to the curb. As he passed, Esán touched his arm. The man shook his head and faced them. His expression changed. Suspicion melted away. "Okay. We watch out for one another. Time to go back to the hotel."

Dwight nodded. "Cool. You lead the way. We'll be right behind you." He waited a moment. "Did you do something to him, Nesá? His attitude did an about face."

Esán grinned. "I just helped him relax a bit."

Their arrival at The Plaza seemed much quicker than the walk to the restaurant. Karl met them in the hall and questioned his henchman.

"They give you any trouble?" Hawk-keen eyes bored into him.

"No, sir. We ate great pizza and came back. If you don't need me anymore tonight, I'll catch some sleep."

Karl seemed satisfied. "Be here by eight." He transferred his piercing gaze to Dwight. "What did you think of pizza, nephew?"

"It was the best." He yawned. "I have a class at ten in the morning. Time to say goodnight."

"Ricco will accompany you tomorrow." His expression hardened. "He will make scheduled reports to me throughout the day."

Dwight scowled and stomped into his suite.

Esán waited, curious how one watchdog would oversee them both.

"In the morning, Nesá, you, Dwight, and Ricco will leave the hotel together. Ricco will divide his time between you. He'll check on you when Dwight is in a class. His job is to watch both of you. Do anything stupid and Penee and your friend, Arienh, will suffer."

Expressionless, Esán nodded, walked into the suite, and closed the door.

29

Brie fashioned holograms of Gar and Spyglass asleep next to the Taylor guitar, and Torgin curled up on the bed in his room. Assured theirs would hold, she pulled the blanket up to her chin and created her hologram. Satisfied all was in order, she masked her movements and slipped into the darkened bathroom. *"Now."* She hoped the single telepathic word would not be detected.

The hall door eased opened. Ghost-like, Gar, Spyglass, and Torgin crowded close to her. She pictured their destination. The dark room morphed into a small, dimly lit studio apartment. Careful to erase their energy trail, she released a long exhale.

"You can relax. We're safe."

Gar wandered the room. "Where are we, Brie? Can that Karl guy find us?"

Brie sank onto a straight-backed chair and looked around before answering. The studio, one large room plus a bathroom, had a Murphy bed pulled down in one corner and the kitchen at the opposite end. The living space between contained a couple of overstuffed chairs, a loveseat sleeper couch, and a small dining table.

She smiled at Gar. "This is the apartment Corvus arranged for Esán and Ira. Neither Karl nor Dwight knows about it. Corvus and now the three of us are the only ones who've been here. Let's get planning. I'm not sure how long my holograms will hold."

Torgin straddled a chair. "Gar? Are you okay?"

The boy stood motionless, staring out the window, his back to the room. His head tilted right, then left; his small hands clutched the sill. Spyglass whined. Gar blew out, misting the windowpane, knelt, and hugged his dog. "I'm okay, boy."

A final glance out the window produced a slight smile. He settled cross-legged on the worn couch. "I know where Penee is. She put a picture in my head. Why me? Why not one of ya guys?"

"She chose you for two reasons, Garon. If Karl can track telepathy, which I doubt, he wouldn't expect her to communicate with you; and you and Penee have a special connection."

"A connection?" Confusion flared, then cleared. "Oh! I know. 'Cause of El Stroma, right?"

Brie smiled. "Exactly right. Tell us what she shared."

His forehead wrinkled in concentration. "She put four pictures in my head real fast: the first was kinda like she was lookin' 'cross the street; the second was a building number; the third was an apartment number. Last, she showed me three men playin' cards in a smoke-filled room."

Torgin moved to the couch beside him. "She was smart, sending the images to you. What could she see across the street?"

Gar chewed his bottom lip. "A side street in a kinda dingy neighborhood. I could see the park between a couple of high-rises in the distance." He squeezed his eyes shut, then nodded. "I know where it's at. Gin and I passed it sometimes on our way ta music gigs in the park. The building's number is two hundred and fifty; the number on the apartment's 8F. It's close ta the Museum of Natural History."

Brie's thoughts took a fast track. *Stay focused, Brielle AsTar.* "Would it make sense to teleport the girls to this apartment? Karl wouldn't know where to look for them."

Deep thought-etched wrinkles crinkling around half-closed eyes, Torgin stared at the wall. He nodded to himself and glanced at the clock. "It's almost midnight. If we're going to do it, now's perfect. Everyone's in bed."

Gar jumped up. "We can bring 'em here, then teleport ta our place. By the time, Karl finds out, we'll be fast asleep." He grinned.

"There's one important thing to consider, Garon." Brie reached for his hand.

He took it. "Are ya okay?"

"I'm fine, Gar." Unblinking, she explained. "You can picture where the girls are. We can't. You must take the lead."

"Lead? Ya mean, I would have ta teleport 'em?"

She nodded. "You'd have to help."

Gar hugged Spyglass close. "What do ya think, Spy? Can I do it?"

The terrier answered with a lick on the chin.

Gar met Brie's gaze. "We'll work together, right?"

Brie hugged him. "Of course. We need you to be our eyes. All three of us will teleport them. Your job is to find them and project a picture in our minds. Can you do that?"

He held her gaze, his unwavering. "We're a team?"

Brie met it with a serious gaze of her own. "We are a team—Torgin, you, and me."

An expelled breath puffed his cheeks. "Tell me what ta do."

"Let's sit in a circle so we can hold hands. I'll walk you through it step by step."

Brie cleared her mind and directed the boys to release the day's debris from theirs. Tranquility wrapped the studio apartment. Next to her, Torgin relaxed. Gar's breath grew steady. The clock chimed midnight. Total calm permeated the air.

Brie looked at her companions. "It's time, Garon. Torgin and I will focus on Ari and Penee to help you project your psychic essence to where you believe they are. Squeeze my hand when you see a detailed image of them in your mind."

Gar's feelings and thoughts flowed into her. Torgin's presence supported them both. The studio apartment ceased to be their reality. Gar's etheric essence stood on the street, looking up at a building. Ghostlike, he floated upward, hovered by a window, and vanished through a wall.

The inside of a room focused. Penee and Ari lay curled together on a dirty mattress. Gar stared down at them.

Small fingers squeezed Brie's hand. She returned the signal. "Keep your attention on the girls. When I say go, teleport them. Torgin and I will help. If you understand, squeeze my hand.

His cool fingers pressed hers. Strengthening her connection to Penee, then Ari, she prepared to bring them to her.

The girls' door opening cast a long rectangle of light across the floor. A man stuck his head in, peered at the bed, and withdrew. The light vanished. Laughter filtered through the closed door.

Gar gulped a breath. Brie squeezed his hand. "Now."

The filthy room and the mattress blurred. Two bodies materialized on the Murphy bed in the studio apartment.

"Penee! Ari! I did it." Gar broke into shuddering sobs of relief.

Torgin embraced him. Rocking back and forth, he whispered words of confidence. "You did great, Garon. You're okay. Everything is okay. Look. Penee and Ari are safe and sound and awake."

Ari jerked to sitting. "What the... Brie! How? Never mind. Help me. Penee's drugged. She couldn't neutralize it, and I can't wake her."

Brie dropped to her knees by the bed and placed a hand on Penee's forehead. Cold flesh shocked her warm palm. The Remembering Stone clutched to her chest, she closed her eyes, her entire focus on drawing the drug into the stone. Little by little, she felt warmth leaking into Penee's chilled body. Each ragged breath she drew became less labored. Brie's racing heartbeat gradually slowed. Her pulse returned to normal. She touched Penee's forehead with the blue stone and sat back on her heels.

Penee's eyes fluttered open. A tiny smile of recognition widened as she looked from Ari to Torgin to Gar. A full-bodied stretch brought color rushing to her cheeks. With a happy grin, she allowed Torgin to help her to sitting. "You brought us here?"

He grinned. "Gar did most of the work. Brie and I tagged along."

She smiled. "You're my hero, Garon."

His expression unfathomable, he flashed a timid smile. "I'll always take care of you, Penesert."

Torgin took his hand. "Time to go."

Brie handed Ari the key to the apartment. "See you tomorrow."

Ari hugged her. "Thanks. What do you think Karl will do when he finds out we're missing?"

"He'll be angrier than The MasTer's Reach. I've warned Esán that he and Dwight better be ready." She hugged Penee. "You rest. Stay inside and don't use DiMensionery, just in case. The Mindeco is on the loose, so stay alert."

Torgin tugged at her hand. "Gotta go, Brie. I checked the apartment. It's clear. The holograms are working, but won't be for long. We need to be in bed before the jailers find out their prisoners have vanished."

Gar's small hand clutched hers tighter. She pictured the 72nd Street apartment.

• • •

Esán got Brie's message just past midnight. An hour later, the door to his room flew open. Karl stormed in. "Penee and Ari have disappeared. What did you do? Brie and the others were in their beds fast asleep."

Esán rubbed his eyes. "I have no idea what you're talking about. I've been right here in bed."

Karl yanked the covers back. "Get up, Nesá Zervos, and tell me where they are."

"I don't know where they are." Esán met Karl's angry gaze and clamped his mouth shut but completed the thought... *I wouldn't tell you if I did.*

Karl's face twisted into a hate-filled mask. His arm jerked back.

Esán held his ground. "If you hit me, I cannot be responsible for my actions."

The man's narrowed features, a picture of violent rage, showed his inner fight to contain his instinctual behavior. His mouth worked around a response. He curled his fingers and lowered his hand.

Heedful of his danger, Esán suggested another possibility. "Have you considered that your men might have fallen asleep on the job?"

He responded with his own. "Why are you here with the girls? Brie is a VarTerel. Torgin has math skills. What do you have?" Frowning, he turned the doorknob. "Dwight is sure you're their unknown weapon. I agree. Go back to bed. Stay there. I have ordered Ricco to come back to the hotel. He will be outside your door. I'll decide what to do with you in the morning."

The alarm going off at seven-thirty roused Esán from a light sleep. Senses alert for trouble brought him upright. Ricco glared down at him.

"Mr. Sorda wants you in The Penthouse in twenty minutes." He marched to the door. "Dwight's up already."

Esán grabbed his clothes and headed to the bathroom. A quick shower cleared his head. Dressed for the day, he walked into the sitting room. Dwight waited by the door, checking his watch.

"Fifteen minutes and forty-five seconds... Not bad. Let's go."

Jonas met them at The Penthouse door. "He's expecting you in the study."

Dwight led the way, knocked, and entered without waiting. "Good morning, *Uncle* Karl. I suppose we're in for more scolding?"

Sorda's lean features narrowed even more. His eyes snapped. "Your hunt for the stones begins today. We hid them in the theater. I thought Upori had them. He was certain I did." He scowled. "Neither of us does. Find them and bring them to me. Understood?"

Esán let worry creep into his response. "Yes. Any word about the girls?"

Sorda circumvented the desk to glare from one boy to the other. "You're wasting my time. I don't know why your mother thought you might be useful, Dwight Anders." He sneered. "You, Nesá Zervos, had better prove your worth, or I might change my mind and get rid of you sooner than later. Both of you—out of my sight."

Dwight dodged through the door. Esán made it through as it slammed shut. Without speaking, they returned to their suite. Esán checked the contents of his book bag, found a small recorder, and tossed it in the waste basket. Dwight pulled everything from his dance bag, held up a matching one, and tossed it. He looked straight at the recording device wedged in the bookshelf. "You're wasting equipment, Uncle Karl. Once it's gone, you can't replace it in this time and dimension."

Sorda marched into the suite and slapped Dwight across the face. "You destroy anything else—"

Dwight shoved him. "Keep your hands off me, Karlsut Sorda.

Esán grabbed their bags and ushered Dwight into the hall. "Here." He held out his dance bag. "Let's go before he locks us up or worse."

Ricco met them at the elevator and shot them a sly look. "Boss ain't happy." He glanced behind them. "Better hurry."

The door slid open. They darted inside. Dwight waved at Sorda through a one-inch gap. "Bye, bye."

Esán shook his head. "How old are you, Anders?"

Ricco glanced from one to the other. "He's got men stationed in the lobby. Not sure what their orders are, but I'd stay alert if I was you."

Esán hit the stop button. "Listen, Dwight. I have enough to manage without babysitting you. Are you finished throwing tantrums?"

A nasty comeback almost jumped from Dwight's mouth. Esán grinned. "Nice control. Keep it up. Ricco, how many men in the lobby?

"He hired four of us. That's all I know."

"Okay. We exit through the lobby like we have no idea we're being watched. We take a cab like we normally do. You can drop me at Fordham and go on to the Juilliard Building. Ricco will escort you to class and come back and check me." He grinned at Dwight. "Say hi to Rayna for me." He pushed the down button.

Leading the way from the elevator, Esán asked the doorman to hail a cab. A quick backward glance caught two men watching them through the doors.

A taxi pulled up to the curb. Esán pulled the back door open. "Fordham University, please." He slid across the vinyl seat.

Ricco climbed in last. "Looks like we're clear."

Morning dawned with anticipation fluttering like butterflies in the 72nd Street apartment. Brie shaped Rayna, dressed, and packed her dance bag. A scratch at the door hinted impatience on Gar's part. She smiled down at a tail-wagging Spyglass waiting at her door and raised an eyebrow at his master.

"Ya ready to go, Miss Rayna?"

Gar fed a scrap of bacon to Spyglass. "Torgin says come eat. He's got an early class."

Rayna stuffed her purse in her bag and hefted it to her shoulder. "Lead on."

Gar grinned and darted down the hall into the kitchen.

After depositing her bag by the door, she followed. "Smells good in here." She sat down and picked up a fork.

A grinning Torgin placed a plate piled high with eggs and bacon in front of her. "What's your schedule today?"

"I have morning technique class with Madame Dolavina, then *pas de deux* class with Mr. Tansley, and rehearsal for *Gems* this afternoon. How about you?"

Torgin, his back turned to the tiny recording device in the corner, winked at Gar, then spoke extra loud. "I have composition and piano this morning. This afternoon, I rehearse *Gems* with the ballet orchestra. How about you, Gar?"

Gar pressed his lips together to hide a smile. "I have ta guard Rayna. That's my job. I'll be wherever she is."

Torgin cleared the plates. "Sounds like a busy day. We'll do the dishes later. Let's brush our teeth and get going."

The elevator door closing allowed them to drop the pretense. Rayna sighed. "I'd flush Sorda's recording devices down the toilet, except I'm certain he'd find a way to replace them."

Torgin pushed a button. The elevator halted with a jerk. "Gar, you know what you're to do?"

"Yep. I'll find Mira. Then I'll poke around the theater ta see what I can find. I'll meet ya to eat lunch at the Juilliard cafeteria."

Rayna nodded. "I'll see if I can isolate Dwight from his watchdog long enough to share what I learned yesterday. Once he knows, I can tell you."

Torgin pushed the button. The elevator descended. Doors slid apart.

An aggressive, muscular man stepped into view. "What took you so long? Telling secrets in the elevator?"

Torgin regarded him with distaste. "You are interested...why?"

The man glowered. "I'm an associate of Karl Sorda. That means—"

Spyglass growled and nipped at his ankle.

He jumped back. "Get that damn dog away from me."

Gar whistled. "Spyglass, heel." The terrier dropped to his haunches by his master. "Ya afraid of dogs, mister?" He slid his hand under the rope collar.

The man made a point of ignoring him to give Torgin a hard glare. "I'm stickin' with you today. Sorda figures Ricco can keep an eye on both Rayna and Dwight."

Torgin shrugged. "Suit yourself."

The man glowered at Spyglass and strode from the building.

Rayna scanned the empty lobby. With a wicked grin, she linked elbows with Torgin. *Teleport.*

Gar touched her bag.

They arrived in the cubicle in the silent, dark costume room in the theater. Exit lights illuminated the doorways.

Gar laughed. "Hey, that guy's gonna get a surprise."

Torgin pulled the curtain aside. "Was that wise, Rayna?"

She raised her chin. "I couldn't help myself. Besides, I put a thought in the doorman's head. He'll tell your guard we went out through the basement."

He shook his head. "Ari would be proud. Speaking of which... I wonder how she and Penee are this morning?"

A light came on. Mira entered the costume shop. "They, unlike you, are doing their best not to draw unwanted attention."

Rayna considered defending herself, thought better of it, and closed her mouth.

Mira put an arm around her shoulders. "Restraint is a good thing." She released her. "You and Torgin had better go. I know you have classes to attend. Gar, you and Spyglass will stay with me."

Torgin caught Gar's eye. "Be careful today."

The boy grinned. "Always am. Ya, too."

Rayna hiked up the stairs after Torgin. At the top, he kissed her cheek and hurried toward the exit.

"Hi, we've been waiting for you, Rayna."

She turned to find Kelsia and Lois standing by the casting board.

Lois, her perpetual scowl in place, tucked a stray hair in her bun. "Do you always enter the building through the costume shop?"

Rayna stifled a sigh. *The day has begun.*

30

Esán poured over manuscripts pertaining to time in relationship to distance, sound, and light. He buried himself in works on theoretical physics, especially the writings of Albert Einstein. A stack of books on quantum mechanics sat on the shelf, awaiting his attention.

He drummed his pencil on the edge of the desk and pondered the effects of centrifugal force and the Coriolis effect on objects in space. *I wonder how these might impact the spin of a time tunnel.* His desk drumming continued, stopping and restarting with his fluctuating thoughts. Memories of Torgin creating a musical composition from every rhythmic sound projected his ideas in a new direction.

A knock at the door jolted him from abstract thoughts to the reality of Joe Shyro standing by his desk.

"Mr. Shyro, aren't you supposed to be in Bermuda?"

"I was. May I sit down?"

"Of course." Esán glanced around for another chair.

Halfway to standing, Mr. Shyro stopped him. "No need to get up. I can fetch a chair." He brought one from a corner table, locked the study room door, and closed the blinds.

Esán regarded his actions, puzzled by his visit and his behavior. "Is everything alright, sir?"

"When we're not in class, please call me Joe." He rubbed his hands over his thighs. "I'm fine, but I have a concern I'd like to share with you. May I go on?"

"Please."

"Since I last saw you, several strange things have occurred. At first, I brushed them aside as my imagination working overtime. An event two days ago forced me to admit I have a problem, one that begins and ends with Karlsut Sorda." Anger crept into his expression. "How is he treating you?"

"We're having some differences. Tell me what's been happening and why you came back early."

Joe folded his arms. His jaw tightened. "I returned to New York for several reasons. Concern for my wife, Kathy, and you topped the list. A man followed us to Bermuda. I didn't consciously notice him until he showed up in our hotel. After that, I noticed him everywhere we went. When I tried to speak to him, he left in a hurry. Not long afterward, I received a phone call, one threatening the safety of my Kath and myself. We checked out of our hotel to spend the night at one nearer the airport. The next morning, we departed on the early flight." He rolled a pencil between his fingers.

Alarm raised red flags in Esán's mind. "Where's your wife?"

"She's safe." Joe pointed at a blank piece of paper. Esán handed it to him. The scratch of lead accompanied his concentrated scribbling. He reviewed what he had written, laid the pencil aside, and slid the paper across the desk.

After a quick read, Esán met Joe's gaze and nodded.

Retrieving his missive, Joe tore it into tiny pieces which he divided into two piles and threw away in different waste baskets. With a furtive peek between the blinds, he returned to his chair, his intense gaze fastened on Esán. "You can't continue to work for Sorda. The caller threatened your life if I don't 'behave'."

Esán narrowed his eyes. "You're certain Karl is behind this?"

He nodded. "In my business, you meet a variety of interesting people. I have a friend who owed me a favor. He agreed to track down the calls made to my phone. Someone called three times from The Plaza Hotel. You need to leave town, or barring that, you need to return full-time to school. I'd feel a lot happier if you were working with me at the theater so I can keep an eye on you."

Esán glanced at the clock. "I'm being watched. My 'keeper' is due in five minutes. He'll stay about an hour. Then he goes back to SAB. Meet me at the Carnegie Deli. We can discuss a plan."

Joe drummed his fingers on the desk. "I have a better suggestion. Come and find me backstage at the theater. We'll slip into a dressing room. More private, don't you think?"

Esán unlocked the door to check the hallway. "I'll be there as soon as Ricco leaves. Go. I don't want him to see you."

"You be careful." He strode from the room, glanced back once, and dodged through an exit.

Esán closed the door and raised the blinds. He took his seat, opened a book in front of him, and glanced up as Ricco strolled into the room and plopped down on Joe's vacated chair.

"So, you discover anything fascinating?" He peered at the stack of books and papers. "You read all that stuff?"

Indicating a need for quiet, Esán scribbled several notes, including two math formulas. He looked up to find Ricco shaking his head.

"You're pretty smart, huh? Why's Sorda so worried about you gettin' away? You enjoy what you're doin', right?"

Esán shrugged. "Sorda's a strange guy." He laid his pencil along the spine of the opened reference book. "How's your day going? Is Dwight behaving?"

"He's doing that ballet stuff. Pretty feminine, if you ask me. Never could figure out why a guy would want to prance around like that." He scratched his head. "He ain't a pansy, is he?"

Esán flipped through pages of his book, found what he was seeking, and regarded Ricco with a look halfway between pity and annoyance. "Listen, I've got work to do. Sorda won't be happy if he thinks you've been keeping me from doing it. When is Dwight finished today?"

Ricco folded a blank sheet of paper into an airplane. "'Round five-thirty." The plane glided across the room. He reached for another piece.

Esán moved the paper out of reach. "Why don't you take a break. Dwight and I will be busy until then. I'll meet you at the fountain at six o'clock."

Ricco retrieved his airplane, smoothed a bent wing, and let it fly. It landed on top of the book. "Don't do anything dumb, okay. I'd hate to see how the boss'd react." On that note, he turned about face and departed.

Esán glanced at the clock. *I have forty minutes before I meet Joe.*

He focused on the manuscript, his goal to track down an elusive piece of data.

Rayna completed a triple, partnered *pirouette* into *a ninety-degree arabesque*. With a lengthening breath, she tipped forward into a *penché*, and returned to *arabesque*, her arms in *fifth high*. Dwight released her, allowing her to balance on her own. The accompanist nodded. Rayna finished on her knee with the last note of the music.

The studio, full of dancers, broke into applause. Dwight offered a hand, escorted her forward, and stepped back. She took a solo bow. He returned to her side for a bow together.

Mr. Tansley gave corrections to the class, complimented the dancers on a good day's work, and dismissed them.

Rayna noted the sparkle in Mr. Corvino's eyes and flashed him a brief smile as she wiped the sweat from her face and neck. A biting pain reminding her to shift shape caught her by surprise. She glanced at the clock. *Where has the day gone?*

Stuffing pointe shoes in her bag, she made her way to the door. Lois blocked her exit. "So, are you and Dwight an item? I mean... You spend a bunch of time together." She peered over Rayna's shoulder. Her scowl hardened. "Where is the dear boy, anyway?"

Rayna edged around her. "See you in rehearsal." Hurrying to the girl's changing room, she zigzagged between benches filled with chatty dancers and dodged through the back entrance as Lois' high-pitched voice penetrated the room.

"Anyone seen *Rayna Deejara?*"

In the public restroom, Rayna ducked into a stall at the back. Her bag slipped from her fingers. The suddenness of the shape shift to Brielle brought a gush of anticipation with it. While she assimilated the change, Brie leaned against the wall to review the day.

A decision to enjoy her time in the studio had allowed her to immerse herself in the persona of Rayna. Every moment in class had been a delight. Madame Dolavina had given her alternate persona excellent corrections, praised her when she applied them, and placed her in the first group in the center. Lois had glared from the sidelines, jealousy making her pouty expression even more unattractive. Kelsia had beamed at her each time she did well.

Brie sighed. *Are humans everywhere driven by such insecurity and fear?*

The main lavatory door squeaking open reminded her to pay attention. Rayna materialized, flushed the toilet, and picked up her bag.

The girls' empty dressing room provided her the opportunity to exchange her sweaty dance clothes for a clean, dry set before donning her bell bottoms to run across the plaza to rehearsal. Rayna's reflected image in the mirror snagged her attention. Deep inside, The MasTer's alter ego, Fisaco, stirred. She remembered Etoile's response to the renegade personality and his quick withdrawal. Her imitation of the demi-goddess sent her nemesis into retreat.

"Is something wrong?"

She turned to find Kelsia watching her. "Hi. I thought you had a practice session with the Demo Program this afternoon."

"I just finished. You're going to be late for company rehearsal if you don't get a move on." She stepped aside. "Maybe we could meet for dinner after you finish?"

Rayna slung the strap of her bag over her shoulder. "I can't tonight, but I'd love to go another time. Let's make plans tomorrow."

She felt Kelsia's sad gaze follow her as she hurried from the room.

From a quiet spot by the Metropolitan Opera, she scanned the area near the fountain. Dwight strolled toward her.

She met him halfway. "Where's your watchdog?"

Dwight grimaced. "He's checking on Esán. I imagine he'll appear soon. How are we going to manage time alone with our full schedules and my constant companion?"

She smiled. "We'll find a way. Better get moving. Rehearsal begins in fifteen minutes." Her arm linked through his, she matched his long stride. Five minutes later, they entered the studio, found a place for their dance bags, and a corner to warm up in.

Torgin's day had been crazy. He arrived at his composition class to find his classmates talking excitedly and his instructor's teaching assistant scribbling on the blackboard. The TA brushed the chalk dust from his hands and faced the class.

"Mr. Byron will be out of town for the next couple of days. I've written your homework on the board. If you have questions, I will be in the teacher's lounge."

Torgin pulled out a notebook. The assignment, to compose a solo melodic composition for the wind instrument of your choice—flute, saxophone, oboe, clarinet, horn, or bassoon—made him smile. That it was due in two days brought a groan from several of his classmates.

The door flew open as he stuffed his notes in his bag. Sorda's man, anger gleaming in his eye, motioned him into the hall. "You ever try to dump me again, I'll make your life miserable." He poked him in the chest. "Got it?"

The impulse to slap the man's hand away made Torgin clutch his shouldered bag tighter. "I have another class. Care to join me?"

"I ain't here ta go ta classes." He scowled. "My job's ta watch ya. How long will ya be?"

"Maybe an hour." Torgin shrugged. "Do you have a name?"

"The guys call me Pike. Where's your class?"

Torgin strode past him. "Follow me."

Pike trailed him, sat outside the practice room while Torgin worked a difficult section on the flute, and paced the hall while he took his conducting class. At lunch, he sat with him in the cafeteria. Cole waved from across the room but chose not to join them.

Pike finished his meal and shoved his tray aside. "What's next?"

"I have rehearsal with the ballet orchestra."

"How long?"

"A couple of hours, perhaps longer."

"I ain't hanging out here for another boring instant." Pike slit his eyes. "If you don't tell Sorda, I'll trust ya to head home when you're done."

Torgin finished his juice. "Isn't he paying you to know where I am at all times?"

"Yep. That's why you're gonna keep your mouth shut. If you don't—"

"You're gonna make me sorry." Torgin picked up his tray. "I get it. I won't tell Sorda if you promise not to hang around me all day tomorrow. You can meet me at the apartment, escort me here, then meet me later to go back. What do you say?"

Pike chewed his lip. "Deal. See ya at your place in the morning."

He left the cafeteria with a lightness to his step that made Torgin shake his head.

Cole strolled over. "He didn't look happy. Is he a friend of yours?"

Torgin stacked Pike's tray with his. "Absolutely not. A friend asked me to show him around. I think he got pretty bored. Music isn't his thing."

They left together, chatted for a time by Revson Fountain, and then separated. Cole had a dinner date. Torgin watched him go, then glanced at his watch. *Rehearsal's in twenty minutes.* He sighed. *Will this day ever end?*

31

Ari gazed down at Penee curled up on the Murphy bed. Brie had removed most of the sedative from her system, but Ari feared some remained. Penee tossed and turned, moaning as though in pain. When Ari tried to wake her from her senseless stupor, she roused briefly, mumbled a series of delirious remarks, and slipped back into a semi-sleep state.

Pacing to the window, Ari reached for Efillaeh then glared at her empty hand. *You sure messed up, Arienhe AsTar. I know you left the knife behind to keep it safe, but you knew you were all heading into a dangerous situation. You should have kept with you. Learn to think ahead.* She glanced back at her drugged friend. Bitterness rose in her throat. "Sure wish I had your talents, Brielle Ralyn." She gripped the windowsill and swallowed. "But I don't want to be a VarTerel!" The unbidden words just popped out.

Penee moaned. Her eyes fluttered open. A loud gasp accompanied her struggle to sitting. With a lost look, she hugged herself and shivered.

Ari hurried to her side. "How can I help you?"

"N-n-need to n-neutralize what remains of the d-drug. C-can't do it alone."

Her pleading look left Ari shaken. "I'm not my sister, Penee. What if I can't do anything without the sacred knife?"

"You're s-stronger than y-y-you think. Sit."

Ari sat next to her. "Tell me what to do. I'll try my best."

A deep inhale stopped Penee's shaking. "Hold my hands. Concentrate on...the drug."

Ari clasped her friend's cold hands. Heat tingling at the base of her spine crept upward, sending gooseflesh racing. Her heartbeat quickened. Her mouth grew dry. Filled with thoughts of failure, she lowered her chin to her chest. Tears of frustration tumbled down her cheeks.

Penee's arm encircled her. "We did it." Her whisper rustled her hair. "You are amazing, Arienh AsTar."

"I just sat here." Ari sniffed through her tears and stared in surprise.

Penee handed her a tissue. "You absorbed the remains of the drug and neutralized it. All I did was let you." She smoothed back her long, caramel-blonde hair. "I want a shower and something to eat. How about you?"

Ari helped Penee to her feet. "You go first. I need a moment."

Again, Ari gazed out the window, trying to get a grip on her chaotic thoughts. The shower formed a background chorus to her repeated invocation: *I do not want to be a VarTerel. I want to be myself.*

The words punctuated her march from the window to the door and back. When the shower stopped, so did she. Feet planted, hands on hips, chin high, she announced out loud, "It is my choice. Nobody can make me become a VarTerel."

Penee, one towel wrapped around her body and another around her head, regarded her with alarm in her lovely eyes. "You sound angry. Has something happened?"

Ari struggled to find an answer. "I didn't know or, at least, I didn't want to recognize my power. I always thought when I healed someone using Efillaeh, it was all the sacred knife. Now, I have to face the fact that I helped." She frowned. "I want my life to be my own, Penee. Brie is happy in the role of VarTerel. I'd hate it."

Penee rummaged through a drawer of boys' clothing, found a sweatshirt and sweatpants, and pulled them on. For a moment, she scrubbed a towel over her hair in silence, then lowered it to study Ari. "I believe you'll discover the Galaxy Guardians know who to ask and who to leave to their own devices. Neither you nor I would succeed as VarTerels. Brie has the right temperament and a warehouse full of gifts. She will become a great VarTerel. That doesn't mean we have to hide our power. We're responsible for developing the gifts we're given. I intend to use mine to rebuild my home planet."

Ari met her gaze. "I intend to help you do it." Adrenalin-fueled stress drained away. She felt totally depleted. "Now that that's settled, let's eat."

Penee combed her fingers through her hair. "I'll find us a snack. You shower. It will make you feel much better."

Ari headed to the bathroom and stared at herself in the mirror. "I am me. I will use my powers in my own unique way to protect the solar system and to save El Stroma." She undressed and climbed in the shower. Soaping up, she allowed the steamy water to wash her fear of losing control of her life down the drain along with the suds.

G ar, Spyglass, and Mira entered the costume shop to find it alive with activity. Women pinned flimsy patterns to silky fabric, cut out bodices, or gathered tulle on noisy sewing machines to make beautiful tutus. Other women cut out and assembled tunics for male dancers.

Mira smiled, greeting her fellow seamstresses with a nod or a gracious "good morning". At her workstation, she positioned a tutu on her lap, scratched Spyglass under his chin, and spoke to Gar in a low-pitched voice. "Please use your gifts to search for the Corps Stones. Try not to draw attention to yourself." She straightened. "Why don't you explore a bit? You'll find some fun things to see." With a nod, she busied herself, clipping stray threads from the short, layered skirt of one of the ballerina's tutus.

Gar left Spyglass curled under her chair, tuned into his senses, and wandered the perimeter of the large room. At first, he sensed nothing. As he rounded a rack of costumes, his instincts kicked in. Like small, twittering birds, they guided him to a cardboard box in a dim corner.

Footsteps headed his direction sent him ducking between racks. A hand shoved several garments aside to hang new costumes on the bar. Gar waited until the retreating footsteps stopped, then tiptoed back to the hidden box.

Excitement hummed. He knelt to rummage inside. *I coulda sworn...* He dumped the soft packing paper on the floor and stared into the empty carton. *The stones were in this box. I can feel 'em.*

The room grew quiet with the approach of the day's end. He carried the carton to Mira and set it on the table. "They hid the stones in this, Mira. I'm sure of it."

She scooped the packing paper up in her hands. "I believe you're correct, Garon. Did you find anything else?"

"No, ma'am." He wandered over to a rack of costumes. Fascinated, he touched a net ruffle. "Girls wear tutus, right?"

"Yes. Tomorrow we'll do fittings with the dancers."

She stuffed the paper back in the box and set it on the floor. "Rayna is in rehearsal with the company. She'll finish soon. Perhaps it's time you resumed your guardianship duties. What do you think?"

His heart leapt with happiness. He gave a soft whistle. Spyglass trotted to his side. "I enjoyed being with ya today, Mira, but I missed Rayna. Do I come to the costume shop tomorrow?"

Mira's beautiful smile warmed him. "Check in with me once she's in class, and we'll decide what we need to accomplish. Thank you, Garon. You helped me a lot today."

Gar rubbed the blush from his cheeks. At the door, he turned to wave. "See ya tomorrow."

He arrived outside the practice studio in time to watch Dwight and Rayna perform a dance variation with several couples. At its conclusion, the rehearsal director gave a series of notes and left with the accompanist. Dancers wandered from the studio, chatting about their day. When Rayna didn't appear in the hall, Gar poked his head in the studio.

She smiled at him. "Please stand watch, Gar. Let me know if anyone is approaching." She left him alone in a hallway now devoid of activity.

Sitting cross-legged on the floor, his senses tuned to warn him of danger, Gar draped an arm over Spyglass. He let his thoughts drift to Gin and a simpler time in his life.

Esán stacked his research materials on a shelf, stuffed his notebook in his satchel, and closed the door behind him. The walk from Fordham to the New York State Theater helped disperse his unexpected fatigue from sitting all day bent over a desk.

In the theater, Joe appeared deep in conversation with Rich Drazah, a lighting tech who worked both at the theater and the Forum. He glanced up at Esán's approach. "Hi, Nesá, you know Rich. We were just discussing the lighting design for *Gems*. Please join us."

Rich nodded a welcome. "I understand we might be working together."

"I'm hoping so. We'll see what my boss says."

Joe handed Rich a thick folder. "Excellent work today. Let's meet here tomorrow. If Mr. Sorda is agreeable, I'll bring Nesá up to date so he can join us." He pursed his lips. "How's eleven o'clock sound?"

Rich tucked the folder under his arm. "See you in the morning." His retreating footsteps echoed in the quiet of the empty theater.

Joe led the way backstage to a deserted dressing room, switched on the light, and blocked it from escaping with a towel placed along the crack between the floor and the bottom of the door. He pulled out a wooden chair from under the counter and slid it toward Esán. "Take a seat. Let's do some brainstorming."

Esán dropped his book bag on the floor. "Do you know why Sorda is threatening you?"

Joe straddled a chair. "No, but I'm betting you do. I did some research at the library in Bermuda. Tell me why Sorda is interested in time travel?"

You are one smart man, Joseph Shyro. Esán hid his surprise behind a puzzled expression.

Joe rested his arms on the chair back. "Please don't play games with me. My life, my wife's, and yours depend on how we handle this. Let me help. I discovered quite a bit about time travel in Bermuda. Did you know some people believe the Bermuda Triangle is a dimensional portal?" He didn't wait for an answer. "I've read enough science fiction to understand if you're messing with time, you don't want to change anything. If you do, a trickle-down effect can change lives and histories. Correct?"

Esán licked his lips. "We are in a situation not of our making, one that can get us killed. I'm bound by an oath of integrity not to share the details."

A spark of determination gleamed in Joe's eyes. "I don't care about the damn details. I want my wife safe; I want my life back. If you have the power to travel through time, you can erase information from my mind." His eyes narrowed. "You need to deal me in to whatever game you're playing." He looked up and gasped.

Corvus materialized at the room's center. Joseph launched to his feet, stumbled backward, and raised his chair, ready to defend himself.

Esán jumped up. "Joe, he's a friend. He won't hurt us. I promise."

Joe's gaze leapt from Esán to Corvus. The chair shook. He set it down but kept his white-knuckled grip in place.

"This is Corvus." Esán explained. "I'm betting he's here to help us find an answer to our dilemma."

A wide, amiable smile deepened the dimple in Corvus' cheek. "I apologize for startling you, Joe, but I felt my arrival in this fashion would make it easier to believe what we are about to share."

Joe studied him intently, reclaimed his seat, and folded unsteady hands in his lap. "I'm listening."

Corvus pulled up a chair and nodded.

Incredulity replaced Joe's defensiveness as Corvus gave him a summary of who they were and why they were in New York City, 1969.

"Questions?" Corvus finished with an open smile.

Joe pressed a trembling hand to his forehead. "I asked you to deal me into the game, didn't I." His lowered the hand to his lap. "I'm assuming if we make it through this in one piece, you will remove what you've shared from my memory?"

Corvus smiled. "We will."

A heaved exhale erased the 'deer in the headlights' expression from his face. "Okay. Where to from here?"

Corvus glanced toward the door. "First, Esán—you know him as Nesá—needs to leave. His guard will arrive soon. Please remember to call him Nesá when anyone else is around. Now, I suggest we go to your apartment, Joe. We need to discuss how to free Esán from Sorda to work with you. Esán and Ricco will meet Dwight to return to The Plaza. Questions, either of you?"

Esán smiled. "Sounds great."

Corvus replaced his chair and turned to him. "Sorda can't know you've spoken with Joe. Act surprised when you learn he's back in New York. Ricco's almost at the fountain. I'll be in touch." He rested a hand on Joe's shoulder. "Picture your apartment. I'll teleport us there. Let me know when you're ready."

Joe gave Esán a bemused smile, then nodded. The duo vanished. Esán straightened the dressing room, picked up his book bag, and walked through the theater. When he reached the stage area, he paused in the wings. A single blue light tossed his shadow across the sprung wood floor, where dancers danced and actors presented their stories.

He remembered a quote he had read by an English playwright named Shakespeare:

> *"All the world is a stage,*
> *And all the men and women are merely players.*
> *They have their exits and their entrances,*
> *And one man in his time plays many parts..."*

Esán left by the stage door and made his way to meet Ricco. *I wonder how many parts I will have played before this drama draws to a close?*

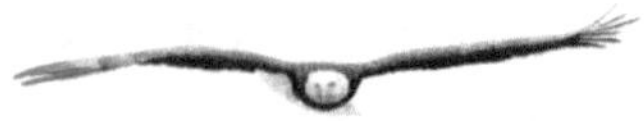

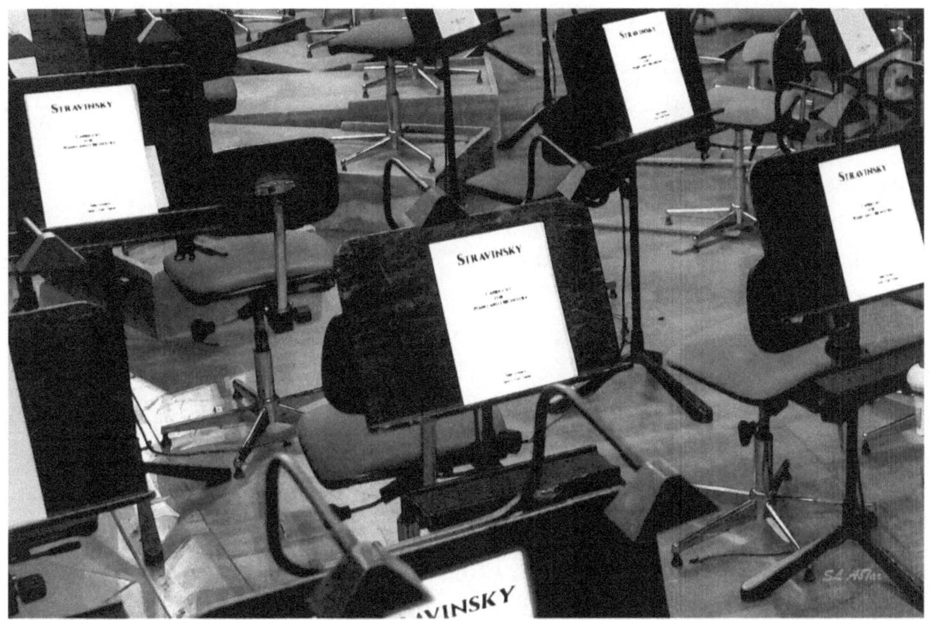

32

In the ballet studio, Rayna drew Dwight down on the piano bench. "I'm not sure where to begin, Dwight." She tapped her knee. "Have you heard of the Décussate Zone?"

He shook his head.

"It is where the Inner and Outer Universe intersect in space and is also referred to as the Rim. Beyond the Décussate, there are solar systems, planets, and suns like we have in the Inner Universe. In the solar system closest to the Rim in the Outer Universe lies a planet called El Stroma, the home of two disparate cultures, the Pheet Adole and the Eleo Preda. The RomPeer of the Pheet Adolan empire, an industrial, economic based culture, initiated a war with the Eleo Preda, who followed a more agricultural, spiritual path. His goal to annihilate the Eleo Predan people and lay claim to their homeland evolved into a war for dominance of the planet."

Spyglass's sharp bark pierced the studio quiet. Dwight grabbed her hand.

The door swung inward. Gar darted through, slammed it shut, and stood panting. "He's out there. The Mindeco." He scampered behind Dwight. Spyglass scratched at the door, growling.

Brie flashed into being. "Dwight, take Gar. Leave by the back exit. I'll deal with the Mindeco."

Dwight looked at Gar. "You go. Take Spyglass with you."

The boy shot him a disgusted look. "Not leaving Ray—Brie ta fight alone. You go."

Brie rolled her eyes. "Cool it, you two. He's right outside. Stay behind me."

The door exploded open. Rikell, Mindeco of RewFaar, lumbered into the studio. His singular gaze darted from one occupant to the next. Spittle dripped from his bone-yellow jaw. He wiped it away with a hairy hand, his attention fixed on Dwight.

"Sorda promised me your body. I'm here to collect." He lurched forward.

Shields shot up, surrounding Brie and the boys. She stood, feet apart, fists on her hips, her gaze riveted to the massive bear-skull head swinging from right to left in front of them.

The head halted. Mindeco's single eye blazed fiery red. "Do not interfere, VarTerel." He snapped his teeth together. "Or I will take the boy."

Spyglass strained against Gar's hand on his collar. A series of sharp barks ended in a low, continuous growl.

"Dwight is not what he seems, Rikell. He is worth more to you as an ally than if you take possession of him." She glanced at Gar. "You know you would burn up Gar's body in an instant. Besides, he is my guardian. You touch him, you answer to me." Her staff flashed into her hand.

The Mindeco cowered. A door slammed somewhere nearby. He shot up to his full height, sniffed the air, and stooped, his single oculus level with Brie.

"Remember, Brielle AsTar, I want the stones by week's end." He swung his enormous head toward the exit, lumbered from the room, and loped down the long, empty hall.

Brie released the shields. Her staff vanished. Gar closed the door and knelt to hug Spyglass.

Dwight cleared his throat. "Um... Can I create shields like that? Vygel told me about them, but said I wasn't strong enough."

Understanding struck Brie like a lightning bolt. "Vygel Vintrusie?"

"You know him?" Dwight looked confused. "He's the one who taught me to teleport and to sense telepathy."

Brie gabbed her dance bag. "When we get to the apartment, I'll tell you all about him. Where are you meeting Ricco?"

"By the fountain."

"Good. Gar and I will meet you there."

Dwight hesitated. "Shouldn't we stick together?"

She shifted to Rayna. "Walk me to the dressing room. Gar and Spyglass will stand guard. We'll change and go out to the fountain together. How's that?"

He looked relieved. "Much better."

Gar checked the hall. "All clear."

Rayna, flanked on both sides, felt a wave of relief as she entered the empty changing room. She sank onto a bench and covered her face with her hands. *I am ready to go home, back to my own solar system.* A sense of urgency crept over her. *If we don't find the stones, we won't have a home to return to."*

T orgin exited the rehearsal hall as the sun sank below the skyscraper-obscured horizon. Rehearsal had been a nightmare. He had barely made it on time. Two other musicians wandered in ten minutes later. To make matters worse, the orchestra was working on the second act in *Gems*, when the solo pianist became ill and hurried from the room.

Matt Harwood, the conductor, had put his baton down, and alternated rustling through the score with glaring at individual members of the orchestra.

Strain stretched the atmosphere thin. Musicians squirmed. Chairs squeaked. Music stands scraped over the floor. No one even whispered.

Mr. Harwood cleared his throat. "Several of you play the piano. I need a pianist for this rehearsal. Who will volunteer?"

A wall of silence greeted his question. Torgin kept his eyes glued to his music. A pair of feet appeared in his line of vision.

Trying not to flinch, he met the conductor's narrowed gaze. "Thank you for volunteering, Mr. Whälen. Please prepare to begin."

Torgin ignored the murmur of discontent rippling through the orchestra, put his flute in its case, and gathered his music. With a sinking feeling in the pit of his stomach, he moved to the piano. Stravinsky's "Capriccio for Piano and Orchestra" required an exceptional pianist. Torgin groaned. *Wish I had thought to look over the piano part.*

Mr. Harwood glared. "You sight read, do you not?"

"Yes, sir, but..."

Harwood tapped his baton on his stand. "Let us begin at the beginning."

The rehearsal tumbled downhill from there. No one emerged unscathed, least of all Torgin. When Mr. Harwood dismissed the orchestra and marched from the hall, frustrated mumbling rapidly transformed into a clamor of discontent. Several members made snide remarks to Torgin as they passed him on the way out.

An older woman stopped by the piano. "Don't let today discourage you." She glanced at a group leaving together. "We have a faction who are always ready to squabble. Ignore them. You did well, which makes them even grumpier." She offered her hand. "My name's Lana."

He shook it. "Torgin." He smiled. "You knew that, right?"

She chuckled. "I'm just glad I wasn't the target today. Matthew is a good man. By tomorrow, he'll have his sense of humor back. Go home and relax." With her violin case tucked under her arm, she made her way from the hall.

Torgin packed his score and sat in the quiet of the empty space. When the janitor shuffled in and began straightening chairs and stands, he left, his heart saddened by the negativity but warmed by Lana's kindness.

As he exited the building, he scanned the plaza. A few people lingered near Revson Fountain. Several others drifted toward Columbus Ave. A stealthful movement on the far side caught his eye. The Mindeco slipped between buildings. Panic chained Torgin to immobility. Worry about his friends set him in motion. *I need to find Gar.*

A rat terrier padded into the fountain's warm light. Gar followed. Dwight and Rayna strolled after them. Ricco crossed at the crosswalk, climbed the stairs, and intersected with Esán in front of the theater.

Torgin hurried to the fountain, grinned at Gar, nodded at Dwight, and hugged Rayna. "I just saw—"

"We know." Rayna turned to greet Esán and Ricco. "Hi."

Ricco glanced around. "Where's Pike?"

Torgin looked at the shorter man. "I promised to go straight home. Pike's meeting me at the apartment in the morning."

The man glanced at his watch. "Dwight and Esán, Sorda's expecting you at the hotel for dinner. We'd better go."

Dwight scowled. "Give me a minute. I need to talk to Rayna about tomorrow's schedule." He drew her to one side. "When are we going to talk?"

She squeezed his hand. "An opportunity will present itself. The information isn't going anywhere. You might even be better off not knowing while you're dealing with Sorda. Remember not to let him know you have more power than he realizes." She stood on tiptoe and kissed his cheek. "I'll see you in the morning." Ricco barked, "Let's go. I ain't got all night." He walked toward Columbus Circle.

Dwight and Esán said goodnight and ambled after him.

Torgin looked from Rayna to Gar. "Let's find somewhere to have dinner so we can compare notes without Sorda eavesdropping." He glanced at the spot where the Mindeco had disappeared. A chill skated up his neck.

Linking arms with Rayna, he guided her toward Columbus Circle.

Karl greeted Esán and Dwight with a sneer. After a meal fraught with tense moments and long silences, he sent Dwight to their suite and led Esán to the study. Taking a seat behind his desk, Sorda picked up the dagger-shaped letter opener, stood it point down on the leather desk blotter, and balanced it with the tip of his finger. Cold, penetrating eyes fastened on Esán.

"What did you learn today, Nesá? Anything important?"

Esán forced himself to appear relaxed. "If you would share what exactly you need to know, I could make faster progress. As it is, I'm learning what's known about the science of time today. What I haven't discovered is how to relate it to your time machine."

The dagger hit the blotter. Sorda repositioned it, point to Esán. "I received a call from the head of Fordham's research department. They have requested you suspend your research for a week while they do some scheduled maintenance." He paused, his expression unreadable. "I don't suppose you knew Joe Shyro was back in town?"

"No, sir. I thought he planned to be in Bermuda until the end of the month."

Sorda gripped the hilt-like handle of the letter opener. "Never lie to me, Nesá." Placing it in the desk drawer, he folded his hands on top of the blotter.

"Tomorrow, you will join Shyro at the theater. He would like you to work with him on a ballet he's lighting." He rose to walk around the desk. "I agreed only because it will give you an opportunity to search for the Corps Stones. Upori stole them from The Penthouse. I'm almost positive they're hidden somewhere at Lincoln Center." His features hardened. Steel-eyed, he loomed over Esán. "Have Penee and Ari been in touch with you?"

Esán maneuvered his chair backward, stood, and met Sorda's demanding gaze. "As far as I know, they haven't tried to contact me."

"How about your friends?"

"I have not conferred with them. What time do I meet Mr. Shyro tomorrow?"

Sorda's chin jerked up. "He's requested you be at the theater by ten o'clock." He blocked Esán's path to the door. "You will, of course, continue to stay at The Plaza."

Esán allowed a note of rebellion to seep into his response. "I assumed as much. It's late. May I go?"

The older man moved aside. "Ricco will monitor your movements. Don't do anything stupid. You are expendable." He let that sink in. "So is Joe Shyro. Goodnight, Nesá."

Jonas escorted him from The Penthouse. In the hall, Esán exhaled a long-held breath. *What I wouldn't give for some privacy.*

On cue, Dwight opened the door to their suite. "How about a walk? Ricco can come with us?"

Ricco appeared behind him. "You gotta stay in the suite tonight. Boss's orders."

Dwight marched into the suite and fired a dirty look at the recording device in the sitting room. "Thanks, *Uncle* Karl. See you tomorrow." He strode to his bedroom, flung the door wide. "Goodnight one and all."

Esán cringed at the loud slam that followed.

Ricco raised his eyebrows. "A little annoyed, huh?" He prepared to depart. "Jonas is watching, so I'd stay put, if I was you."

After Ricco left, weariness hit Esán like a storm surge. Weighted steps carried him to his room. He dumped his bag on a chair, used the bathroom, and prepared for bed. Stripping off his t-shirt, he tossed it over the 'hidden' recording device and, grinning to himself, stretched out on the bed. "Goodnight, Karl. Sleep tight."

Half expecting Jonas to come marching in, he pulled his blanket under his chin. A yawn ended in a fatigue-heavy sigh.

33

Morning dawned with storm clouds blotting out the sun. Brie woke early, feeling angry at the world. She found Torgin already in the kitchen cooking breakfast. "You're up early, Torgin."

"Couldn't sleep. I kept dreaming about yesterday's rehearsal. Sure hope the solo pianist is back today." He juggled a hot piece of toast, dropped it on a plate, and lathered it with butter. "You're looking grouchy."

"I woke up cross at the world and couldn't go back to sleep." She separated a peeled orange into segments. "Maybe a walk would help me feel less blue." She bit a segment in two and wiped the escaping juice from her chin. "Tell Gar I'll be back in an hour."

Torgin's eyes alight with mischief, he jerked his chin toward the hall. "Tell him yourself."

Gar glared at her from sleep-blurred eyes. "What did I tell ya about keeping me close?" He snatched her toast. "Thanks. I'll get dressed."

Seriousness replaced the humor in Torgin's expression. "Gotta admit he's doing a great job." He handed her fresh toast. "I'm glad."

Brie spread on a thick layer of peanut butter and blueberry jelly and took a bite. "Thanks, Torg." She spoke around a mouthful then swallowed." What's your schedule?"

"Pike's meeting me downstairs in thirty minutes. My conducting class begins at nine-thirty. I considered skipping it to search for the stones." He shrugged. "Until we know more, it seems like a waste of time."

She followed her last bite of toast with a juicy segment of orange. "I think you're right. I need to run something by you."

He dropped another piece of bread in the toaster. "Shoot."

She chuckled. "You sound like you've been in 1969 forever." At the sink, she turned the tap on full and held a dirty dish under the gushing water. In an undertone, she shared her thoughts.

"Remember, I told you about the tracker disc in Penee's neck, the one Aunt Henri removed with the crystal on her staff?"

He dried the dish. "I remember."

She swished soapy water around in a bowl. "I'm pretty sure Dwight has one in his neck. Should I try to remove it?"

Torgin watched her rinse the bowl. "You're asking me? Why?" He took it from her and wiped it dry.

"You think differently than I do. What's your gut reaction?" She grabbed a couple plates. One slipped through her wet fingers, hit the floor, and shattered. "Oh no!"

Torgin grabbed a whisk broom and dustpan and knelt beside her. "If you can disable it so Sorda continues to believe he's tracking Dwight, I'd say do it. If you can't, removing it will only complicate matters and might put Dwight in more danger than he's in already."

She stood up. "Thanks for the helping to clean up my mess. I need to go. I'll get my things. Will you check on Gar for me?"

"Sure thing." He emptied the dustpan.

She smoothed her hair back and frowned. The temptation to stay home, destroy all the recording devices in the apartment, and hide from the world, tugged.

"Brielle, come here." The frantic ring in Torgin's voice sent her scurrying from the kitchen.

He pulled her into the bathroom, out of the recording device's range. "Gar's gone. There's no sign of him."

Panic surged through Brie, ready to plunge into a power packed wave. Spyglass trotting from the music room alone made it dissolve. A flash of light illuminated the room. A grinning Gar appeared and grew serious. "What's happened?"

Torgin rounded on him. "You. You're what happened. Where were you?"

A sheepish grin flickered. He shut the bathroom door. "I went to make sure the studio apartment is safe for Brie to visit. Ari and I got talkin'." He smiled at Brie. "Your sister's pretty cool, ya know."

Brie, arms folded across her chest, gazed down at him. "You'd better practice what you preach, Garon. Next time, you tell us what you're up to."

"Never frighten us like that again." Torgin knelt to look Gar in the eye. "Understand?"

Gar squirmed. "Sorry. Didn't mean to scare ya."

Brie relaxed her arms. "Tell us what you discovered."

"Everything's fine. Penee's better. Ya know what she told me? Ari helped neutralize the rest of the drug." He grinned. "Ari couldn't believe she did it. She told me Penee needs rest and to come over later and bring dinner." He grinned. "I told 'em we'd bring a surprise."

Torgin looked from one to the other. "I gotta go. You two be careful today."

Brie nudged Gar toward the bathroom door. "So do we. Let's go together. I'll meet you two in the hall." The door shutting behind them triggered her shift to Rayna. Corralling her scattered thoughts, she double-checked her dance bag, grabbed an umbrella, and walked through her room to the hall.

Gar cocked his head. "Why do ya need that?"

The distant rumbling of thunder supplied the answer.

He shook his head. "Ya know everything before me."

The subway to Lincoln Center, packed with people and smelling of urine and trash, did little to enhance Rayna's foul mood. Gar and Torgin gave her a wide berth. When they reached 66th Street and exited the train, she stomped up the cement stairs, muttering under her breath as she opened the umbrella.

Torgin shot Gar a sympathetic grin. "Good luck." He raised a brow at Rayna. "Hope you figure out what's causing your grump, Rayna Deejara." He strode into Juilliard.

Rain dripping from the umbrella into her shoes didn't improve Rayna's mood. At the door to SAB, her attempt to smile at her young companion ended in a grimace.

Gar looked contrite. "I didn't mean ta ruin the day. I was takin' care of ya, that's all."

"This isn't about you, Gar. I woke up grouchy and haven't been able to shake it. Panicking about you didn't help, but it's not what's making me edgy. I sure wish I knew what was." She rubbed the back of her neck. *The Star of Truth, even hidden by Rayna's persona, should warn me of trouble.*

Gar tugged at her shirt. "I bet dancin'll make your day better." He held open the door.

"Sure hope you're right." She closed the umbrella and hiked up the stairs.

※　　※

Esán arrived at the theater to find Rich working backstage. "Hi. Have you seen Joe?"

The lighting tech jerked his thumb toward the auditorium. "He's front of house. Said he needed some quiet time."

Esán walked on stage and scanned the rows of red seats.

"I'm out here." Joe waved from midway back in the dimly lit theater. "Join me."

Esán used the exit from backstage and walked up the red-carpeted aisle. He sat next to Joe with his bag on the seat beside him. "I expected to see Summer here."

Joe resettled in his plush red seat. "I suggested she take a few days off to catch up on her classwork. There's no point in exposing her to danger, too." He wrote a note on his clipboard, then raised his critical gaze to examine Esán. "You look rested."

"Karl forbade us to leave the hotel, so I managed a good night's sleep. What's on the agenda for today?"

"You tell me. The lighting plot for *Gems* is about done. The ballet will premier in another week. That gives us some time to search for the stones."

Esán heard the fatigue in his mentor's voice. "You know we could send you and your wife somewhere safe. You don't have to stay in New York."

"Corvus and I talked about that." A smile made a quick appearance. "I like him, by the way." He pursed his lips in a distracted fashion, then shook himself. "I've committed to help with the search. Corvus seems to think Upori was the last person to handle the stones. If you were him, where would you hide them?"

Esán considered all the options. "There are only two buildings in Lincoln Center Upori, as Michael Mazer, had access to: SAB's facilities in the Juilliard Building and the State theater." He sat back. "I'll see what I can discover from here. Maybe I can pinpoint a place to begin."

Joe blinked. "From here? How?"

"It's called a mental probe."

"Never mind." Joe stood up. "I'll be backstage. Come find me when you're done." He side-stepped along the row and strode down the aisle.

Esán centered his thoughts, closed his eyes, and began a scan of the theater and the buildings close by.

The whisper of leather soles in the aisle stopped next to him. "Find anything?" Corvus perched on the arm of a seat.

"No. You?"

He shook dark hair back from his face. "Nope. Almiralyn is pretty sure they were in the costume shop. Gar found a box filled with packing paper that reeked of the stones. Neither of us can track them from there. They've vanished without a trace. How's Joe holding up?"

"He's overwhelmed but managing. What's next, Corvus?"

"You keep Joe occupied and safe from Sorda and from himself. I'll check in with you later." He disappeared into the darkness.

Ricco marched down the aisle, his expression blazing with curiosity. "Who was that?"

The desire to be flippant almost won over common sense. Instead, Esán rose and reached for his bag.

Ricco gripped his wrist. "Answer me. Sorda wants to know everyone you and Dwight talk to. Who was the guy?"

Esán pulled his hand away. "I believe he's an accompanist at SAB."

"Why was he talking to you?"

"Because I was here, Ricco. He'd never been in this theater and was asking questions."

"Like?"

Esán hoisted his book bag. "Like, where's the restroom—where is the grand piano kept—do I know the stage manager's name?" He looped the leather strap over his shoulder. "I have work to do. Come with me or stay here. Your choice." He turned and exited the row at the opposite end.

Ricco, grumbling to himself, trudged up the aisle to a side exit.

Esán shook his head and went in search of Joe.

R ayna glared at herself in the floor to ceiling mirror. *Concentrate.* She struggled to focus on dance while her rebellious thoughts played leapfrog. *We need to find the Corps Stones. Dwight's anxious to know his lineage. How do we convince the Mindeco to work with us?* Her thoughts scrambled like eggs in a pan, leaving her confused and frustrated.

"Miss Deejara, are you in *this* room or somewhere else?"

Rayna, cheeks flushed scarlet, glanced at the studio reflected in the mirror and realized the entire class waited to hear her reply. Lois smirked. Kelsia shot her a worried look. Corvus, a brow raised, observed her from behind the piano.

She made a slow pivot. "I am so sorry, Madame Dolavina. I promise to pay attention."

The teacher's eyes flickered with a spark of concern. "See me in my office at the end of class. Please dancers, we will do the *ronde de jambe* combination from yesterday. Mr. Corvino."

The shuffle of students preparing to begin the exercise covered Rayna's embarrassment. Promising herself she would stay present, she attempted to immerse herself in the combination. Midway through, a knife-sharp pain left her gasping. A spasm turned her knees to rubber. She crumpled to the studio floor.

Madame Dolavina signed to her accompanist to stop playing. "Please, Mr. Corvino, help Rayna to the dressing room. Kelsia, go with them. Rejoin us when you can.

Her words barely penetrated the wall of pain overflowing Rayna's awareness. Muscular arms lifting her to standing helped her to cling to reality. Relieved to have support on the laborious walk down the hall, she leaned on the man beside her. Through a blur, she recognized Mira waiting at the dressing room door.

"I'll help her from here, Mr. Corvino. Please tell Madame Dolavina if Rayna can't manage the rest of the day, I'll make sure she gets home."

Mr. Corvino waited by the door, his gaze sympathetic and questioning, while Mira helped her to a bench.

"I'll see you after class, Rayna." Mr. Corvina closed the door and left.

Kelsia set her dance bag on the floor. "Should I stay and help take care of her, Miss Mira?"

"She'll be fine." Mira peered at the wall of lockers. "Show me which locker is Rayna's. Check with me after class, and I'll let you know how she's doing."

When the door clicked shut for the second time and Kelsia's footsteps had faded, Mira sat down. "Rayna, look at me. I'm going to touch your forehead."

Soft fingers brushing her temples steadied Rayna's trembling limbs. Her confused thoughts cleared. "What's wrong with me, Mira? I woke up this morning edgy, even a bit angry. Now, I feel as though I have the flu."

Mira pulled her street clothes from the locker. "Change. What you're experiencing is the pull of our time and the tenuous balance being maintained by the Guardians. The Clenaba Rolas Solar System is in trouble.

"We must find the Corps Stones. Gar is already searching the other costume areas. Torgin is scouring the hall and the orchestra pit in the theater. Esán and Joe are working on the backstage area, dressing rooms, and catwalks."

Rayna pulled her Kelly green T-shirt over her head. "Does Dwight know what's going on?"

"No. We left him in men's class. We don't want Sorda to suspect anything." She studied Rayna, her sapphire eyes alight with worry. "How do you feel?"

"Shaky, but okay. Am I the only one reacting?"

"The Star of Truth gives you dimensional awareness the rest of us lack. The Guardians enhanced its ability for this trip to the past. You are a barometer to alert us when changes occur."

Rayna shivered. "Now what?"

"Let's go to the costume shop. You can shift to Brielle, and we can check on Gar's progress. Then we need to find the Mindeco. Corvus and I believe he was the last to touch the stones. I made a subtle mental scan of Dwight and Sorda. Neither one has any knowledge of their location."

Rayna stuffed her dance bag in the locker, her mind a whirlpool of what ifs.

34

Torgin, at Mira's behest, searched the rehearsal hall and the orchestra pit for the Corps Stones. When he found nothing to suggest they had been in either, he ate a quick lunch at Juilliard's cafeteria and slipped into an empty practice room. *I hope Mr. Pauley will be at rehearsal, but if not, I intend to be ready.*

Stravinsky had written the piano part in the Capriccio to showcase his own virtuoso skills. Torgin didn't intend to let Stravinsky or himself down. With meticulous care, he practiced each section. His confidence grew little by little until an hour later, he straddled the bench, a grin on his face and excitement churning. "Today's my first rehearsal in the orchestra pit."

With Stravinsky's music buzzing in his brain, he collected his flute case, hurried past the fountains, and entered backstage a few steps behind Lana and a young harpist.

Lana led the way downstairs to the orchestra pit and paused. "How's your mother doing, Yvonne? I understand she hasn't been well."

The harpist smiled. "She's doing much better since I arranged with her supervisor to let her work on costumes at home. Having something to keep her occupied seems to have helped her recovery."

"I'm delighted to hear it." Lana waved at a fellow violinist and made her way through the pit to the string section.

Torgin watched the harpist take her seat. A question struggling to surface faded as the excitement of playing in the orchestra pit demanded his attention. Today, the pit would remain in the basement; tomorrow, they would raise it to floor level. He grinned, took a preparatory breath, and entered.

Lana's supportive smile caught his eye. He returned it with a smile of his own.

Behind him, a sneering male voice announced, "If it isn't the conductor's pet."

Someone shushed him as Matt Harwood wove his way to the podium, sorted his music, and picked up his baton. He tapped the music stand. "Glen Pauley continues to be under the weather. Since you helped us out yesterday, Mr. Whälen, I'd appreciate it if you would do so again today."

He waited for Torgin to adjust the piano bench and organize his music, then stood poised to begin. "Let's warm up."

The orchestra went through a set of established exercises. At their completion, Mr. Harwood waited for the shuffling of musical scores to grow quiet, then tapped the podium and raised his baton. "Act II from the top please." He gave the downbeat. Stravinsky's music filled the pit.

Torgin, immersed in the thing he loved most in the Universe, let memory carry him through the *presto* and slip him effortlessly into the calmer *andante* movement. At its close, Mr. Harwood tapped the top of the stand, guided the orchestra through several difficult sections, and with a smile of satisfaction lowered his baton.

"Take a fifteen-minute break. We'll work on the *allegro* when we reconvene. Mr. Whälen, I'd like to speak with you."

Chairs scraped. Orchestra members wandered backstage. Torgin waited for the conductor to finish conversing with an older musician, then joined him at the podium.

"You did well today." Humor sparkled. "I noticed you played from memory. That's quite a feat. How long did you practice last night?"

Torgin grinned. "Awhile. I hope Glen is on the mend."

Harwood sobered. "That's what I want to talk to you about. He's not doing well. How would you feel about being the official understudy? I can't promise you an evening performance, but I think we can arrange a matinee. What do you say?"

"I'm happy to help, sir. Thank you for the opportunity."

Harwood smiled. "Good. I'll extend the break five minutes, so we can both catch our breath." He left the pit, deep in conversation with the first violinist.

The need for quiet sent Torgin slipping from the theater. He stood near the stage door, breathing in the freshness of rain-moistened air and allowing his mind to wander. A telepathic message flickered. *Find Corvus after rehearsal.*

Disquiet erased his moment of content. Torn between the desire to know what had transpired and the pull of the piano, he returned to the pit and the music that enlivened his soul.

Harwood called the orchestra to order. "I have an announcement. Glen Pauley is unable to return for another week. I have asked Torgin Whälen to be his permanent understudy." His gaze flicked to the oboist. "If you have negative thoughts about this, please keep them to yourselves. We have work to do."

The rest of the rehearsal flew by. The third movement required the most work. Repeated sections echoed through the theater. Woodwinds, brass, percussion, and strings practiced separately, then together. By the end of the hour, Matt Harwood beamed. "Thank you for a great rehearsal. See you tomorrow."

As the musicians dispersed, Lana walked up to the piano. "You were amazing today." She glanced over her shoulder. "I think you even impressed your favorite opponents." She nodded before joining the exodus of bodies.

Torgin ran a hand over the Steinway grand's ivory keys. *What a marvelous instrument! The sound is so much richer than the apartment piano.*

Wariness sounded an alarm in his head. He gripped the handle of his flute case and came to his feet, eyes scanning the exit. A shadowy form dodged to one side. A single blazing eye peered into the pit.

Torgin tensed. A raven landed on his shoulder. The Mindeco's disappointed howl pursued him as he teleported with the raven to a dressing room near the stage door.

Corvus materialized. "You're learning to use your gifts. Well done."

"Thanks. What do we do about the Mindeco?"

"You warn the others. I'll track him. With luck, he'll lead me to his hideout." Corvus' dimple deepened. "I heard you playing. I had no idea how talented you are. Never stop, Torgin." He stepped back. "I'm off. Brie and Mira are in the costume shop."

"Wait. Where's Gar?"

"He's with Brielle. Stay alert." He flashed from view.

Torgin absorbed the peaceful emptiness. *Wish I could stay right here.*

Leaving the quiet dressing room behind, he hurried from the theater.

The Mindeco skulked through the early evening in Central Park, his thoughts in a jumble, his frustration ready to boil over. He reached the eastern side and crouched in the shadows. Eyeballing the people coming and going from The Plaza Hotel, he reviewed his actions over the past two weeks.

I hid the three stones in the costume shop. I went to check on them. His anger rumbled. *The box was there, but no stones.* He caught a bug on the tip of his tongue, sucked it down, and spit. *Dwight must have found them.* He growled under his breath. "The boy knows nothing. That leaves Sorda." A wave of hatred almost choked him. *I will pay you back, Karlsut. If you had lived up to your end of the deal, I'd still be enacting the role of Michael Mazer.*

The futile wish to shape shift a bird and soar over the city left him scowling. Mindeco could only change shape by seizing and merging with a Human. Resentfulness rubbing him raw, he sank deeper into the night's muggy darkness and glared at the hotel.

He had threatened to seize a series of bodies that he would then leave whole to be found and mourned. Canines clicked together. He knew doing so would bring unwanted attention in his direction. *I have no desire to become the hunted. In this crime infested city, fear would spread like wildfire.* Fear, he realized, made Humans do things they might not otherwise even consider.

I require a body no one would expect me to appropriate. A wicked gleam lit his central oculus. *I know just the one, but I need to plan with care.*

To avoid being seen, he zigzagged his way back to Central Park West. Crouched within a group of trees, he prepared to wait. Getting to his hideout meant exposing himself to discovery if he traveled before the dinner crowds thinned.

A yawn reminded him he had not slept in several turnings—days on this planet. Tucking his head between his knobby knees, he covered it with long, leathery arms. His internal alarm set to wake him at midnight, he relaxed into a sleep state light enough to keep him safe.

Brielle and Mira re-examined the cardboard box Gar had discovered. The faint residue of the Corps Stones' power remained. A search of the costume shop and sewing rooms nearby netted them nothing new.

Gar trailed Spyglass between fabric-covered tables. "The stones were in that box, in this room. Where'd they go?" He angled a chair to face the women. "Could Upori Athai hide 'em without the Mindeco knowin'?"

Mira shook her head. "When the Mindeco seizes a body, he usurps his victim's mind. That Upori maintained any control is unusual."

"In the box one minute, gone the next." Gar's brow crinkled. "Dwight didn't take 'em. Sorda's never been ta this place. So, who walked off with 'em?"

Torgin strode into the room. "Hope you found something 'cause I came up empty-handed at the theater."

Esán descended the steep steps, attention fixed on Brie. "I understand you've had a rough day. How are you feeling?" He placed a protective hand on her shoulder.

Brie sighed. "I'm fine. I had a bit of a meltdown. Mira tells me it's a sign our solar system is reacting to the three missing Corps Stones. We're trying to decide where to search for them next."

Torgin pulled a chair into the circle. "Are you positive Rikell didn't abscond with them?"

Brie rubbed the back of her neck. "The Mindeco is as eager to find them as Karlsut Sorda. Personal gain tops their lists of reasons why they want them, so they'll be after us once we're in possession of the stones."

She acknowledged the concern on Esán's face with a small smile. "I'm fine, Esán." She squeezed the hand resting on her shoulder. "Did you discover anything?"

He planted a kiss on the top of her red curls, grabbed a chair, and joined the group. "Nothing. I sent Joe home with explicit instructions to stay put. We plan to meet at the theater to put the final touches on the lighting plot in the morning."

Corvus entered from between costume racks. "Good call. I'll stop in to see him later tonight. Where are the watchdogs, Ricco and Pike?"

"I told them Torgin, Dwight, and I were attending a special presentation and we'd see them by the fountain at eight o'clock. I also left a message at the hotel for Sorda." He glanced at the stairs. "Speaking of Dwight, has anyone seen him. He said he'd meet me here."

The Star of Truth tingled. Brie frowned. "Why didn't he come with you?"

Esán snapped to attention. "What's wrong, Brielle?"

She rubbed her neck. "I'm not sure. The star's tingling... Not sufficient to shout imminent danger, but enough to say something's not quite right."

"The Seeds have been restive, too. Stay alert everyone."

Torgin set his flute case on the table. "Corvus, did you find out where the Mindeco is hiding?"

"No. I left him sleeping on the west side of the park. He's up to something. Reading his thoughts is a tricky business, so I'm not sure what. Has anyone checked on Penee and Ari today?"

Gar squirmed in his chair. "I saw 'em this morning before Rayna and me left the apartment. Penee still doesn't feel so good. Ari's keepin' her busy practicin' stuff."

"What stuff?" Brie sat straighter.

"Bet ya didn't know they're the openin' act at a concert in the park next weekend, right?"

Brie shook her head. "Wow! Their music ploy is real, not something to distract Sorda's attention from Ira. My goodness, we are all up to our ears in learning new things."

Mira laughed. "Isn't that what life's all about?" She glanced at a small clock on her sewing table. "We have just under two hours to plan our next move. It appears the stones were in the costume shop but aren't any longer. Someone, we aren't certain who, removed them from their hiding place. Think. Have you seen or heard anything that might help us?"

A concentrated silence fell over the group. After a brief interval, Brie sighed. "We're wasting time. Let's take a break."

Gar shot her a sheepish glance. "Don't suppose we could eat soon? That would be a good use of our time, right?"

Brie gazed from one member of the group to the next. "We have about an hour and a half before the boys meet their keepers. "What do you say to dinner at the Juilliard cafeteria? It has great food."

Mira nodded her approval. "I think that's a grand idea. You go. I have things to do here." She walked them to the exit. "Keep your eyes open and take care of each other."

Brie hugged her. "You sound like you're saying goodbye forever."

"Our forevers are intertwined. Go." Mira walked back toward her sewing table.

Brie stared after her, foreboding tugging her lips down at the corners. She hurried to catch up with Esán and slipped her hand into his.

He searched her face. "Is something wrong?"

She glanced back. "I'm not sure." Giving herself a shake, she urged him faster.

35

A rush of foreboding paused Esán at the door to the cafeteria. "You go ahead, Brie. I'd better find Dwight."

"Are the Seeds acting up?"

He hugged her. "I'll just feel happier if I'm sure he's okay."

"I'm coming with you." Brie clutched his hand. "Torgin and Gar, you eat. We'll join you when we can."

Gar rolled his eyes and folded his arms. "You keep forgettin' your promise. Where you go, I go."

Torgin gave a low chuckle. "Guess that means postponing dinner. Where do we begin the search?"

Corvus stepped from the shadows. "The Mindeco has Dwight. He wants the stones, or he'll invade his body and find them himself." His solemn gaze found Brie. "You'd better tell us Dwight's identity. Is he powerful enough to hold Rikell at bay?"

A shiver of dread skimming over Brie pressed her closer to Esán. He put an arm around her. "I suggest we eat while Brie share's what she knows. Do we need to include Mira, Corvus?"

"She's on the way." He held open the cafeteria door.

Esán led his companions through the food line to a quiet corner near the back entrance. The sounds of chairs and trays and people settling gradually quieted. Torgin surveyed the room and nodded at Gar. A soft whistle brought Spyglass padding in from the hall to lie down at his master's feet.

Esán, noting Brie's far-off expression, decided to let her direct the conversation and savored a bite of cheese ravioli.

She poked at her salad, sighed, and put down her fork. A VarTerel's dignity cloaked her. "My instincts rebel at sharing Dwight's true identity without his knowledge. It feels like betrayal." She frowned. "I would prefer that he hear it first and tell you in his own way. What I will share is that Dwight is far more powerful than his mother led him to believe."

Corvus leaned forward. "Dwight knows he can teleport and use telepathy, correct?"

Brie nodded. "Yes, he does; so does the Mindeco."

Mira walked through the cafeteria and pulled up a chair next to Corvus. He filled her in on what she had missed. When he finished, her attention shifted to Brie. "Can you send a message to Dwight without alerting the Mindeco?"

"Rikell isn't telepathic." Brie shoved her food back and forth on her tray. "My concern is Dwight might give himself away."

Mira nibbled a French fry from Corvus' plate. "Eat up, Brielle. You need all the fuel you can get." She pilfered another bite. "Does Sorda realize Rikell has Dwight?"

Corvus shook his head. "Did you know he promised the Mindeco Dwight's body if he found the stones?"

Esán ate the last of his ravioli. "I bet Dwight falling victim to the Mindeco is not part of Karl's deal with his mother." He placed his folded napkin on the tray. "Dwight has a tracker disc in his neck. Once Karl learns he's missing, he'll be able to find him."

Torgin stacked the empty trays. "Does Sorda know who Dwight really is?"

"If he knew, he wouldn't have promised the Mindeco his body." Esán slid his tray toward him. "What's our plan?"

Brie touched the star. "Rikell is unpredictable. Rescuing Dwight needs to be our priority."

Torgin wrinkled his brow. "I'm guessing we can't go into the past again." He stood up, trays in hand. "I'll be back."

Esán looked at Corvus. "I saw you shake your head in response to time travel."

"Rikell isn't stupid. He'll be watching for any repeated behaviors. He warned me not to follow him to his hideout, or he would invade Dwight's body immediately."

Gar flicked a crumb from his new blue shirt. "I bet Spyglass and me can find him." He wrinkled his nose. "His smell is a dead give-away. Ya think he'd expect me ta be lookin'?"

Mira rested an elbow on the table. "Perhaps not, but if he caught you, he'd have two hostages, both of whom we would do anything to keep safe."

Gar reached down to scratch Spyglass' ear. "That Mindeco ain't gonna catch me, 'specially if I have a raven close by." His eyes bored into Corvus, whose dimple formed a valley in his right cheek. "What do ya say, Corvus, wanna be my partner?"

Mira frowned. "Is that a good—"

Corvus stopped her with a smile. "What's your plan, Garon?"

Gar pursed his lips. "Rikell likes prowlin' at night, right?"

Corvus tipped his head. "He does."

"If we're gonna find 'im, maybe night's the best time. He won't expect us ta be out in the dark, so he might mess up. I say we go ta where ya last saw him. I'm bettin' his scent's still strong. We find his trail and play it by ear."

Reminiscent of his raven persona, Corvus cocked his head. "I believe we have a plan. Do you know how to shape shift?"

"Ain't tried."

"Then, it's time you did."

Gar, bursting with excitement, hugged his dog. "Stay with Brie, Spyglass. Protect her good."

The black and white terrier rested his nose on the edge of her chair.

Corvus rose. "Mira, can you check on Joe?"

"Will do." She smiled. Seriousness erased any levity from her expression. "You both be vigilant."

Torgin checked the clock over the register. "The watchdogs are our next challenge. How do we explain Dwight's absence?"

The shuffling of four people extricating themselves from cafeteria chairs took precedence over conversation. They filed through the back exit to regroup in the hall.

Mira fixed a serious gaze on the boys. "Don't tell Ricco and Pike anything. You know nothing about Dwight—except that you're worried. Brie and Torgin, stick close to the phone in case Rikell checks on you. Esán, handle Sorda with kid gloves. Don't let him out of your sight. If you need help..." She tapped her temple. "I'll come as soon as I can. I'm off to see Joe."

Esán clasped Brie's hand and followed Torgin across the street. They paused at the corner of Philharmonic Hall. Ricco and Pike waited at the fountain. Esán, steeling himself for the encounter, stepped past his companions into the open.

Ricco squinted through the dancing water and marched to meet them. "Where's Dwight?"

Esán schooled his features to a worried expression. "We can't find him. We've looked everywhere."

Pike joined them. "The kid and the dog? They gone too?"

Torgin changed his flute case to the other hand. "Gar headed to the apartment to make sure it's safe. He takes his job seriously, you know."

Pike scowled, then focused on Esán. "When did you see Dwight last?"

"I saw him after his men's technique class. He was going to change and said he would meet us at the cafeteria."

Ricco snarled under his breath. "Better get back to the hotel." He groaned. "Sorda's gonna have my head." He eyed Esán. "You got money for a cab, or do we take the subway?"

"I have money."

Ricco snorted and marched toward the street.

Esán hugged Brie, then paused beside Torgin. "Take care of her." Not waiting for a reply, he jogged after Ricco.

Through the rear window of the cab, he watched Brie, Torgin, and Pike climb into a taxi down the block.

"You be careful, Brielle AsTar."

"You too, Esán Efre."

The Checkered Cab nosed its way into traffic, joining an endless stream of yellow.

Gar and Corvus arrived in a darkened ballet studio to the silence of night. Light shining through the windows created rectangular shapes on the floor. After pulling the blinds on the observation window, Corvus walked to the center of the studio.

"I know you have never shifted shape. Do you have questions?"

Butterflies bouncing into one another in Gar's stomach threatened to steal his voice. Small hands pressed against his belly; he did his best to reply. "Brie told me I have ta remember I'm Human. She said if I forget, I might get stuck in a shifted shape for always." He shuddered. "I'll remember."

"The beauty and magic of an animal's form can be overwhelming, Gar. You must cling to your humanity, no matter how much you cherish your chosen shape." Seriousness gave way to a reminiscent smile. "I know this because I love my raven form." His gravity returned. "Awareness of my attachment to it is vital. I almost lost myself one time." He shivered. "Never again." Raven-black eyes moved from Gar's head to his feet and returned to his face. "What form would be best for you?"

Gar raised a hand. Corvus' eyes sparkled. "Yes?"

"Could I be a raven like you?"

"Why a raven?"

"Gin used to tell me stories of the raven." Gar rubbed sweaty palms on his jeans. "He was born a long way from New York. His granddad told him stories, and Gin told me.

"The raven's a trickster. You know, like a joker. It used its cunnin' to create the world. Then it stole the stars, the moon, and the sun from a rich man and put them in the sky to light it. It tricked another man so it could bring water to the world so plants and animals could grow.

"Gin told me the raven was his totem animal. It watched over him." Emotions broke like waves on the beach. A tear leaked and dripped from his chin. He forced a smile. "I want to shape a raven 'cause of Gin and 'cause it's black like me."

Corvus stared in silence at the studio mirror. A pivot brought his sharp gaze to rest on Gar. "Give me your hands and shut your eyes, young Garon."

Mentally crossing his fingers, Gar held out his hands. Warmth flowed from Corvus' palms to his. A mental probe made him gasp. Discipline and desire kept him from pulling his hands away. The probe withdrew. His palms cooled.

Corvus released his hands. "You can open your eyes."

Gar shoved a nervous tremor away. "Do I get ta shape a raven?"

Corvus, his expression more serious than Gar had ever seen it, knelt and looked him in the eye. "You are young to assume a raven's form. If you didn't possess the power you do, I would say no. They are tough birds to control, Gar —highly intelligent and clever." His gaze intensified. "Promise me you will never ever give in to their cunning."

Gar rested steady hands on his mentor's shoulders. "I promise on the memory of Gin I will not give in ta the raven's cunnin'. I vow ta use its form ta help me achieve my destiny."

The dimple in Corvus' cheek quivered and deepened. "Mira told me you're special. Let's get to work. Is there anything else you want to share about the raven."

Gar controlled the desire to jump for joy by reaching back in his memory.

He knelt in front of Spyglass. "I'm nine years old today, and I get ta play chess in Washington Square Park with Gin." He stuffed the box containing the chess pieces in his raggedy backpack, whistled for his dog, and hurried to meet Gin at the subway.

They got off at the park and hiked up the stairs. A raven swooped overhead and cackled a greeting. Gin gazed after it. "I believe that raven just wished you a happy birthday, young Gar." Spyglass gave a sharp bark and strained on his rope leash.

Not far along the walkway, the raven landed in a tree above an empty stone table. Gin, his eyes twinkling, sat down. "This is our table, boy." He brushed a few stray leaves off the chessboard painted on the tabletop and accepted the box of chess pieces. "Since you are the birthday boy, you get to begin."

Gar grinned and set up the white pieces on the black and white squares. He glanced at Spyglass, then at the raven watching them from one shiny, black eye, and sat down. "Ya think he's good luck, Spy?" His dog rested his pointy nose on his paws and looked up at him. Gar studied his pieces, moved a pawn forward one square, and nodded at Gin. Move by move, they attacked and counterattacked.

The game was nearing its end when the raven fluttered to a lower branch. Gin looked up and smiled. Gar reached for his queen, heard a flurry of wings, felt a rush of air brushing his cheek, and watched the raven flying off with the chess piece in its black beak. He shot to his feet to chase it. Gin shook his head, reached a wrinkled, arthritic hand out to hover over his king. With a low, gurgling sound, he picked it up. The raven landed on the table, dropped the white queen on a black square, cawed, and soared upward. It landed on the branch, bobbing its head up and down. Gin chuckled his delight.

Gar jumped up and down. "Whoopee! I won the game!"

Gar swallowed a lump in his throat. "When I was a kid—" He eyed Corvus from beneath his thick lashes. The man's serious expression did not falter. "Gin taught me all about 'em. I've studied 'em by watchin', too." He bit his bottom lip. "Gin said they have a faster heartbeat than other birds and super quick minds. They're real smart. They can figure stuff out and communicate with other creatures. What else do I need ta know?"

Corvus looked down at him. "It sounds like Gin taught you well. Create a raven's picture in my mind."

Gar shut his eyes, his thoughts concentrated on every detail he could remember. The image formed. He placed it in mind.

"Excellent. Next, I'll place an image in your mind. Tell me when it's clear."

A young raven took shape.

"I can see it, Corvus."

"Okay, nod when you feel its heartbeat."

Gar pressed a hand against his chest and gulped a startled breath. "Oh!"

"Let your mind embrace the raven's. Do nothing else."

The quickness of the raven's mind intertwining with his caught Gar by surprise. He yelped. His eyes opened full-wide. His fingers curled. From a distance, he heard panting and forced himself to take a long breath. His gaze darted to Corvus.

"You're fine, Gar. Keep your eyes on me and your focus on the raven. Breathe."

Gar sighed and relaxed his fists.

"Good. If you feel stable, blink."

Gar's lids lowered and opened.

"When I tell you, shut your eyes, picture the raven's inky black feathers, its black eyes, beak, and legs. Imagine yourself in its body. Allow its quick, intelligent brain to become yours. Embrace its heartbeat as your own. Do nothing else. Understand?"

He blinked.

Corvus stepped back. "Close your eyes, Garon. See the bird in all its glory. On my count, make it your own. One... two... three... NOW!"

The change from Human to raven flowed with the ease of morning into day. Gar, his black talons resting on the smooth, gray flooring in the studio, marveled at his good fortune. Raven eyes picked out minute details. Raven wings unfurled, shook, and folded against his sleek body. He opened his beak, tasted the air on his raven tongue, and let loose a caw which made him jump in surprise.

"Gar, if you can hear me, ruffle your feathers."

His feathers lifted, quivered, and settled into place.

Corvus knelt. "I am going to shape Karrew. We will fly together two circles around the studio. I'll land and change. You'll land on my arm and wait for me to tell you when to shift. Are your ready to fly?"

Gar's feathers trembled. Karrew appeared beside him. The word 'fly' drifted between them. Karrew fanned his wings and lifted into flight. Gar imitated his every move. Air whispered around him. The studio floated beneath him. His raven heart sang. Wings pressing against air sent him higher. Circle one... circle two... Too soon, Karrew alighted at the studio's center. Corvus materialized and raised an arm.

Gar landed, wrapped his claws around human muscle and bone. Confusion shook him. Corvus ran a hand down his feathered back.

"Easy, young Gar. Flutter to the floor. Picture your authentic form. On my count, shift to Human."

Raven wings carried him floor-ward. His taloned-feet touched down. He folded his wings, pictured his human shape, and cocked his head to see his mentor.

"One... Two... Three... Shift!"

Corvus' command triggered the change from raven to Human. Gar doubled over, seeking reality. Air entered his human lungs. Blood pulsed through his veins. Human thoughts soaking in a chaos of emotions almost dropped him to his knees. A tremor straightened his spine. He looked at Corvus. "I wish Gin had been here ta watch me fly." He shook his head. "I had no idea. Thank you."

A powerful arm encircled his shoulders. "You are a brave young man. Are you ready to find the Mindeco?"

Gar leaned his head against Corvus' solid side. "Will we fly?"

A laugh shook the ribcage. "Yes, but not until we're outside." Corvus moved away, raised the blinds, and held open the door.

Karlsut Sorda met Esán and Ricco at the door of The Penthouse. "Where's Dwight?" Anger underscored every word.

A scowling Ricco jerked a thumb at Esán. "Have to ask him, Boss."

Sorda stepped aside. "In here, now. I'll meet you in the sitting room." He marched to his private office. From inside, a howl of frustration erupted. The door flew open. He emerged red-faced and fuming.

"Who sabotaged my equipment? I can't track Dwight without it." He glared down his long nose at Ricco. "I want him found. I want him right here. You have two hours."

Ricco stuttered. "I d-don't even know where to b-begin looking."

Sorda rounded on Esán. "Go with him, Nesá. Be back with Dwight at your side by ten-thirty, or I will have Joe Shyro brought to me." His anger sliced the air like cut glass. "I will make his life more miserable than you can imagine. Understood?"

Esán grabbed Ricco by the arm. Half dragging him, he marched him from The Penthouse to the elevator. The metal door slid shut. He glared at the panel of numbered buttons, his arms folded, his mind racing. *What are you up to, Dwight Anders?*

Ricco snarled. "He was with you when he disappeared. You'd better—"

The elevator stopping at the third floor cut him short. A couple dressed for a night of dancing entered and moved to the opposite side of the car. At the main floor, Esán and Ricco followed them into the lobby.

Ricco strode out the main exit and turned toward Central Park South. At the corner he stopped. "*You'd* better find him, Esán." His voice was hard-edged, his eyes narrowed. "I'm not goin' with you. I'll only be in your way. At ten-fifteen, I'll meet you in our favorite pizza place. Go do your thing." He shoved his hands in his pockets and walked west.

Esán, relief as tangible as the night breeze, crossed to Central Park; strolled down a moonlit path; and, when the coast was clear, stepped off the trail.

Gar jogged beside Corvus, who led the way from the Juilliard Building onto Amsterdam Avenue and strode uptown to a pass-through several buildings away.

"Alright, Gar, this is the plan. We'll fly to the park and land in a tree above the spot where the Mindeco hid. The common raven lacks a developed olfactory gland, but we retain all our individual gifts in our shifted forms. I'm hoping your acute sense of smell will pick up his scent. Stay close to me. If we get separated, land. Aerial views are confusing, so stay put. I'll find you. Are you ready?"

Gar sucked in a breath. "Yes, sir, Corvus."

"Good. You change, then I will."

Gar pictured the young raven, embraced its heartbeat and its quick intelligence, and counted to himself. The air shimmered. Blue-black feathers ruffled and settled close to his bird body.

Corvus nodded. *"Good job. My turn."*

Karrew flashed into being. Waddled steps carried him along the pass-though. His wings spread. A dark, glistening eye glinted Gar's direction.

Gar opened his wings. Karrew shot upward. With a clumsy lift into the air, Gar steadied and soared after him. An odd assortment of roofs passing beneath them formed a foreign-looking landscape. A river of lights flickered along the distant streets. The faint sounds of honking horns floated upward. In no time at all, the trees of Central Park reached toward them. Karrew flew between leafy branches to land above a cluster of large rocks hidden amongst several hackberry trees.

Gar alighted, took a moment to stabilize, then lifted his beak. The odors of earth, dog feces, and animal decay almost made him dizzy. He fluttered to the top of a large, gray rock, hopped to the ground, and, with a waddling strut, followed the fading aroma of the Mindeco.

Corvus fluttered to a landing beside him. *"You lead. I'll warn you of danger."*

The Mindeco's decaying odor led them past the 72nd Street Station to 73rd Street. Flying low, they rounded the corner onto Riverside Drive. Midway down the block, nestled between more modern, taller buildings, a high wooden fence obscured what lay beyond. Gar flew to a square opening cut in the fence. His raven eyes peered into a jungle of weeds surrounding a once grand house. From his perch, he could make out splintered boards and shingles scattered on the ground beneath a dilapidated turret. Support beams kept the balcony from toppling. Moss-covered siding, long devoid of paint, soaked up the moon's cool light. A sign on the porch read *Construction Zone - No Trespassing* in fading red letters. The powerful stench of Mindeco saturated the night breeze.

Corvus flew into the darkness created by the close-growing trees in a park across the street and shaped Human. Gar, landed beside him, shifted, and grinned.

Corvus nodded his understanding but remained serious. "I'll see what the situation is inside. You keep watch."

Gar opened his mouth to argue. Corvus shook his head. "The Mindeco is smart; so is Dwight. We can't afford to give our presence away. If I'm not back in ten minutes, go to the apartment." His smile flashed. "You've done well today."

A soft shimmer later, Karrew soared over the fence. Gar fought the temptation to follow. Instead, raven wings carried him to a leafy branch of a large elm. Well-hidden, he gazed up at the distant stars. Wonder flooded his senses. *I can shape a raven!*

rie stood in the living room with Sorda's mini recorder in her hand. Her nostrils flaring in disgust, she dropped it on the floor and ground it into shattered pieces under her heel. *Privacy at last.*

Plopping down on the couch, she closed her eyes and listened to the soft strains of Torgin's playing drifting down the hallway. *How can you play such serene music when life is such a mess?* She bit her bottom lip. *Where are you, Dwight Anders? What are you up to?*

"That's what I've been wondering." Esán's kiss brushed her cheek.

"Esán!" Jumping to her feet, she threw her arms around his neck. "I am so glad you're here."

He held her close, his eyes focused on the small pile of shattered electronics." He stepped back and pointed. "Do you think that was wise?"

"Maybe not, but I wanted some privacy."

Spyglass scampered into the room and sniffed Esán's pant leg. Torgin leaned against the archway, noted the fragmented electronics, and shrugged. "I thought I heard your name. How did you ditch the boss and the hired hand?"

Esán grinned. "You sound like you grew up here, Torg. Ditch... hired hand..." He laughed. "It's good to see you, too. Sit. Sorda turned me loose to find Dwight." He glanced at his watch. "We have less than two hours."

Brie wiggled free and pulled him down on the sofa.

Torgin leaned back in his favorite chair, crossed his long legs at the ankles, and gazed from her to Esán. "What happened at the hotel?" He rubbed Spyglass's nose. "Lie down, Spy."

The rat terrier curled up by his feet.

"Good boy." Torgin's gaze fastened on Esán. "Well?"

Brie folded her arms. "How mad was Sorda?"

"He was angry Dwight was missing. The discovery that someone had sabotaged the electronics hidden in The Penthouse study...I'm certain they're not replaceable...made him even more furious. Without them, he can't trace Dwight, nor can he monitor us." He gave her a crooked grin. "So, we have lots of privacy, at least for a time."

A frown replaced her elated smile. "I bet the only person who knew about his monitoring equipment was Dwight."

Esán nodded. "Exactly. I'm pretty sure Dwight did the damage. My question is why? I understand not wanting to be monitored all day every day, but—" He folded his arms. "We explained to him that Sorda needed to think everything was normal."

Torgin planted his feet on the floor. "Sure wish Corvus and Gar would show up. I'm getting worried."

Footsteps in the hall halted the conversation. Brie's eyes widened in surprise. Penee and Ari stood in the archway. "A warning would have been nice, Arienh AsTar."

Ari dropped into the chair next to Torgin, looking only slightly chagrinned. "It was much more fun to scare you to death. Sorry, that wasn't the plan. We needed to share something important but couldn't use telepathy."

Penee sat at the end of the sofa. "Gar sent me a message. They've found the Mindeco's hideout. Dwight is with Rikell."

Ari twitched her braid over her shoulder. "Guess what else? He isn't a prisoner, so what's he doing there?"

A key in the apartment door produced an expectant silence. Gar dashed into the room, his triumph splashing its occupants. "*I* shaped a raven and led Corvus to the Mindeco." He knelt to greet Spyglass. The excited terrier jumped up to lick his face.

Corvus grinned. "Gar's done a terrific job today." He walked past him. "We need to talk." Grabbing the desk chair, he rolled it over to the group.

Gar scrambled to sit cross-legged on the floor at Torgin's feet. Spyglass settled in his lap.

Corvus rubbed his knees and rested his hands on the leather arm of the chair. "Dwight has joined forces with Rikell. Their plan is simple—take over the body of Karlsut Sorda, find and sell the stones, and use Sorda's machine to return to our time."

Torgin relaxed back in his seat. "Oops. Guess he doesn't realize the time machine is stuck in 1969."

Ari scowled. "What's going on with Dwight? Even *I* felt his acceptance of us as friends."

Brie's mind churned. "Everyone he has trusted as family or thought were his friends—his mother, Karl, Upori—have betrayed him. Even I failed him by not finding time to tell him who he is."

Penee sighed. "I understand how he feels. Until I met you, Brie, I'd never had a genuine friend." She smiled at her companions. "Now I have all of you, but it took me awhile to realize I belong." She bit her bottom lip. "If you hadn't helped me to accept my true identity, I might have continued to be angry and suspicious. Dwight is carrying a load of hurt. How do we get through to him?"

Brie glanced at Corvus. "I need to speak with him, to share his true identity."

Corvus held her gaze. "We can't help Dwight if we don't understand what he's facing. I think you have to tell us who he is."

Spyglass gave a sharp bark. Torgin grabbed his collar. Gar scrambled to his feet and stepped closer to Brie. Ari raised a brow as Penee jerked around.

Dwight Anders materialized in front of the room's mask-covered wall, his expression blank, then expectant, then fearful.

Brie moved toward him. "We're so glad to see you." She took another step. "Dwight, I'm so sorry. I didn't mean to let you down."

He looked beyond her, then searched her face. "More than anything, I wanted to hate you, to hurt you—all of you. I thought if I joined forces with the Mindeco, the hurt and anger might go away." His shoulders hunched. "Instead, I felt worse treating you the way people have treated me all my life. It made me sick." He wrung his hands. "It made me hate myself more than I hate the people who betrayed me."

Shaking fingers smoothed long bangs from his forehead. "I've done something awful."

Penee patted a spot on the sofa. "Come. Tell us what's happened. Perhaps we can help."

"Why would you help me? I was ready to destroy our solar system and you with it."

Brie held out her hand. "You and I need to talk alone. When we're done, we'll come out here. Then you can tell us how we can help."

Curling his fingers into a fist, he raised puppy-sad eyes to her face. A sigh sent a shiver through him. The fist relaxed. He rested his ice-cold hand on hers.

Corvus preceded them into the hall. "Dwight, what's happening with the Mindeco? Has he gone to The Plaza Hotel?"

Dwight lowered his gaze. "You know about that?"

"I heard you suggest the Mindeco seize Sorda's body."

"I was so angry—" he shook himself. "Rikell prefers not to merge with a

Human on an empty stomach. He's out scavenging." Dwight grimaced. "He goes through trash cans and eats rats and dead stuff. Once he's full, he'll sleep. He'll venture out when he wakes up."

"Thanks." Corvus withdrew.

Brie pushed open the dining room door, flashed him an encouraging smile, and motioned him ahead of her. He sat down, propped his elbows on the table, and rested his face in his hands.

Brie angled a chair toward him. Quiet settled over them.

37

The Mindeco skulked through the alleys of Manhattan, feeding at the trash cans of his favorite restaurants. In search of dessert, he crossed to the riverfront to feast on small crabs, shellfish, muskrats, and frogs. The biggest impediment to his banquet—Humans. The hunt would be on if anyone saw him. More times than he could count, he walked away from a delicacy to protect his anonymity.

On this night, excitement accompanied him on his quest. Dwight had shown up on his doorstep. The Mindeco licked his lips and loped across the highway to Riverside Park. *The boy has no idea how close he came to having his body snatched.* Rikell crouched amidst bushes and trees to watch a drunk stumble by. Across from his hiding place, a homeless man pulled soiled newspapers from a trash can, spread them on the ground beneath a tree, and stretched out for the night.

Rikell forced himself to remain vigilant. *Patience. Patience, Rikell, Mindeco of RewFaar. You can sleep soon.* When traffic thinned, he slouched low and loped to a break in the wooden fence surrounding the old house. Merging into shadow, he reached the back entrance, entered, and descended the rickety stairs to his favorite basement corner. A yawn stretched his skeletal mouth wide. Digestion took all his body's energy. He shoved a filthy, tattered blanket beneath his head, and slept.

Brie studied Dwight. Despondence shrouded his dancer-lean body. Although she could discern the slight expansion and contraction of his ribs, he seemed not to breathe.

A shudder brought his head up. An uncertain gaze met her solemn one. "Why are you willing to trust me?"

Her smile made a fleeting appearance. "I always recognize the truth." She sobered. "Why are you here?"

He swallowed, took a long breath, and folded trembling hands in his lap. "I realized that, of all the people I've dealt with in my life, you and your friends have treated me better than anyone. Our solar system is in danger because of my selfishness. I want to help save it." He rubbed his palms together. "Most important, I wish to understand who I am and my part in this."

Brie listened with her heart and her VarTerel's instinct for truth. The Star sent a wave of warmth through her. Nothing triggered distrust of the young man regarding her. Serious but softening, she offered encouragement. "I'm not here to judge you, Dwight. It's more critical to me you recognize your truth so you can make the right choices. That's what's important."

Sincerity flooded his expressive face. "I pledge to help you find the Corps Stones and to save the Clenaba Rolas System."

The Star's warm tingle confirmed his honesty. "I hear the truth in your words." She waited a breath. "Do you?"

His earnestness changed to realization. "I do. I hear it. I feel it." Satisfaction blossomed. "I *know* it."

Relief removed any remaining uncertainty from Brie's smile. "I suggest we get busy. Let's talk about who you are. Do you need a moment?"

He leaned his head back, squeezed his eyes shut, and inhaled a long, deep breath. As his lungs emptied, he straightened and met her steady gaze with his own. "I'm as ready as I'll ever be."

"Your birth name is Rethson Jacy Vilandree. Rethdun Torin Vilandree, also known as Relevart, and Rayn Jaradee Palmira, are your blood-parents."

"Rethson Jacy Vilandree." Tears glistened in Dwight's eyes. "My father—Wait! Relevart? Are you saying my father is the Universal VarTerel?"

"Relevart is your blood-father. His given name is Rethdun. A process called Protariflee was used to create you and your parents. Rethdun and Rayn are birth-mates. Their genes are different, although they were birthed from the same womb."

"Do I have a birth-mate?"

Brie smiled. "No. Your mother, Rayn, wanted a child who bore her genes and Rethdun's. The MasTer, a story for another time, forbade it. Your Aunt Rasiana and a Protariflee technician made your mother's wish come true. Soon after your birth, The MasTer found out. He ordered Vygel Vintrusie to hide you somewhere safe. Relevart found out you existed two sun cycles ago."

Hurt crept into Dwight's handsome features. "He knew, and he didn't search for me?"

"As soon as he found out about you, Relevart sent Almiralyn and Corvus into the past to bring Vygel Vintrusie to him. Vygel refused to tell them anything. He and his fellow Mocendi, Thorlu Tangorra, escaped. The hunt for you dead-ended. Relevart's goal was to reconvene the search as soon as the Corps Stones were back on their home planets."

Dwight's dark brows bridged. "So, my father, put the Corps Stones ahead of finding his lost son?" He nodded to himself. "I would have made the same decision." Curiosity bloomed. "How about siblings?"

Brie wanted to hug him. She controlled the urge. "Your older brother, Den, was just found. You also have a half-brother, Elf, who is on Myrrh. Penee is your sister... sort of. She's Elf's birth-mate but not blood related to either of you. Close your eyes. My mother created a painting for Relevart and Den. I can share its image with you."

She let the painting take shape in her imagination. When it was clear, she projected the image into Dwight's mind.

His sharp inhale made her open her eyes. His eyelids fluttered. Tears spilled down his face. "I have a family. They never told me. I want to meet them all."

Sadness leaked into Brie's heart. She lowered her gaze.

He touched her hand. "Are you alright?"

She let memories flicker from her mind to his: Rayn at Soasi, Rayn shaping a galee, Rayn with Relevart during her last hours. At first he looked startled, then sad, then calm.

"Thank you, Brie. I'm sorry I'll never meet my mother."

She smiled through her tears. "She loved you, even though she never met you. You carry the genes of two powerful VarTerels, Rethson. We will all help you, but be careful or you might cause more harm than good." She gave him time to absorb what she had told him. "Are you alright?"

He smiled a jubilant smile. "I'm grateful. Thank you, Brielle AsTar. Do the others know?"

"I wanted you to tell them in your own way."

He pointed at himself. "Is this what I really look like?"

"At the moment, yes." She pulled him to his feet. "When we've resolved our present dilemma, we'll explore whether Roween and Vygel changed your appearance."

After kissing her cheek, he strode down the hall. Everyone turned as he entered the living room. He waited for Brie and clasped her hand. "I am Rethson Jacy Vilandree, the Protariflee son of Rethdun and Rayn. I have an older brother, a half-brother..." He beamed at Penee. "...and a sister named Penesert." He paused, connecting with each person who supported him "You are my friends. Thank for not giving up on me."

Everyone surrounded him. Smiles, tears, and hugs later, they resettled, their faces flushed with the pleasures of friendship.

Dwight grew serious. "Out of a sense of loyalty to the woman who raised me, I have not shared something important." He seemed to gather his courage. "Roween Rattori is my foster mother. She's the queen pin of this operation."

Corvus took the lead. "Thank you, Dwight. Your honesty will help us all moving forward." He nodded his appreciation. "Tomorrow, we must each play our roles. Mira and I will continue our search. Has anyone thought of anything else that might help us find the Corps Stones?"

Torgin rubbed his brow. "I heard a conversation that keeps coming back to me. One orchestra member's mother is a seamstress. She's been recovering from an illness. Someone delivered work to her at home. Since the delivery arrived, she has recuperated faster than expected."

Corvus nodded. "I'll have Mira check on who it might be."

Ari grinned. "Hope she has the stones so we can finish this and go home."

Corvus interjected. "It's vital that we don't attract more attention to ourselves than necessary." A Karrew-like tip of the head focused his gaze on her. "When we leave with the stones, the fewer minds we need to wipe clean the better."

Dwight fidgeted. "What about the Mindeco?"

Corvus rubbed his chin. "I believe he'll sleep a couple of days. Hopefully, by then we'll have the stones."

"What do we tell Karl about Dwight's disappearance?" Esán twisted to see him better.

Dwight laughed. "We tell him Rayna and I went on a boat ride around Manhattan."

Brie grinned. "Great." She blew him a kiss. "Rayna will hold you to that."

Esán shot her a sidelong glance. "How about the electronics?"

Mira appeared in the doorway. "Taken care of. I erased Karl's memory of anything connected to their breakage." She walked up to Dwight and offered her hand. "Almiralyn Nadrugia."

He stood and bowed over it. "Rethson Jacy Palmira, at your service."

Brie watched Dwight surrounded by those who would love him for the rest of his life. A brief discussion with Almiralyn had left him smiling. He hugged Penee and grinned at Ari. Hope filled the apartment.

Mira joined her. "You did well today, Brie. We haven't found the stones, but we're closer. Dwight is a key player." She nodded and moved to Corvus' side.

Esán drew Brie into the hall. "You're sure Dwight isn't playing a game with us?"

She smoothed her hair. "What do the Seeds tell you?"

"They tell me Dwight thinks he loves Rayna. That could be a problem."

"He knows *I* love *you*. He's coming to terms with the fact that he is not Dwight Anders, but the son of the Universal VarTerel. It's a lot. Give him time."

Mira and Corvus joined them. "I did not fix Sorda's tracer, Esán. I put the suggestion in his mind that he has a faulty part. He replaced one of the recording devices in your suite. It's in the sitting room." She glanced at her watch. "Time to go. We can trust Dwight to work with us, at least for now."

Corvus summarized Torgin's information for her. "Please find out which seamstress has been out sick, Mira." His attentive gaze turned to Brie. "You need some sleep, Brielle AsTar. Thanks for all your work today."

She yawned. "The power of suggestion. You two go. I'll shoo the others out the door."

Corvus kissed Almiralyn's cheek. "I promised Joe I'd stop by." He vanished.

Almiralyn hugged Brie and flashed from sight.

Esán shook his head. "You never know who's gonna turn up in 1969, do you?" He kissed her. "Dwight and I need to leave, or Ricco will have a coronary. See you tomorrow."

Esán and Dwight met Ricco at the pizza place at ten-fifteen to walk to The Plaza Hotel. Karlsut Sorda pulled open The Penthouse door at the instant the elevator opened. Broadcasting his frustration, he motioned them into the suite, led the way to the sitting room, and rounded on Dwight.

"Explain yourself, Dwight Anders. You've been gone all day. What have you been up to?"

Dwight, looking sheepish, answered, "I'm sorry I worried you, Uncle Karl. I invited Rayna to dinner that turned into a cruise around Manhattan." He shrugged.

Sorda glared. "You didn't think I'd worry?"

Dwight rubbed his neck. "Why? You track my whereabouts, day or night." Folded arms and a petulant expression shouted rebellion.

"The tracer has malfunctioned, Dwight." His nostrils flaring widened the tip of his long, narrow nose. "It will be fixed by tomorrow. Do not make me regret keeping you around."

Dwight's full lips pressed into a thin line.

Esán jumped in. "We need to get some sleep. Tomorrow's a big day. Rehearsals begin in the theater." He stifled a yawn. "Our search for the stones continues as well."

Sorda's chin lifted. His piercing gaze moved from one to the other. He shrugged. "See me in the morning before you leave the hotel."

Dwight marched out the door and strode into the suite across the hall. Esán ambled after him. The Penthouse door shut in chorus with theirs. They headed to their own rooms. As prearranged, Dwight waited for several minutes before easing Esán's door ajar.

"It's safe. Come on in." Esán grinned. "You were perfect in there." He paused. "It's been a big day. How are you doing?"

Dwight plopped down on the bed. "I'm fine. A bit overwhelmed. I'm relieved that I am more than Roween's puppet." Earnestness glowed in his eyes. "I realize you love Brielle. You know Dwight's personality is falling for Rayna." He gave him a rueful smile. "Rethson understands he can't fall in love with Brie's altered shape, but..." He shook his head. "What a brain teaser."

Esán studied Relevart's youngest son. "You remind me of Den. You'll like him. His life wasn't any easier than yours." He grew thoughtful. "All of us, except Torgin and the twins, have just met our families. We were scattered all over the solar system. Our destinies have finally brought us together with our families and with each other." He yawned. "We'd better get some sleep, or tomorrow will be even tougher."

Dwight rose. "Thanks for understanding...about Rayna." His crooked smile transitioned to a full-bodied yawn. "See you in the morning."

Esán sat on the bed, staring at a blurred spot on the wall. *The day's been an eye-opener. The sooner we have the stones in our possession, the better. Old Earth year 1969 is interesting, but I'm ready to go home.*

38

Rayna walked from her room the following morning with a smile on her face and anticipation in her heart. Today, her first rehearsal with the ballet company excited and terrified her. Her confidence that she and Dwight were up to the challenge warred with the knowledge she had little actual training and had never performed on a stage, let alone one the size of the New York State Theater's.

Étoile's voice in her mind calmed the frantic flutter in her stomach. *"If you have questions or feel insecure, think of me."*

Torgin poked his head out of the kitchen. "Hey, Rayna, you look hot."

With a cheerful grin, she turned to show off her tight-fitting jeans and royal blue silk top. "What's for breakfast?"

"I made French toast with bacon curls, yogurt, and maple syrup. Yours is ready."

She closed the kitchen door so they wouldn't disturb anyone and took a seat at the table. "Is Gar still sleeping?"

Torgin set her plate in front of her. "Nope, he took breakfast over to the girls. He should be back soon. Hey, last night was pretty amazing. I sure hope Esán and Dwight hoodwinked Sorda." He sat down, munching on a piece of crisp bacon. "Who would have thought Dwight was Rethson? Won't Relevart be surprised?" He poured juice from a flowered pitcher. "Or will he? Maybe he's known all along. Did he send us to New York to find the Corps Stones or Rethson?"

Rayna picked up her glass. "You'll have to ask him." She relished the tang of orange mixed with mango, swallowed, and set the empty glass on the table. "Tell Gar I'll meet him at Lincoln Center."

"Tell me yourself, Rayna Deejara." Gar grinned at her. "Hard to believe I think myself from one place to the other." He gave her a quick hug. "That's from Ari." He hugged her a second time. "That's from Penee. They said to have a great rehearsal. They meet their back-up group for the first time today. Cool, huh." Grabbing a piece of bacon from her plate, he plopped down on a chair. "Kitchen sure smells yummy."

A grinning Torgin set a plate stacked with French toast in front of him. "It's hard to believe Ari can sing. Can't wait to hear her with Penee."

Gar chuckled. "They sound great." He crunched a bite of bacon. "I'm not s'pposed to tell ya, though."

Rayna gave him a playful glare. "You've heard them, and I haven't? Not fair!"

Torgin returned to his seat. "Maybe not fair, but it sure helps build the suspense." He tapped a fork on the edge of his plate. "Speaking of suspense... Today the orchestra is working with the company soloists. I am so nervous. This is the first time I've played for live dancers. Glen is still home sick, so I'm playing the piano solo."

Rayna dredged a bite of French toast in lots of maple syrup. "You'll be great! We're rehearsing with the *corps de ballet* and *demi soloists* of the company. If I think about it, I get sick to my stomach, so I'm treating today like any other day." She popped the toast in her mouth and licked the maple-sweet syrup from her lips. A big smile accompanied her last bite. "Sooooo delicious, Torg."

She washed her dishes and left to clean her teeth. After a quick inventory of her bag, she stuck her head in the kitchen. "Gotta run. Let's go, Gar."

He looked at his almost clean plate, swiped a chunk of French toast through a puddle of syrup, tossed Spyglass the only remaining bite of bacon, and wiped his mouth on a sticky napkin. "I'm ready."

Rayna shook her head. "No, you're not. Go brush your teeth. I'll do your dishes."

He dodged past her down the hall.

She grinned at Torgin. "I'm sure glad he came into our orbit. Can't wait to hear what Mira found out about the seamstress. You coming?"

"Pike's showing up in about fifteen minutes. I'll see you in the cafeteria at lunchtime."

"Great. Have a great rehearsal."

Gar darted by her to hold open the door. "After you, Miss Rayna."

Torgin trailed after them. "I'll lock up. Be careful."

Rayna gripped the pole on the packed subway, wishing she had taken a cab. The man behind her pressed against her back, sniffed her hair, and wiggled closer. She turned. Her message-filled gaze canceled his lewd expression. He cringed. The breaking train pitched him backward. She dodged onto the platform, a knowing gleam in her eye. *He'll never harass another woman.*

Gar and Spyglass met her by the steep cement stairs. She peered at her watch. "Class starts in twenty minutes."

He jogged up the steps with his dog at his heels, crossed the street, and hurried toward the Lincoln Center Plaza.

Esán, alone by the fountain, welcomed her with a quick hug. "Dwight's getting ready for men's class. He said to tell you, he'll see you at the theater." He stepped back and pursed his lips in a silent whistle. "You look hot!"

Eyes twinkling, she kissed his cheek. "Thanks. You look pretty snazzy yourself. Will I see you later today?"

"Yep. I'm headed over to the theater to finish focusing the lights with Joe. By the time the company arrives, we should be ready. The actual tech rehearsal is Friday."

She smiled. "I need to go. Thanks for hanging around. My day's always better when I start it with you." Halfway to the Juilliard building, she glanced back. He waved, waited until she reached the street, and strolled toward the theater.

Gar accompanied her to the dressing room door. "Stay alert, Rayna. I'll be with Mira."

She entered to find Kelsia, the last occupant, preparing to leave.

"You're going to be late." She waved her hand towel. "I'll save you a spot at the barre."

"Thanks. I'll hurry." Dropping her bag on a bench, Rayna unlocked her locker. "What the—" She gagged and stepped back.

Kelsia peered over her shoulder. "Oh, my goodness!"

Inside, a dead rat hung by its tail. Drawn in its blood on the wall was a single eye."

Kelsia hurried to her side. "Who did that?" She gaped in horror.

Rayna sank onto the bench. "Go to class. I'll take care of this. Please don't tell anyone."

Doubt clouded Kelsia's pretty features. "Are you sure you should be alone?"

With a tight smile, Rayna urged her friend to the door. "I don't want you involved in this. Go. I'll see you after class."

Kelsia shot a worried glance at the locker and left.

Gar slipped into the room. His eyes as big as saucers, he stared at the mess. "What the heck?"

She pulled him closer. "Doesn't Mira need you today?"

He gulped. "Mira isn't there. No one's heard a word from her. I came to tell ya somethin's not right." A finger pointed. "Who do ya suppose did *that*?"

Rayna pulled him down on the bench to face her. "We have to clean up the mess, then find Corvus."

Gar licked his lips. "The Mindeco has Mira, right?"

She fought to keep her answer calm. "I think he might. You know where he's hiding. I need you to show me."

"We goin' alone?" He sounded doubtful.

"Not if we can help it." She looked at the rat and shivered. "I sorta hate to touch it."

"Geez, Rayna, it's only a rat." He grabbed it by the tail, tossed it in the wastebasket at the end of the bench, and pulled out the garbage bag. "I'll get rid of this. You clean up the blood." He tipped his head. "Think you can do that?"

She grinned at the concern in his eyes. "I can."

"Good. Don't go anywhere 'til I'm back. Promise."

"I promise."

With a quick nod, he dodged into the hall.

Rayna scooped her things from the locker, stuffed her soiled clothing in an extra trash bag from the bottom of the wastebasket, and wiped the blood from the wall with a wet paper towel. By the time she crammed the bag of clothes in the locker, Gar peeked in the room.

"You alone?"

"I am. Come in." She closed her locker.

Gar strode to her side. "Corvus is playin' for class. What do we do?"

"We find Esán." She wiped her hands on a paper towel. "I don't want to search as Rayna. How busy is the costume shop?"

"Everyone's helpin' ta transport the *Gems* costumes to the theater 'cause it's easier to do last-minute fittin's over there."

"Good." She tossed the towel in the trash. "Lead on."

They arrived to find the large sewing space deserted. Rayna slipped into a changing booth and composed herself for the change to Brie.

"Rikell." Gar's telepathic message froze her into stillness.

A costume rack slammed against a wall. She peeked from behind the curtained entrance. A box flipped into the air, landed, then skidded to a stop close by. Light flooded the room. Heavy breathing and the odor of decay swept ahead of the Mindeco. His enormous head swung one way, then the other. A clawed hand swiped items from a sewing table onto the floor.

In the changing booth, Rayna drew a soft breath; Brie materialized, steadied herself, and walked into the costume shop.

Rikell, midway to throwing a chair, lowered it. Shoulders rounded, long arms dangling, he fastened his oculus on her. A low growl built to a roar.

She folded her arms. "Go ahead. Alert security. They'll come running. You'll be trapped."

The roar faded. "I gather you found my gift, Brielle AsTar. I have your friend Almiralyn. She's trapped by her own magic." He laughed a silent laugh. "You didn't know I could do that, did you? You think I am just a dumb old Mindeco from the Trutore Mountains." The skeletal head swept closer. "Find the stones. I'd hate your friend to end up like the rat in your locker."

The heat of his putrid breath scalded her cheeks. Tears burned her eyes. She held her ground.

Small paws clicked on the linoleum flooring. A sharp bark commandeered the Mindeco's attention. His head swung toward the sound. Spyglass trotted to his side, his shrill bark echoing through the costume shop.

Gar jumped up from his hiding place. "Spyglass! Come!"

A clawed hand darted toward the terrier. Spyglass bit down. Rikell's single oculus bulged. A surprised chuckle escaped the toothy mouth. He lifted the hand, dog and all. "You are a brave pup." A drop of gray-blue blood dripped to the floor. Spyglass released his hold and landed on all fours.

Gar started forward. Brie pulled him back to her side.

The Mindeco lowered his head. Spyglass lifted his nose. For a moment, they remained, noses almost touching, then Rikell swept his head back to Brie and Gar.

"I am not Upori Athai. I will not kill a harmless creature." He sucked the bite on his hand. "I will, however, end the life of an enemy. Bring me the stones, or Almiralyn dies." He lumbered from the room.

Gar knelt. Spyglass jumped into his waiting arms, licked his face, and wiggled free. Gar scratched his ears. "Never scare me like that again, Spy." He stood up. "What do we do now?"

Dwight strode into the room. "Kelsia told me about your locker. I guessed you'd be here." He looked at the mess, sniffed the air, and scowled. "I take it you've been dealing with the Mindeco. Why didn't you call me?"

"Because we didn't have time to alert anyone. He has Almiralyn, Dwight. I knew yesterday something was up. I'm almost positive she let him catch her. Now she needs to be rescued, and we have a rehearsal this afternoon and—"

"Hush. We'll manage. I alerted Esán. He'll be here as soon as he can. So will Torgin. I haven't involved Penee and Ari. I left that to you if you feel it's necessary."

She walked over to Almiralyn's tidy workspace. A small, folded piece of paper pinned to an orange and green cushion caught her attention. As she removed the pin, Corvus marched into the costume shop.

He surveyed the mess and took stock of those present. "It appears we have a problem. Where's Mira?"

Brie handed him the note. "It's addressed to you."

After reading it, he again took stock of those who watched him. "It says: I will take care of M. Find the stones; take them home."

Brie pulled her long hair over her shoulder. "Rikell was here, as you can see. He says he's trapped Mira with her own magic. Can he do that?"

Half expecting a knowing smile, her stomach clutched when Corvus folded the paper and slipped it in his pocket. "We need to do several things. Brielle, change to Rayna and go with Dwight to rehearsal. I've told Esán and Torgin to stay at the theater. We can't blow our cover. There's too much at stake. Gar, you come with me. We'll take Spyglass to the apartment."

He picked up the rat terrier and clasped Gar's hand.

Brie touched his arm. "Did you know about this?"

"No. Have a good rehearsal. Keep your eyes and ears open. Mira didn't check on the seamstress who was out sick. Please ask Torgin to see what he can discover. Gar and I will see you at the apartment." They vanished.

Brie shook her head. "Sometimes I just want to—"

Dwight's dark brows rose almost to his hairline.

She heaved a sigh. "Help me clean up the mess, so we can go."

Dwight studied her. "You're worried, right? Almiralyn is a VarTerel, so she should be able to control the Mindeco, shouldn't she?"

Brie didn't answer. Nothing she could say would make either Dwight or herself feel better."

39

Esán and Torgin had been halfway to the costume shop when Corvus intercepted them to send them back to the theater. Unable to shake the worry Dwight's message had prompted, Esán considered following Corvus just to make certain Brie was alright. Torgin's suggestion that he might regret disobeying elicited a childish response: 'Corvus is not my boss. He doesn't get to tell me what to do.' Torgin had shaken his head and walked back toward the theater.

Esán watched a child crawl up on the fountain's rim, toss in a coin, and make a wish. Envious of the innocent act, he sighed. *Wouldn't it be nice if life were that easy...pay a penny; get your wish? Time to grow up, Esán Efre.*

He picked up his pace, caught up with Torgin, and matched his long stride. "Thanks for stemming my need to rebel against something. My increasing edginess is making me cranky."

Torgin glanced down at him. "The pressure of not finding the stones is triggering different reactions from each of us. I withdraw to hide in my music.

Ari rebels. Brie gets busier." He paused. "We're dealing with a dangerous situation that affects the woman you love. I'm not sure how you remain calm at all. Dwight and Penee aren't as familiar to me, so I can't gauge what drives them in what direction."

Esán chuckled, then sobered. "You amaze me, Torgin Whalend. I remember the scaredy-cat kid Ari and Brie brought to Myrrh the first time." He glanced up at his friend. "Have I changed, too?"

Torgin grinned. "Four years is a long time. We've all grown up a bunch." He punched him in the arm. "Race ya to the stage door."

They arrived out of breath and laughing like a couple of kids. Esán gulped in air. "I needed to do something silly. Thanks, Torg. See you after rehearsal." He stepped into the dim interior of backstage.

Torgin, close behind, waved at an older woman who had entered ahead of them. A long stride caught him up with Esán. "Can't wait to see the lighting for *Gems*, Nesá." He hurried past him.

Esán called after him. "Can't wait to hear you play."

Torgin shot him a wide smile over his shoulder and joined the woman, waiting by the door to the pit. Watching them walk away, Esán smiled to himself. *You are better prepared to function in 1969 than any of us.*

From the wings on stage right, he watched a tired-looking Joe discussing cues with Rich. The stagehand nodded, scribbled on a pad, and strode into the stage left wings.

Joe waved Esán over. "Good to see you." He examined him with a critical eye. "Corvus told me what occurred. I imagine Sorda wasn't happy. Did you get any sleep at all?"

"Some. How about you?"

Joe flashed him a cynical smile. "Who can sleep when they've just learned what I've learned?" Moving ahead of him, he glanced back. "By this evening, we should have almost everything ready for the technical-run on Friday. If we accomplish enough this afternoon, I might even sleep tonight."

Esán followed him through the door into the front of the house. *Unless Gar and Corvus find and rescue Mira, none of us will be sleeping.*

Gar and Corvus took the elevator to the basement of the apartment building, propped opened the door to the pass-through, and, merging into the shadow, shifted to soar skyward in the muggy morning air. Karrew took the lead. Chiwaa, the name Gar had chosen for his raven form, soared at his side. They glided to a landing in Riverside Park opposite the ramshackle house.

"Stay put." Karrew shot upward, circled, and vanished into debris and overgrown bushes.

Chafing at being left behind, Gar focused on his shifted form. Brie had helped him pick his raven name. He ruffled his feathers and cocked his head. *Chiwaa means wind raven in my ancestral language. Someday, I will fly over my homeland of Charnlandia on El Stroma.*

The smell of decay snapped him back to the present moment, his raven eye locked onto the Mindeco skulking from a shaded pass-through. He skirted the fence and swung a loose board to one side. Maneuvering his enormous body through the opening, he pulled the board into place.

Chiwaa pranced from one foot to the other. *"Karrew, trouble!"* He cocked his head, listening intently.

"Chiwaa, meet me by the river."

Relief lifted him into flight. At a prearranged spot behind a highway scaffolding, Gar alighted. His human gaze roamed the gray-green water. He inhaled, filling his lungs with humid air as Karrew glided to a landing and Corvus materialized. "The Mindeco has imprisoned Almiralyn in her bird form beneath a heavy-duty metal milk crate. He returned before I could move it. Now he's curled around it, pretending to sleep."

Gar frowned. "Isn't Mira powerful enough to escape?"

Corvus paced to the river and back. He pulled a syringe from his pocket. "This was by the cage. It contained a sedative. I'm wondering if it's what Sorda was using on him. If so, and he gave Mira a full dose, it means she's in danger of losing herself in her bird form. Somehow, we must maneuver Rikell away from her. We need to get her to Ari."

Gar swallowed a wave of panic. Corvus' internal struggle played out like a living drama on his face. Gar shivered. *Corvus knows the danger better than me.* "What do we do?" His anxious question met with distracted silence. He cleared his throat. "I helped teleport Penee and Brie away from Sorda's men, Corvus. Can't we teleport Mira from the basement to the studio apartment?"

Corvus stared from glazed-over eyes toward the Mindeco's hideout. Frustration carved fine lines at the corners of his mouth. His dimple vanished altogether. "The girls aren't at their place."

Gar slipped a hand in his pocket. His fingers curled over the crystal Brie had given them. "They had rehearsal today, remember? Wanna let Brie know what's up?"

"We don't want to jeopardize her cover or her search for the stones." A quick march beneath the elevated highway underscored Corvus' mounting turmoil.

Gar gathered his courage to speak. "I'll find Ari while you guard Mira. As soon as we're back at the apartment, I'll let ya know. Then we can teleport her there."

Corvus' restless pacing ended. He put a hand on his shoulder. "Gar, thank you for being the grown up. When someone you love is in danger, it's hard to be rational. Are you alright flying on your own?"

A moment of insecurity scuttled upward. Gar rubbed his palms together, his gaze flicking across the sky. "I know this part of the city pretty good. I'll be in touch."

The shift to raven happened without conscious thought. Corvus offered his arm and waited until Chiwaa perched on it. "You be careful."

Chiwaa soared over the highway and buildings lining Riverside Drive to 72nd, followed it to the park, and flew south to the 65th Street Transverse. When he reached Sheep Meadow, a large grassy area that hosted concerts and rallies, he landed in the trees near a mobile stage set up on the northeastern side.

Stagehands scurried back and forth, securing the stage area. To one side, a crowd clustered. A flash of red hair acted like a signal fire. Circling the area, he alighted within a stand of elm trees. A quick change to Human left him moseying into the open. Unsure how to attract Ari's attention, he angled toward the stage and walked the periphery until he could see her.

A hand clasped his shoulder. "What are you doing here?" Penee gazed down at him.

His startled inhale hissed between clenched teeth. He edged her away from the milling throng of people. "We got trouble. How long will ya be?"

"We're just finishing up. Come with me."

She zigzagged toward Ari. A tall, angular guy with a beard and pierced ears stopped them. He jerked a thumb at Gar. "He ain't allowed by the stage."

Penee put an arm around Gar's shoulder. "He's my little brother. I'll watch him."

The guy laughed. "You're kiddin', right? No way is *he* your brother." He scowled at Gar. "Get lost, kid."

Penee flashed a dangerous smile. "He stays with me. If *you* have a problem, take it up with your boss."

The man's scowl transformed to a full-on sneer. "I told ya he's not welcome here."

Penee's sunglass-covered eyes hardened. He flinched, looked confused, and, muttering under his breath, wandered away.

Ari waved and made her way to join them. "Mira's in trouble, right?"

Gar nodded. "Mindeco's got 'er. How'd ya know she's in trouble?"

Ari took his hand. "Brie shared her concern. What's the plan?"

"We need to teleport her to your place." Gar led them beneath the low-hanging branches of a large sourwood.

Ari peered through the leaves at Sheep Meadow. "What's the quickest way to reach the apartment?"

Penee scanned the area. "Too many people to teleport."

Gar stepped behind the tree, shaped Chiwaa, and fluttered to a low branch.

Ari frowned. "I can't shape a bird. You go. I'll meet you at the apartment."

Penee hesitated, then in the shape of an American kestrel, she fluttered to the branch beside Gar's young raven.

Chiwaa soared high above the meadow. The kestrel streaked past him. By the time he reached the west side of the park, she soared over Broadway. Raven wings pressing against the muggy city air, he cut a diagonal to their building and shifted shape in the pass-through. He walked to the front entrance, stuck his hands in his pockets, and leaned against the wall.

A falcon glided between buildings across the street. Penee ambled onto 72nd with a smiling Ari at her side. They stopped beside him. Penee grinned. "Look who I found."

Ari pulled open the door. "After you, Garon."

He marched ahead, an upsurge of belonging washing over him. The warm feelings changed to worry when they reached the studio apartment. *Has Corvus rescued Almiralyn?*

Hidden in the trees in Riverside Park, Corvus masked his presence behind subtle shields and shifted shape to Karrew. Circling above the derelict mansion, he swooped through a broken window into the Mindeco's lair, flew through dusty rooms and dim hallways, and touched down on what remained of a kitchen counter. The door to the basement, which had long since fallen from its hinges, lay to one side. The Mindeco's huge footprints, barely discernible in the dusky light, tracked down the steps.

Karrew flew down the stairwell to a wooden rafter in search of his quarry. Rikell sat on the cracked cement floor, the metal milk crate between his feet and his long, lanky arms raised in a full-bodied stretch. His mouth yawned wide. He dropped his arms. The gleaming oculus focused on the immobile white bird in the makeshift cage.

"Hope I didn't give you too much of the drug, Almiralyn Nadrugia. I want you aware enough to know you're trapped." Hunger growling in his belly rumbled through the basement. Saliva dripped from his protruding jaw. "Your friends have deserted you." He purred his delight, then sniffed the air. "Dinner time. Don't go away. I won't be long." Rising to his feet, he rested long, taloned fingers on the top of the cage, fixed his oculus on his prisoner, and then trudged up the rickety staircase.

Karrew waited until he could no longer sense Rikell's energy or smell the decay that enveloped him. Fluttering to the ground, he shaped Human and knelt by the milk crate. A single blue eye opened. The white bird's feathers shivered.

Relief flooding his sense, Corvus rested a hand on the top of the woven metal. A slight tingle hummed under his palm. Instinct snapped his head up. Blinding light flashed. An explosion hurled him through the air. Pain coursed through him as he slammed into a wall and slide to the floor. The last thing he remembered—white feathers floating in slow motion to the cement floor.

. . .

Corvus regained consciousness to the sounds of sirens and shouting. His head pounded. His body throbbed. Groaning, he pushed himself to sitting. Debris filled the basement. No sign of Almiralyn's white bird remained. He forced himself to focus. Her energy signature, through faint, had not disappeared. His heart wrenched. *I have to find her.*

The dull thud of heavy boots on the floor above and urgent voices calling to one another brought his instincts for survival to the fore. Climbing with painstaking slowness to his feet, he took stock of his body. Nothing alarmed him.

A fireman's silhouette paused at the top of the stairs. "I'll check the basement."

Karrew materialized and fluttered into dust and shadow beneath the stairway.

The man's search of the big, open area progressed quickly. A second man appeared at the kitchen door. "You need some help down there?"

"Nope. All done." The first man plodded up the stairs. "Someone's been living down there, but no sign of them now."

When the commotion at last died down, Karrew surveyed the basement one final time. No evidence the white bird had ever been there gave him a moment of hope. Fear for her safety eroded it. He flew up the stairs into the heat of late afternoon. Unencumbered by the back wall of the house, a barrier that no longer existed, he alighted on the fence and surveyed the chaos. *Did Rikell set the trap? Why would the Mindeco destroy his hideout. He wouldn't.* Karrew flew to the top of the turret. *So, if not him, who?"*

40

Rayna stood backstage, wiping sweat from her neck with a hand towel and watching Dwight practice turns with the only black male dancer who performed with the company. The rehearsal had gone well. Mr. Thompson, the ballet master, had beamed and announced the next day's rehearsal would be onstage with a full cast.

Dwight shook hands with his fellow dancer and hurried to her side. "He was great. Did you see me do five turns in that pirouette?"

She grinned. "I did. I think we're both going to miss this."

Gar darted from the shadows. "Corvus sent me. Both of ya gotta go to Ari's place fast as ya can. He said no telepathy or teleporting."

He moved to leave. Rayna grabbed his arm. "Is Mira alright?"

"Don't know. Gotta find Esán and Torgin."

She released him. "See you at Ari's."

Like a shadow, he disappeared into the wings.

Rayna picked up her dance bag, draped her towel over her shoulder, and headed for the dressing room.

Dwight matched her stride. "I'll meet you in the hall. Don't leave without me."

"I won't." She slipped inside.

Laugher and chatter filled the room. A good rehearsal meant good humor all around. The positive atmosphere soothed Rayna's fraying nerves. Lois entered, sat down across from her, and began untying her pointe shoe ribbons. "You and Dwight were beautiful today."

Rayna masked her surprise by pulling on her jeans. "Thanks."

Lois looked apologetic. "I can be a bitch when someone better than me shows up. Sorry."

Rayna zipped her pants. "No apology necessary. You and Peter did great as well." She checked herself in the mirror and picked up her bag. "See you tomorrow."

Dwight met her in the hall. They hurried outside, where Torgin and Esán waited with Gar.

"Taxicab or subway?" She looked past the fountain. "It's rush hour. What do we do?"

Gar shot her a mischievous grin. "Corvus didn't say no shape shiftin'."

Torgin groaned. "That means I catch a cab for sure. I'll take your bag, Esán."

Dwight matched his groan. "Me too. Give me yours, Rayna." He slid the strap over his shoulder. "Let's try Amsterdam Avenue. Sometimes it's less crazy this time of day." He led the way.

Gar pulled Rayna with him into an alcove facing away from the crowd. Esán leaned against the wall to survey the area. "Go."

Gar shifted. Chiwaa flew uptown. Rayna in the shape of a falcon soared after him. Esán's kestrel flew parallel to her. They reached the studio apartment, landed side by side in the pass-through, and assumed their human forms.

Darted around the corner onto the street, Gar grinned. "Look, the guys are here already."

Rayna arrived at his side as a cab pulled up to the curb. Torgin and Dwight climbed out.

Gar ran up to them. "What did ya do to get here so quick?"

Torgin grinned. "We got into a taxi with a real cool driver. That's it." He handed Esán his bag.

Dwight handed Rayna hers and motioned her into the waiting elevator. Ari met them at the apartment door and, with a worried nod, ushered them into the one large room. Corvus stood to the side of the window. Penee, looking pensive, lounged on the Murphy bed.

Rayna dropped her dance bag. Brielle materialized. "Where's Almiralyn?"

Corvus, a bruise blossoming on his cheek, faced the group. "The Mindeco imprisoned her beneath a metal milk crate. He left to feed. I attempted to lift the crate. An explosion hurled me across the room and knocked me out. When I came to, the overturned crate was empty. All that remained of Almiralyn's bird form—" He shivered. "A few white feathers."

Gar's eyes filled his face. "Do ya think she's okay?"

Corvus sank down on the end of the bed, unsteady hands tugging his dark hair. "I tell myself I'd know if she were dead. We have to find her."

Torgin pointed. "I think she found us."

Two long strides carried Corvus to the window. His gaze froze on the white bird perched on the building across the street.

Brie slipped her hand into his. "She's not dead, but she's not good either. Look at her breast. How do we—"

Corvus flashed from view.

The white bird launched into flight. White wings glowing in the last light of day carried her into the distance. Corvus appeared on the roof opposite. His silhouetted figure vanished. A raven streaked after the injured white bird.

Gar shook his head. "Thought no teleportin'."

Brie peered at the fading color splashing the sky. "Love makes its own rules. I suggest we share information—" She gasped. White hot pain, igniting fire in her veins, dropped her to her knees.

Esán's strong arms helped her up and supported her to the end of the bed. "We need to leave Almiralyn to Corvus and find the stones."

"Our time is slipping away." Brie sagged against him. "The pain's getting worse."

Her twin dragged a chair from the dining table and sat down in front to her. "If you can sense our solar system destabilizing in the future, shouldn't you be able to feel the stones in the city?"

"Their presence has been illusive since we reached New York, Ari. Either I haven't been close enough to them, or..." she sighed, "...I'm not strong enough."

Esán hugged her. "You're more than powerful enough. My guess is they haven't been near Lincoln Center since we arrived."

Penee broke her thoughtful silence. "Gar mentioned they might have gotten mixed up with the trim for the new *Gems* costumes, right?"

Gar, who had stationed himself by the window, turned. "I found a box Mira said reeked of the stones." He shrugged. "They never turned up. I'm bettin' whoever took work to that sick seamstress got the stones mixed up in her stuff."

Torgin snapped his fingers. "Almost forgot. I spoke with Natalie, the harpist. It seems that a strange woman called on her mother, the seamstress who's been ill. Since the stranger's visit, she's gotten worse. Natalie's not sure why and neither are her mother's doctors. Haven't the costumes been delivered to the theater? Chealim told us proximity to the stones affects people in different ways. If they were with the costumes she was working on, maybe they made her better. Their removal might be the reason she's relapsing."

Easing her aching body upright, Brie clasped Esán's hand. "Partial dress rehearsal for some dancers occurred today. Dress rehearsal for the entire company isn't until next week." A wave of pain hit. She held her breath until it abated. "Costumes for the principal couples didn't arrive at the theater with everything else." She gripped Esán's hand harder. "We need to go back. If the costumes are there, maybe the stones are with them."

A buzzer sounded.

Ari stood up, grinning. "That'll be the pizza I ordered."

When no one responded, she put her hands on her hips. "We can't do what we have to do if we're starving. Right, Torg?"

He pulled out his wallet and handed her a couple of bills. "Right you are. Dinner's on me."

The buzzer rang again. Ari pressed the button. "Yes?"

A crackling voice replied. "You ordered a pizza."

"I did. I'm on the way." She beckoned. "Come on, Gar. I could use a little help."

When the door closed, Penee hopped up and, with Torgin, began setting the table. Brie rested her head on Esán's shoulder. "Do you think Corvus has found Mira?"

Esán kissed her coppery curls. "He'll let us know when he does. I'm worried about where the Mindeco is going to hide. An investigation of the explosion makes the old house on Riverside Drive unapproachable."

Brie stared out the window. *If I were Rikell, where would I hide?*

Corvus kept Mira's bird form in sight until she vanished into the woods on the far side of The Pond. His unsuccessful search brought him to the ground in human form beneath Gapstow Bridge. A frantic scream propelled him up the bank to the path. Another shrill scream increased his pace along the edge of the water. He rounded a bend to find several people gathered around a hysterical woman.

"A monster came from over there. It was a giant, leathery thing as tall as a tree. One huge eye in the center of its bony head glared at me so hard I screamed." A sob shook her. "It growled and ran away."

An older man handed her his handkerchief. "Which way did it run?"

She pointed. "It ran that way." A sob choked her. "Toward Fifth Avenue."

Excited chatter erupted.

Corvus ambled past the clustered bystanders into early evening shadows cast by a small copse of evergreens; placed a message in Brie's mind; and, satisfied she received it, he shifted.

Karrew lifted into flight, his eyes peeled for the Mindeco and the white bird.

Esán felt rather than saw Brie tense. She swallowed her bite of pepperoni pizza, gulped a drink of cola, and set the paper cup on the table. "Corvus updated me. He said the Mindeco is near The Plaza Hotel. What if he's pursuing Sorda?"

Dwight lowered his slice of pizza and muttered to himself. "You are so dumb, Dwight Anders."

Ari leaned an elbow on the table. "Care to clarify, or would you rather we guessed?"

He brushed his bangs aside. "I totally forgot. My mother—" Loathing flared his nostrils. "Roween told me if the Mindeco went rogue, I was to listen to a message disc she secreted in my boot." He pushed back his chair, removed the boot, and pried the inner sole free. After a brief hunt, he held up a small, black disc and wedged it in his ear. His expression made the rounds from chagrin, to shock, to outrage. Removing it, he stared at it in horror. "Esán, you'd better listen; then I'll share what it says with everyone else."

Esán tucked it in his ear. His eyes hardened. His mouth formed a firm line. With a sneer of disgust, he removed it, his expression mirroring Dwight's.

Torgin groaned. "Well? What's the bad news?"

Dwight swallowed. "Prior to leaving RewFaar, Vygel injected a small ampule into my neck and Sorda's. He explained it was an immunization against the diseases we might encounter in the past. Roween's disc explains that it's a drug to protect us against the Mindeco. If Rikell takes over one of our bodies, the ampule will dissolve. The drug delivered into our system will trap Rikell in the host-body until the host dies. Worse: he can't take over his host's mind, so he must share it." A shudder shook him. "I hate Sorda, but I don't wish this nightmare on him."

Esán placed the disc on the table. "I'll call the hotel. You get yourself together." At the small desk behind him, he lifted the telephone receiver and dialed. After several rings, he left a message and replaced it. "No one is answering at The Penthouse, not even Jonas."

"I'm going to warn Karl." Dwight gripped the edge of the table, stood, shivered, and made a disgruntled return into his seat. "If the Mindeco is with Sorda, how do I control him? I may have the power, but I don't understand how to use it." He cast a pleading gaze at his companions.

An oval of glowing light formed at the room's center. Corvus walked free. "You all look like I feel. I haven't found Almiralyn, and a woman spotted the Mindeco in Central Park. It won't be long before the police get involved."

Dwight dropped his head in his hands. Esán offered Corvus the disc. "I suggest you listen to the message on this. We need a plan of action, the sooner the better."

Corvus, his expression unfathomable, removed the disc from his ear, and handed it to Dwight. "I suggest you keep this close. Rikell isn't dumb. If we can convince him to listen to it, we might have a chance. Let's split up. Gentlemen, you will come with me. Ladies, go to the theater. See if the soloists' costumes have arrived."

Gar jumped to his feet. "What about me? Who do I go with? The guys or girls?"

Corvus almost smiled. "What do you think would be best?"

The boy's mouth worked. He looked at Brie. "Do ya need me?"

Brie kept her expression serious. "I'll always need you, Gar, but today I have Penee and Ari to help me. You should go with the men, don't you think?"

His smile lit up the room. "Okay! Penee and Ari, take *good* care of her." The smile widened to a full-on grin. "Spyglass, stay. I'm ready, guys."

Esán kissed Brie's cheek. "See you back here." He clasped Gar's hand. "How do we travel, Corvus?"

"Gather 'round. I banned teleporting because I didn't want to alert whoever blew up the Mindeco's hideout. Right now, expediency matters more." He gripped Gar's other hand. "Girls, take care."

T he crescent moon's dim light turned the park into a spooky unknown. Corvus had selected a spot on the west side near 62nd Street to materialize. Evergreens obscured their presence and camouflaged their arrival. Esán glanced at his companions. No one moved. Lighthearted laughter drifted through the trees. Corvus, a finger to his lips, moved closer to the path, checked both directions, and rejoined his companions. "Any ideas where to begin?"

Esán spoke up. "Dwight and I will find Sorda. Torgin and Gar can go with you to search for Rikell."

Torgin glanced around. "What if we find the Mindeco? Dwight has the disc. I think he should stay with us...or the disc should."

Dwight looked doubtful. "Next scenario: The Mindeco has already found Sorda but hasn't taken him over... We'll need the disc with us."

Corvus intervened. "Dwight keeps the disc. If we find Rikell, I'll send you a message. Go."

Esán urged Dwight ahead of him. A sprint brought them to the corner of

59th. The red light changed to green. They crossed the street and hurried to the main door of The Plaza Hotel. Alert to everything in the lobby, Esán pressed the elevator button. Once inside, silence reigned. Dwight's harried expression mirrored Esán's racing thoughts. *I can only guess what we'll find in The Penthouse.*

41

While he waited for Corvus to explain his plan, Torgin contemplated a dandelion blooming amidst tree roots and gray pebbles. *I'd sure feel safer in the air. Wish I thought I could shift shape like my ancestor, Kuparak.*

Corvus studied him with introspective attention. The dimple in his cheek deepened. A satisfied gleam shone in his eyes. "We need to discover if you carry the gift of shifting shape."

Torgin's head came up. "Is this the right time to try something that complex?"

Corvus beckoned Gar closer. "Shift to Chiwaa. Remember, ravens are a rarity in the city. Don't call attention to yourself. Alert me if the Mindeco or anyone else wanders this way."

"You got it." Gar disappeared. A young raven flew to a high branch.

Self-doubt sent a shiver through Torgin's body. He met Corvus' questioning gaze. "I'm terrified it won't work."

The dimple smoothed. "Nervousness, my friend, is just another form of excitement. Embrace it. Now, listen." With the efficiency of one who understood every aspect of the art of shape shifting to another form, Corvus explained the process step by step.

Torgin snuffed out his lack of confidence with the reminder he had been in the company of shape shifters since he met the twins.

Corvus completed his explanation. "Questions?"

"No. You were precise in your description."

"Good. Then I believe it's time to discuss what form you would like to assume."

Torgin felt a thrill of anticipation as he replied without pause. "Kuparak shaped a galee, which is akin to a bald eagle. I would like to follow in his footsteps."

Much to Torgin's delight, Corvus did not negate his choice. Instead, he nodded. His smile beamed. "You have chosen well. I sense you are familiar with this bird?"

"I am, Corvus. When Relevart told me about Kuparak, I researched birds resembling the galee. I've even imagined myself in an eagle's form from the beat of its heart to the working of its mind. Tell me what to do."

"You never cease to surprise me, Torgin Whalend. Stand over there. We have little time, so pay attention."

Torgin moved to a clear spot between trees. Corvus' words about fear equaling excitement calmed his doubts. He shut his eyes and forced himself to breathe. The image of a bald eagle gazing at him from a golden eye came into focus.

Corvus' instructions filled his mind. "Experience the eagle's heart beating in *your* chest. Good. See the world through eagle eyes. Embrace its keen mind. Steady, Torgin. Do not shift. I'll tell you when. Embody the eagle's essence. Good. On my three, make it your own. One, two, three...

Torgin cocked his raptor head to gaze at his mentor. Gar's excited voice filled his mind. *"Yipee!"*

A woman's frantic shout eclipsed the moment. "He stole my purse!" Running feet headed their way.

Karrew materialized and flew to a leafy branch.

A man dodged between the trees, a purse clutched in his hand.

Eagle's wings unfurled. Torgin assessed their power, then lifted into flight.

With talon's extended, he dropped toward the escaping man. A howl of surprise sliced through the night air. The thief sprinted into the trees, throwing the purse away as he ran. Torgin soared upward. Heady with the thrill of success, he landed on a high branch, folded his wings, and ran a long, brown feather through his beak. A golden eye scanned a world encompassing a multitude of minuscule details. *Wow! I am an eagle!*

A large raven landed near him, then soared aloft with a smaller raven in its wake. Torgin contained his desire to follow as several flashlight beams pierced the darkness, pooling on the ground in a search for the missing purse. An officer's light picked out the handbag. He retrieved it, strode to the path, and melted into the night.

Powerful wings carried Torgin skyward. Eagle-sharp sight picked out the slightest movement in the world below. Flight captivated him. Elation sent him higher. Through his growing intoxication, he heard Corvus in his mind. *"Find the Mindeco."*

Swooping lower, he trained the eagle's long-distance vision on the night-darkened terrain and winged his way from one end of the park to the other. Many interesting things attracted his attention. The Mindeco, however, remained elusive, as did Mira's white bird.

A raven shot to his side. *"Land."* It swooped to the spot where the police officer found the purse. Torgin alighted on a tree root and folded his wings. A younger raven fluttered to a rock nearby.

Corvus materialized and stood listening to the night sounds: the traffic, the occasional honking horn, the strains of music drifting through open car windows, a dog barking in the distance.

A grinning Gar flashed into human form. Corvus' thoughts touched Torgin's mind. *"On my count, embrace Human and shift. One, two, three!"*

Torgin blinked in the moonlight. His knees almost buckled. He gazed at his hands as though they belonged to another. Wiping sweaty palms on his pants, he looked up. An expressionless Corvus observed him. Gar grinned from ear to ear.

Corvus extended his hand, his dimple deepening. "Congratulations, Torgin. A scant few succeed at shaping an eagle; you achieved it on the first try. We'll talk more another time. I found no sign of the Mindeco or the white bird. Did either of you?"

Gar shook his head. "Nope."

"I saw nothing." Surprised his vocal cords worked, Torgin added an afterthought. "Did either of you fly over the hotel?"

The boy wrinkled his brow. "No."

Corvus stepped away. "Stay here. I'll take a quick look."

Karrew flew through the canopy of branches.

Gar grinned up at Torgin. "Have ya named your eagle form?"

Torgin grinned back. "Kupar after Kuparak, of course."

Esán and Dwight arrived at The Plaza and went straight to The Penthouse Suite. The door stood ajar. In the sitting room, a white-faced Jonas sat staring at nothing, his jaw slack; his eyes wide and glassy. Esán laid a gentle hand on his shoulder. "Jonas, it's Nesá. Can you hear me?"

A shudder ran through the man's body. He blinked, wrapped his arms tighter around himself, and, rocking back and forth, sobbed.

Dwight knelt. "Jonas, where is Uncle Karl?"

The house boy hiccuped. "I...he..." A sob shook him. Momentary clarity produced one word. "Rooftop." A shudder doubled him over.

Dwight rose. "Are you thinking what I'm thinking?"

"That Rikell paid Sorda a visit? Yes." Esán strode to the office. "Jonas needs help." He pressed the telephone receiver to his ear. "This is The Penthouse. Our house boy requires medical attention. Good. Thank you." He hung up. "Someone will be right up."

"Are you sure it's wise to bring an outsider into this, Esán?"

"I doubt anyone will give credence to a story about a one-eyed monster. We need to get to the rooftop."

Dwight peered into the hall. "All clear. Let's take the stairs."

They crept from the stairwell into the ambient glow of night in the city and skulked from shadow to shadow to a huge air-conditioning unit. A snarl rattled in a large open space near the roof's center. Esán pulled Dwight behind him. From their hiding place, they watched the Mindeco and Karlsut Sorda countering each other like tango dancers in a ballroom. Rikell shuffled forward. Sorda edged back. The Mindeco's leathery arm shot out. Sorda dodged to the side.

Rikell growled. "Play this silly game if you wish, Karl. I will get you in the end."

Dwight stepped from the cover of the air conditioner into the city's sallow glow. "Rikell, listen to me. If you snatch his body, you—"

"Shut up, boy." The Mindeco's gaze remained fixed on Sorda. "I will have you or Sorda. No one will seek a one-eyed monster in a man's body."

A raven swooped over the rooftop. Corvus walked from the darkness. "Listen to Dwight, Mindeco. If you don't, you'll regret it."

Sorda inched closer to Dwight. Esán stepped between them. "Stand still, both of you. Rikell, Mindeco of RewFaar, if you won't listen to Dwight, listen to me. Vygel gave both Sorda and Dwight a drug to protect them from death by your withdrawal. If you invade either of them, you will remain imprisoned together until you both die."

❧ ❧

Rikell whipped his gaze from Sorda to Dwight. The fire of lust bloomed in his oculus. His gaping jaw produced a rattling howl. Sorda raised the dagger-like letter opener. Rikell launched forward. Strong, talon-tipped fingers gripped the man's wrist. The dagger clattered to the rooftop. A hard yank forced the human male into Mindeco arms. Rikell snorted, tipped his head back, and fought the instincts tearing his psyche to pieces. He snuffled the fragrance of Human. Lost in desire, he positioned his chest against Sorda's spine, pressed his jaw against the man's occipital bone, and merged.

Yells of those around him dimmed. The dizzying pain of entering a human body left him staggering. He shook himself free of the searing spasm and blinked. His laugh of delight froze in his throat. Sorda's horrified thoughts burned in his brain. Denial shuddered through him. *Why is Sorda's essence still here?"* Human eyes darted over the rooftop. Confused, he rounded on the three men, who stared at him in dismay.

Dwight held out the message disc. "I suggest you listen to this—both of you."

Sorda's trembling hand pressed the disc to an ear. Rikell's rage mixed with Sorda's blistered with the heat of volcanic lava. A moan escaped quivering human lips. The disc sailed through the air and fell at Dwight's feet. "How long have you known?"

Dwight pocketed the disc, his eyes never leaving the man in front of him. "I found out an hour ago. I tried to tell you. Neither of you listened." He sneered. "Now your lives are intertwined forever." Turning on his heels, he marched to the stairs.

Rikell breathed in the man's essence. He gazed from human eyes at his human hands. *"I understand your rage, Karlsut Sorda, but..."* A triumphant laugh echoed over the rooftop. Human face muscles contorted into a crooked grin. *"I, Rikell, Mindeco of RewFaar, inhabit a human body."* He snorted with glee. *"I have access to a human brain—a conniving, unprincipled brain—a human brain, nonetheless.* The comforts of living as a man outweighed his dislike of sharing his existence with Karlsut Sorda.

His human eyes narrowed. Fresh scents filled his nostrils. He turned to find Torgin and the young black boy had joined Esán and Corvus. His thoughts joined with Sorda's. "You haven't won the game. If you do not bring us the Corps Stones, we will kill the VarTerel Almiralyn Nadrugia."

Mindeco and human luxuriated in the aroma of their fear. "She lingers in bird form, forgetting moment by moment who she is." A taunting chuckle accompanied the merged life forms to the elevator.

Esán turned to Corvus. "Does the Mindeco know where Mira is?"

Corvus looked up at the sky. "If not, he believes he'll find her before we do."

Gar squirmed. "They changed into one person. Never thought the Mindeco could really do that. Wow."

Corvus gave him a quick hug. "You and Torgin do a sweep of the park. I'm certain Mira is there. Then find the girls. Esán, you come with me. We'll collect Dwight and pick up Joe. He shouldn't be on his own."

Esán pressed the button on the elevator. "Let's all meet at the apartment on 72nd." He followed Corvus into the lift. As the door slid shut, he gasped. "Did I just see Torgin shape an eagle?"

Corvus smiled. "You did. He'll share his story later. Dwight's in danger as long as he's close to Sorda. I'll feel better when we have him with us."

At The Penthouse level, Esán led Corvus to the suite he shared with

Dwight and hurried inside. Sorda towered over his 'nephew,' who sat on the sofa, expression blank and arms folded.

"You let this happen, Dwight Anders. Your mother planned it. Did you think I wouldn't know, that I'd let you go free while I'm trapped in a body with a monster?"

Dwight remained stoic.

Sorda stepped closer. His eyes bulged. "I cannot control the savage. He is fighting to take over."

Corvus positioned himself to intercept Sorda's gaze. "You have more important things to deal with than Dwight. I suggest you and Rikell figure out how you're going to share a consciousness and a body. You'll find it easier if you negotiate a way to move forward."

Sorda pressed a hand to his temple. "Why should I listen to you?"

Esán moved to Corvus' side. "He is the representative of the Universal VarTerel, Karl. I'd listen if I were you."

Dwight rose to look his would-be uncle in the eye. "We have a solar system to save. You can help or not. It's up to you."

Karl sneered. "Do you really believe you can be of use? You're a talentless foundling left on a doorstep." He rounded on Esán, hunched his shoulders, and stuck his chin forward. "The Mindeco shared who you are, Esán Efre." His agitated gaze fastened on Corvus. "Bring me the stones, or Almiralyn dies." He stumbled into the hall. A gait between Human and Mindeco carried 'them' to The Penthouse. The door slammed shut.

42

B rie, Ari, and Penee arrived at the theater as dress rehearsal for the principal dancers in *Gems* finished. From seats in the balcony, they watched Cerril Thompson give notes and dismiss the cast. The crew swept the stage area for the following day's rehearsals, left a single blue light glowing at center stage, and departed.

Silence settled over the auditorium. Brie led her companions backstage. Her heightened senses picked up nothing. She sighed. "I doubt the stones are in the theater. Let's make a thorough search, just to be safe."

The girls split up to check dressing rooms, restrooms, and the backstage area. Brie finished a frustrating search of her sections. Empty-handed, she wandered into the wings near the exit. Fists on her hips, she stared into the vast emptiness. The quiet magic of a theater filled with performance memories lulled her sense of urgency. The blue light at center stage wavered.

A white bird's faint shape formed. *"Tell Corvus stones hidden—"* White feathers trembled. The bird faded into the velvet darkness.

Penee, tugging her long hair into a low ponytail, strode onstage. "No sign in my section. Are you alright?" Her gaze swept over the rows of red seats. "You look like you've seen a ghost."

Brie described Mira's brief appearance. "Why can't she shed her bird form. I wish I understood what's happening to her." She pulled her attention from the empty auditorium. "Did you find anything?"

"Nope. Why can't we find the stones? If the seamstress used them to decorate the costumes, shouldn't we be able to detect them?"

Ari walked across the stage, holding up a tiara. "A Corps Stone looks like this, right? We've all been expecting their energy to guide us. Could the thieves have muffled it somehow?"

After examining the headpiece, Brie handed it back. "They resemble this. It's a sapphire. We're looking for a ruby, an emerald, and a diamond encased in a quartz crystal. The only representation I've seen was about the size of my palm. Relevart said they can change proportions." She shrugged.

Ari frowned at the tiara. "So, this one isn't a Corps Stone?"

"Correct. We're all sensitive enough to feel the pulsing energy of the real ones."

"Something's up." Penee directed their attention to the far side of the stage.

Gar sprinted from the wings. "Hey, guess what! The Mindeco swallowed Sorda." A lopsided frown flashed. "He didn't swallow him, but—"

"He merged with him." Torgin strode up behind him. "We have lots to share." He surveyed the empty theater. "This isn't the place." He considered each girl. "You didn't discover anything, right? We didn't spot Mira either."

Brie frowned. "I saw her. At least, I saw a projection of her white bird. Something strange is going on. We need to find Corvus. I hope he knows more than he's sharing.

Torgin clasped Gar's hand. "Dare we teleport. The theater's deserted."

"We do." Brie offered Gar her hand.

Ari held up the tiara. "Better put this back." She darted into the wings.

Gar slipped his free hand into Brie's.

Ari jogged on stage and clasped Penee's.

Brie exhaled. "Concentrate on the apartment on 72nd. Ready?"

The theater vanished; the living room came into focus. Dwight, Esán, and Joe sat around the coffee table.

Joe, looking somewhat shell-shocked, jumped when they appeared, then chuckled under his breath. "Am I caught in the middle of a fantastical, futuristic novel?" His expression confounded, he scanned the group. "I know life is a series of short stories." He shook his head. "Mine are just more mundane than yours."

Esán patted him on the back. "Soon, you'll return to your life. How's your wife holding up?"

Joe's eyes twinkled. "Kath's doing fine. She's enjoying her sister's family. If it weren't for her, I'm not sure I'd want to give up this adventure."

Torgin and Gar got comfortable on the floor. Penee and Ari followed their example.

Esán made room for Brie. "From your worried expression, I gather you didn't find the stones."

"We didn't, but the white bird's image materialized in the theater with a message for Corvus." She squirmed to search the room. "Where is he?"

Torgin leaned against Dwight's chair. "He sent us to pick up Joe and find you. He said he needed to check on something."

Locks clunked. The door squeaked open. The locks resetting echoed down the hall. Footsteps on the hard wood floor became muffled as Corvus walked into the carpeted room. "Sorry I'm late."

Brie's serious gaze explored his face. "Please sit down. I have a message for you—also a question."

Esán shot her a sidelong glance.

Corvus pulled the desk chair into the circle. He directed a look containing unfathomable emotions at Brie. "You heard from Mira?"

She described what had taken place in the theater.

He sank into the chair. Distress washed all else from his bearing. "The stones are hidden... Did she mention where?"

"No. I think something frightened her. She vanished. Tell us what you know, Corvus. We can't help if we aren't in the loop."

Stillness, so intense he seemed to melt into it, enshrouded him.

The Star of Truth pulsed, sending a chill up Brie's neck. Esán's hand on her knee tensed. Ari's brown eyes narrowed. Penee froze, her hand entangled in her long hair. Torgin angled his tall body to see Corvus better. Dwight held his breath. Joe shrunk further into his chair. Only Gar appeared unaffected as he scratched Spyglass's pointed, black ears.

A shake of his head brought Corvus from his trance-like quiet. "The bird trapped under the Mindeco's milk crate, was not Almiralyn. The one we saw on the rooftop was another plant. I wanted it to be her, so I let myself believe it. It wasn't until the Mindeco merged with Sorda that I saw the truth taking shape. After the boys left The Plaza, I slipped into The Penthouse. You will never guess who I discovered conferencing in the living room." He lowered his head, raven-dark hair curtaining his bruised cheek.

"Ya goin' to tell us?" Gar wiggled closer to Brie.

Corvus smoothed his hair behind his ears. "The Mindeco squatting next to the couch where Karlsut sat beside—"

"Wait," Ari spit out. "Why isn't Sorda dead? If Rikell left his body, it should have decomposed."

"From what I could tell from their conversation, Sorda was given an antidote to the original shot, one which allowed the Mindeco to release him without harming him."

"Who sat next to Karl?" Dwight demanded.

Disgust twisted Corvus' mouth. "Vygel Vintrusie."

Torgin, who had reclined on the floor, launched upright. "If Vygel is in 1969, does that mean Thorlu Tangorra is, too?"

Corvus shook his head. "That's something I can't answer. I can tell you someone else unexpected was in the room." He looked at Dwight. "Roween Rattori is in New York City, 1969."

Dwight choked. "My moth—Roween!" He gagged. "How? She didn't come with us. Neither did Vygel." His brow creased. "Or did they?" He murmured through his confusion, "I remember Upori and Sorda getting into the time machine. After that, I recall little until I woke up at The Plaza."

"I can understand Vygel traveling back in time." Esán mused. "But why would Roween make the trip?"

Corvus grimaced. "Roween is many things; stupid is not one of them. While Vygel and Sorda argued about the stones, I watched her expression grow more and more annoyed. She rose like a queen, glared at the subjects of her disgust, and delivered a scathing lecture." He waved a hand. An image of the exchange formed above the coffee table.

Roween Rattori's disdain dripped from her words. "I knew you would botch this up. Do you think I made this trip for my good health? No. I came because

I realized you, Karlsut Sorda, Upori Athai, and..." She glowered at the Mindeco. "And you, Rikell, were incapable of managing a simple task. You only had to follow my plan." Her scathing glare fastened on Vygel. "Whatever made you blow up Rikell's hideout? What a fool thing to do." She motioned Vygel to his feet. "Come, Vintrusie! We have things to attend to."

The image faded. Corvus sighed.

Shooting pain left Brie panting. "I need a moment."

Esán put his arm around her. "Corvus, we have to find the stones. Brie can't tolerate much more of this. I'm betting, based on her reoccurring pain, that our solar system can't either."

Brie spoke through clenched teeth. "Does Roween have Almiralyn?" She gasped.

Corvus moved to her. "May I touch your head, Brielle?"

She forced a response between gulps of air. "Yes."

He pressed his palms against her temples. Through tear-filled eyes, she witnessed her pain twist his features. Her distress eased. He lowered his hands.

"Thank you, Corvus."

"You're welcome. I can't promise it won't come back. Every day the stones remain missing adds to the instability of the Clenaba Rolas System." He returned to his seat. "After Vygel and Roween bragged that they have imprisoned Mira in her bird form, Vygel formed a vortex and they vanished."

Dwight brushed his bangs from his forehead. "Bet Karl wasn't happy."

Penee hugged her knees to her chest. "Did you follow their energy signatures, Corvus?"

"I tried. Vygel was too clever. I lost them close to the Metropolitan Museum." He squinted. "I'm almost certain they're staying somewhere near it."

Brie fingered the velvet pouch containing the Remembering Stone. "We have to find them, Corvus. What do you suggest?"

"I assume Vygel is monitoring our every move, so we need to be careful. I advise against teleporting except in an emergency. If you use telepathy, shield it. Shape shifting is okay if we're careful."

Ari folded her arms. "Are you suggesting we shape shift to search for Roween? What are we going to do? Fly around peeking in windows?"

Ignoring her flippant tone, Corvus addressed Dwight. "You and I should investigate the area around the Met. You're well acquainted with Roween's energy; I know Almiralyn's. Between us, I believe we can pinpoint their location."

Esán drew Brie closer. "Do you think the stones might magnify their signatures?"

Corvus shrugged. "Possibly."

Gar gazed at Corvus over Spyglass's head. "What do we do while you're checkin' stuff out?"

"You get some rest." Corvus glanced at the clock on the desk. "It's eight o'clock. We have an important masquerade to keep up. Our adversaries will be watching. If they think we know about Vygel and Roween, they will disappear. Tomorrow is Friday, a big day at the theater. I presume you will have the weekend off?"

Torgin folded his long legs under him. "Mr. Harwood won't call an extra rehearsal of the orchestra on Saturday unless he's not happy with tomorrow's. Other than that, I should be free."

Joe looked at Corvus. "If I may..."

"Of course, Joe, please always join the conversation."

"Thanks. Esán and I aren't required at the theater until Monday afternoon. The light plot is complete, and we've hung and focused the lights. We're ready to go."

Corvus' dimple twitched. "Thank you, Mr. Shyro. Dwight, what's your schedule?"

"No rehearsals this weekend unless something unforeseen happens tomorrow."

Corvus contemplated the group. "Penee and Ari, what about you?"

Penee smoothed her hair. "Saturday, we have a rehearsal with our musicians on stage. We'll know more after tomorrow's run through."

He smiled. "Thank you. I'm scheduled to play for company class. Based on what you've shared, tomorrow's a workday. Dwight and I will do a little reconnaissance tonight."

Torgin pushed himself to his knees. "I have a concern. Vygel can't watch all of us at once, so who is his most likely target?

Brie gave Torgin a nod of appreciation. "Torgin's concern is valid. I think Vygel and Roween want to keep track of Dwight. They know he's Relevart's son and, therefore, a bargaining chip they can't afford to lose."

Esán nodded. "I agree. I'm also certain—since they have Almiralyn—that you, Corvus, are at the top of the list." He pulled Brie closer. "Vygel knows Brie is a powerful VarTerel and that she's Wolloh's apprentice. Sorda informed me Vygel told him who I am, so I'm under the microscope, as well."

Torgin ran a hand along Spyglass' back. "They are likely to dismiss Gar, Penee, Joe, and myself as unimportant. *We* should hunt for Roween; you should go about the business of doing what they expect."

Dwight's chin came up. "You don't know Roween. How do you propose to find her?"

Brie altered her position on the sofa to meet his eye. "You can provide them with an imprint of her energy. Corvus will do the same for Almiralyn. I agree with Torgin and Corvus. The more naturally we behave, the better. It's late. The girls will sleep in the studio apartment. We'll be back for breakfast in the morning."

Esán got up with her. "I'll walk you over."

"Me too." Gar jumped up.

"Wait." Dwight came to his feet. "I think we should do a quick search for Roween tonight. Maybe we just fly over the museum and the blocks surrounding it. They don't know we know anything, so they won't expect us."

Torgin moved to his side. "I'm happy to do a fly-by, but you need to stay put. Vygel knows your energy like the back of his hand. He doesn't know mine or—"

"Mine." Gar chirped.

"Or Gar's." Torgin finished, noting Corvus' negative stance. "We can go. Corvus, you can come as far as the Museum to keep an eye on us." He held out his hands. "Give me a feel for Roween, Dwight."

The stubborn light in Dwight's eyes flared brighter.

Brie moved to his side. "He's doing us a favor, Dwight. Help him out."

"Are you asking me or ordering me, VarTerel?"

"You're my friend, not my subject. I think you should take Torgin and Gar up on their offer. It's your choice. Do what *you* think's best." She walked down the hall to the kitchen, sat at the table, and rested her head on her arms. *Too many personalities...too much hurt...too much anger.* She yawned. *I am so, so tired.*

43

Torgin, Gar, and Corvus rode the elevator to the basement, each immersed in his own thoughts. Exiting into the pass-through, they prepared to shift shape.

A grinning Gar rounded on Torgin. "I wanna watch you become Kupar. Please."

Corvus' affirming nod prompted Torgin to open to the energy of the eagle. The beat of its heart filled him; its keen mind enlivened his desire to become Kupar. Gar's gasp penetrated his raptor hearing. He looked up at the boy from one eagle-gold eye. A clipped eagle's song prompted Gar's shift to Chiwaa. Karrew materialized, to follow the young raven skyward. Kupar, wings wide, soared after them.

The trio reached the east side of the park to the chiming of the Delacorte Clock and headed north, following the flow of lights along Fifth Avenue. Landing in a tree near Alexander Hamilton's statue, they spent a few moments in quiet reflection before executing their prearranged plan.

Chiwaa left to investigate the buildings between 86th Street and 91st. Kupar soared south along Fifth Avenue from 78th to 72nd, then crossed over to Madison Avenue to make his way back to the statue.

Corvus watched them go with misgivings. Although he had agreed to remain hidden, his urgent need to find Almiralyn prompted him to fly to the roof of the Robert Goldwater Library at the Met to scan the buildings across the way. Nothing sparked his interest. A flight between Fifth and Madison Avenues ended in the trees bordering a small park near 89th Street. Raven head cocked, he focused on the far side of Fifth Avenue.

Disappointed by his failure to discover Almiralyn, he flew to a maple at the corner of 85th. His neck feathers prickled. On the opposite corner, Mocendi shields formed a cloud over the upper stories of the apartment building. A cautious mental probe picked out Vygel Vintrusie's essence.

Corvus carefully withdrew, masked his thoughts, and waited.

A short time later, the shields shimmered into nothing. Vygel Vintrusie, with Roween on his arm, strolled from the building east along 85th Street. Wrapped in a cloak of protective wards, Karrew soared high above them until they entered a restaurant on Park Avenue. Circling back to Hamilton's monument, he touched down in human form. An eagle and a raven landed in a tall oak.

Corvus gave a soft whistle.

Chiwaa fluttered to the ground. Gar materialized, his coal-black eyes glinting with hope. "Ya found something, right?"

The eagle, Kupar, cocked his head to listen from the branch of the oak tree.

After describing what he'd seen, Corvus sketched out an alternative plan. "You will both patrol between Fifth Avenue and Park Avenue. I will search for Almiralyn. My goal is to discover where she's imprisoned before Roween and Vygel return."

Karrew flew to the museum roof, where he landed as Corvus. Gar and Torgin landed in human form and paid close attention as he pointed out the building he would be searching.

"Don't take a chance on being seen by Vygel. Remember, Torgin, he has highly developed senses and knows your energy signature. The minute they leave the restaurant, alert me. I'm going to see if I can find the unit they're in. Once we know that, we'll go back to the apartment."

The boys shifted and soared high above the city. Karrew alighted on the roof of Vygel's building. Corvus materialized. Humanities' vibrations penetrating from below, from the buildings surrounding him, from those strolling on the streets palpitated his skin like the soft touch of a moth's wing. *So many people.*

Ambient light glowing around him, he knelt to press his palms to the rooftop. *Almiralyn Nadrugia, where are you?*

T hree floors below Corvus in an eleventh story corner apartment, a diamond-white sapphire and obsidian cage imprisoned a white bird the size of a raven. Cerulean blue eyes gleamed in the light of a single lamp. A shiver ruffled its feathers. It tipped its head one way, then the other. Somewhere deep in its mind, a hidden secret demanded attention. In the presence of the man and the woman, the bird's consciousness fought the promptings. Since their departure, the calls for recognition grew more persistent—*Almiralyn, Almiralyn, Almiralyn, remember your humanness.* The same message repeated over and over.

The bird pranced from one foot to the other. An impulsive peck at the bars sparked an electric-like charge that raced over the surface of the cage. The bird jerked back. *What did you do, Vygel Vintrusie?* A soft squawk of surprise followed the human thought. Head cocked to one side, the bird fought to reclaim its sense of self.

A faint flash of light near the cage made it shrink into itself. A human male's dark eyes peered between the bars. Recognition sent goosebumps scurrying beneath white feathers. Fear amplified by something it could not define brought only one word to its struggling bird-human mind. *Danger!*

A key turned in the lock. Panic shot through the white raven. The man with the dimple in his cheek disappearing diffused it, leaving in its place dread of the couple who entered, their laughter edged with malice.

orvus, Gar, and Torgin arrived at the 72nd Street apartment at ten-thirty to find everyone waiting.

Gar dashed to the front room. "Corvus found her!"

Brie shot an inquiring look at the subject of his exclamation. "Weren't you going to stay hidden, Corvus Karrew Castylim?" She moved closer to Esán. Penee sat beside them.

His dimple twitching, Corvus settled into Penee's vacated chair. "That was the plan. It soon became apparent, however, that the sheer number of buildings was inhibiting Torgin and Gar's ability to make headway." He became more intense. "It seemed important to cover as much territory as possible before Roween and Vygel figure out we know they're in the city, so I joined the search."

Penee's mismatched eyes gleamed. "Where did you find Almiralyn?"

He rubbed his dimpled cheek. "In a corner apartment on the eleventh floor of a building on 85th and Fifth Avenue. They've imprisoned her in a white sapphire and obsidian cage that Vygel has shielded to keep her in *and* others out."

"Almiralyn is..." Esán paused.

"Fading." Corvus bit his lip. "That's why we have to extricate her as soon as we can."

Dwight frowned. "How do we rescue her without giving ourselves away?"

"We substitute another bird in her place?" Corvus massaged his forehead. "Even if we had one, we'd need to bypass Vygel's energy shield." Frustration tugged at his dimple. "Besides, he knows all of us, except Gar."

Penee cleared her throat. "Corvus, I'm not that familiar to him. If you imprint me with Mira's energy signature, I can take her place. We make the exchange when Roween and Vygel are absent from the apartment. With luck, they won't notice a difference. Once Mira is safe, you teleport me back to the apartment." Her brow wrinkled, then smoothed. "Or I stay put to spy. I have a special connection with Gar. He can be our go-between."

Esán looked worried. "If they discover the switch, you'd be—"

"Vygel knows enough about me to realize I'm worth more to him alive and unharmed. I doubt he'd hurt me. I don't know about Roween."

"My mother…" Dwight bit his lip. "Roween won't hurt you if she realizes she can use you."

Gar marched over to Penee. "Ya'd better not get caught, Penesert." Assuming a fighter's stance, he faced Corvus. "I'll be stayin' close to her, so I can alert ya to trouble."

Corvus gazed from one to the other. "I can't ask you to do this. Almiralyn would never forgive me if they hurt either of you."

Brie clasped Penee's hand. "I'm betting this will work. It will leave the rest of us free to go about the business of maintaining our cover and convincing them we're unaware they're in New York."

The phone ringing forced a lull in the discussion. Torgin answered it, listened, and held the receiver out to Esán. "It's Mr. Sorda."

Esán pressed it to his ear. "This is Esán. Yes, Dwight's with me. No, we plan to stay where we are tonight. I'll call in the morning. Goodnight."

Dwight folded his arms. "Well, that was a civilized conversation. What did *he* want?"

Esán returned to the couch. "Sorda seemed concerned about our sleeping arrangements." He surveyed the room. "What do you suppose Rikell will do now he's free of Sorda's body? He needs to hide since rumors are flying about a one-eyed monster in Central Park."

Ari walked to the window and gazed down at the street. "If I were the Mindeco, I'd take over another body." She sat down. "Which one of us would he consider expendable?"

Torgin raised a hand. "Me. Rikell thinks, along with the rest of them, no one would miss me in this timeframe. Don't worry. I'll keep my wits about me." He yawned.

Ari punched him in the arm. "You'd better b'cause I'd miss you, Drotti." She refocused her attention. "I want to help Gar protect Penee, Corvus."

Torgin's brows rose. "Thought you didn't want to shift shape to any form but Ira Raast."

"I don't. Ira can stay close enough to help if needed. Gar can keep me posted; I'll update you."

Brie stifled a yawn. "That means no information comes straight to any of us. With luck, Vygel won't notice. He can be pretty unaware." She snuggled closer to Esán. "Okay. We have a plan to protect Penee. If she changes places with Almiralyn, when do we make the exchange?"

Corvus rested his forearms on his knees. "Right now, we all need to sleep. Gar, you watch Roween's apartment starting early in the morning. The first thing we require is their movement pattern throughout the day. If they leave, you send a message to Ari, who will contact me. Since we'll all be busy at the theater tomorrow, they'll be less watchful than they'll be this weekend. Let's hope they give us an opening sooner than later."

"When they do, how do we make the exchange?" Penee asked.

"I will teleport to Almiralyn then teleport you there. I'll create a warding shield to disperse your energy essence. After I imprint you with Almiralyn's energy signature, they won't notice a difference." Corvus stood up. "Ladies, you need to go. Do you want an escort to the studio apartment?"

Brie smiled a weary smile. "We'll be fine. I'll call when we get there."

After goodnight hugs, Corvus walked them to the door. "Please stay alert." Framed in the opening like a palace guard, he watched them file into the elevator. *Take care of yourselves.*

44

Breakfast the following morning was a restive meal. Joe, who appeared not to have slept at all, said little. A withdrawn, distracted Dwight nibbled at a burnt piece of toast. Torgin grabbed a glass of juice and locked himself in the music room. Only Esán and Brie appeared ready to face the day.

Penee watched her companions leaving with an increased sense of foreboding. *Whatever made me think I could take Almiralyn's place? What if I can't shape her white bird? What if Vygel or Roween guesses something's amiss?*

Memories of Den Zironho helping her five-year-old self feed an apple to the sable mare B'hean helped to ward off her uneasiness. She slouched into the softness of the overstuffed chair, restless fingers clutching the well-padded arms. *I miss you so—*

Tingling air brought her to her feet. The dizziness of being teleported without warning made her stumble. Corvus, impatience tinged with fear buzzing like hornets, regarded her. A white bird peered between glistening cage bars, its feathers a mass of restless ruffling.

"I'm sorry I frightened you, Penee, but we have to hurry. Are you ready to make the shift?

"I'm ready." She shivered. "I'm just scared."

A hand steadied her. The next instant, Corvus held the trembling white bird in his arms. "Place your hands on her. Absorb her essence."

Penee shuddered as she realized the distance to which Almiralyn's humanness had fled. When her psyche had soaked in everything possible, she removed her hands. "You better take her to Ari. She needs Efillaeh's help."

"Make the shift. I won't leave until you're inside the cage."

Penee calmed her agitated breathing; stared at glistening bars; and, wrapped in Almiralyn's energy, looked at Corvus from human eyes one last time.

The speed and forcefulness of her shift sent icy cold skittering over the skin beneath her white feathers. She cocked her head to study the obsidian beneath her feet, noted the rippling current in the glistening bars surrounding her, and shrunk smaller. A soft breeze wafted over the cage. Corvus, his beloved Almiralyn in his arms, flashed from view.

"They come." Gar's warning, a mental whisper, gave Penee just enough time to camouflage what remained of her essence in the fleeting humanness of Almiralyn Nadrugia.

The sounds of entry preceding the murmur of two voices alerted her to the return of Vygel and Roween. The gawky Mocendi peered down at her. "Almiralyn, I feel less of you. It is sad, is it not, that your friends have no idea of your whereabouts?"

A tall, angular woman with hard, penetrating eyes walked to his side. She leaned closer, a sneer twisting her unattractive features. "By the time they find her, she will be beyond hope." A cruel laugh blew a heated breath between the white sapphire bars. "What a pity, Almiralyn Nadrugia, that you will never be Human again."

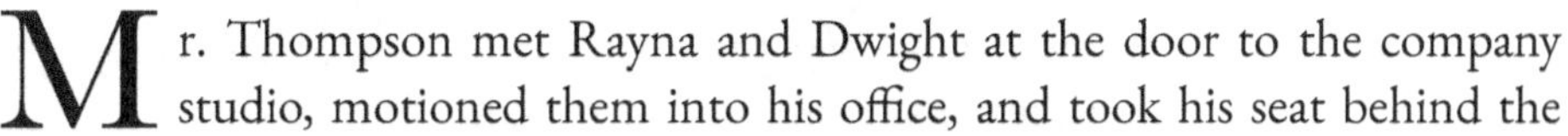

Mr. Thompson met Rayna and Dwight at the door to the company studio, motioned them into his office, and took his seat behind the desk. "We have received a request from the public radio station to interview the apprentice dancers invited to perform in *Gems*. Madame Dolavina recommended you. Lois and Peter will rehearse in your place today." He handed them a slip of paper. "That's the address. If you hurry, you'll just make the scheduled time."

Rayna glanced at the note. "Mr. Thompson, Dwight and I are not company apprentices."

With a smug smile, he presented them each a business envelope. "You are if you sign your contracts and leave them on my desk by the end of the day Monday."

Hugging the envelop, Rayna smiled her best smile. "Thank you, sir."

He held open the door. "Have a good interview."

Rayna preceded Dwight into the hall, her mind racing. At the girls' dressing room, she shot him an anxious look. "You're awfully quiet, Dwight. What's up?"

"We can't sign a contract. We won't be here."

She rubbed her neck. "One day at a time. First, we do the interview, then we go back to the apartment. My instincts tell me events may escalate."

He studied her with narrowed eyes. "How much longer can our solar system remain stable without the stones?"

"I don't know." She flinched. "The pain has intensified. It's also more frequent." Gripping the doorknob, she did her best to project a calm front. "Meet you at Revson Fountain in fifteen minutes. The radio station is at the Empire State Building, so we'll grab a taxi."

Dwight's tension eased. "I've always wanted to visit The Empire State Building. See you in a few."

Rayna, dressed for the interview, strolled from the Juilliard Building into the morning sunlight, and, mingling with tourists, made her way toward the fountain. As she rounded the corner of Philharmonic Hall, she caught sight of an awkward figure in a shadowy portico on the opposite side of the plaza.

"Hey, Rayna, I'm over here." Dwight waved and strode toward her.

Relieved to turn away from the portico, she hurried to meet him, slipped her hand into his, and walked with him toward the street.

He glanced down. "Are you okay?"

She shifted her dance bag. "Keep your eyes on me. Vygel's over by the theater watching us. Let's find a taxi and see if we can lose him."

Dwight flagged down a Checkered Cab, opened the door for her, gave the driver the address, and climbed in. The cab pulled away from the curb into traffic. Vygel limped down the steps, frustration twisting his toothy mouth as it disappeared into the stream of yellow cabs.

Rayna grinned. "I think we gave him the slip." She relaxed. "I wonder what the interviewer will ask?"

"Guess we'll find out soon enough." Dwight leaned back and closed his eyes. When they exited the cab at 34th Street and Fifth Avenue, he paid the driver, linked arms with her, and stared up at New York City's tallest building. "After we're done, let's ride to the top."

She laughed. "You're such a tourist."

"I'll never have another chance to explore it." He pushed open the door and escorted her to the elevator.

At the radio station, a pretty woman guided them to a recording studio. "Please have a seat at the table. Steve will be with you shortly."

Intrigued by the mics, headphones, and the large rectangular window separating them from a room filled with equipment, Rayna settled in a chair beside Dwight.

A young man sporting a dirty-blond ponytail and a warm smile entered, clipboard in hand. "Hi, I'm Steve Garnem. I'll be doing your interview." He sat opposite, studied the clipboard, and looked up. "Rayna Deejara and Dwight Anders, have—" A man knocked on the window.

Steve stood up. "Be right back."

Dwight frowned. "That was weird."

Another taller man entered. His mane of brown hair pulled back with a headband exposed the strain etching his countenance. "Steve had to go. My name's Dave Quinset." Hazel eyes darted from one to the other. A fiendish grin twisted the sensual mouth. "He will reschedule your interview. Are you available on Monday morning?"

The odor of decaying flesh made Rayna gag. "We'll check our schedules."

The man shot a suspicious glance over his shoulder. "I'll be watching you. Bring the stones with you on Monday. If either of you tell anyone where I am..." He leaned closer. "You know who I am?"

His hissed question sprayed saliva on Rayna's cheek. She wiped it off with the back of her hand. "We know."

He smoothed his leather vest. "Find those stones." He left and reappeared in the room beyond the glass.

Rayna grimaced. *Rikell has taken a new body. I wonder how long he will keep it?* Her bag in hand, she glanced at her watch. "I suggest a little sightseeing, then a quiet lunch."

Dwight grinned from ear to ear when they exited the elevator at the Top Deck on the 102nd floor. The breathtaking view of New York City and beyond left Rayna awestruck.

"We need you." The words whispered in her mind along with a quick image. She nudged Dwight toward the elevators and pushed the down button.

At the eighty-fifth floor, the elevator doors opened to a woman exiting her office across the hall. "Can you hold that? I'm running a bit late."

"Of course." Dwight pressed the stop button. Rayna exited, her thoughts racing.

The woman locked her office and hurried into the elevator. "Thanks."

Dwight dodged between the closing doors. "Are you alright, Rayna?"

A finger to her lips, she crossed to the woman's office, whispered a charm, and tapped the lock.

They slipped inside. The instant the lock clicked back into place, Brie appeared. "We have to go. Mira's in trouble."

Dwight squeezed her hand. "Where to?"

She placed an image in his mind. The office vanished.

👁 👁

Corvus, Ari, and Almiralyn's white bird form materialized at the center of the deserted studio apartment. Ari hurried to prepare the Murphy Bed. Corvus sat down, placed the trembling creature next to him, a gentle hand resting on her winged back. "Mira, we need to change you to Human. Do you understand me?"

A tremor ruffled limp feathers. A feeble peck on his hand suggested she understood.

Ari withdrew Efillaeh from its hidden scabbard. The amethysts in the hilt gleamed in the light streaming in the window. "Did you contact Brie, Corvus?"

"I did. She'll be here soon."

The bird's shivering demanded attention. He picked her up to cradle her chilled body next to his heart. Dread gripped him. Her fading humanity stole the warmth from her body one drop at a time.

"Mira! Don't leave me. Mira!"

Ari moved to his side. "Let me use Efillaeh. Maybe it can keep her here until Brie—"

Light flashed. Brie, followed by Dwight, appeared by the kitchen table. Clutching the blue velvet pouch in her hand, she hurried to the bedside. "See if you can corral her. She doesn't have much time."

Corvus guided the bird to the center of the bed and lay down beside her. Brie knelt next to him with Ari. Dwight, looking lost, glanced from one to the other.

"Kneel at the foot of the bed, Dwight." Brie tipped the Remembering Stone onto her palm. "Concentrate on helping her to reclaim her humanness."

"I've never done this. I—" He looked away.

"Look at me." Brie held his wavering gaze with a steady one. "You have the power to help. Just do what I ask." She focused on the white raven. "I'm going to hold the Remembering Stone to her heart. Everyone concentrate on drawing her humanity back to the present." The quivering bird scuttled to the side, dodging her hand. After two more tries, Brie frowned. "Corvus, see if you can discover what she's afraid of."

With the white raven in his arms, he rolled onto his back. Closed eyelids twitched. "Vygel gave her a drug intended to keep her in bird form forever." Stillness enshrouded him. His face blanched wheat-flour pale. A pain-filled groan escaped up his throat. He passed Brie the becalmed bird. "I need Efillaeh. Hurry!"

Ari pressed the sacred knife to his heart. The amethysts glowed. He gagged, then grew quiet. A deep inhale brought color seeping back to his complexion. Reclaiming the white bird, he placed her on the bed with a hand on either side of her body. "She's ready for the Remembering Stone."

Brie inched closer. When the bird remained placid, she rested the gold-flecked blue stone on the white chest. Ari held the healing blade above the ruffled feathers on her head. Dwight watched, his expression expectant. Brie chanted.

"Almiralyn, remember the form of your birth.
Let humanness reclaim you and return you to Earth.
Release your bird form 'til a time of your choosing,
A time when you call it to respond to your musing."

Brie touched Corvus' arm. "Release her."

The white raven cocked her head. Dulled sapphire eyes enlivened. White wings unfurling, fanned the air. Motion ceased. Nothing stirred—not the blink of an eye, the ruffling of a single feather, nor breath filling the chest. Then, motion resumed with the fanning of wings and their coming to rest against white feathered sides. The bird vanished, leaving a pale, motionless Almiralyn in its place. As beautiful as the Grimms Brothers' *Briar Rose*, she lay in a trance state, her silvery-white hair forming a robe around her.

Corvus leaned over her. "Almiralyn's body has returned." He kissed her cheek, then lifted tear-filled eyes. "She does not inhabit it." A flash flood of emotion left him shaking. "Arienh. Brielle." Sobs quaked.

Brie and Ari exchanged glances but did not place the Remembering Stone or the knife on the death-quiet body.

45

In the white sapphire cage, Penee's fear-induced shudder puffed up her neck feathers. She wanted nothing more than to escape the influence of the Corps Stones and Roween Rattori's rage. The slap of leather soles against the hardwood floor announced the woman's angry approach. Shrinking into herself, Penee quaked as the woman marched straight to the cage.

Steel-hard eyes peered between the sapphire bars, her homely visage filled with malice. "Not dead yet, Almiralyn? I'm surprised you have lasted this long." She withdrew a small, obsidian key on a long chain from beneath her starched cotton blouse. The drawer in the obsidian base slid open. An exhaled breath wafted between the glistening bars. A ring-bedecked hand held up an egg-size emerald encased in quartz crystal. "Ahhh. What a beauty." Cradling it in her hands, she carried it to the antique rosewood coffee table and placed it on the silk scarf draped over it. After retrieving the other stones, she sat down to examine each one, her sharp features twisted into a Cheshire-grin.

Penee reveled in the slow return of her strength. She had felt the stones diffusing her energy. Not until Roween removed them, did she realize why Almiralyn could not escape. The Corps Stones drew their power from everything in their vicinity.

Roween's crooning voice floated through the room. "You are so beautiful—so powerful. That silly woman had no idea what she possessed." Her salacious laugh cut short. "Now, you're mine to control. You will serve my needs."

A laugh of delight, cut short by a ringing phone, produced a series of profanities. Long, angry strides carried her to the far side of the suite. Her face twisting into a scowl of distaste, she pressed the receiver to her ear.

Grateful for the distraction, Penee created an internal curtain-like barrier behind which she channeled her returning strength. She focused her thoughts on Gar. *Roween. Stones.*

Tension stiffened Roween's spine. She slammed the receiver into the cradle and hurried back to the coffee table. One by one, she returned the stones to their hiding place, locked the drawer, and hid the small obsidian key beneath her blouse.

A short time later, Vygel strode into the room, surveyed it with a sour expression, and glared into the cage.

Penee subjugated her energy to what little remained of Almiralyn's. Her breath wheezed. Her feathers drooped.

He shrugged. "What a waste. I didn't believe her friends would let her die."

Roween lowered onto the couch. "They have no idea we're in the city, so why would they seek her here?"

Vygel wiped the sweat beading on his upper lip with a silk handkerchief. "We have done well, have we not." He refolded it into a perfect square and tucked it in his pocket. "Soon, the stones will be ours." His tongue slipped over his yellowed teeth. "I can't wait to sell them for enough money to travel the Universe."

Roween gazed at the large ring on her right hand, the ring that marked her as a LaChette on the planet of RewFaar.

Vygel scowled. "I'm going to check on Sorda. Would you care to come?"

She twisted the ring from her finger, held it up in the light, and slipped it back into place. "You go. I have things I wish to accomplish."

His eyes bulged. "Things?"

An indifferent yawn brought her to her feet. "You know. Girl things. Boring things. Go check on Karlsut. When you return, we can go to out to dinner."

Vygel pursed his lips, pivoted, and left the room. The apartment door slammed shut.

Penee shivered as the stones began absorbing her energy.

$\sim$

Brie gave Corvus time to regain his composure before slipping the Remembering Stone back in its velvet pouch. "Almiralyn lingers in Surazal, the gray land between life and death. If I were certain she would return to this reality, as Wolloh did, Ari would give you Efillaeh to drive through her heart." She bit her lip. "Something else holds her, something I don't understand. We dare not do more. You must take her to the Guardians."

A lighting-sharp pain blazed between her temples. Brightness saturated her vision. An image flashed into being and dissolved, leaving her shaking and her thoughts in turmoil.

A gentle hand touched her shoulder. "Brie, can you hear me?"

Through a blur of confusion, she gazed into her twin's worried face.

"Ari, I—" Trembling hands pressed to her throbbing temples, she forced one word between clenched teeth. "Roween—" Another stab of pain pierced her chest. She doubled over, panting.

Gar materialized at the room's center. "Roween has the stones. I heard her tell the white bird she's usin' 'em to track ya." His gaze darted over the group. "Ya can't stay here."

Dwight moved to the end of the bed. "Penee?"

Gar squinted at him. "She's okay, right now. Vygel's off to check on Sorda, but he won't be long. He doesn't get it that Roween has the stones. She hides 'em in the drawer in the cage's shiny black bottom." He looked at Almiralyn's prone figure. "Mira was close to 'em for too long."

Ari knelt, her hand on his shoulder. "How do you know all of this?"

His nostrils flared. "I shaped a spider so I could watch through the window, and, like Brie taught me, tuned my hearin' to listen. When Vygel left, Roween bragged to the white bird that she bribed a seamstress to give her the stones. She unlocked the drawer. I saw 'em...the Corps Stones! They're hidden there. That's why Mira's so sick. That horrid woman laughed. "Death will claim you before the night is over, Almiralyn Nadrugia." He clutched Ari's hand. "What do we do?"

Brie bent down to look him in the eye. "You're positive the stones are in the drawer?"

"Roween locked em in. She wears the key on a chain 'round her neck."

Corvus slid off the bed. "Brielle, you saw something before Gar appeared. What?"

She rubbed sweaty hands on her thighs. "Roween in New York with Vygel. Then, the Corps Stones destroying the planet Earth. We have to restore them to their natural home planets—" A shudder of pain ripped her thoughts into pieces.

Corvus embraced her, soaked the pain from her body, and stepped away panting. "Roween is directing the stones to create your pain." He crawled onto the bed beside Almiralyn and pulled her onto his lap. "We have to leave!"

Brie put a hand on his shoulder and motioned their companions closer. "Ari, I need you to put shields up around us."

Ari nodded. Dwight and Gar joined them. Glistening shields surrounded them.

With her increasing discomfort simmering, Brie placed an image in Corvus' mind. He nodded.

Pain ripped through her, dumping her at the edge of consciousness.

S trong arms steadied her. "Brielle, we need you."

Esán's urgent words pulled Brie from the precipice to a place of no pain. She breathed in his scent and allowed his warm embrace to center her.

He released her. "Brie, Corvus told us what's been happening. We need you to tell us what our next step is."

Brie gazed at the group assembled in the lounge in SAB's costume shop. Esán sat beside her. Torgin and Joe watched her with intense interest. Almiralyn, still trapped in Surazal, lay on the much-used couch, her head in Corvus' lap. Ari and Dwight waited, their attention fixed on her.

She frowned. "Where are Gar and Spyglass?"

"Here we are." Gar poked his head in the door. "Standing guard."

"Please come in." She closed her eyes to sift through the happenings of the past few hours. Memories prancing in her mind like restless horses sorted themselves into one urgent message—leave with the stones or they will destroy Earth. She swallowed. "We have to rescue Penee and the stones. All of us, including Joe, must leave 1969, and we can't do it from the costume shop."

Joe's distressed expression stopped her. "Joe, are you alright?"

"Are you sure I won't be more trouble than I'm worth? I can leave the city —maybe take my wife on a second honeymoon."

Corvus left Almiralyn's side. "Joseph, you realize Rikell or Vygel or both will find you. How do you plan to protect her? You know too much. They can't let you live, Joe."

"Wipe my memories clean. Then I won't be a threat."

Esán shook his head. "Erasing your memories would leave you and your wife even more vulnerable. You won't recognize the danger when they come for you."

Brie nodded. "Even if they found out we wiped your mind clean, I doubt that it would protect you. Don't you want to visit our time?"

He sagged. "I don't want to leave Kathy."

Brie touched his arm. "I can't imagine leaving Esán either. But, Joe, we have no choice. If we don't leave now, there won't be an Earth to return to."

Corvus held her gaze. "What aren't you sharing, Brielle?"

"There's only one place in New York where it's safe to enter Mittkeer. The fewer who know, the harder it will be for Vygel to track us. We need to hurry. Corvus and Joe, protect Almiralyn. Dwight, you can help me. Torgin and Ari, I need you to give me a high note on your time whistles. Esán use the Seeds of Carsilem to move us forward in time..." She glanced at the clock. "...three hours."

Torgin handed Dwight the Compass of Ostradio. "Do what I tell you, Dwight." He held up his whistle. "I'm ready."

Dwight bit back a reply and stared at the compass.

"So am I." Ari's deep voice rang like a bell.

Brie noted the excitement in Gar's eyes. "Please hold on to Spyglass, Garon."

With a grin, he scooped the terrier up in his arms.

She tapped the dog on the head. "No noise, little one. Okay, Dwight, when I put the image of where we're going in your head, you focus your intention on the compass and take us there. Ready, everyone. Ari and Torgin, go!"

A soft light flared. Ari gasped; Dwight laughed. Esán hugged her and whispered, "You are amazing, Brielle AsTar." From a dizzying height, a panorama of New York City spread out below them. The clear night sky, sprinkled with stars, provided a backdrop for the moon's descent to the distant horizon.

Gar grinned. "The Empire State Building. How'd ya know it'd be empty?"

Dwight smiled. "We explored it earlier today."

Joe's eyes widened. "That's why we needed to travel ahead three hours...so the building would be closed. I'm gonna miss all this."

Gar tugged at Brie's shirt. "What about Penee?"

"We teleport her to us. It's past midnight. Vygel and Roween should be sleeping. Gar, you work with Torgin to transport the cage with Penee. Esán will stand by with me to help." She slowed her racing thoughts. *One step at a time, Brielle AsTar.*

"Corvus and Joe, please continue to guard Almiralyn. The sooner we leave after we rescue Penee and the cage, the better. Dwight, be ready to support them. Ari, work with Torgin." She took a rejuvenating breath. "Gar, see if the apartment is quiet."

Gar slipped a hand into Torgin's. His eyeballs darted behind closed lids. He blinked. "All clear."

Torgin took his other hand. "Are you ready?"

The boy licked his lips. "Ready."

Torgin looked at Brie. "At your command..."

◈　◈

The light from a standing lamp cast the giant shadow of the white sapphire cage on the wall behind it. Penee shrunk lower, one blue eye peering between the bars. Her adversaries had long since retired, yet worry plagued her. *If they discover I'm not Mira, what will they do?*

The slightest tingle of a mental probe suspended all thought. She did not move. Gar's withdrawal from her mind, leaving no message, alerted her to be ready. Forcing a calm she did not feel, she tucked her head beneath her wing.

A siren whining in the street below made her cringe. She peered from under the long feathers. Nothing in the apartment stirred. The cage quivered. The bars glowed diamond bright as the power of Gar and Torgin engulfed it. A bedroom door crashed open. Footsteps stumbled down the hall. Vygel limped across the living room, his arthritic hands reaching toward the white sapphire and obsidian cage. His dismayed howl, cut short, left Penee gazing between the bars at two happy, grinning faces.

Torgin slapped Gar on the back. "We did it! Terrific work!"

Penee flashed into human form next to them. "Thank you. Thank you all. I have much to share."

A loud guffaw brought a surprised gasp from the companions. A tall man with a mane of dark hair, his hazel eyes darting over the group, stood at the periphery of their circle. "What a lovely little reunion you're having." His gaze lowered. A brow arched. "I imagine Vygel and Roween are not happy about their missing cage." He sniffed the air. His demeanor changed from sardonic to conniving. "Do I sense the stones?" He darted forward, grabbed Joe's arm, and yanked him into a tight embrace. "Give them to me, or I will release this body and merge with your friend."

Joe's eyes, rounded in terror, did not leave Brie's face.

Her VarTerel's shaft solidifying in her hand, she stepped forward. Rainbow light from its crystal crown pooled at the man's feet. Her voice rang out. "You have a choice, Dave Quinset, aka Rikell of RewFaar. Look around. On this rooftop are some of the most powerful people in the Inner Universe. One word from me, and they will all join forces against you. Release Joe, and you may travel with us to the future. Make the choice to harm him, and you forfeit your existence. It's up to you."

Dave, his face an open book, worked through and rejected several scenarios. A grimace telegraphed his acceptance of defeat. "I'm outnumbered." A rough shove sent Joe stumbling away from him. "I'll behave."

Esán pulled a dazed Joe behind him.

Corvus continued to hold Almiralyn in his protective embrace. "Joe, sit with me. Dwight and Penee, since we know Rikell isn't always true to his word, please stand guard while the others prepare to create a time tunnel."

Penee and Dwight stationed themselves on either side of the Mindeco's human victim.

Dave glared at the group. "We have our own time machine, you know."

Torgin grinned. "You mean the one that's stuck in 1969?"

"How did you—" The man's lips pressed into a thin line. "Never mind." His nose wrinkled. "At least show me the stones."

"You can see them when we are safe in the future." Brie turned to Gar. "Take Spyglass and guard the cage."

The Mindeco's stolen persona fixed his attention on the boy. "You charge a mere child with the care of the cage? I gather they didn't hide the stones there."

Dwight touched Dave's shoulder. "Quiet, Mindeco."

Goose bumps skittered up Penee's spine. She scanned the Top Deck. "We need to go. Something's not right."

46

Brie's brows shot together. "Torgin, show me Ostradio."

He took it from Dwight's trembling hand. At Brie's signal, he touched it to the tourmaline crystal.

She chanted,

> *"Compass of Ostradio, recalibrate, reform.*
> *The settings last used must return to their norm.*
> *Focus intent ahead of this time;*
> *Secure our destination with power sublime."*

The compass needle spun in a blur of gold and stopped. Torgin flipped it over. The constellations reformed. "Done." He looped its leather cord over his head and pulled out the time whistle.

Ari moved to his side. "I'm ready.

Brie held the staff high. The panorama of New York City melted into

Mittkeer's starry night sky. With her staff's crystal, she drew an oval window. On the eighty-sixth floor observation deck at the Empire State Building, Vygel and Roween searched for them without success. Brie closed the window. "We need to go. They can't enter Mittkeer, but Vintrusie can cause us problems. Torgin and Ari, begin."

The harmonic notes infused the Land of No Time and All Time. Esán clasped Brie's hand. Her tourmaline crystal's rainbow light illuminated the land of ever-night. She pressed his fingers and felt the response of the Seeds of Carsilem controlling the magnetic spin of the forming tunnel. Torgin increased the power of his higher pitched whistle. Ari kept her lower notes steady. The speed of the spin increased. Brie concentrated on balancing the colors shooting from her crystal. The forward momentum of the passageway accelerated. Dimensions streaked past. Spyglass barked and squirmed. The body of Rikell's human victim dissolved. The Mindeco yowled. His lean, leathery body cannoned backward through time, leaving Penee and Dwight on their knees, battling the magnetic drag of his unexpected departure.

Cage bars glowed bright diamond white. The crackle of them breaking changed to tiny chimes ringing as white splinters joined the spin of the time tunnel. At Gar's feet, the obsidian base of the cage quaked with repeated tremors.

Esán hissed, "Protect Spyglass."

Gar crouched next to Penee, shielding his small dog.

Light shot through the keyhole in the obsidian drawer. The base shattered, revealing the three Corps Stones encased in swirling colors.

Torgin strained to hold the high notes steady. The spin of the tunnel increased. He riveted his gaze to Ari's. Together they fought to stabilize their tempo.

The staff clutched in both hands, Brie fell to her knees. The Emerald Corps Stone's vibrating phosphorescence infused the quartz crystal, cocooning it. Like a rocket of green light, it shot up the tourmaline's rainbow path, penetrated the time tunnel, and, trailing a sparkling tail, streaked across Mittkeer's starry dome. The Ruby and Diamond Corps Stones shot through the spinning tunnel, following individual trajectories across the star-lit heavens.

Torgin and Ari played a final long harmonic note. The spinning of the passageway slowed. Esán dropped to his knees, trembling hands covering his face.

Consummate silence cloaked them. Darkness engulfed them. A soft breath penetrated the silence. A glimmer of light floating their direction blazed brighter. Chealim, in all his celestial glory, towered over them.

Joe gasped.

Gar whispered, "Are we dead?"

The Guardian's voice tolled. "Garon, son of Ralara Aureka and Tane Anaru, you are very much alive." He waved a hand. The subterranean cavern beneath Tao Spirian's ocean wavered into being. "Welcome to the future. Well done, all of you."

Brie clambered to her feet. "The Stones?"

Chealim's smile widened. "Your time tunnel has returned them to their rightful places. Not what we expected, but we are delighted. I believe Almiralyn needs some attention. He knelt, touched her forehead, and recited:

"From the Land in Between, Surazal its true name,
Release death's cold hand, your life you must claim.
Loved ones await you, your destiny too.
Come back to us now, you have much more to do."

An inhale raised Almiralyn's chest. Color washed her cheeks a tender pink. Her eyelids fluttered open. A slow smile shaped her beautiful mouth. "Chealim." She sighed.

His feather-light touch brushed her forehead. "Sleep, Almiralyn Nadrugia." He rose to his magnificent height. "I believe a life was lost in the tunnel. When you have replenished your energy with a good meal and sleep, we will discuss your return to the time before the death occurred and what you must do to withdraw from the 1969, leaving it unscathed by your visit."

His gaze came to rest on Dwight. "I have someone who is waiting to meet you." He offered a hand.

Dwight hesitated, brushed his bangs off his forehead, and reached up to clasp it. In a glow of shimmering iridescence, he and Chealim evaporated.

As though invisible gags vanished, everyone began talking at once.

Brie smiled at Esán, who draped an arm over her shoulder and grinned.

Dwight gazed through a window at the beauty of Tao Spirian's Ocean of Mālie and tried to ignore the loud beat of his heart. *I'm going to meet my father. Will he like me? Will I like him?*

"Hello, Rethson."

The voice, deep and mellow and gentle, washing over him, subdued his doubts. A slow pivot ended with him facing the man whose honey-gold eyes, glowing with love, brought him to tears.

"I am Rethdun Torin Vilandree, otherwise known as Relevart. I am your father."

Dwight swallowed a lump in his throat, attempted to speak, and failed. Gazing up at the aging face where fine lines crinkled as the generous mouth curved upward, he rediscovered sound. "I'm Dwight. I mean Reth—" Words tumbled over themselves. "I've wanted to meet you. I didn't know...I had no idea...I thought you didn't care."

A variety of emotions flitted across the older man's face. "Had I known of your existence, Rethson, I would have searched the universe to find you sooner. Can you forgive me? Since I learned of Rasiana's incredible gift, I pursued every course I could think of except wringing Vygel Vintrusie's neck."

Dwight's mouth twitched. "I doubt that would have been helpful."

The older man chuckled. "Truly. Let's not waste any more time lamenting what could have been. Let's celebrate what is. I imagine you have questions. What do you want to know?"

"I'd love to see what I, Rethson, look like. Roween and Vygel made certain I wouldn't guess I was anything more than an unwanted child."

Narrowed amber eyes studied him. "May I touch your forehead?"

Dwight nodded his permission.

The touch, as fleeting as a butterfly's kiss, produced a current of warmth that ran up his spine. Like a snake shedding its skin, he shrugged away Dwight's physical characteristics. His awareness returned with the steadiness of the rising sun. Cool palms eased the heat from his flushed face. "Do I favor you or my mother." He laughed. "My voice is deeper."

"There's a mirror across the hall. Shall we take a peek?" Rethdun strode into a long, gleaming corridor, pushed open an entrance, and motioned him through.

His reflection in the floor to ceiling mirror triggered a gasped. "My eyes are amber." He fingered his jet-black hair and gazed at his body. He had retained the lithe build of the dancer, but broader shoulders and more muscular arms defined his upper torso. His father's reflection made him smile. "Brie told me you had amber eyes." Shyness overwhelmed him. "She placed the image of a painting in my thoughts, a family portrait painted by her mother. I've met Penee. Will I ever meet my brothers?"

"We'll make certain you do." Rethdun looked bemused. "I always longed for a family. I am joined now to my life-mate, Henrietta, whom I believe you will like. When I met Den, Elf, and Penee not long ago, my heart overflowed. Finding the Corps Stones had to take precedence over my search for you." His laugh rang out. "The Universe works in interesting ways, does it not? You, my youngest son, right here because of that choice."

Dwight grinned. "I am your son, Rethson, not a child no one wanted." He accepted an embrace, returned it, and stepping back, faced the mirror. He gazed from his father's reflection to his own. "I definitely see a family resemblance." A laugh of delight made his father smile."

A tall, dark-haired man strode into the room. "Hello, little brother. I'm Den." He flashed a grin and offered a hand. "You look like me, too. How does it feel to discover you are part of a family?"

Dwight regarded him with interest. "I understand you just found yours. How do you feel?"

Den chuckled. "Extremely lucky." He grew serious. "Chealim sent me to collect you both. We have decisions to make." He held open the door. "Do we call you Dwight or Rethson?"

"I expect to be resuming Dwight's persona soon, so let's keep things simple. I am Dwight until all the loose ends are tied up." With a final glance in the mirror, he followed his father and brother from the room. "I can't wait until my friends see the real me."

Penee pulled a chair away from the group. *I wonder how Dwight and Relevart are faring?* Eyes fixed on the diversity of the ocean world beyond the clear wall, she mused about everything that had occurred since her rescue from Soputto's moon. *I'm so glad TaSneach's ever-winter is behind me. I sure wish—*

A reflected movement on the glassy surface widened her eyes.

The reflection spoke. "Hello, Penesert."

She jumped to her feet, her gaze fastened on the handsome face of the man she adored. "Den!"

A second man peered over his shoulder, laughter sparkling in his amber eyes.

Momentary confusion snapped to realization. "Rethson! You look like Den, except for the color of your eyes."

Den's arms embracing her demanded all her attention. The hum of everyone's excitement at Rethson's appearance covered his whispered, "I have missed you." A soft kiss brushed her lips as he let her go.

She slipped a hand into his, then turned to observe the reactions to how much Rethson resembled him. Relevart watched from the doorway, his smile widening as he soaked in the presence of his children.

Penee sighed. "I'm sorry Elf isn't a part of this reunion."

Den grinned down at her. "Watch."

Relevart moved aside to allow a young man into the space. Elf acknowledged them all, introduced himself to Dwight, and beamed a thoughtful smile at Ari, who dragged him to the couch where she talked non-stop.

Gar, with Spyglass at his heels, marched to Penee's side. "You're Den, aren't ya?"

Den raised a brow. "I am. And you are?"

Penee grinned. "Den, this is Garon. He is my Eleo Predan partner in the fight to restore El Stroma. Gar, this is Relevart's oldest son."

Gar gazed up at him and held out a hand, palm up. "Good ta meet ya, Den."

After touching the offered palm, Den smiled. "Penee's shared a bit of your story. I can't wait to hear more of it from you."

Relevart cleared his throat. "Chealim has asked me to tell you we will reconvene in the morning. At that time, he will confirm that the Corps Stones made it to their home planets. He will also present a plan for your return to the past. Now, please join me. I am to take you to a special dinner arranged in your honor."

The shuffling of chairs, feet, and excited chatter filled the room. Gar pulled a hesitant Joe into the group. A soft flash of light left them on a beach where the twin suns of the Clenaba Rolas System slipping below the horizon tossed rays of golden orange into the heavens. Torches defining the dining area highlighted a long table covered with Tao Spirian delicacies. A scattering of tables in varying sizes, each lit by the warm glow of a lantern, lined the beach a good distance above the high tide line.

Penee glanced at Den. "Dare we sit on our own?"

His extraordinary smile warmed her. "I believe that's why the assortment of tables." He escorted her to the buffet and followed her through the line. Their plates heaped high with treats of all kinds, they settled at a table set for two beneath a palm tree.

Penee absorbed the beauty of the night and the welcome presence of the man across from her. Her gaze roamed the cheerful faces of her friends. *I am so lucky I found you.*

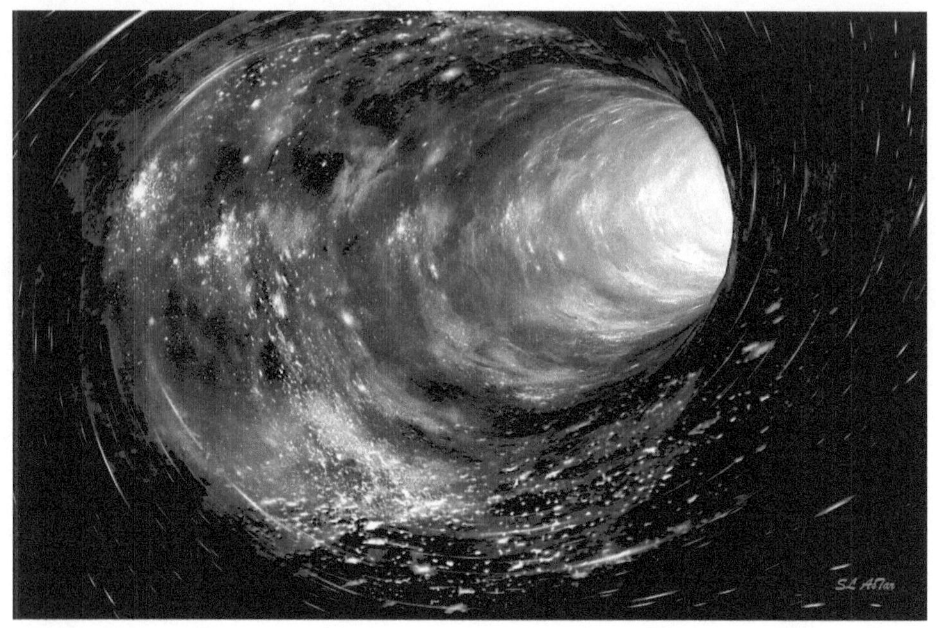

47

Mittkeer's ever-night stars shone brighter than Brie remembered. She glanced at her companions. The high-pitched hum of their apprehension made her backbone stiffen. Esán put a protective hand on Joe's shoulder. Dwight's gaze roamed the endless night sky. Gar, dark brown eyes huge and filled with wonder, gripped Spyglass by his rope collar. Torgin and Ari, time whistles in hand, faced each other. The Compass of Ostradio, recalibrated for their return to Earth, gleamed against his tie-dyed t-shirt.

Gar fidgeted and pressed closer to Penee. He glanced up at Brie. "How long do we have to wait?"

Relevart materialized, his VarTerel's staff in hand. "Everything is ready." His words echoed through the Land of All Time and No Time. "Take care of yourselves."

Brie held her staff higher. Musette's tourmaline light cast its rainbow colors into the dome of starlight. Torgin raised his time whistle. A long, clear, high note rang through Mittkeer. Ari's response in a lower key set the time tunnel in motion. Esán focused the power of the dual seeds of Carsilem to control its magnetic spin. Relevart's presence receded into the future. A howl from the past escalated to a roar. The tunnel spun faster. Dave Quinset, Rikell's last victim, reformed molecule by molecule. Rikell flew up the spinning passageway, merged with the body, and fell to his knees, muttering.

The compass wobbled, changed its destination, and steadied. The tunnel slowed, loud music swelled, a recording studio enclosed the Mindeco and its victim. Growling low, Rikell exited Dave's body. Eyes rounded in horror, the terrified man moved backward toward the door. Little by little, his expression eased. Step by step, he backed into an office with his name on the door, sank into a chair behind the desk, and picked up his headphones. The office melted away as the spinning tunnel continued to pull them into the past.

The corridor outside The Penthouse Suite at The Plaza Hotel took shape. Rikell leapt free of the tunnel. Landing on the plush carpet, he swung his enormous head left, then right. The single blazing oculus focused. He lumbered along the hotel corridor toward the stairs to the roof. Sorda's sitting room came into focus. Roween, Vygel, and Sorda lunged to their feet. Musette's rainbow light engulfed them and teleported them into Mittkeer. The time tunnel reversed its spin. A distant figure walked from the future, a staff raised high. Its crystal gleamed brighter. A ray of shimmering white light shot down the tunnel, encapsulated the trio of thieves in a luminescent glow, and reversed its direction, carrying them back to their own time.

Brie refocused Musette's rainbow path into the past. Ari played a final note and lowered the whistle. Torgin performed a breathy musical phrase that melted into the fabric of Mittkeer. The time tunnel evaporated. Late afternoon light flooded the 72nd Street apartment on the day before they had gone home to the future.

Silence engulfed the companions. Ari, her expression unreadable, tucked her whistle beneath her blouse, and sank onto a chair. Joe, looking shell-shocked, followed her example. Shaking hands covered his pale, sweat-soaked face. Gar pulled Penee with him to the window. Spyglass, tail wagging, trotted after them.

Dwight sank cross-legged to the floor. "What will happen to them?"

Esán drew Brie down on the sofa. "They have broken Universal Law. They will have to face the Galactic Tribunal."

Torgin lounged in his favorite chair, his long legs crossed at the ankles. "You look like you're worried about them, Dwight."

"Roween raised me. She may have used me, but I still care about her."

Brie nodded. "Of course, you do. I'm sure Relevart will share more when we return. Let's check our schedules, so we're ready to resume our lives in 1969."

Ari glanced at the clock. "Speaking of resuming our lives, I'll be right back." She hurried from the room.

Joe lowered his hands. "What happens to me? Do you erase my memory now or wait?"

Esán smiled. "When the time comes, Chealim will be the one to expunge them. He will do whatever you prefer."

Joe wiped sweat-damp palms on his pants. "I'd like to finish this adventure with you. If it's okay, I'll keep my memories as long as possible."

"Sounds good to me. "Esán's eyes widened. "Oops. Almost forgot. Chealim asked me to tell you to select a memory to keep tucked away in your mind. It needs to be one that won't impact anyone else. Think about it."

Gar spoke over his shoulder. "Hey, guys, does the Mindeco remember stuff?"

Penee transferred her gaze from the street to Brie. "Our memories are intact. What about Rikell's?"

"He didn't return to the future, so he's caught in his memories of 1969."

Ari strolled into the room and joined Penee and Gar by the window. "Which means... He's out there, searching for the stones." She groaned. "We're still his target, right? Why didn't we send him back with the others?"

Brie rested her head on Esán's shoulder. "The Council decided that catching Vygel, Roween, and Sorda was more important. They felt we could manage Rikell, especially when he discovers the stones are no longer in this time and dimension."

A buzzer sounded.

Ari grinned. "That'll be the pizza I ordered. Since we don't want to change anyone else's reality more than we need to, I called to have it delivered to this address rather than the studio apartment."

Torgin pulled out his wallet and handed her a couple of bills. "Excellent work, Ari. I'm starving. Dinner's on me."

The buzzer sounded again. She pressed the button. "Yes?"

A crackly voice replied, "You ordered a pizza?"

"I did. I'll be right down." She beckoned. "Come on, Gar. I could use some help."

Dwight trailed Torgin down the hall. They returned with plates, napkins, and utensils to set up the coffee table for a pizza party.

Brie snuggled closer to Esán, her thoughts drifting back to Almiralyn's rescue. "I'm glad Mira's okay. Corvus was more scared than I have ever seen him."

Esán kissed the top of her head. "I'm worried about where the Mindeco's going to hide. The last thing we need is to deal with another of his victims."

Brie stared out the window. *Where did you hide before, Rikell of RewFaar? One thing I know for sure—we must beat you to Dave.*

A festive atmosphere accompanied the pizza dinner. Brie smiled to herself. The return of the stones to their home planets and Almiralyn's recovery had taken the pressure off. Lighthearted teasing and lots of laughter eased the fatigue of the past few days.

After cleanup, Joe announced he was too tired to think. A yawn underscored his statement. Exhaustion escorted him to bed. Ari and Dwight sat down at the kitchen table, deep in conversation. Torgin, Gar, and Penee slipped away to the music room.

Brie picked up Gar's terrier. "Bet they need music time, huh, Spy? You can come with us." She followed Esán into the living room and snuggled next to him on the couch. "I'm exhausted. Are you?"

He scratched Spyglass under the chin. "I'm pretty beat. I think we're all in let-down mode."

Soft strains of the piano accompanying the guitar drifted down the hall. Penee's clear soprano joined in.

Esán smiled. "I had no idea Penee could really sing."

The music stopped.

Dwight poked his head in the room. "Come and listen with me."

Brie jumped to her feet. She, Esán, and Dwight huddled at the music room door.

Penee and Ari stood together beside the baby grand piano. Gar, guitar in hand, faced them. Torgin played an introduction. Gar picked up with the melody. Ari's eyes sparkled with delight as she and Penee sang the first chorus.

Brie listened in amazement to her sister and friend. Her eyes brimmed over. Tears dampened her cheeks.

Esán's arms encircled her. "I can't believe what I'm hearing."

At the end of the second chorus, the girls sang a harmonizing note together. The piano grew silent. Gar strummed a final cord on the guitar and smiled.

Brie let out a soft breath. "Oh, my."

Ari grinned. "Surprised ya, huh!" She hugged Penee. "Thanks, Pen."

Brie hugged everyone. "That was wonderful. I'd ask for an encore, but it's getting late. We have a long day tomorrow." She kissed Esán's cheek. "Ready, ladies? Sleep is beckoning from the studio apartment."

Ari yawned. "Do we walk or teleport?"

"I don't know about you and Penee, but I could use some fresh air." Brie led the way into the hall.

Ari kissed Esán on the cheek. "Goodnight, soon to be brother."

Dwight ambled over. "What about me? Don't I get a goodnight kiss?"

Brie nodded at Ari. One on either side of him, they stood on tiptoe and planted a kiss on each cheek.

Penee pretended to pout. "Hey, what about me?"

Gar ran up to her. She bent down to receive his kiss with a beaming smile.

Ari grabbed her hand and reached for Brie's. The apartment morphed into the smaller studio.

Brie raised a brow at her twin. "I thought we were walking."

Ari grinned. "It felt like a good time to disappear." Grabbing a baggy shirt, she prepared for bed. "We all sleepin' on the Murphy?"

Penee collected a pillow and a couple of blankets from the cupboard. "I'm happy on the floor. See you in the morning."

Ari crawled onto the bed. Brie stepped from bell-bottomed jeans, lay beside her twin, and let thoughts of Esán woo her to sleep.

The following morning Rayna and Dwight traversed the plaza at Lincoln Center, heading straight to the theater, their focus on reaching Dave Quinset at the Empire State Building before Rikell merged with him. Mr. Thompson walked up as they arrived and escorted them to his office. They left a short time later with their apprentice contracts.

Sitting in the back of the Checkered Cab, Rayna half expected to see Vygel's bent figure on the curb. She glanced at her watch. "If we don't run into traffic, we have enough time to find Dave and make it to our interview."

They arrived at the radio station with time to spare, slipped past the reception area, and hurried down the hall to the recording studios. Alert for any sign of Rikell, they knocked on Dave Quinset's door.

"Come in."

They entered to discover him hunched over a tape recorder, headphones in hand, one ear pad pressed to his ear. His side-long glance produced a frown. He pushed a button on the recorder. "Do I know you?"

Rayna offered her hand. "I'm Rayna and this is my friend. We have an—"

The Mindeco dodged in the door. Dave's eyes bulged. His face paled to the white of a bleached sheet. Brie gripped his hand.

Dwight snapped at Rikell. "Close the door."

The lock clicked. The Mindeco's toothy lower jaw protruded. "How'd you know I'd be here?"

"The stones are no longer in New York City, 1969, Rikell, nor are Karl, Vygel, and Roween. Behave and we'll take you home to the future with us."

The boney jaw dropped. "You're lying. You want the stones. Find them or I will..."

"Please, Rikell, listen to Dwight." Rayna touched Dave's temple and lowered his head to rest on the desk. "We don't have time to argue. Go to The Plaza Hotel. See if Karl's registered." She walked up to him. "Let me help you." She touched his arm.

His cry of protest faded with him.

Dwight shook his head. "You sent him to—"

"Visit his time machine. He'll have to stay hidden until the museum closes." She returned to Dave. A light tap on his temple brought him to. He picked up the conversation without missing a beat.

"Thank you for stopping by. It has been a pleasure. The receptionist will show you to Steve's studio." He pressed the ear pad to his ear, his attention on the recorder.

In the hall, Dwight smiled down at her. "You continue to amaze me."

The receptionist greeted them with a gracious smile and guided them to the recording studio. "Please make yourselves comfortable. Mr. Garnem will be right with you."

Dwight sat furthest from the door. Rayna settled in her chair as a young man entered, clipboard in hand.

"Hi, I'm Steve Garnem. I'll be doing your interview." Sitting opposite, he studied the clipboard. "Rayna Deejara and Dwight Anders, have either of—" A man knocked on the window.

Steve stood up. "Be right back."

A few minutes later, the receptionist entered the studio. "Steve had to go. He asked me to reschedule your interview. Are you available on Monday morning?"

Rayna pushed her chair back. "We need to check our schedules. Do you have a card, so I can call you?"

After a quick stop at the front desk, Dwight led the way into an almost full elevator and pushed the button to the 102nd floor. Rayna, feeling claustrophobic, hugged her dance bag to her chest, trying not to panic.

They exited at the Top Deck, enjoyed the spectacular view, then took the elevator to the eighty-fifth floor. The doors opened as a woman exited the office across the way. "Can you hold that? I'm running a bit late."

"Of course." Dwight followed Rayna into the hall, his hand keeping the door from shutting.

The woman smiled and hurried inside. "Thanks."

Dwight waited for the doors to close then grinned. "We've got a couple hours of our own time. Let's do some real sightseeing."

Brie laughed. "Okay with me. Where do you want to go?"

He pushed the elevator's down button. "The Metropolitan Art Museum! Can you think of a better way to understand a culture than to study its art?"

A cab deposited them at the front steps of the museum. Two hours later, they emerged in the sweltering heat of the July day. "What a great idea! I loved every minute, Dwight. How about you?"

He squeezed her hand. "I'll never forget it." His intense gaze switched from the building's facade to her face. "I'm glad Chealim gave us time to finish what we began, aren't you? I mean, at least we get to perform in the opening weekend of the show."

Rayna smiled. "He realized we have all loved what we are doing. With Karl and gang gone and the Mindeco trapped, it almost feels like we're on holiday. Anywhere else you want to visit before we go back?"

"The city is full of things to explore, but I'm full of art and culture. I'd rather just take the time to digest it. You?"

Her gaze followed a group of young people climbing the museum steps. Their obvious excitement made her smile. "I'd suggest we stop by Sheep Meadow to check on how the girls' rehearsal is going, but Ari made me promise to wait until the show." She flashed a crooked smile. "Guess I'm ready to go back. Cab or subway?"

He stepped to the curb and hailed a cab. As it pulled into traffic, he sighed. "I just wanted to be quiet."

"I'm glad." She let herself relax.

The ride provided some time for reflection. Rayna gazed out the window. *It's nice to just enjoy the experience of New York, 1969. Even if the Mindeco is on the loose.*

48

Friday, everyone departed early, leaving Ari and Penee to spend the morning at the 72nd Street apartment, preparing for their Sunday afternoon performance. The coordinator directed them to open the show with three songs. After they finished rehearsing each of them, Ari kicked her sandals off, sat down on the couch, and sipped ice water from a tall, glass tumbler.

"You okay, Penee? Your attention's been somewhere else all morning."

Penee picked up an artifact from the shelf, turned it over, and sighed. "I'm worried about Rikell. Will he continue to focus on finding the stones, even if he's aware his fellow thieves are no longer in this time and dimension? He is so unpredictable."

Ari propped her feet on the coffee table, her gaze fixed on the ancient masks decorating the opposite wall. "Since I'm pretty certain he doesn't want to create a panic, I expect he's in hiding. I'm worried he'll snatch a body, and we'll lose him all together." She checked the time. "Rehearsal is at two o'clock; it's noon. I suggest we eat a bite of lunch before heading to Sheep Meadow."

Penee replaced the artifact, paused to glance out the window, and trailed her into the kitchen. Forty-five minutes later, they walked onto the street.

Ari linked her arm through Penee's. "Let's take the subway to 66th Street. We can walk from there."

At Broadway, they descended the stairs to the dingy underworld of New York City's subway system. The Friday lunch crowd surged around them. Ari scanned the platform. Beneath the angled slope of a staircase at the far end, a figure she knew all too well merged with graffiti-covered walls.

"We've got company." She kept her voice low. "Don't look back."

Fear flickering in her eyes, Penee mouthed a single word. "Mindeco?" Her grip on her purse strap tightened. "Why doesn't anyone else see him?"

"Because they don't expect to." Ari eased her into a group of rambunctious teens dancing to music blaring from a boombox.

The roar of the train approaching muffled the music. Brakes squealing cancelled it. Doors slid open. People poured onto the platform. Pulling Penee with her into the last car, Ari made her way to the end door. "Turn your back, Pen, so he won't recognize you." Ari tucked her long red hair beneath the neckline of her shirt and pulled her wide-brimmed hat lower.

The doors rattled closed; the train leapt forward into the tunnel. Ari grabbed the pole. A quick glance between packed bodies assured her Rikell hadn't boarded their car.

At 66th Street, the crowd carried them through the turnstiles to the stairs. A brisk walk later, they crossed Central Park West and made their way to Tavern on the Green. A server guided them to a table by the window.

Penee settled on the bench seat with her back to the park. "Did he follow us?"

Ari surveyed the open space behind her. "I'm sure he realized he couldn't stay hidden on the train. We're safe at the moment." She picked up the menu. "Let's enjoy a lemonade before we venture over to the Meadow."

Penee checked her watch. "We have almost an hour. I'll have some lemonade."

Ari grinned. "Just might join you."

. . .

They emerged from the restaurant with twenty minutes to spare. A quick-paced walk brought them to the raised stage on the northeastern side of the meadow. They reported to the stage manager and found a spot to watch the hustle and bustle.

Ari scanned the area. The stage, backed by an open space enclosed on three sides by trees, was about three feet high. The crew had added a dark red skirt since the previous rehearsal. They had also set up light stands on both sides of the stage area.

Penee nudged her. "Weren't we supposed to meet the headliners today?"

The harried assistant stage manager waved them over. "Thunderstorms over Boston have kept planes on the ground, so the stage is yours this afternoon. Make good use of the time. Tomorrow will belong to the headliners. You're up."

Their backup musicians, three guitarists whom they had liked right away, joined them. An excellent rehearsal left everyone feeling excited about Sunday's show.

After checking in with the stage manager, they strolled through the meadow. Midway across, Penee halted Ari with a hand on her arm. "Hold on. I'm just checking to see where I might watch from if I were Rikell. What if—"

Ari shook her head. "No 'what ifs'. One day at a time." She linked arms with Penee. "Let's get a cab. I can't wait to hear how Dwight and Rayna saved Dave Quinset from Rikell."

Esán and Joe spent the morning in the New York State Theater. They completed their lighting cue-to-cue of *Gems* with enough time to grab lunch at the Juilliard cafeteria. The sounds of orchestra members gathering in the pit and dancers warming up on stage greeted them when they returned.

Esán sat down at the lighting table. Unexpected butterflies fluttering in his stomach made him gulp a breath. "I think I'm nervous, Joe. What if I mess up?"

Joe Shyro shot him an understanding look. "Now you know how I've been feeling lately." He shuffled through his notes. "*Gems* is almost two hours long, so it has a lot of cues. You, I have noticed, have a photographic memory, so I'm not worried. Today's a tech run; expect things to go wrong. This is our opportunity to fix any problems." He smiled. "Better now than during performance, right?" He studied his notes. "Bet Torgin's in the pit. Why don't you go check?"

Glad to walk off his nerves, Esán strolled down the aisle to the center of the first row. He settled on the edge of a red velvet seat and leaned on the balustrade, fascinated by the musicians setting up in the pit below him at basement level. To one side, he spotted Torgin speaking with the conductor. After a brief conversation, he wove his way between the chairs to the piano.

"Pssst! Torg."

Torgin glanced over the pit.

Esán waved. "Up here."

Summer green eyes tracked his voice. "Hi, up there. How'd your cue-to-cue go?"

"It went. I gather you're playing the piano today. How's Mr. Pauley doing?"

Torgin shook his head. "He's a little better—"

"Time to warm up," the concertmaster announced from the podium. "Everyone please take your seats?"

"See you later." Torgin turned and placed his score on the piano's music rack.

Esán murmured to himself. "Can't wait to hear you play, Torgin Whalend."

He strode up the aisle to the sounds of instruments tuning and instructions being given.

Joe glanced up at his approach. "Saw you talking. Is Torgin playing the solo today?"

"He is. You've never heard him perform, right?"

"Only snippets. This is my intro to his work." Joe handed him a clipboard. "Your job is to keep me on track and to take notes. When we're ready to start, put on your earphones so you can listen to the Stage Manager call the cues." He checked his watch. "We've got about ten minutes. If you need to do anything, now's the time."

Esán settled at the table. "I'm good." He fiddled with a corner of a piece of paper on his clipboard. "Thanks, Joe, for letting me work with you. I'm really sorry you got mixed up in my stuff."

Joe leaned back in his chair. "I have to admit, our time together has kicked me out of my comfort zone. Not a bad thing." He nodded toward the stage. "Better pay attention. We're getting close."

W hile Dwight dumped his bag in the bedroom at the empty apartment, Brie materialized, shook her red curls loose from her ballet bun, and ran her fingers through her hair. A growling stomach sent her foraging in the fridge. Dwight clearing his throat behind her made her glance back.

Rethson, his amber eyes alight with wonder, stood in the doorway grinning. "I couldn't resist the urge to see the real me." He shifted to Dwight and peered over her shoulder. "I sure could use a snack."

She handed him two bottles of cola. "Me, too. Let's finish the last of the pizza." She slid two small pieces from the box onto a plate and preceded him into the living room. With her back against the arm of the couch, she slipped off her sandals, stretched her legs, and wiggled her toes. "It's amazing how things work out. Who would have guessed when Chealim sent us into the past, we'd find you?"

Setting the cola on the end table, he reclined in an over-stuffed chair with his hands behind his head. "It's hard to believe I met my father and my brothers. Somehow it feels more like a dream than a reality." He took a swig of cola and held the bottle up in the light. "I'll miss a few things about this time." He savored another bubbly swallow. "This, pizza is just as good cold as it was last night. I wish we weren't eating the last two pieces. They're making me want more." His brow furrowed. "What happens after the opening night performance? How will Chealim and Relevart erase memories of us and leave everything intact?"

A shiver surprised her. She glanced from her cola to the window. *Did the cold bottle or else something else trigger it?*

"Brie, are you okay?" Dwight's gaze darted to the window.

She shrugged. "My instincts tell me we're being watched." She savored a bite of pepperoni smothered in cheese and chased it with a tingling swallow of cola.

Dwight raised a brow and stood up. "I'll check." He crossed to the window, scanned the street in both directions, and returned to his seat. "Nobody's out there. At least, not now. Who'd be watching anyhow?"

Brie closed her eyes. A quick mental search of the street produced nothing. "It might have been Rikell." She shrugged. "You asked about erasing memories. Chealim will use the patterns and designs that were already in motion when we arrived. They will form a framework to maintain the integrity of life's course into the future and guide things along their natural path. From what I understand, it's like keeping a swelling river within its banks." She noted his confusion, drank the last of her cola, and swung her bare feet to the floor. "For example, Lois and Peter will assume our roles in the remaining performances of *Gems*. They along with everyone involved—audience, dancers, technical staff, orchestra members, etc—will remember the brilliance of the opening night performance with them dancing. The Guardians are being generous by giving us the gift of a performance. I'm grateful. I've loved every minute of my experience in the dance world." She raised her eyes to the heavens. "Thank you, Étoile!"

He pursed his lips, then relaxed them. "Will we remember being in New York City, 1969?"

"Always and forever." Brie slipped on her sandals. "You want to keep the memories of learning who you are and meeting your father, right?"

"I do." A smile took shape. "I want to remember so many things. He counted on his fingers: partnering with Rayna, turning five rotations in a *pirouette*, landing a *double tour* without even a bobble." He laughed. "It's been pretty cool, huh?"

"It has." Brie grinned back. "I have a question. How did you become the wonderful dancer and partner you are? Terpsichore sent Étoile to teach me about ballet."

He looked puzzled. "One day I knew nothing about dance; the next I was in a practice studio with everything I needed to know to join the dance community."

A key turned in the lock.

Brie jumped up. "Hope that's Ari and Penee."

Two more locks clicked.

He tipped his head. "Can't you tell?"

The door opened and closed, accompanied by the clank of a single lock.

She laughed. "Sometimes surprise is fun."

Spyglass bounded into the room, pawed Brielle's leg, and licked her hand. Gar strode in behind him. "I did what ya told me to do, Brie. The Mindeco followed Penee and Ari. He was waiting outside. They got on the train and lost him. Guess what? They sounded so good in rehearsal. They have a backup group playing with 'em. You're gonna love it!"

One lock preceded the creak of the door. Ari walked in and plopped down in the big chair next to Dwight. "You didn't tell us Gar was guarding us today."

Brie arched her brows. "You didn't ask."

Penee entered the room. "Thanks for watching our backs, Gar. I saw you at the subway station. You sure made yourself unnoticeable."

Gar's mouth worked. "So how'd you see me?"

She chuckled. "It's more like I felt you."

Ari shot Penee a dejected look. "*Why* didn't you tell *me*?"

Penee shrugged. "Thought you knew."

"Harrumph." Ari scowled.

Again, the door opened. "Anybody home?" Torgin preceded Joe and Esán into the room.

Dwight swiveled in his chair. "How was rehearsal?"

Torgin straddled the straight-backed chair. "Great! I played the solo piano in the second movement. I might get to play it on opening night." He held up crossed fingers.

Esán and Joe joined Brie on the couch. Slipping an arm around her shoulders, Esán let out a happy sigh. "The lights look wonderful, Joe. What do you think?"

"By the opening we'll be in good shape." Joe scanned the group. "Anyone else besides me hungry?"

A chorus of eager yeses made him laugh.

"I know an excellent East Indian restaurant which delivers on the Upper West Side. If you're game to try it, I'll buy."

Affirmatives filled the apartment. A grinning Joe sat at the desk, scribbled a list, and called to place the order.

During the wait for dinner to arrive, conversation centered on the Mindeco following Ari and Penee and its potential hiding places. The buzzer announcing their order's arrival ended it with no resolution.

Joe and Esán hurried from the apartment to meet the delivery man in the building's foyer. The aroma of exotic seasonings accompanied their return. Everyone gathered at dining room the table. Soon dal, shrimp curry, and chicken tikka masala brought murmurs of appreciation. Raita helped to cool the spices, and naan soaked every last drop from every plate. Dessert, a delicious selection of sweets, finished a meal fit for a king.

Not long afterward, the companions bid each other goodnight. When the girls arrived at the studio apartment, Brie pulled Ari aside. "I didn't mean not to tell you about Gar. Things just got crazy."

Ari hugged her. "It's okay. I'm glad he was there. He's quite a kid."

Brie experienced a wave of premonition. "He is. I can't wait to see him grow up." She yawned. "So glad I don't have rehearsal this weekend. Do you?"

Ari crawled onto the bed. "Since the headliners are arriving late, we did everything we could today. Tomorrow we're off. I'm looking forward to doing nothing."

Penee stretched out on the floor. "Me, too. I can't remember when I've been this tired." She rolled onto her side, covered her head with a pillow, and slept.

Brie whispered, "How does she do that?"

Ari snorted. "She closes her eyes and... Here, let me show you." She curled up and shut her eyes. Soft snores floated into the darkened room.

Brie lay in the quiet, thinking about the evening. Joe had played host to a roomful of young people from another time as though he did it every day. His adaptability and willingness to accept the strange situation he found himself in impressed her. *I wonder what you will choose to remember from this adventure, Joe Shyro?*

She gazed out the window at Earth's waxing crescent moon. *A walk on the moon is scheduled on Sunday. What an amazing time to be on Earth.* She yawned. *I am so glad it's the weekend.*

49

Ari woke Sunday morning to nervous fluttering in her stomach and the fear she had overslept. The drawn blinds blocked the sunlight. Brie, who always slept later than she did, was absent. Ari peered at Penee's blankets, folded in a neat stack to one side. *Guess you're up, too.*

She scooted to the edge of the bed. Padding into the bathroom, she splashed water on her face and stared in the mirror. *"Whatever made you think you could sing in front of an audience?"* She dried her grimacing face. *"The bigger question is why Chealim and Relevart thought you could?"*

The apartment door closing interrupted her self-negation. Giggles stifled by whispers piqued her curiosity. A stealthful look from behind the door showed her roommates unpacking a large brown bag. Brie set out paper cups of steaming liquid on the kitchen table. Penee added paper plates.

Bet that's breakfast. Ari grinned in the mirror. A quick flick of her wrist draped her towel over the rack. She ran a comb through tangled curls and walked into the main room.

Brie looked up. "Morning, sleepyhead."

Ari picked up an insulated cup. The aromas of cinnamon and cardamom assailed her senses. "Smells yummy. What is it?"

Penee sipped hers. "It's a type of tea. The lady at the deli called it Chai." She took another sip. "If you don't like it..." She chuckled. "...it won't go to waste."

Ari tasted an experimental sip. "Yum! This is great." She checked the contents of her plate. "Aren't these called bagels?"

Brie lathered hers with a thick white spread. "Correct."

"What's the white stuff?"

Her sister added a layer of red jam. "It's cream cheese." She returned the spoon to the jar. "This is raspberry jelly." She bit into a half a bagel. "Super good, but you can have dry cereal if you'd prefer." Her eyes twinkled.

Ari looked from her to Penee. "You two make quite a team. Pass me the cream cheese—*please*."

The morning passed in a flash. Ari slid into the back seat of a taxi next to Penee, her pulse rate escalating. They reached Sheep Meadow an hour prior to their start time on a gorgeous July day. A slight breeze helped to cool the summer heat; occasional puffy clouds drifted overhead. Concession stands set up at the perimeter of the performance area scented the air with delectable aromas.

Gar had left the apartment early to save a spot for Brie and the boys. His excited wave caught their attention. Waving back, they zigzagged through the crowd to a roped off area defining backstage.

Excitement building in the meadow created jostling butterflies in Ari's stomach. She sucked in a breath. "Aren't you nervous, Penee?"

A soft laugh preceding a sidelong look provided a clear answer.

They arrived backstage to the crew and musicians greeting three ordinary looking people, a blonde girl and two guys, as though they were royalty. Ari nudged Penee. "Bet that's our headliners. I checked out their music. They're great!"

The woman excused herself and walked over. "Hi, I'm Mary. I understand you're our opening act."

Ari nodded. "I'm Ari, and this is Penee. We call ourselves The VarTerels. It's a pleasure to meet you."

Mary smiled. "What an interesting name. What does it mean?" Before Ari could answer, Mary acknowledged a wave from the stage manager. "Nice meeting you both. See you following the show."

Penee blew out a breath. "I know nervousness and excitement feel similar, but..." She inhaled. "I can't wait for this to be over. How about you?"

Ari surveyed the flurry of activity. "I think it's kinda fun. Let's find a place to warm up." She led the way to the boundary of the backstage area. A look at Penee's pale face made her smile. "We're gonna be great. After all, the VarTerels are on our side."

Penee cracked a small grin.

• •

Brie, Esán, Torgin, and Dwight left Joe at the apartment to enjoy much needed time on the phone with his wife. They arrived at Sheep Meadow about thirty minutes before showtime to find Gar protecting a spot in the middle of the crowd. Soon they were sitting together, their excitement magnified by the people surrounding them.

Brie scanned the jam-packed meadow. People sat on blankets with their coolers close at hand, lounged in lawn chairs, or sat on the grass. Anticipation triggered by the blaze of stage lights transitioned to a round of applause as a tall, slender man stepped to the mic.

"Ladies and gentlemen, thank you for joining us on this gorgeous, sunny day!" Grinning from ear to ear, he thanked a list of presenters and backers and made quick work of a few rules regarding shows held in the park. Like a barker at a carnival, he shouted, "What do you say we get this show on the road?"

A burst of enthusiastic clapping quieted at the raise of his hand. "Please welcome a duo never before seen in New York! The VarTerels!"

To thunderous applause, Ari and Penee, their long, flowing skirts accenting their graceful walk to center stage, removed their mics from the stands. Ari's deep voice boomed. "Thank you! We are delighted to be with you today. I am Ari and this is Pen. We'd like to begin with one of our favorites by Bob Dylan!"

More applause stilled as they began the opening chorus of "Blowin' in the

Wind". The song, performed a cappella, caused the crowd to grow even more quiet.

Brie experienced a wave of amazement. Dwight stared at Ari with stark admiration. Esán caught Brie's eye and beamed in appreciation; Gar swayed to the music; and Torgin grinned from ear to ear. "Who would have guessed Ari could sing like that!"

The song ended with the crowd's delighted whistling and clapping. A guitar trio took their places onstage, strumming the opening cords of "Turn, Turn, Turn" by the Byrds. Penee picked up the melody. Ari sang a syllabic counterpoint, which created an intriguing percussive effect. Their last song, "This Land is Your Land", rang out. A woman's scream slashing through the music ended it.

"There! Over there!" She shrieked. "I saw it—the monster with one eye."

The performers clustered together. Audience members scrambled to standing, frantic eyes searching the meadow, their fear spreading with the speed of a wildfire.

Esán pulled Brie to her feet. "Surround Gar." Covered by the hysteria of the crowd, they moved into a circle. "Shift, Gar. See if you can spot him."

A young raven materialized. Black wings lifting it into flight, it soared over the swarming throng.

Onstage, the announcer sprinted to the mic. "Please stay calm and stay put. The police are on the way."

Even as he spoke, the crowd scattered. Esán gripped Brie by the hand. "If we stay, we get trampled; if we run, we get trampled. What's the plan?"

Torgin cast a glance behind him. "I'll go to Ari and Penee. You'd better find Gar."

Brie dropped to her knee. "Tell me when."

Esán glanced around. "Now."

Brie cocked her kestrel head and waited.

Esán knelt, his eyes on Torgin.

Torgin's gaze darted over the meadow. "Go."

Brie soared over the park. Kestrel-keen eyesight alerted her to stealthful movement in the trees. She landed in a leafy maple. *"Gar. Esán."* The message would bring them to her.

Fluttering lower, she materialized. "I know you're here, Rikell. We must talk."

A single, glowing, red oculus glared from the bushes and undergrowth. "We have nothing to discuss. I have no intention of returning to RewFaar. All that awaits me at home is a cold, dirty cave."

Esán walked from the trees. "You can't stay in the city without creating problems. We'll help you hide. When we're ready to go back, you can come with us."

A young raven landed on a leafy branch, its head cocked.

Rikell's growl of dissatisfaction rumbled. "When I was in Upori's body, I did some research. What if I find a person to snatch, one whose body I can live in and die with?"

Brie struggled to find an answer which would not incite his anger. The silence between them grew heavy.

Esán stepped into the breach. "We can't make that call—only the Galactic Guardians can. Let me teleport you to the abandoned house on Riverside Drive. It's no longer being watched. You'll be safe until it's time to leave New York." He held out a hand.

Rikell glared at it. "How do you know I won't snatch your body?"

Esán didn't move. "Because you're not dumb, Rikell. You realize my power has multiplied a hundred-fold since we last met. I will not allow you to hurt me or anyone else. Come with me now."

The Mindeco shuffled from the bushes.

The words, *Tavern on the Green,* whispered through Brie's mind. Esán and the Mindeco flickered out like a candle's flame.

❦

Torgin met the astonished gaze of a young woman who had turned as Esán shaped a kestrel and flew after Brie.

"A b-b-boy—" She gulped. "He was right t-there—"

A long stride carried him to her side. He touched her shoulder. "It's okay. My name's—"

Her eyes blurred. A man grabbed her arm and pulled her into a wave of frantic humans racing by them.

Torgin, with Dwight at his heels, wove his way to the stage. They reached the police barricade as Ari squatted on the edge of the platform to speak with an officer. The man nodded and held a walkie talkie to his ear.

An officer in the barricade broke ranks for them to step through the wall of men.

A kestrel swooped overhead. Torgin and Dwight reached the back of the curtained platform as the girls descended the steps. The four huddled, speaking in soft voices.

Ari, her eyes shaded with a hand, looked at Torgin. "Is Rikell still in the park?"

Dwight surveyed the crowd of police officers. "Not if he's smart. I suggest we go home. I'm betting today's concert is over."

Penee sighed. "I'm pretty sure you're right. The stage manager rushed the headliners into a big car the minute chaos erupted. Ari, let's check in with him to see if we're needed. If we're not, I agree with Dwight. We should go to the apartment. The others will hang out to make certain Rikell is no longer a danger."

Torgin watched them mingling with the crew and musicians. "I can't believe how beautiful their voices are. I wonder if they'll keep singing when we get back to our time?"

Dwight looked downcast. "At least, it'll be easier to find a place to sing on El Aperdisa than to dance."

The girls returned, looking chagrined. Ari expressed her frustration by folding her arms. "They plan to reschedule the concert at Wollman Rink Theater at the end of the summer. I'm going to let Rikell have it. We'll never get the chance to sing "This Land is Your Land", again. Besides, I wanted to hear Mary and her fellow singers perform."

Dwight draped an arm over her shoulders. "You can sing it for me anytime. You and Penee have amazing voices."

"Ah. Thanks, Dwight." Ari blushed.

Penee looked amused. "Thanks. I just received a message from Gar: Tavern on the Green. Let's check with the police to make sure it's safe to leave this area."

Torgin conferred with an officer who waved them over. "You've signed out with the stage manager, right?"

"Yes. He said we can go when you feel it's safe."

The officer spoke into his walkie talkie, listened to the reply, and nodded. "You're free to go. Whatever the woman saw is long gone. Still, stay alert while you're in the park."

Penee flashed her beautiful smile. "Thanks for taking such good care of us."

"You're welcome, miss. Be careful." He turned his attention to another performer.

Torgin took Penee's arm, Dwight linked his with Ari's, and the four of them walked from the enclosed perimeter across the almost empty meadow.

They reached the Tavern on the Green to find Gar outside the restaurant.

"Hi. Brie says to tell ya we got a table. Hear the food's pretty good."

Penee grinned. "Finally, I get to try the strawberry shortcake. I'd say we're in for a treat. Lead on, Garon."

Brie waited on a bench seat by herself at a table set for eight near the back. Gar slid onto the bench. Torgin pulled out chairs for Penee and Ari, received glowing smiles in return, and sat next to Gar. "Where's Esán?"

Brie shared their encounter with the Mindeco. "He teleported Rikell to the old, abandoned house and then went to pick up Joe. They should arrive soon. Let's decide what we want to order, so we're ready."

Ari picked up her menu. "So much to choose from! Can you imagine coming straight here from Idronatti and The Plan? You'd never figure out what to eat."

Torgin chuckled. "If you were hungry enough, you'd manage." He glanced up. "Here come the boys."

Esán and Joe slid into their seats, grabbed menus, and studied them while the server took everyone else's orders. By the time he'd finished, they were ready. He scribbled theirs on his pad and hurried away.

Gar fiddled with his silverware. "Do ya think Rikell will stay put, Esán?"

"Keep your fingers crossed. We don't have time to babysit him." He grinned. "Tech week and then showtime!"

The conversation turned to culinary delights, sharing stories of the past week, and speculating about the upcoming walk on the moon.

Torgin sat back, determined to enjoy time with his friends. His printed schedule suggested the week ahead would be dauntingly busy. The knowledge their time on Earth raced toward the finish line tempered his excitement about the approaching performance, but only a little.

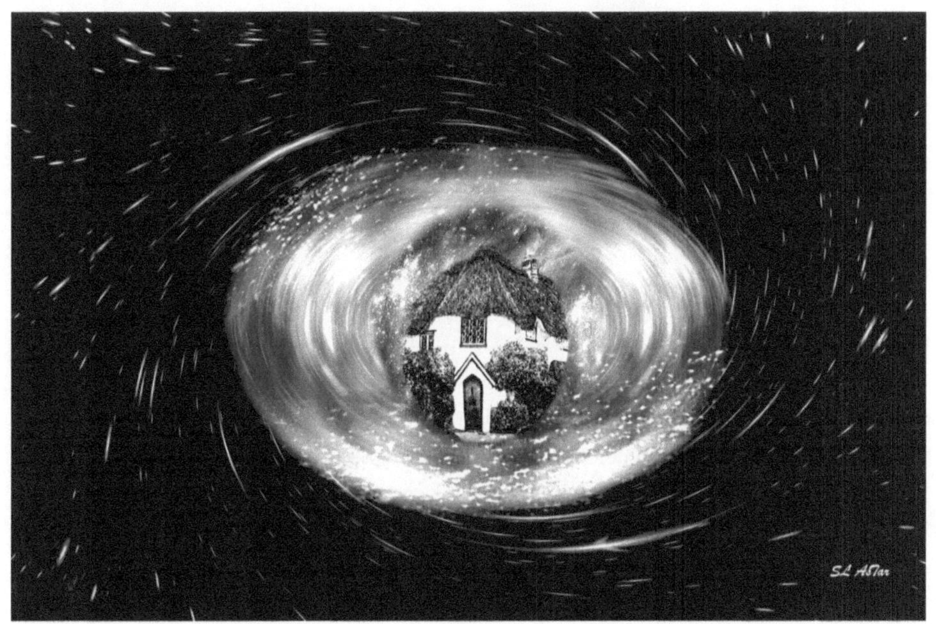

50

The week had flown by. Monday night Rikell disappeared. Their search turned up no clues to his whereabouts. Esán recommended they give up the hunt to concentrate on their last days in the city.

Tuesday, Rayna and Dwight arrived at Lincoln Center to discover a flurry of frantic people fleeing the theater. The stage manager stopped them at the stage door. "We just got word a bomb is hidden in the auditorium. All activities are cancelled until we receive an all clear. Dancers are requested to gather in Juilliard's cafeteria."

Rayna gripped Dwight's hand. Together, they hurried across the plaza toward 65th Street, dodging panicky people as they went. Torgin met them in front of the Juilliard Building and led them inside. "Did I hear right? There's a bomb in the New York State Theater?"

Half listening, Rayna performed a mental scan of the buildings comprising The Performing Arts Center. A gentle nudge brought her attention to her friends' questioning expressions. "The area is clean. No bombs. Just lots of scared people." Her eyes narrowed. "I almost wish we were home." She clutched the strap of her dance bag. "But then we'd miss all the fun of opening night. Let's grab a snack and wait for the all-clear."

Within an hour a voice over the loudspeaker announced that class and rehearsal for the company dancers would resume at one o'clock. The rest of the day went as planned: ballet class, rehearsal, notes, and, finally, a subway ride home.

Wednesday arrived with everyone in good spirits. The day flew by. All too soon, Rayna gazed in the dressing table mirror. Full dress rehearsal was about to begin. Esán was with Joe in the lighting booth. Torgin warmed up in the orchestra pit. Ari, Penee, and Gar sat in the center of the auditorium. They would see the results of weeks of work for the first and last time. A grin erased her nervous jitters. "What an adventure we are having!"

"Places for the first act." The stage manager's words sent a prickle of excitement skittering up her spine. Dress rehearsal was about to begin.

At the end of the third act, the curtain lowered. The ballet master gave his corrections, complimented the cast on a job well done, and dismissed them with an admonition to get plenty of rest. Brie met Dwight outside her dressing room and hurried to meet their friends at the backstage door.

Ari threw her arms around her neck and sobbed. "You were so beautiful. I'll never forget what an amazing dancer Rayna is."

Rayna brushed the tears from her sister's cheek. "And I'll never forget what a gorgeous voice you have."

Penee grinned nonstop. Gar nodded as if he'd known all along she and Dwight would be brilliant.

The subway ride to 72nd Street seemed somehow nostalgic. They walked to the apartment, each lost in their own thoughts. Joe, Esán, and Torgin met them at the door to escort them into the dining room where an array of Moroccan delicacies awaited. Rayna shifted to Brie, shook out her long red curls, and prepared to relax. Lots of laughter and discussion about the great food in 1969 ended the late-night meal with everybody smiling. Clean up completed, they adjourned to the living room.

Gar and Spyglass dashed ahead. "What the heck!" The terrier's sharp bark echoed his master's surprise.

Brie hurried down the hall with everyone crowding behind her.

A vortex swirled at the room's center. Relevart stepped free. "I've come at the request of the Guardians. Gar, Penee, and Ari, you have completed your time on Earth, 1969. Please leave anything not from the future. Bring only what you came with."

Gar stared up at him with questions rounding his eyes.

Relevart smiled. "Yes, Gar, you may keep your new clothes." He chuckled. "Of course, Spyglass gets to come." Seriousness draped him. "Girls, please hurry."

Ari and Penee left to change.

Joe cleared his throat. "Excuse me. Are you erasing my memories, now?"

Relevart's eyes twinkled. "Our preference is that you remain a part of the what's occurring until the end. Chealim would appreciate knowing what memory you wish to keep."

Joe gave a relieved huff and smiled at Esán. "If I may, I'd like to remember the subtle beauty of Esán's lighting design for *The Gift of Balance*, please."

Esán grinned.

The Universal VarTerel nodded his approval. "I'll tell Chealim. I have one more thing to share. Rikell has snatched the body of a young man from Manhattan's Upper East Side, who is wealthy, spoiled, and as conniving as the Mindeco. The Guardians have left him where he is." Relevart glanced at the hall. "Let's go, ladies."

Ari hurried into the room. "I understand 'merde' is good luck in the dance world." She hugged Brie. "Merde, sis!" On tiptoe, she kissed Dwight's cheek. "Merde, Dwight." With a wave, she jumped into the portal.

Penee followed her example and hugged Esán and Torgin. "See you soon."

The glowing vortex swirled faster. Gar hugged everyone, picked up Spyglass, and jumped into the fading portal. Light in the room dimmed. Brie felt an ache of loneliness. Esán hugged her. Dwight embraced Penee.

Torgin gave them a wistful smile and sank into his favorite chair. "That was unexpected. How do you think we'll leave?"

Brie sat with Esán on the sofa and leaned her head on his shoulder. "I expect we will find out all too soon."

B rie turned slowly, taking in every detail of her bedroom at the 72nd Street apartment. "I can't decide which is more nerve-wracking, the end of our stay in New York City, 1969 or dancing in the world premiere of a ballet that will be world famous."

A soft knock interrupted her thoughts. Esán poked his head in. "You ready to go?"

"I'll be out in a minute." She shoved her pointe shoes into her bag and shifted to Rayna. A quick look in the mirror at the outfit she had worn the day they arrived in Central Park, 1969 brought a gleam to her eyes. *We met Gar that day. What a gift.* She stepped into the hall.

Esán and Torgin, each looking dashing in a rented tuxedo, greeted her with wide smiles.

She grinned. "You look so cool, gentlemen! You've got your other clothes, right?"

Torgin held up his leather book bag. "All set."

Dwight strolled from the living room dressed in his bell-bottomed jeans and bright shirt. "Better go. We don't want to be late."

R ayna rode the subway to Lincoln Center with butterflies emerging from their cocoons to flutter non-stop in her stomach. *I am performing with New York City Ballet in the New York State Theater!* The train jerked to a stop. Dwight and Torgin forged a path along the crowded platform. Esán escorted her up the stairs. At the theater, he wished her a brilliant performance, then left to join Joe. Torgin gave Dwight his bag and hurried to the pit to warm up with the ballet orchestra. Dwight smiled down at her. "This is it, Rayna." He kissed her cheek. "Merde! See you on stage."

Dressed for company warmup, Rayna stood in the wings. Nostalgia washed over her as the crew set up barres and pushed an upright piano into place. *My last ballet class...* A rush of bittersweet memories overpowered her. *I knew I would miss it, but I didn't realize how much until now.* Dabbing the tears from her cheeks, she walked between the rows of portable barres to a spot near the back of the stage.

Mr. Thompson preceded the pianist from the wings as a few straggling dancers hurried to the barre. After a thorough warmup and a pep talk, he dismissed the company to prepare for performance.

Rayna did her hair and makeup, put on her pointe shoes, and slipped a thigh-length, silk, flowered robe over her leotard. Slipping backstage, she prepared to enjoy the opening act of *Gems* from the wings.

Excitement built. The stage manager called 'places'. Dancers in emerald green costumes prepared for the top of the show. Work lights dimmed. Music filled the stage. The deep garnet-red curtain opening sent gooseflesh racing over Rayna's skin. Poetic mystery created by the choreography combined with the delicate strength of the petite, blonde soloist mesmerized her. A storm of applause at the end matched the pounding of her heart.

As the curtain closed, she slipped away to get ready for her debut performance. She sat staring in the mirror at the contours of her face, touched up her makeup, and bent to tuck a renegade pointe shoe ribbon out of sight. Before pinning her headdress in place, she examined its central diamond-like stone. *I'm so glad the Corps Stones are back on their home planets!* Draping her robe over the chair, she stepped into her silver trimmed, white tutu.

Lois strolled over. "Shall I hook you up?"

Rayna smiled. "Please. You look lovely, Lois. Are you excited?"

Lois met her eyes in the mirror. "I am. You and Dwight are wonderful. I'm glad you're dancing tonight. Merde." She moved away to join her friends.

Kelsia poked her head in the door and hurried over. "You look beautiful, Rayna. I came to say 'merde' and invite you and Dwight to go out afterward."

Rayna kept her expression happy. "We'd love to."

"Great. Meet you by the fountain." A jaunty walk carried her from the dressing room.

Relieved the Star of Truth had remained quiet, Rayna adjusted a tutu strap and turned as a dancer she only knew by sight walked over to hand her a white rose. "Phillip, your young admirer, asked me to give this to you."

Rayna inhaled the sweet scent. "Thank you. Merde."

The dancer grinned. "You, too. You and Dwight make magic together."

A wave of nostalgia accompanied Rayna backstage. She found a quiet place to watch the final flurry of red at the end of *Gems'* second act. The applause muffled by the closed curtain sent premonition skittering up her spine. Dancers exiting the stage flooded the wings. Happy chatter accompanied them to their dressing rooms.

Rayna dipped the toe of her pointe shoe in the rosin box, listened to the tiny crunch, and switched feet. She glanced up to find Dwight observing her.

She clasped his hand. "Do you think Torgin and Esán are as nervous as we are?"

The arrogance of 'old' Dwight flared. "Why should *I* be nervous?"

Her brow arched.

He laughed. "I'm kidding. Can't you feel my hand shaking?" Curiosity gleamed. "Do you know what's going to happen when we're done?"

She gazed onstage at crew members preparing it for the third act. Dwight's arm encircled her waist. "You are so beautiful, Rayna." He released her. "I understand you love Esán, but please let me adore you tonight."

"Oh, Dwight. Let's love every moment! Come on, we have the okay to go onstage."

After warming up, Torgin smiled at himself in the dressing room mirror. *I sure look handsome in a tux.* He straightened his bow tie. *I wish I knew what the plan is at the end of the performance.* Organizing his own clothes for a quick change, he left.

The excitement filling the pit almost made him dizzy. His fellow artists dealt with pre-performance jitters in their own ways. Violinists reviewed cords in silence; the young harpist sat with the soundboard resting on her shoulder, staring into the distance; flutists practiced the fingering on invisible instruments. House lights dimming produced a breathless silence.

The pit rose to floor level. A spotlight picked out Matt Harwood entering the pit to take a bow. He waved the orchestra members to their feet, bowed with them, and took his place at the podium. His baton raised, he waited. The lights intensified; the curtain opened. With his downbeat, music flooded the theater and dancers filled the stage.

The opening act ended, the pit lowered, and Torgin moved to the piano. His hands wiped dry on his pants, he soundlessly reviewed the fingering of the piano solo. Too soon, the orchestra returned; Matt Harwood stood, ready to enter. House lights dimmed. From the moment of the conductor's downbeat, Torgin's nervousness evaporated. The beauty of the score and his fingers caressing the ivory keys became his soul's truth. Thunderous applause brought him from immersion in his art to the reality of taking a bow.

Intermission found him gazing once more at himself dressed to the nines. His smile twitched. *What a night! I played the flute in the opening act, the solo piano in the second, and I will finish by playing the flute for the final time in 1969.*

"This is your five-minute call. Five minutes until curtain." The stage manager's voice crackled over the loudspeaker.

Torgin picked up his flute, made his way to the fountain, drank in deep gulps of water, and followed his fellow musicians into the orchestra pit of the New York State Theater for the last time.

E sán worked the show with Joe in the lightening booth. Rehearsals of the ballet had inspired him. Now, as he watched Dwight partnering Rayna in the third act, their fluid clarity and musicality took his breath away.

I will never forget this as long as I live.

Joe cleared his throat and swiveled in his chair to look at him. "I wish I would remember how beautiful they are, what an amazing musician Torgin is —" His eyes glazed over. A slow rotation faced him toward the auditorium. He resumed his concentrated attention to what was happening onstage.

The Seeds of Carsilem sent a thrill rushing upward from Esán's feet to his face. He reached for his clipboard, only to have it fade beneath his fingertips. Slipping from the booth, he closed his eyes. When he opened them, he stood in the darkness behind a fly rail backstage as the curtain closed on the ending pose of *Gems.*

Rayna floated through the third act, her passion for dance carrying her from one step to the other. Dwight's partnering made her feel hummingbird-light. The curtain closing with the music's final chord made her heart want to cease beating. Dwight's hand clasping hers kept her reality bound. He glanced toward the wings. Her gaze followed. Esán, his eyes filled with love, smiled. Heady with relief, she saw Torgin join him.

Allowing Dwight to guide her to the back line, she took her place for the curtain calls. Led by the principal dancers, the company moved forward, then back to the thunderous applause of a standing ovation. The company's famous director/choreographer entered with Matt Harwood to take a bow. A final forward and back with the company dancers brought the garnet-red curtains down. No one moved. The stage manager stepped from the wings. Grinning, he raised his thumb. The dancers broke from the lines, flowing together in a flood of congratulatory joy.

Rayna gripped Dwight's hand tighter. Her eyes closed. She opened them to the fading sounds of laughter and excited chatter. Her VarTerel's staff materialized in her hand. The star-scape of Mittkeer came into focus.

A long, low note filled the night. Torgin withdrew his time whistle and responded in kind. Then he removed Ostradio from its pouch. Dwight cupped the magic compass in his hands, his intent focused on the future. A continuous flow of high and low notes blended. Musette shot its rainbow light up the tunnel, guiding them from past to future. Costumes and tuxedos morphed into bell bottoms and t-shirts. Ostradio's needle spun, blurred, and stopped with the constellations of the future gleaming on its deep blue back. Torgin switched to a higher key. Brie directed her crystal's rainbow ray further up the spinning shaft of light. Their forward momentum acting like a magnet flooded the tunnel with all remembrances of them from their sojourn in 1969. In a murmuration of tiny, white sparkles, the memories flew one direction and then another across the midnight sky of All Time and No Time, fading out of existence.

Afterword

In Mittkeer beneath the Constellation Bilar, Ari waited, time whistle in hand, her eyes on Relevart. At his signal, she placed her fingers. The harmony formed by her whistle with Torgin's shrilled in her ears. She heard it, saw the swirl of rainbow colors, and felt the pressure of time rushing toward them. A final long note finished with her on her knees, panting.

Relevart's hand touched her shoulder. "Arienh, you have done well. Look who's home."

She lifted her head. A smile tickled, then exploded. Brie embraced her. Esán, Torgin, and Dwight followed suit. Her own deep laugh made her grin even broader. "It's about *time* you all came home!" She grabbed Brie's hand. "I watched you dance in the time window in Mittkeer." She turned her around. "We all did."

Applause filled the garden at the Guardian of Myrrh's cottage, floated over the Terces Wood and The Grasslands, and seeped into the caverns of the Dojanack Mountains.

Esán squeezed Brie's hand. She wiped tears from her eyes. They were all there: her parents, Aunt Henri, Relevart, Penee, Rethson, Almiralyn, Corvus,

Elf, Den, Gar, and Spyglass. Everyone who had helped to save their Solar System.

Chealim materialized with the sun blazing high in the sky. His smile washed over them all.

He opened his arms. The deep toll of his voice rang out.

Tao Spirian prophecies speak of a man
With two seeds of Carsilem, who took a hard stand.
A journey through time with a young VarTerel
Saved their home planets and galaxy as well.

GLOSSARY LINK

A searchable glossary for the
VarTerels' Universe™ is available online at:

www.skrandolph.com/glossary

ACKNOWLEDGMENTS

I have learned over the years the value of a team of readers who are willing to look for errors and inconsistencies in my writing. Because my writer's brain sees what it expects to see, I am not good at editing my own work. Critical eyes on my chapter headings, book covers, maps, etc help me to provide you, my readers, with clean, professional novels for your enjoyment

I am deeply grateful to the following:

A special thank you to Linda Lane, my editor and mentor, whose demand for perfection and clarity helps me continue to raise each book to a new level. Her eye for detail and her ability to catch those elusive moments that require additional information to help the reader's understanding of the story are greatly appreciated.

Ann McEntire, my beta reader and proofreader, finds the little stuff better than anyone I know and keeps me smiling as she does so! Thank you for your humor and your delight in what I do.

Doing the research and consulting the right people is vital to my need for providing my readers with correct information. Corps Stones gave me the opportunity to learn from two men whose expertise contributes to the story and the character development in this novel.

Alfred Martin, Jr., PhD one of my former dance students, now a media and cultural studies scholar. Alfred lent his expertise to the development of my black and inter-racial characters and his knowledge of the dance world to *Corps Stones*. To learn more about Dr. Martin and his book *The Generic Closet:*

Black Gayness and the Black-Cast Sitcom visit his website at: www.alfredmartin.com

Joseph P. Oshry owner of Designed Lighting LLC in Florida. His assistance in guiding and reviewing my theater lighting design and technical descriptions in *Corps Stones* was brilliant! In my former role staging dance productions, I had the great pleasure of working with Joseph as he lit my work for the stage. I am honored that he included a photo from one of my ballets in his book, *Studies of Light: In the World and on Stage*. Visit his website to see images of his beautiful lighting and how to obtain his book: josephoshry.com

Heartfelt thanks to Tom Krantz, whose range of experience and talents make him a multitask master. He not only formats my books for paperback, hardback, and ebooks, manages my website and my newsletter, publishes my novels, and critiques my work, both written and graphic, but he is also my partner in life...my anchor and my sanity.

And to Leslie Randolph and Salley Yorke whose support buoys me up. Thank You!

As a digital artist, I require models who provide me with a visual of my characters.

To Madison Harvey, Courtney Krantz, Jared Olmsted, Sean Krantz, Charles Lawrence, and Guy Molnar: A very special thank you for allowing me to use your images to represent characters in my illustrations.

Although I prefer to use my own photography to create my digital art, sometimes I don't have the breadth of material and visuals required. I thank all the talented artist who contribute to www.pixabay.com, www.stock.adobe.com, and nasa.gov for the supplemental photos that allow me to create detailed illustrations for my novels.

ABOUT THE AUTHOR

FROM DANCE STAGE TO WRITTEN PAGE

STORYTELLER

Dance, humanity's most ancient narrative art, captivated S.K. Randolph as a child living and dancing in the British Crown Colony of Bermuda. After graduating from the University of Utah with a BFA in Ballet, her dance career spanned four decades of performing, mentoring, teaching, choreographing, and directing. Over sixty of her original choreographic works were brought to life for theatre audiences around the globe, establishing her deep foundation in pacing, movement, and narrative structure. She was the Ballet Mistress of the Colorado Ballet and the Alberta Ballet as well as cofounder of the Bermuda Dance Theatre. For the last two decades of her dance career, she educated the next generation of creatives, as Director of Dance at Interlochen Center for the Arts, named the "#1 Best High School for the Arts in America", and at St. Paul's School.

S.K. at the helm of her forty-foot boat leaving Seattle, Washington on a transformative seventy-five day voyage up the Inside Passage to Sitka, Alaska. Then a decade writing while living afloat swinging on the anchor rode in one remote Alaskan cove or another. 2010

DIGITAL ARTIST

S.K., a pioneer in the digital art sphere, has been creating original digital art since 1997. Utilizing a unique, self-taught technique, she transforms photographs into vibrant, otherworldly masterpieces using Adobe Photoshop. Today, her VarTerels' Universe™ series features nearly 500 of these hand-crafted digital illustrations.

VOYAGE TO WRITING

In 2010, S.K. retired from the dance world to live with her partner on their boat in the world's largest temperate rainforest along the remote and rugged coast of Alaska. Isolated in nature, she spent a "gap decade" afloat honing her writing, refining her digital art style, and mastering shipboard skills (including catching dinner). It was during this creative voyage that she transitioned her storytelling from the dance stage to the written and illustrated page, self-publishing her first novel, *DiMensioner's Revenge*, in 2011.

TODAY

Now, in 2026, S.K. is currently writing the twenty-first installment of her saga. She and her partner reside in the lower-48 states, living on the side of the largest flat-top mountain in the world. From her mountain studio, she continues to cultivate her "Illustrated by the Author" Science Fantasy series, VarTerels' Universe™, dedicating her life to the timeless journey of a true storyteller.

S.K.'s website
www.skrandolph.com

Facebook
facebook.com/skrandolph11

Substack
skrandolph.substack.com

Fishing

VarTerels' Universe™ Book 14
Part II- CoaleScence
Novella
30 pages

A twelve-year-old boy with extraordinary powers must survive slavery, betrayal, and the relentless pursuit of a deadly league that murdered his parents and will stop at nothing to control him.

Available in the paperback *Agothany 2* and as an individual eBook.

An epic science fantasy saga told through art and words
in companion shorts and illustrated novels,
available as paperbacks and eBooks.

Illustrated by the author, color in eBooks
and black and white in paperbacks.

Presented in suggested reading order.

DiMensioner's Revenge

Illustrated by the Author
VarTerels' Universe™ Book 1
Part I - UnFolding
Novel
642 pages, 73 illustrations

Four young people from a regimented city discover their destiny when they journey to Myrrh—the hidden remnant of Old Earth—only to find themselves hunted by a vengeful DiMensioner, his death shadow, and alien mercenaries determined to destroy everything they've come to cherish.

Available as a paperback with black & white illustrations and eBook with color illustrations.

Gifts

VarTerels' Universe™ Book 2
Part I - UnFolding
Novella
34 pages

A pregnant art student must deceive a ruthless surveillance state about her twin daughters' true father, the brother of a powerful Guardian, or become the perfect hostage in a deadly political game.

Available in the paperback *Agothany 1* and as an individual eBook.

Discovery

VarTerels' Universe™ Book 3
Part I - UnFolding
Novelette
32 pages

Fourteen-year-old Torgin must choose between protecting his passion for music and spying on the only friends who understand him in a dystopian city where the government controls every aspect of life.

Available in the paperback *Agothany 1* and as an individual eBook.

Rescue

VarTerels' Universe™ Book 4
Part I - UnFolding
Novella
31 pages

In a dystopian city where surveillance is constant and conformity is mandatory, twin sisters Ari and Brie must navigate secret portals and evade ruthless patrollers to rescue a lost boy and return him home before their forbidden act lands them all in the dreaded Five Towers.

Available in the paperback *Agothany 1* and as an individual eBook.

ConDra's Fire

Illustrated by the Author
VarTerels' Universe™ Book 5
Part I - UnFolding
Novel
504 pages, 59 illustrations

Kidnapped to a hostile desert planet, Esán must survive while his friends race to rescue him, unaware that their rescue mission will unleash ancient powers and reveal family secrets that could destroy three worlds.

Available as a paperback with black & white illustrations and eBook with color illustrations.

Encounters

VarTerels' Universe™ Book 6
Part I - UnFolding
Novella
29 pages

When a vengeful DiMensioner forms an unholy alliance with a death shadow to steal a legendary crystal and destroy the Guardian who banished him, he discovers that the children he saves along the way may hold the key to his own redemption—or his ultimate damnation.

Available in the paperback *Agothany 1* and as an individual eBook.

Metamorphosis

VarTerels' Universe™ Book 7
Part I - UnFolding
Novella
31 pages

Wrongfully banished from his home planet and left disfigured by a catastrophic magical accident, Laurent must shed his arrogance and accept his broken reflection before he can master the ancient art of dimensional magic and discover his true purpose.

Available in the paperback *Agothany 1* and as an individual eBook.

MasTer's Reach

Illustrated by the Author
VarTerels' Universe™ Book 8
Part I - UnFolding
Novel
686 pages, 60 illustrations

As the UnFolding reaches its climax, teenagers wielding legendary artifacts must evade deadly hunters across multiple worlds while uncovering shocking truths about The MasTer's identity and a centuries-old conflict that threatens to destroy the Eleo Preda people forever.

Available as a paperback with black & white illustrations and eBook with color illustrations.

Wanted

VarTerels' Universe™ Book 9
Part I - UnFolding
Novella
33 pages

A fugitive with a dark past escapes prison only to discover he's being hunted by a powerful mystical league that wants to control his untapped ability to bend reality itself.

Available in the paperback *Agothany 1* and as an individual eBook.

Jaradee's Legacy

Illustrated by the Author
VarTerels' Universe™ Book 10
Part I - UnFolding
Novel
336 pages, 51 illustrations

Separated as children during a brutal genocide, birth-mate twins Rayn and Rethdun must survive across galaxies while carrying the genetic legacy that could save their dying civilization or destroy them both.

Available as a paperback with black & white illustrations and eBook with color illustrations.

Agothany 1

An anthology of
the Companion Shorts
Gifts, Discovery, Rescue Encounters,
Metamorphosis, and *Collision*
in VarTerels' Universe™
Part I - UnFolding
256 pages

Available as a paperback.
Each Companion Short also
available as an individual eBook.

Incirrata Secret

Illustrated by the Author
VarTerels' Universe™ Book 11
Part II- CoaleScence
Novel
428 pages, 45 illustrations

Racing against ruthless enemies across mystical dimensions, the Universe's youngest VarTerel and a prophesied leader with legendary eyes must rescue kidnapped mentors from a cloud-shrouded island where a phantom octopus guards secrets that could reshape their world—or destroy it.

Available as a paperback with black & white illustrations and eBook with color illustrations.

Lessons

VarTerels' Universe™ Book 12
Part II- CoaleScence
Novella
26 pages

On the desert planet of DerTah, blind oracle WoNadahem Mardree must overcome devastating loss and her deepest fears when a mysterious shape-shifting DiMensioner arrives seeking knowledge, challenging everything she believes about fate, power, and love.

Available in the paperback *Agothany 2* and as an individual eBook.

Corps Stones

Illustrated by the Author
VarTerels' Universe™ Book 13
Part II- CoaleScence
Novel
438 pages, 52 illustrations

A young VarTerel and her friends journey to 1969 New York City to recover three stolen Corps Stones before their entire solar system collapses into chaos.

Available as a paperback with black & white illustrations and eBook with color illustrations.

Fishing

VarTerels' Universe™ Book 14
Part II- CoaleScence
Novella
30 pages

A twelve-year-old boy with extraordinary powers must survive slavery, betrayal, and the relentless pursuit of a deadly league that murdered his parents and will stop at nothing to control him.

Available in the paperback *Agothany 2* and as an individual eBook.

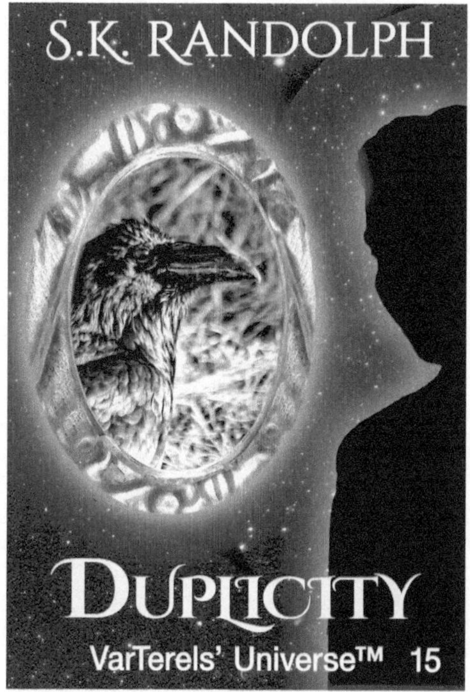

Duplicity

VarTerels' Universe™ Book 15
Part II- CoaleScence
Novella
30 pages

A sworn protector with shapeshifting abilities and a future Guardian destined to unite worlds must outwit a ruthless League of sorcerers determined to claim her before she can fulfill her destiny.

Available in the paperback *Agothany 2* and as an individual eBook.

Mocendi's Gambit

Illustrated by the Author
VarTerels' Universe™ Book 16
Part II- CoaleScence
Novel
328 page, 35 illustrations

Stripped of her protective Star of Truth and held captive aboard an enemy ship young VarTerel Brielle AsTar must trust an unlikely ally—a former enemy seeking redemption—and escape through folded time before The MasTer's followers destroy everything she loves.

Available as a paperback with black & white illustrations and eBook with color illustrations.

Destiny

VarTerels' Universe™ Book 17
Part II- CoaleScence
Novella
32 pages

Brielle AsTar, the youngest VarTerel in the Inner Universe, must hide her genetically engineered babies and their surrogate mother from ruthless spies while battling a dangerous gene threatening to resurrect an ancient evil.

Available in the paperback *Agothany 2* and as an individual eBook.

Cimondeli

VarTerels' Universe™ Book 18
Part II- CoaleScence
Short Story
12 pages

Sixteen-year-old Desty has never seen the sky, but when she ventures beyond her underground refuge for the first time, she discovers her telepathic gifts, befriends a majestic flying lizard, and learns that healing a poisoned world may begin with bridging the divide between enemy tribes.

Available in the paperback *Agothany 2* and as an individual eBook.

Queen's Quest

Illustrated by the Author
VarTerels' Universe™ Book 19
Part II- CoaleScence
Novel
420 pages, 44 illustrations

A young VarTerel, a bearer of cosmic seeds, a musical genius, and a street-smart boy with magical spectacles must unite their extraordinary powers to shatter an impenetrable dome, defeat a rogue demi-god, and complete a universal cycle before time runs out.

Available as a paperback with black & white illustrations and eBook with color illustrations.

Collision

Prequel to VarTerels' Universe™
VarTerels' Universe™ Book 20
Part II- CoaleScence
Novella
64 pages, 14 illustrations

A genius physicist barely out of university must lead a team of Galactic Guardians wielding ancient instruments of power to rescue Earth from total annihilation, even as enemies from his past conspire to ensure the planet's destruction.

Available in the paperback *Agothany 2* with black & white illustrations and as an individual eBook with color illustrations.

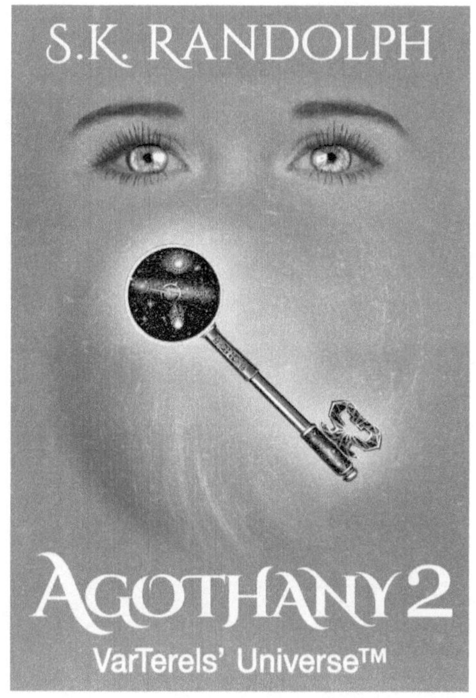

Agothany 2

An anthology of
the Companion Shorts
Lessons, Fishing, Duplicity
Destiny, Cimondeli, and *Collision*
in VarTerels' Universe™
Part II - CoaleScence
284 pages

Available as a paperback.
Each Companion Short also
available as an individual eBook.

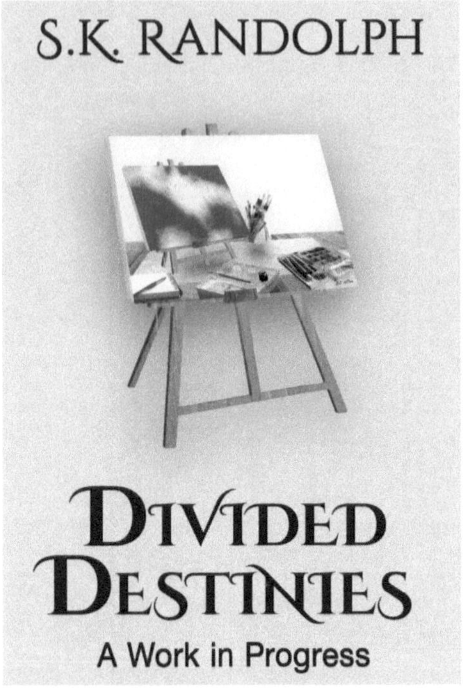

Divided Destinies

Illustrated by the Author
VarTerels' Universe™ Book 21
Part III- QuicKening
Novel
a Work In Progress

Divided Destinies is a work in progress with a targeted release date of late 2026. An illustrated novel, it starts QuicKening, Part III of the VarTerels' Universe™.

See www.SKRandolph.com for current status and subscribe to S.K.'s newsletter to receive progress updates.